WHEN YOU'RE DESIRED

"Why did you choose me?" Simon asked.

"I thought you were the finest man in London," she answered, closing her eyes briefly, as if to summon the memory from the depths of her consciousness. "And you wanted me so much; more than the others, I thought. When I told you I would meet you in Brighton when the theatre closed, I meant it. I would have gone. I planned to go. But . . ."

"But you got a better offer. I understand."

"If you understood me at all, you would not be jealous," she said, laying her hand on his arm. "You would know there's no one else."

He looked down at the hand on his arm but did not shake it off.

"I never loved anyone but you."

He seized her hand, pressing it to his face. "I wish I could believe you, Celia."

"You need not believe me," she said, "to take what I am offering."

He could bear no more. Taking her in his arms roughly, he pressed her close to him, kissing her hungrily . . .

Published by Kensington Publishing Corporation

When You're Desired

Tamara Lejeune

ZEBRA BOOKS
KENSINGTON PUBLISHING CORP.
http://www.kensingtonbooks.com

ZEBRA BOOKS are published by

Kensington Publishing Corp.
119 West 40th Street
New York, NY 10018

All Kensington titles, imprints, and distributed lines are available at special quantity discounts for bulk purchases for sales promotion, premiums, fund-raising, educational, or institutional use.

Special book excerpts or customized printings can also be created to fit specific needs. For details, write or phone the office of the Kensington Special Sales Manager: Attn.: Special Sales Department. Kensington Publishing Corp., 119 West 40th Street, New York, NY 10018. Phone: 1-800-221-2647.

Zebra and the Z logo Reg. U.S. Pat. & TM Off.

ISBN-13: 978-1-4201-2391-3
ISBN-10: 1-4201-2391-2

First Printing: December 2012

10 9 8 7 6 5 4 3 2 1

Printed in the United States of America

Chapter 1

"I do wish Lord Simon would not go out into society," Lady Langdale declared, her booming voice cutting across the idle chatter in the crush room of the Theatre Royal like a flourish of trumpets. "He always makes one think the war is starting up again!"

Mr. George Brummell had been the first to say it—once, in passing, in 1815. It was now the spring of 1817, but like many of the Beau's offhand remarks, this one had remained stubbornly in circulation. (Sadly, Brummell himself had *not* remained in circulation, having been obliged to remove to France to escape his creditors in 1816; his well-publicized break with the Prince of Wales had ruined him.) Mr. Brummell had meant to pay Lord Simon a sort of left-handed compliment, but Lady Langdale, apparently, saw nothing to admire in that gentleman.

"What does his lordship mean," she squawked, "coming to the theatre bristling with weapons? Does he mean to frighten us? Should we all scatter before him like chickens?"

Though situated at the other end of the room, Dorian Ascot, the Duke of Berkshire, could not help overhearing her ladyship. Rather startled, he turned to look, and discovered to his surprise that it was indeed his younger brother, clad to advantage in the gold-braided blue coat, glazed white leather breeches, and polished black top-boots of his cavalry regiment, whose appearance had so offended Lady Langdale. He was not, Dorian was glad to see, "bristling with weapons." By no means the only military man at the theatre that night, Simon's sword was but one of many, but unlike the other officers, he seemed ready to draw his sword at any moment and cut someone in half. Perhaps that was what her ladyship meant.

As Lord Simon stalked through the crowd, his cold green eyes seemed to be in search of an enemy. His left hand never left the pommel of his saber. He was tall and powerfully built, magnificent in appearance if not precisely handsome, with beautifully barbered black hair, and yet he attracted no flirtatious glances from the ladies. Quite the opposite. Averting their eyes, the ladies ceased their chatter as he passed by, and the gentlemen, as though suddenly made aware of their own inadequacies, quickly got out of Lord Simon's way—almost, Dorian noted with amusement—scattering before him like chickens.

Quickly, the duke excused himself from his companions. Making his way through the crowd, he clasped Simon warmly by the hand.

Simon had the distinction of being the taller, but the Duke of Berkshire was the handsome one, with clear-cut, patrician features and fashionably pale skin. His chestnut hair was streaked with gold, and his eyes, not as green as his brother's, were warm and hazel. Slim and graceful, he had a body built for dancing. Just thirty-six, he looked even younger. His income was an astonishing forty thousand a year, but what was most remarkable about him, perhaps, was that his good fortune and good looks were exactly matched by his good manners. A childless widower, he was considered the most eligible *parti* of the London season.

Simon was Dorian's only sibling, and as boys they had been very close. The bond had been loosened somewhat when Simon, at the age of fifteen, had been packed off into the army. War had changed Simon into a rather harsh, unyielding man, while Dorian had remained more or less the same.

"Have you lost your way, sir?" the elder brother teased the younger. "This is Drury Lane, you know, not Covent Garden. I trust you have not quarreled with Miss Rogers?"

"What a romantic you are, Dorian! You know I never quarrel with females."

Lady Langdale's voice again carried across the room. "They say Lord Simon is soon to be elevated to the peerage, but don't you believe it, my loves," said she, addressing her three daughters, who were all Out, and had been for some time. "They have been saying it for years, but nothing ever comes of it."

"Hush, Mama! The gentleman will hear you," her eldest girl begged her, to no avail.

"Nonsense, child! I was speaking sotto voce," screamed her mother.

"Look, girls! Look! *There* is the Duke of Berkshire! Isn't he the handsomest man you ever saw? Lord Granville without his smirk, as Mr. Brummell used to say—though, for myself, I say the duke is far handsomer than Lord Granville or anybody else! Forty thousand a year! Now, *that* would be a great catch for *you*, Cat'rine, if you would but try harder. The girl who gets *him* shall be a duchess, you know!"

"Come, Mama," Catherine Langdale said firmly, dragging her mother up the stairs.

Dorian felt sorry for the very tall and awkward Cat'rine, whom he had known for years, and pretended not to hear.

"You are very late, sir," he chided his brother. "You've missed more than half the play, if that matters to you."

"That would depend on the play," Simon replied coolly. He, too, had pretended not to hear Lady Langdale, though not because he felt sorry for Cat'rine, whom he also had known for years.

"A most charming revival of *She Stoops to Conquer*," Dorian said with enthusiasm.

"A trifling farce," Simon said, brutally dismissing Mr. Goldsmith's most popular work.

"Perhaps," Dorian admitted, "but I'll take a trifling farce in Drury Lane over a grand tragedy in Covent Garden any day. Mr. Kemble, for all his classical airs and graces, leaves me quite cold. Though he be rough and uneven, give me the dark fire of Edmund Kean!"

"Edmund Kean ain't here," Simon pointed out. "He's taken his dark fire on a tour of America."

"We do miss Kean, of course, but we still have St. Lys. Her style is not the Kemble style, to be sure, yet I think no one would ever call her rough or uneven."

"No indeed," Simon drawled. "I believe she is quite smooth and symmetrical."

Dorian frowned slightly. "I find her manner of play very pleasing and natural. Certainly she brings something to the role of Miss Hardcastle."

Simon snorted. "To be sure! She brings her golden hair and her perfect breasts."

"I am speaking of her talent, sir," Dorian protested.

Simon lifted his brows. "Forgive me! I didn't realize you'd been stricken with St. Lys fever. I thought you were come to London this season to seek a bride, not a mistress."

"Can't a man have both?" Dorian said lightly.

Simon frowned. "A word to the wise, Dorian—St. Lys

doesn't take lovers; she takes *slaves*. You mustn't confuse the actress with the part she plays."

"What?" said Dorian, with sarcastic energy. "You mean Miss Hardcastle doesn't really marry that painted ass, Marlow, after the play? I am glad to hear it! She is an honest child and deserves much better."

"By all means, worship your false idol," Simon said grimly. "Throw yourself into her power. But don't come crying to me when she rips out your heart and feeds it to her dogs."

Dorian laughed aloud. "She keeps dogs, does she? Surely a woman who keeps dogs cannot be all bad."

Unsmiling, Simon shook his head. "Be warned, sir: in *her* world, it is *men* who wear the collars. That golden-haired saint you worship on the stage doesn't exist—*except* on that stage. In reality, Celia St. Lys is a devil's daughter."

"If that is so, then at least you must allow her to be an excellent actress," Dorian retorted. "I'd never have guessed she was a devil's daughter! Simon, what have you to accuse her of?"

Simon compressed his lips but did not answer.

"Well?" Dorian demanded.

"She ruined one of my officers," Simon said reluctantly.

"Did she? How?"

"Her usual method," Simon replied. "She lures men to their destruction in the gaming hells, keeping them at the tables with her charming ways. Then, when they are ruined, she discards them. London, my dear sir, is full of her empty bottles! Think of *that* while you are enjoying her smiles and her shapely ankles."

Dorian only laughed. "If that is all—I am not a green-horn, Simon. Nor am I a gamester. I thank you for your warning, sir, but you need not worry about *me*."

By now the interval had ended, and the crush room was

emptying out. "I'd best be getting back," Dorian said presently. "Her Grace will be wondering what happened to her favorite son. Will you not come up and pay your respects to your mother?"

"Of course," Simon replied.

"We have two guests with us this evening," Dorian went on as the brothers joined the last of the stragglers going up the grand staircase. "Mama invited them, not I. I suppose you will have to meet them. I was sorry to do so myself, but you may feel differently. The father is called Sir Lucas Tinsley, and Lucasta is the daughter—his only child and heir."

"Yes," said Simon. "I have some business with Sir Lucas. When I called at his house, his man told me I would find him here."

Dorian recoiled in dismay. "Business? But, Simon, the man is in *coal*!"

"In coal?" Simon repeated, amused. "That's rather like saying Midas was in gold. From what I hear, Sir Lucas is the king of the Black Indies, and the fair Lucasta is its crown princess."

Dorian groaned. "Mama has been throwing that girl at my head for nearly two weeks now. Her dowry is quite three hundred thousand pounds. A man would have to be a fool not to take her. And yet . . ."

"And yet?"

"I don't know," Dorian said gloomily. "I just don't like her well enough, I suppose."

"As reasons go, that is paltry, sir. Paltry! What is the matter with her that a dowry of three hundred thousand pounds cannot cure? Is her body covered in scales?"

"I'm happy to say I have no idea."

"What, then?"

Dorian thought a moment. "She talks over the play."

"You are too fastidious," Simon told him, smiling a rare smile.

"*I* am too fastidious?" Dorian protested. "*You* would not marry Miss Arbogast. *She* was perfectly unexceptional, but you turned your nose up at her, for no better reason than that *Mama* approved the match. As reasons go, sir, *that* is paltry," he added, throwing Simon's words back at him with relish.

They had reached the top of the stairs. Gloved attendants opened the doors leading to the foyer for the private stage-boxes, and the two gentlemen passed into a corridor softly lit by sconces and elegantly appointed with neoclassical statues.

"Miss Arbogast had but twenty thousand pounds," Simon said, as the door closed behind them. "For three hundred thousands, I should be ashamed not to marry anybody. And so should you be."

"We are not talking of me," Dorian said firmly. "If you had married Miss Arbogast, your mother would have made your inheritance over to you. That is the material point. Her fortune is nothing to yours. You could have sold out last year, and kept Miss Rogers, too."

"These are excellent reasons to marry in your estimation, perhaps, but not in mine!" Simon retorted. "I should not have to marry Miss Arbogast in order to keep Miss Rogers."

"I will speak to Mama on the subject again," said Dorian. "She must be made to see that this is not what my father intended when he made out his will. You are one and thirty. It is absurd that Mama still pays you an allowance. You should be master of your own estate."

"I'd rather you not interfere in the matter," Simon said sharply. "Such appeals, as we know all too well, only serve to increase the woman's obstinacy. My mother enjoys wielding her power over me too much ever to relinquish it. What the pater may or may not have intended is of little concern to his widow. There was just enough ambiguity in our father's will as to give our mother lifelong control over my inheritance, and that suits Her Grace very well."

They reached Dorian's stage box, and the footman opened the door for them.

The Dowager Duchess of Berkshire was seated at the front of the box with her two guests. Though a titan in society, Her Grace was physically tiny, a frail-looking bird wrapped in lace. Diamonds blazed at her throat and ears, and more diamonds crowned her tightly curled iron-gray hair, granting her all the consequence that nature had not. In one gloved hand she held her fan, and in the other her lorgnette—as the monarch holds the symbols of his power. From her Simon had inherited the pale green eyes and aquiline nose of the Lincolnshire Kenelms.

Though it was clear she took no pleasure in it, the dowager presented her younger son to Miss Tinsley while Dorian quietly slipped into the velvet-upholstered seat closest to the stage. The play had started up again, but hardly anyone in the place was giving it their attention. Society did not come to the theatre to see the play, after all; they came to see and be seen. A great deal of attention was focused on the Duke of Berkshire's box. The *on dit* was that His Grace very soon would announce his engagement to Miss Tinsley and her three hundred thousand pounds.

Simon made a swift assessment of the heiress's charms as he bowed over her hand. Apart from a slight cast in one eye, and a sallow, spotted complexion, there was nothing much wrong with Miss Tinsley. Her fashionable gown of puce satin flattered her plump figure as much as possible; her thick brown hair had been elegantly styled, and her rubies were magnificent. Her maid was to be congratulated, Simon thought.

"Lord Simon!" Casting her eyes over him with warm approval, the heiress spoke with a slight, childish lisp. "I vow, 'tis high time we met."

"Have you been wishing to meet me, Miss Tinsley?" he asked politely.

"Yes, of course!" she replied. "I have always wanted to have a brother."

Beside her, Dorian looked over his program and pretended not to hear.

"What a remarkable coincidence," Simon replied, giving the girl a wicked smile. "I've always wanted to have a sister—several, in fact."

Lucasta giggled, but without, he was sure, understanding his meaning. "You did not tell me your younger son was so charming," she murmured to Simon's mother, while glancing provocatively at Simon over her shoulder, her left eye twitching.

Miss Tinsley, Simon noted with much amusement, had all the vanity and caprice of a beautiful woman, and none of the beauty.

"Pray, don't encourage him, Miss Tinsley," said the dowager, opening and closing her beautiful tortoiseshell fan.

Simon turned to Miss Tinsley's father. "Good evening, Sir Lucas," he said politely.

As lampooned in *Punch* magazine, Sir Lucas wore an ill-fitting brown wig and a waistcoat that strained at the buttons, but there was something magnificent about his massive, oddly shaped head. His face, too, was ideal for caricature: protuberant eyes; a bulbous, red nose; and thick, rubbery lips. His strabismus, more pronounced than his daughter's, made him look foolish, and yet Simon knew he must be cunning as the devil, for a fool does not rise from poverty and obscurity to become one of the richest men in England. Sir Lucas owned most of the coal mines in the north of England. Dorian, with his forty thousand a year, was a pauper to him.

"Lord Simon." Sir Lucas's left eye stroked rapidly from side to side like a trapped animal pacing its cage. "Thank you for coming so quickly. Tomorrow would have sufficed."

"Our mutual friend is most anxious to put the matter behind him," Simon answered.

Sir Lucas chuckled. "'Our mutual friend!' Let us not be coy. You mean the prince regent."

"I have the honor of serving that gentleman, yes."

"Odious man!" Lucasta broke in. "I wonder you can serve him, Lord Simon. In your place, I would not do it. I believe he has treated his wife shamefully. And the P. Charlotte, too! Everyone knows he tried to *force* her to marry Prince William when all along she was in love with Prince Leopold. His own daughter!"

"The Prince of Wales has indulged the princess too much," said Sir Lucas, shaking his massive head. "Prince William was the better match; a good father would have *made* her marry him. Why, Leopold is penniless!"

"What about *love?*" cried the heiress.

"You are nonsensical," said her father. He glanced at Simon; at least Simon thought he did. With that roving left eye, it was rather hard to tell.

"You may speak to Papa after the play, Lord Simon," Lucasta said before Simon could answer. "*We* are going backstage to meet St. Lys, but Papa hates the theatre and has no opinion of actresses. You may keep him company while we are gone."

"Go backstage, child?" cried her father. "No indeed! I won't have my daughter mingling with *actresses*. You would be tainted by association. What would your dear mama say if she should look down from heaven and see you in company with such women?"

"Nonsense, Papa!" laughed the young lady. "What fustian you talk! You took me to see the inmates at Bedlam, and I did not go mad. I think I can safely meet an actress without losing my character!"

"Mrs. Siddons, perhaps," said Sir Lucas. "Mrs. Siddons is a respectable married woman. But not St. Lys. I forbid it."

"Who cares about old Mrs. Siddons?" said Lucasta. "At her last performance, she was so fat, the stage creaked. These actresses all get fat, sooner or later. Miss St. Lys will be fat, too, one day. How I shall laugh!"

Twisting in her seat, she addressed Simon, who had seated himself behind her. "Your mama and I have made a wager, my lord. Her Grace says that St. Lys's golden ringlets are natural, but I am sure they cannot be so. We must go backstage after the play. How else am I to prove that I am right?"

"Do you plan to pull her hair?" Simon inquired politely.

"No one is going backstage," Dorian said firmly. "I have told you before, Miss Tinsley, *ladies* do not go backstage. It would be most improper."

Accustomed to getting her way, Lucasta frowned at him. "Don't be silly! If your mama goes with us, who would dare say it was improper?"

"Indeed," Simon put in dryly. "Who would censure the Dowager Duchess of Berkshire?"

"I confess I have a strong curiosity to meet St. Lys," the duchess announced, surprising both her sons. "If the management will undertake to remove all undesirable persons from our path, I see no reason why Miss Tinsley and I couldn't visit the—the Green Room, I believe it's called."

"Mama!" Dorian protested. "The Green Room! Have you lost your wits?"

"Would you have me forfeit a bet?" she responded calmly. "Miss Tinsley is our guest, Dorian," she added. "One does not argue with a guest, after all."

"Madam, I protest," Sir Lucas began, growing red in the face. "I really cannot allow my daughter—"

"Pshaw!" said the duchess, forgetting that one does not argue with a guest. "There is nothing whatever to be feared, Sir Lucas. His Grace and I shall go with her. I think it a very good notion. How else are we to settle our wager?"

Sir Lucas opened his mouth, but his tongue failed him as, all around them, an enraptured hush fell over the brightly lit tiers of the theatre. As if ensorceled, the audience abruptly stopped talking. All eyes swung to the stage, and three thousands caught their breath in an audible gasp.

St. Lys had arrived.

She flitted onto the stage, a tall, willowy, golden-haired beauty. Pink, as all the world knew, was the actress's favorite color, and she always had a touch of it about her person, whatever the character. Tonight, she had a bright pink ribbon tied at her throat.

London adored her. "As a goddess sometimes must assume human form to walk amongst us mere mortals," Mr. Hazlitt had written in a review of *Hamlet* two years before, "so St. Lys comes to us in the guise of Ophelia."

Tonight she was in the happier role of Miss Kate Hardcastle: sometimes a proper young lady, and sometimes a barmaid, but always a ravishing flirt. Mr. Charles Palmer, as Young Marlow, tried desperately to make his presence felt, but it was not to be. No one needed him. No one wanted him. He had as well quit the stage.

Lucasta moved her chair closer to Dorian's. "I prefer the opera to the theatre. Music is so edifying. Would you not agree, Your Grace?"

If Dorian even heard her, he gave no sign of it. He had eyes—and ears—only for St. Lys. Opening her lorgnette, Miss Tinsley leaned forward to scrutinize the actress.

"I don't see what all the fuss is about," she said, giving

a toss of her head. "She is rather pretty, I suppose, but I'd hardly call her the English Venus, as some do. They call her the Saintly One, too, but that doesn't make it so! I have heard—"

Leaning closer to him, she began to whisper. "I have heard countless tales of duels and suicides. They say she has had dozens of lovers, but no one has ever seen her with a white swelling. That's because, at the first sign of trouble, she heads straight to the apothecary for a dose of pennyroyal."

Try as he might, Dorian could not ignore this revolting accusation. "If you are insinuating that Miss St. Lys is a *murderer*, I would caution you, Miss Tinsley. That is slander."

"I don't say it; others do," she protested. "I have better things to talk about than Celia St. Lys, I promise you, even if others do not. Walk into a shop and the clerk will tell you which soap Miss St. Lys favors—'Pear's Almond Blossom, madam. We cannot keep it in stock.' The Saintly One polishes her teeth with Essence of Pearl. And for the complexion, we are told, nothing but Milk of Roses will answer. She has her own color, too—St. Lys pink, if you please, and a rose to go with it! They sell prints of her in Ackermann's, and cameos of her in Bond Street. Her face is in every shop window in town, it seems."

She went on in this manner for the rest of the play and finished, as the curtain came down, with, "I am sick to death of Celia St. Lys!"

St. Lys came out for five curtain calls and kissed her fingers to them all. Two adorable children, a boy dressed as Harlequin and a girl dressed as Columbine, came out with her to gather the roses that had been tossed at her feet. At the fifth call, St. Lys slowly pulled the pink ribbon from her neck, smiling cruelly as her adorers in the pit—gentlemen, bank clerks, and footmen all jumbled up together—clamored to be awarded the prize. She seemed unable to choose. She loved them all equally, perhaps. Covering her eyes with one hand, she tossed the ribbon into the pit with the other.

Anyone would have thought it was a pearl of great price. There was punching and kicking and gouging, until at last a victor emerged with the prize. By that time, of course, St. Lys had left the stage.

Chapter 2

Lifting her skirts high, much to the appreciation of the stagehands below, Celia St. Lys ran down the narrow spiral of steps leading from the bright and lofty stage down to the dark, damp depths of the theatre. Legs flashing white in the gloom, she ran through the maze of corridors to her dressing room.

This was a small apartment divided into two parts. The first was a tiny sitting room prettily appointed with a French sofa and chairs upholstered in pink damask. Here, when so inclined, St. Lys received her visitors, and made them wait. Celia went straight through the sitting room to the alcove, kicking off the high-heeled mules she had worn in the final act just to annoy Mr. Palmer, who was two inches shorter than she. In her stocking feet she stood before the full-length mirror, watching impatiently as her dresser unlaced the back of her costume. The scent of roses filled the air. Dozens of bouquets, all composed of pale pink blooms, crowded the outer room, where the actress sometimes received select visitors. She was hungry, and the overpowering scent of roses made her feel light-headed.

"I am sick of roses!" she declared.

Her adorers would have been shocked to hear it; the

St. Lys they knew loved roses, especially pink roses. Then again, the St. Lys *they* knew was never cross or sad or sick or nervous. She was always happy and beautiful. "I never should have let them name a rose after me. I wish someone had named a peach after me; one can eat a peach, after all."

Stepping out of Kate Hardcastle's heavy skirts, she kicked them away.

Clucking her tongue, Flood picked the old-fashioned brocaded skirts up off the floor, placed them gently over a chair, and continued undressing her mistress.

"Sure madam is in a pet this night," observed the Irishwoman, as she always did, every night, because madam was always in a pet after a performance.

Bit by bit, she stripped St. Lys down to her chemise, a garment so fine it scarcely concealed the slim, graceful form underneath. Men—the dirty creatures—were forever offering Flood money to let them spy upon her mistress, but to their continuous disappointment, the Irishwoman could not be bribed. She loved madam as no man ever could, and would have cut off her skinny, freckled arm rather than betray her. Lest madam catch cold, Flood tenderly wrapped her in her favorite old dressing gown of golden velvet. Once it had been sumptuous as a lion's pelt, but now it was shockingly shabby. But when Flood had threatened to sell the old thing to the rag-and-bone man, madam had smiled like the sun and said, in her deliciously low, husky voice, "You're *much* older than that, my darling Flood, and I wouldn't sell *you* to the rag-and-bone man, either."

Celia went to her dressing table and, seated at the triple glass, began creaming her face. Though she had been blessed with great natural beauty, the harsh lights of the playhouse made the use of some cosmetics necessary. She used lampblack to darken her blond lashes and brows. She painted her lips red and rouged her cheeks bright pink. The lampblack made her eyes look intensely blue, and the crimson on her lips made her teeth look very white. Her skin was flawless. She never painted it with white lead, as the other actresses did, but made do with a little tinted powder, discreetly applied between acts, lest the Saintly One become known as the Shiny One. Offstage, she never wore cosmetics of any kind—save a little lip balm on her small, plump mouth. Her adorers were always charmed to see St. Lys on the street, barefaced as a child, and Celia, believing herself to be quite beautiful enough without artificial enhancement, was happy to give them what they wanted.

Carefully and gently, as if removing dirt from a butterfly's wing, she slowly removed her stage "face" with a piece of soft flannel. Without the lampblack, her eyes looked round and innocent. Her mouth looked softer and sweeter without the crimson paint.

For the role of Miss Hardcastle, her golden hair had been dressed in a loose pompadour with tight ringlets cascading down her back. Tilting her head, Celia considered the important question of whether to draw the pins, and quickly decided against it. She knew from experience that her hair could be unruly. Once free, it might not allow anyone to wrestle it into a new shape. Besides, her public liked her a little old-fashioned, not quite so à la mode as the haughty ladies of the ton.

Her stomach rumbled, recalling her to more important questions.

"Why *do* they send me flowers? Why don't they send cake? Or champagne?"

Flood was painstakingly inspecting Miss Hardcastle's clothing for stains and rents. She looked up in alarm. "Best you stay away from cake, madam! Let alone champagne!

Your breeches for the new play is made up already—and not an inch to spare in any direction!"

"Nonsense," Celia said indignantly. "If anything, I've lost weight. I hardly know myself, I look so hagged! I vow I must look *thirty* at least."

"Thirty!" Flood cried. "No indeed, madam! Though 'tis true you'll never see twenty again," she added, quite unnecessarily, in her mistress's opinion.

In fact, Celia was twenty-four—positively ancient for an actress. Every day, sleek and ravishing fifteen- and sixteen-year-old beauties turned up at auditions, as hungry for fame and fortune as Celia herself had been when she had first arrived in London.

"It's so unfair," Celia went on. "A player-man can be old and fat, short and smelly, and nobody bats an eye! But let an actress have so much as a *laugh line* at the corner of her mouth—and out she goes on her arse! My time is coming, Flood. Oh yes, it is, I know," she insisted as Flood protested vehemently that that day would never come. "I'll show up at the theatre one day, and there will be another woman's name painted on my door."

"Sure they could never replace *you*, madam," Flood told her firmly. "Did not Mr. Hazlitt himself declare you to be the finest actress in London?"

"Certainly; now that Mrs. Siddons is retired, and poor Mrs. Jordan—" A sudden swell of tears compelled Celia to stop. Dora Jordan, the famed comic actress, had died the previous year, after having fled to France to avoid her pressing debts. She had been Celia's friend. Rushing to console her mistress, Flood encircled her with bony arms.

"It's tired you are, that's all, madam," Flood crooned. "You want a nice, hot bath, and a good night's sleep."

"No indeed," Celia said indignantly, pushing her away.

"I'm not *yet* an old woman! I want a nice hot supper and a night on the town with my handsome young man. Is he here?"

"I'm sure I don't know who you mean, madam," Flood said coldly.

Even though he was the son of Mrs. Jordan, and therefore half-Irish, Flood did not approve of Captain Fitzclarence.

Rising from her dressing table, Celia went behind the lacquered screen—last seen on the stage in Sheridan's *The School for Scandal*—at the very back of the room. "You know exactly whom I mean," she said sharply, snatching a pink silk sacque from a peg behind the screen. "You may tell Captain Fitzclarence that I'll be with him directly. And tell him I'm *hungry*."

Flood might purse her lips and shake her head, but Celia knew her servant would obey. Obedience was delayed, however, by a light tap at the door. Mr. David Rourke, actor and stage manager of the Theatre Royal, stood on the outer threshold, having opened the door before Flood could do it for him. "Are you decent, Celia darling?" he called out, one hand over his eyes.

Though madam was safely behind her dressfold, Flood hurried to close the white muslin curtain that separated the inner sanctum from the sitting room. To Flood's certain knowledge, no man had ever passed beyond that muslin curtain, and no man ever would if she had anything to say about it. For good measure, Flood placed herself in front of the curtain, arms spread wide, a forbidding scowl fixed upon her scrubbed, red face.

"Celia, my love?" Rourke called playfully. Having appeared that evening in the role of Tony Lumpkin, for which he was justly celebrated, the Irish actor was still in full makeup, his face an ochre mask. As far as Flood knew,

Rourke had never done her mistress any wrong, but that did not mean he wouldn't try, given half a chance. He was a man, after all.

"I am not your love, Davey Rourke," Celia called back in the same singsong. "You always call me your love when you cannot pay me. Fifty pounds, if you please."

Rather than his usual excuses, Rourke produced a bank-note, which Flood carried to her mistress beyond the muslin curtain. Celia glanced at it over the top of the screen, and Flood placed it securely in the no-man's-land of her own scant bosom.

"Thank you, Mr. Rourke," Celia called out sweetly while Flood, resuming her post in front of the curtain, glared at him.

"You're welcome, Celia darling," he replied. "And now that that's out of the way, I was hoping we might discuss to-morrow night."

"I'm quite looking forward to it, Mr. Rourke. I haven't had a night off since the season began."

There was a warning in St. Lys's voice, and Rourke hesitated before venturing to speak again. "You've not heard about poor Mrs. Copeland, then?" he said after a long pause.

"What about her?" Celia asked, without much interest. Miss Hardcastle and Miss Neville might be the best of friends in the play, but the two actresses in the roles were no such thing.

"She's breeding again."

"So?"

It was not uncommon for an actress to appear onstage while breeding. Mrs. Jordan had borne the Duke of Clarence a dozen children, maintaining her career all the while, and even the great Mrs. Siddons had played *enceinte*—though, of course, *she* had been a respectable married woman. From time to time, high-toned religious types complained about the appearance of impropriety, but by and large, London audiences had been trained not to notice an actress's expanding silhouette. Celia herself had never been "caught."

"I'm afraid Lord Torcaster has forbidden her the stage in her present condition."

Mrs. Copeland was the Earl of Torcaster's mistress and, as such, had to abide by his lordship's edicts or else lose his lordship's "protection," which was rumored to stand at a thousand pounds a year.

"She's not showing," said Celia crossly.

"His lordship has spoken. She is to be removed to his country house for the duration. She leaves tonight. Indeed, she is gone."

"But who will take her part on Friday?" Celia demanded, coming at once to the part that concerned herself. "We shall have no Miss Neville!"

"Miss Archer has been practicing," he told her. "She's much improved. And Miss Vane is coming from Bath. You'll like Miss Vane. She'll be with us on Monday, God willing."

"Belinda Archer!" Celia cried indignantly, thrusting her stockinged feet into high-heeled slippers. "Are you mad? That girl could scarcely manage her lines *tonight*, and she was only my maid! Her mother has gotten to you, I see."

In her youth, Sybil Archer had taken London—and some said the Prince of Wales—by storm. But tonight she had played Rourke's—and indeed, Celia's—mother, in the part of old Mrs. Hardcastle. Mrs. Archer's glory days were firmly behind her, but she had a daughter, a pretty eighteen-year-old, whom she hoped to bring out to great acclaim.

"Why don't you give Belinda *my* part?" Celia went on angrily. "Why don't I just quit? It's what you all want!"

By now Rourke was used to her threatening to quit and he reacted quickly, pouring oil on the troubled waters.

"Nobody wants you to quit, Celia darling. Everybody loves you."

"Sybil Archer has been trying to get rid of me since the day I arrived," Celia declared, only slightly mollified by his twinkling Irish charm, "but I'm still here!"

As if to prove it, she swept aside the muslin curtain and stood before him, fully revealed, an angry golden-haired goddess with blazing sapphire-blue eyes. Her full, white breasts swelled against the top of her pink gown as she breathed. She was magnificent.

"That you are, darling," Rourke said wistfully as he gazed upon the beauty before him.

"What about *Twelfth Night*?" Celia pursued. "Who will play Olivia—Miss Vane? If so, then we have no Sebastian!"

"Miss Archer knows the part. She has been studying."

"Good God!" Celia said violently. "I might as well retire now!"

"Retire, is it? And you in your prime?"

Celia glared at him. "*In my prime?*" she howled. "Well-preserved! Is that what you mean? You think I'm old, don't you? You want me to quit! Very well; I quit!"

"Nobody wants you to go, love," he murmured softly, softly. That was how one had to tread with these beautiful, brittle butterflies of the stage: softly.

"I shan't be doing *this* when I'm old and gray," Celia declared, her blue eyes suddenly cold and hard as they contemplated the future. "I can bloody well tell you that! And when I go, by God, I'll be sitting on a pile of money, so I will. They say even Mrs. Siddons is hard up these days. But not me, Davey. Not me! All I need is one more good run."

Rourke opened his mouth to pour more oil, only to find that it was no longer necessary; her mood had changed. "I just need one more good run, Davey! Is that too much to ask? Just give me one more good run!"

"*Twelfth Night* should answer, my love," Rourke said gently. "In your first scene you wash up on the shores of Illyria, half-naked and soaked through to your skin. Then you spend the rest of the play in tight breeches. Who wouldn't pay to see that?"

"We've no Olivia!"

"I'll work with Belinda. She'll be grand; you'll see."

Celia sighed. "No, she won't," she said, sounding more resigned than belligerent.

"She will, she will," he insisted. "Anyway, we've a more pressing matter: Mr. Palmer's benefit." He paused hopefully, but St. Lys merely lifted her brows in cool disdain. "As you know, Mrs. Copeland was to play Juliet," he went on glumly. "Obviously, we'll be needing someone to take her place on short notice. Would you be an angel, Celia darling?"

"Why don't you ask Miss Archer?"

"I did; she turned me down."

"What?" cried Celia, rounding on him furiously.

"I'm only joking you," he said quickly. "You're the only one who can do it and you know that well."

She did not laugh as he had hoped. "Mr. Palmer won't want *me* in his benefit, surely. What is it he says about me, Flood? 'Ah! St. Lys! Precious little face; precious little bottom; precious little talent!'"

"If you don't play, Celia darling," Rourke persevered, "he'll have to cancel, poor man, and then he won't be able to feed his five long children. And you know how little Charlotte worships the ground you walk on. Be an angel! Be a saint! Do it for the children!"

As Celia stood unmoved, there was a knock on the door. It opened, as if of its own accord, and a tall young man in scarlet and gold regimentals strode into the room. From his actress mother Captain Fitzclarence had inherited his dark good looks, while his royal father had provided him with something more practical: a commission in the Life Guards. Just nineteen, he was quite five years Celia's junior.

"I am come to fetch you, Celia," he announced.

"High time, too," Celia grumbled, motioning to Flood to fetch her cloak. "I'm bloody starved. I want my supper."

"I was detained by Her Grace, the Dowager Duchess of Berkshire," he protested. "What a sight! She is like a little doll stuck all over with emeralds and diamonds."

"How nice for Her Grace," Celia returned. "May we go now?"

"Not just yet," he replied. "Her Grace has expressed the desire to meet you. She awaits you in the Green Room. I am to take you to her."

Flood, her mistress's cloak in hand, was brought up short by this announcement. Her mouth fell open and her eyes swung to her mistress's face.

"I'm afraid I'm in no mood for one of your jokes, Clare," Celia said, frowning.

"It's no joke," Fitzclarence assured her, seizing her by the hand. "You are desired this instant. Upon my honor, 'tis true," he insisted in response to her obvious doubt.

"Oh, yes?" Celia scoffed at him, her hands on her hips. "And what, pray, does the Duchess of Berkshire want with me?"

"The name of your modiste, perhaps," he quipped. "Or, possibly, acting lessons? I *suppose* she means to congratulate you on your performance. Is it so strange? You were utterly divine tonight."

For once, flattery seemed to have no effect on the actress. "But, surely— Surely I am quite beneath the notice of such a lady," Celia protested. "I'm hardly Sarah Siddons, am I? I'm only an actress, for heaven's sake!"

"Oh, that's perfect," he congratulated her. "That's just the right touch of humility. Play it just like that, my dear, and you'll have the old bitch eating out of your hand in no time at all."

"No, thank you," Celia said tartly. "I'd rather not be nibbled on, if it's all the same to you."

"Her Grace might be after wanting you for a private performance, Celia darling," Rourke suggested. "There's money in that."

Celia's expression hardened. "Celia St. Lys is not available for private performances," she announced. "If anyone wants to see me, he or she can bloody well buy a ticket."

"I wouldn't put it quite like that to Her Grace," Rourke advised her lightly.

"I shan't put it to Her Grace at all," Celia declared. "I haven't the slightest intention of putting myself on display in the Green Room tonight. I'm tired and I'm hungry. I want my supper. Tell Her Grace I've left the theatre already."

"But Her Grace does you great honor," Rourke protested, "and 'tis a great fool you'd be to go offending her."

"He's right, Celia," Fitzclarence told the actress. "She's not just any old duchess, you know. She's one of the patronesses of the ton."

Celia laughed scornfully. "So? I ain't a debutante. What can she do to me? Revoke my vouchers to Almack's? Somehow I think I'll survive Her Grace's disapprobation."

"Don't be a fool, Celia," he cautioned her. "One cannot snub a duchess."

"Why not?" she wanted to know. "Where is it written that an actress may not snub a duchess? This may be my only chance to do so."

"She has brought her son with her," said Fitzclarence persuasively.

Celia lifted her brows. "Which one? The lady has two,

and there is a vast difference between the elder and the younger."

"Is there really? Do tell," said Fitzclarence.

"One can only hope that His Grace is nothing like his brother."

Clare chuckled. "Don't worry," he told her cheerfully. "It is not the cursed younger son. I shouldn't bother if it were only Lord Simon. No, it's the good one: Berkshire himself, in the flesh, the soft, pallid, unmarried flesh. Here is your golden opportunity. You shall have five minutes at least in which to fix the man's interest—plenty of time, if I know you."

Celia sighed. "I suppose it would be foolish to offend them." Fitzclarence pulled her, unresisting, to the door. "It would indeed. 'Twould be the height of folly to keep Their Graces waiting any longer. *You* may be of the aristocracy of talent, my dear, but *they* are the aristocracy."

"I do sometimes think the French had the right idea about the aristocracy," Celia grumbled.

The Green Room was neither green nor a room, at least not by strict definition. It had neither walls nor a door. Situated off the stage, just out of view of the audience, actors waited there to go onstage during a performance. After the performance, it became a place where patrons of the theatre might mingle with the actors and actresses. In this environment, pretty young actresses could easily meet rich admirers, and rich admirers could easily acquire attractive mistresses. Needless to say, it was not a place much frequented by respectable females. For those actresses who valued their reputations, it was a place best to be avoided. Celia regarded it as little better than a slave market, and those admirers who sought St. Lys there did so in vain.

Why had the duchess chosen to meet her in the Green Room? she could not help wondering. And why tonight?

"Did Her Grace say why this honor was to be bestowed upon me?" she asked aloud, tucking her hand into the crook of Fitzclarence's arm.

"Her Grace is a lady very much accustomed to having her own way," he replied. "I'm sure 'tis nothing sinister. I daresay 'tis nothing more than a whim. You're not nervous, are you?" he asked curiously.

"Certainly not," Celia replied sharply. Though more than a little unnerved, she was determined not to show it. "I simply prefer to have these things arranged in advance."

"This is real life, Celia," he informed her. "There are no playwrights or stage managers in real life."

"I don't need a playwright," she said, annoyed. "For your information, this ain't my first duchess. It certainly ain't my first duke. I just hope they don't keep me too long. I might faint from hunger."

"Just be yourself," he murmured, as they drew closer to the curtain that set the Green Room apart from the rest of backstage.

She laughed shortly. "Be myself? Are you wise? It's St. Lys they want, not Celia."

"Are they not one and the same?"

"Lord, no. Chalk and cheese." Celia paused behind the curtain to take a deep breath, then gave her escort a slight nod. "Let's get this over with, shall we?" she murmured, fixing her mouth into a smile of supreme confidence.

The Duke of Berkshire was already on his feet when St. Lys appeared, but he snapped to attention and offered her a full, ceremonious bow. His Grace's companion, a plump young woman in puce satin, merely stared, her eyes almost starting from her head.

"Who's the girl?" Celia murmured to Fitzclarence, without losing her smile.

"That is Lucasta Tinsley, the great heiress. Didn't I mention her?"

"No, you did not," Celia replied, still smiling.

A chair, or, rather, a throne, had been brought from the property room for the duchess to sit upon. Her Grace was occupied with Miss Charlotte Palmer, the pretty little Columbine who, with her brother, had gathered up St. Lys's roses after the play. As Celia moved toward them, the dowager looked up, her green eyes widening in astonishment. "Good heavens, Miss St. Lys!" she exclaimed involuntarily. "You are even more beautiful than I thought."

The famous and beautiful St. Lys seemed not to hear the compliment.

"Come, Charlotte," she said to the little girl, stopping halfway across the room and stretching out her hand.

"Oh, do please let her stay with me, Miss St. Lys," the duchess said quickly. "She is not bothering me in the least. She's so adorable! I'd like to take her home with me," she added, pinching the child's cheeks. "Isn't she adorable, Dorian?"

The Duke of Berkshire, caught staring at St. Lys as if she were a painting or, perhaps, a statue in a museum, gave a start, and said yes. Yes, she was.

"Come here to me, Charlotte," Celia repeated clearly, still holding out her hand. "I will show you the proper way to curtsy to a duchess. One must be taught these things, after all."

The child ran to Celia eagerly. Celia demonstrated the proper form, sinking into a very deep curtsy, her head bowed in tranquil reverence. The child copied the graceful movement as best she could, to the duchess's delight. Her Grace applauded, saying, "I wish you would take some of our debutantes in hand, Miss St. Lys. The last drawing room at St. James's Palace was the most shocking display of gaucherie I have ever had the misfortune to see."

"Go and tell your papa that I will play in his benefit tomorrow night," Celia whispered to Charlotte Palmer, sending her from the room with a kiss.

"Bring her closer, Fitzclarence," the duchess commanded Celia's escort. "Don't be afraid, Miss St. Lys," she added kindly. "I shan't bite you."

Celia laughed. Even her laugh was famous; no one who ever heard that delightful low, throaty purr ever forgot it. "I am very glad to hear *that*, Your Grace," she drawled, coming forward. "One can never be too careful these days."

The duchess smiled indulgently. In her opinion, beautiful actresses ought to be at least somewhat impudent. Certainly they should not behave like prim young ladies straight out of the schoolroom. *That* would be intolerable. "May I present my son, the Duke of Berkshire? Oh, and—er—Miss Tinsley," she added rather vaguely.

Dorian bowed again, but Miss Tinsley did not curtsy.

St. Lys merely inclined her head. "How nice. I do hope you all enjoyed the play?"

"Very much," said the duchess. "Did we not, Dorian?"

"Yes; very much," Dorian murmured.

"You are very kind to say so," said Celia. "Praise, you know, is the lifeblood of the theatre. 'The drama's laws the drama's patrons give, for we that live to please, must please to live.'"

"Is that Shakespeare?" Dorian asked eagerly. "I'm awfully fond of Shakespeare. I did a little amateur acting when I was at Eton."

St. Lys glanced at him. "I'm afraid that was Dr. Johnson, Your Grace."

"Well, you certainly pleased us tonight, my dear," the

duchess told her warmly. "You were charming, from first to last! Absolutely charming! We were in raptures."

"I was not in raptures," Lucasta declared. "You were very good as the barmaid, Miss St. Lys. I grant you that much. But, I suppose, it is a part that comes *naturally* to a person like yourself."

Dorian stiffened with anger, but St. Lys merely laughed. "All my parts come naturally to me, Miss Tilney," she said.

"Tinsley!" snapped Lucasta. "My father is Sir Lucas Tinsley," she added proudly. "You will have heard of him, of course. He is one of the richest men in England."

"Is he?" Celia said politely. "In that case, we must send him one of our letters begging for a donation. Is he a charitable man, your father?"

"Of course. But he only gives to the *deserving* poor," Lucasta replied haughtily. "I hardly think *you* qualify, Miss St. Lys."

"But it is not for *me*, Miss Tinsley," Celia protested. "I am neither poor nor deserving. It is for the *children* of the London Foundling Hospital; they are poor *and* deserving. Indeed, it is a cause near and dear to my heart. Every summer, we hold a benefit for the children."

"One does like to give back, doesn't one?" said the duchess, smiling complacently.

Lucasta sneered. "Foundlings! You mean those horrid little creatures that are dropped in the streets by their parents to be fed and clothed at the expense of the public? My father says it is a mistake to encourage such practices by feeding the wretches."

"Good Lord, Miss Tinsley!" said Celia, prettily taken aback. "May I ask who, if anyone, is included in your father's idea of the deserving poor?"

"My father believes that the good Lord helps those who help themselves."

"The good Lord may indeed help those who help themselves," Celia agreed, "but I think that *we* have a duty to help those who *cannot* help themselves."

"I agree," said Dorian.

"Are we going to settle our bet or not?" Lucasta said impatiently.

"Have you a bet?" Celia asked, smiling.

"Not I," Dorian said quickly. "Miss Tinsley and my mother have."

"And we need you to settle it for us," said Lucasta.

"You will help us, won't you, Miss St. Lys?" said the duchess.

"Certainly, ma'am, if it lies within my power."

"The fact is, this young lady bet me ten pounds that your golden hair is not your own, my dear," said the duchess. "I do not often take bets, but in this case, I felt I could not refuse."

"You are not offended, I hope, Miss St. Lys?" Dorian asked anxiously.

"Not at all, Your Grace," she assured him. "I myself like a good wager now and then."

"I should be very glad to give my winnings to the Newfoundlanders," put in the duchess.

"Foundlings, Your Grace. Thank you."

"You have not won *yet*," said Lucasta. "I still say it is a wig."

Celia smiled at her. "Why don't you give it a tug?" she said.

Miss Tinsley accepted the invitation with alacrity. Marching up to Celia, she yanked her hair hard enough to make the actress wince in pain.

"Are you all right, Miss St. Lys?" Dorian asked.

"She's fine," said Fitzclarence. "Aren't you, Celia?"

"I trust this settles your bet for you, Miss Tinsley," said Celia.

"Yes, of course it does," said the duchess. "You may give Miss St. Lys ten pounds for the founderlings."

"I do not have it with me," Lucasta said crossly.

"No matter," said the duchess. "Dorian can take it to Miss St. Lys tomorrow. What is your address, my dear?"

"Eighty-four Curzon Street," Celia replied.

"Curzon Street," the duchess repeated, impressed. "How delightfully convenient. Why, Dorian, she is practically on our doorstep."

Lucasta scowled.

"I think now we must leave Miss St. Lys in peace," said Dorian.

The duchess dismissed him with a wave of her hand. "Come here, my dear," she said to Celia. "Take my fan." She held it out. "I want to make you a present of it. Come, child. You are not afraid of me, are you?"

Celia went forward and took the fan. "You are very beautiful, my dear," the duchess said softly. "I wish I knew your secret."

"My secret, ma'am?"

"Your beauty secret," said the duchess. "Miss Tinsley tells me that you use nothing but Milk and Roses. I cannot believe it. Why, your skin is *perfect*."

Celia looked back at her, smiling faintly. "Thank you, Your Grace. I do have a little secret, as it happens."

"I knew it!" Lucasta exclaimed in triumph. "I knew it was not all down to Milk and Roses."

"It's very good, whatever it is," said the duchess.

"Thank you, Your Grace. It *is* good. Better than anything

you will find on the market. I daresay, it's like nothing you've ever tried before," she added.

"How do you know what I've tried before?" Lucasta asked sourly.

"It goes on quite invisible, and it won't rub off."

"My dear, *that* is impossible," declared the duchess.

"Are you wearing it now?" Lucasta demanded.

"I am never without it," Celia replied.

"And it won't rub off?" Lucasta asked.

"No. You may try, if you like," Celia invited her.

Rather than risk her gloves, Lucasta took out her handkerchief and drew it firmly across Celia's cheek. To her amazement, the white cambric came away quite clean.

"I told you," said Celia, smiling.

"Good heavens!" cried the duchess with great eagerness. "I should not have thought it possible. How does it feel on the face?" She patted her own cheeks rapidly.

"Like air, ma'am. I don't even know it's there until I look in the mirror."

Rising from her seat, the duchess moved closer in. Opening her lorgnette, she scrutinized Celia's face minutely and with magnification. "I vow!" she breathed. "'Tis *quite* undetectable! And it doesn't collect at the corners of your mouth? It does not dry out and crack?"

"Oh no, ma'am, never. I would not like that at all!"

"If it does all you say, one must have it," said the duchess. "What is it called?"

Celia was now enjoying herself. "Nature's Bloom, ma'am," she said, opening her new fan. Of tortoiseshell, inlaid with mother-of-pearl, it was really quite beautiful and must have been expensive.

For skin like St. Lys's, Lucasta would gladly have sold her immortal soul. "Where can I get it?" she cried.

"I'm sorry, Miss Tinsley," Celia told her. "It's not available to the public."

"Nonsense!" Lucasta said angrily. "Who makes it?"

Celia smiled. "Its creator is in heaven. When my supply runs out, 'tis gone forever."

"Nonsense," snapped Lucasta. "Even if the man is dead, he must have left his formula behind. There must be some way to make more Nature's Bloom. Where did you purchase it?"

"'Twas a gift," Celia replied, "from the Creator himself. He made it for me especially."

"Then I demand that you sell me your supply. Name your price!" Lucasta commanded.

Fitzclarence could take no more of the joke, and laughed aloud. Looking around in amazement, the duchess saw that Dorian was also laughing. All at once, the duchess realized that St. Lys had been fooling. As disappointed as she was to realize that there was no invisible cosmetic that carried away all one's flaws and never wore off, she accepted the joke with good grace, and managed to laugh at her own folly.

"You should not get an old woman's hopes up like that," she chided Celia, wagging her finger. "Nature's Bloom, indeed! Better than anything on the market! Oh! If only it *could* be bottled. I for one would bathe in it."

Lucasta was the last to get the joke, and the only one unamused.

"How *dare* you mock me!" she cried, her face red. Her hand shot out and she slapped Celia hard across the face. "There! That'll teach you, you cheap, vulgar, painted harlot!"

Chapter 3

Sir Lucas Tinsley leaned back in his chair, resting his leonine head on his chest. "Let us come straight to the point, my lord."

"Please," said Simon. He looked out over the theatre. The chandeliers had been lowered and attendants were trimming the candles.

"Your royal master owes me money."

"Our position, Sir Lucas, is that the original amount of the loan has been repaid in full."

Sir Lucas grunted. "The regent signed an annuity. By rights, I am entitled to collect ten thousand pounds per annum. His Highness must pay. He is already a year behind in his payments."

"He is your sovereign, Sir Lucas."

"He is not above the law, Lord Simon."

"We've been through all this before," Simon said impatiently. "Why am I here?"

Sir Lucas shrugged. "I am a rich man. Ten thousand pounds per annum is nothing to me, and as you say, the original amount has been repaid. Upon consideration, I see no real benefit in embarrassing His Royal Highness. I might be willing to cancel the annuity altogether . . . in exchange for . . ."

"Yes?" Simon prompted him. "In exchange for . . . ?"

"In exchange for your assistance, Lord Simon."

Simon raised his brows. "My assistance? I don't understand. Why should you require my assistance?"

"You have had some experience, I believe, in dealing with such matters," said Sir Lucas. "His Royal Highness is forever getting tangled up with some woman or other. Greedy, grasping females—out for all they can get!"

"I may have had some dealings with women such as you describe."

Sir Lucas snorted. "More than that, from what I hear. It was not long ago that you had dealings with Mrs. Cleghorn, the opera singer. I understand your master gave her a bond for ten thousand pounds, but afterward he seemed to repent of his folly. He sent *you* to negotiate with the woman. You persuaded her to return the bond for less than a tenth of its value. Well done."

"I'm afraid I have no memory of that, Sir Lucas."

"Of course not. You are discreet. Your master, however, is not. He boasts of it."

"I see," Simon said, after a moment. "And you want me to perform a similar service for you—and forget all about it afterward?"

"Precisely."

"And if I perform this service, you will cancel the annuity?"

"Yes, of course."

"All right," said Simon, gritting his teeth. "You'd better tell me."

"There's nothing much to tell," said Sir Lucas. "About a month ago, I met a woman. I gave her a very valuable piece of jewelry, a diamond necklace—with the understanding that she would grant me her favors. However, she did not."

"I take it, you want this necklace returned."

"Naturally, I want it returned," said Sir Lucas. "I will not be made a fool of by an *actress*. Miss St. Lys cannot have her cake and eat it, too."

Simon gave a violent start. "Miss St. Lys!" he exclaimed. "Oh, you poor fool."

Sir Lucas scowled. "I beg your pardon!"

"You are by no means her first victim, Sir Lucas," Simon told him. "She is quite practiced in the art of deception, as cruel and cunning as she is beautiful. Mrs. Cleghorn is a model of virtue compared to her. I have crossed swords with St. Lys before," he went on. "She is clever, but she is no match for me, as she will discover to her cost. I'll get your necklace back for you, Sir Lucas. But first, you must tell me everything. Start at the beginning and leave nothing out. If I am to help you, I must know all. Where did you meet her?"

Celia at that moment was in her dressing room, blinking back tears as Flood applied witch hazel to her swollen cheek. Flood crooned to her softly.

Fitzclarence was lounging on the pink sofa in the next room. The muslin curtain had not been drawn between the two areas, and he had an excellent view of Celia at her dressing table. "Well?" he drawled. "Are we going to have a bruise or not?"

Pushing Flood away, Celia inspected her face in the mirror. One cheek did indeed look pinker than the other. "I should have hit her back," she muttered angrily. "One should always hit back. Else the blows keep coming."

"Indeed," said Fitzclarence.

"I ran away," Celia continued bitterly. "In the army, I'd be shot for cowardice."

"You were perfect," he told her firmly. "You showed her how a lady behaves. You curtsied like a princess, and you left the room like a queen. I was proud of you."

"I should have kicked her," Celia insisted. "That bitch!"

"That bitch," said Fitzclarence, "has a dowry of three hundred thousand pounds."

"Worth every penny," Celia sneered. "She will make him a proper duchess."

He laughed. "Oh, *he*'s not going to marry her. *I* am. I've just decided. And when she is my wife, Celia, you shall be avenged. I shall send her to bed without any supper. Worse, I shall send her to bed without *me*."

Celia rose from her dressing table, and Flood, anticipating her mistress's needs, instantly was there with the actress's cloak. As Flood fastened the clasp at her throat, Celia pulled on her gloves. "Of course he is to marry her," the actress said crossly. "Why else would he have anything to do with that cross-eyed pig of a girl?"

"Shall we wager on it?" he said, grinning.

"If you marry Miss Tinsley, I'll give you a thousand pounds for a wedding present."

"And if the Duke of Berkshire marries her, I . . . I shall go into a monastery!"

Celia could not help laughing.

"I am quite serious, you know," he said. "Her Grace remarked on what a pretty-behaved girl you are. The duke could not take his eyes off of you. You have made a conquest there, I think."

She tossed her head. "Another one? How nice for me."

"He has forty thousand a year," Fitzclarence said persuasively. "He is a widower. He has no heir."

"Then he is as good as married," Celia said impatiently.

"And, therefore, no good to me. I don't want to be anybody's kept mistress."

"But you're clever. You could make him *marry* you."

"Naturally, I could," she said airily. "But then what?"

"Well, you'd be a duchess. That's something."

"I'd be his property," she retorted. "I'd be locked in a cage for the rest of my life, and *he* would hold the key. I may be clever, but am not such a fool as that."

He laughed. "Don't you want a husband?"

"Lord, no!" Celia replied, shuddering. "I'd rather have gallstones."

"My father had gallstones," said Fitzclarence. "He suffered greatly. Gallstones are no laughing matter."

"Neither are husbands," Celia said tartly.

"Yet many ladies *do* laugh at them," he said.

"Naturally one laughs at other people's husbands," said Celia. "It's only polite! One's own husband is not so amusing."

"What?" said Fitzclarence, starting up in surprise. "*You* have a husband?"

"We do not speak of him," said Flood, firmly, "and he is moldering in his grave."

"You're quite right, Flood," Celia said contritely. "He left us a little money, anyway, so we should not speak ill of him. Shall we go?" she said, picking up her reticule and her newly acquired tortoiseshell fan.

Celia and Fitzclarence went out of the room together, leaving Flood to finish her work and lock up. "We shall have to cancel our excursion to Vauxhall Gardens tomorrow night, I'm afraid," Celia apologized as they moved through the corridor. "Peg Copeland is breeding, and Lord Torcaster most kindly has sent her down to the country to convalesce. I am to take her place in Mr. Palmer's benefit. I must go straight home and study my lines like a good girl."

"When is the last time you did anything like a good girl?"

"You'd be surprised, Captain Fitzclarence!"

"I don't care what you say," he said, leading her to the stage door with his hand firmly under her elbow. "I am taking you to Crockford's for supper."

Crockford's was a fashionable club much frequented by the aristocracy. One could eat and drink there, to be sure, but that was not its main function. It was first and foremost a gaming hell. Though an indifferent gamester, Celia often found herself in such places, being plied with free food and drink, as well as complimentary gaming chips. The proprietors were always glad to see the famous actress. St. Lys was good for business, and her friends were welcome, too.

"Absolutely not," Celia said firmly as he pulled her through the door into the cold night. "I must go straight home, Clare. It's been three years since I played Juliet. I must study or I shall be laughed off the stage."

"Nonsense. You could stand there drooling for three hours and they'd still pay to look at you."

"Then I'd better brush up on my drooling!"

"You must eat, Celia," he said persuasively. "You're naught but skin and bones. And you know Crockford always lays on a good supper."

Celia's belly rumbled. She could never eat before a performance, and she was always starving afterward. And Mr. Crockford *did* lay on a good supper. "All right," she agreed weakly. "But we mustn't stay long."

"No indeed," he agreed easily.

Celia frowned suspiciously. "I mean it, Clare. We'll have a light supper at Crockford's. *One* glass of champagne. But then you must take me straight home."

"Of course," he assured her, patting her hand as he drew it through the crook of his arm.

"Promise?"

"I promise."

A hackney awaited them at the end of Drury Lane. Fitzclarence handed Celia in, climbing up beside her and closing the door. Celia caught her breath in surprise as her eyes adjusted to the dim light of the carriage lamps. On the opposite seat sat two of Clare's fellow officers. She knew them. Between them sat a third male, also in regimentals. His hands were tied and his head encased in a black silk hood.

"What on earth—" Celia began angrily, as the hackney carriage lurched forward. "Clare! I demand to know the meaning of this."

"Hush," Fitzclarence murmured at her side. "All will be revealed."

At a sign from him, the black silk hood was removed. The rosy face of a good-looking, fair-haired, blue-eyed boy, even younger than Fitzclarence, came into view. He blinked at them like a newborn kitten.

"You said you wanted a greenhorn," Fitzclarence murmured.

"Greenhorn? He's an infant," Celia protested. "He ought to be wrapped in swaddling clothes and laid in a manger!"

"I'll leave that to you, then, shall I?"

The boy was staring at the actress with his mouth open. "Bloody hell!" he breathed. "You're Celia St. Lys!"

"Yes, I know," Celia said dryly. "And you are?"

"West," he said eagerly. "Tom West."

Celia smiled a little doubtfully, then shrugged her shoulders.

"Welcome to the regiment, Mr. West," she said.

By the time Simon made his way backstage to Celia's dressing room, the actress had left the theatre. From the shadows, he watched her Irishwoman come out of her dressing room and carefully lock the door. He knew from experience that Flood could not be bribed. He waited until she had gone, then made his way back through the corridors to the stage door.

Before reaching it, he turned suddenly, whirling around so swiftly that the person creeping behind him cried out in alarm. His gloved hand clamped down on a thin wrist. "Why are you following me?" he demanded.

It was a girl, though not an actress by the look of her. She was too thin and dirty. More likely she was a prostitute, of the more common variety. The alleys behind the theatre were full of such pitiful creatures. Probably she had snuck into the playhouse to get warm. Her frizzy hair was as black as it was wild, and she wore a dress of yellow satin that had seen better days. "Was you looking for Miss St. Lys, sir?" she said, her common accent an insult to the English language. "For a shilling, I'll take you to 'er, I will. For another shilling, I'll let you do what you like," she added, confirming his original assessment of her character.

Simon eyed her coldly. "Not bloody likely," he said, releasing her arm. "Do you really know where I can find St. Lys?"

"I do, sir. I 'eard 'er in the 'allway, talking to 'er young man. 'E's ever so 'andsome."

"Captain Fitzclarence. Where did they go?"

She held out her dirty hand. "Ain't you going to pie me?"

"Where did they go?" he repeated.

Her face fell. "To Crockford's, sir," she whispered.

St. Lys, Simon knew, was fond of the place and often went there with her "friends," but that was no guarantee. "How do I know you're telling me the truth?"

"I wouldn't lie to a fine gen'leman like yourself," she said indignantly.

"Of course you would," he retorted. "You'll get your money when I know you're telling the truth. You're coming with me."

"Oh!" she said, her eyes lighting up. She smiled, showing surprisingly good teeth. "Don't mind if I do!"

Together they went out into the night, the girl shivering in her thin dress as they walked to the nearest hackney stand. The girl had never traveled in such style before, and as the vehicle moved along, she ran her hands over the cushions in evident delight. Simon studied her by the light of the lamps. She was an odd-looking little thing, hardly a beauty, though not, he decided, unattractive. Her skin was pale. Her large gray eyes were set very wide apart. Her nose was short; her lips wide and full. He had already seen her miraculous teeth. He decided he liked her face; it seemed to be cleaner than the rest of her.

"Let me see your hands," he told her curtly.

She held them up. At a word from him, she removed the tattered black gloves. Her hands were clean, too.

"What is your name?"

"Eliza, sir."

Common, like the rest of her.

The carriage rocked gently. Simon tried to imagine her clean and neatly dressed, her wild black hair tamed, but his imagination failed him. He had no mistress at the moment, but he was not yet desperate.

They arrived in St. James's Street. From the outside, Mr. Crockford's house looked like all the other houses. Simon ordered the girl to wait for him outside; she was not presentable. If he found St. Lys inside, he would return and pay her half a crown; if not, he warned, she could look forward to a long walk back to Drury Lane.

Leaving her in the cold, he went in. The proprietor met him at the door with an oily smile. Mr. Crockford did not like Lord Simon. Lord Simon had forbidden his officers to set foot in the place. Occasionally they disobeyed, and their commander came to drag them away from the tables. Such unpleasant scenes were bad for business.

"May I interest your lordship in a game of faro?"

"No," Simon answered curtly. "I'm looking for Captain Fitzclarence. Is he here?"

"You may find the captain in the supper room, my lord."

"With St. Lys?"

The proprietor merely bowed. One must be discreet, after all.

Simon plunged into the smoke-filled club where scores of men and women—mostly wealthy gentlemen and their bejeweled mistresses—huddled around various gaming tables. Here and there a masked female moved through the crowd. These possibly were ladies with reputations to protect, but more likely they were courtesans pretending to be ladies with reputations to protect.

St. Lys, of course, would never be found amongst the incognitas.

As he stood in the doorway of the supper room, the Earl of Torcaster called out to him.

The aging roué was seated at a table with a companion. Simon could not escape the acquaintance. The earl's first wife had been Simon's aunt on his father's side. Rather curiously, his lordship's second wife had been Simon's aunt on his mother's side. Happily, Torcaster's current wife was no relation to Simon at all. Unhappily, he still considered Simon his nephew.

"Good evening, my lord."

"You remember Miss Rogers, of course."

"Good evening, Lord Simon," said the earl's companion. She was a lovely young woman with black hair, lively dark eyes, and toffee-colored skin. She was almost covered in jewels—rubies and diamonds mostly.

"Selina," Simon said, giving her a polite bow. Miss

Selina Rogers, the ranking beauty of Covent Garden, had been his mistress briefly, but she had left him for a rich man. Simon had not loved her, and so they had parted on relatively good terms. He had no regrets and no hard feelings, though he was a little surprised to see her with Torcaster, a man old enough to be her father.

"I am looking for Captain Fitzclarence. By any chance have you seen him?"

Torcaster frowned in concentration. "The D. of C.'s bastard? No, dear boy. But St. Lys is here. If he is not with her now, he soon will be. Lucky bastard."

"Is St. Lys here?" Simon said casually.

"Can't you smell her?" said Miss Rogers, laughing. "You must be the only man here who can't! She was playing at French roulette when last we saw her."

"Yes, dear boy," said the earl, "angels do play at French roulette."

"Thank you." With a slight bow, Simon withdrew, moving swiftly to the next room. He paused on the steps to survey the room, and spotted his quarry almost immediately. St. Lys was seated at the very center of the room with a group of red-coated officers, directly under the chandelier. More men crowded around her table. As they shifted, vying for the actress's attention, Simon caught tantalizing glimpses of the actress: golden hair, pink satin, a white elbow on the green baize table. He was loath to approach her, loath to join the throng of men clustered around her like excited bees around a flower, lest he be mistaken for one of her panting admirers. Sooner or later, he reasoned, she would have to get up from the table, and then he would intercept her.

A flash of scarlet across the room caught his eye. Fitzclarence was making his way to St. Lys, holding aloft two glasses of champagne as he threaded his way through the crowd. Simon watched, his eyes narrowed, as the circle around the actress opened up to admit him. For a moment, he could see St. Lys's face clearly, outrageously beautiful with her golden hair cascading down her back as she gazed up at Fitzclarence adoringly. Laughing, she took her champagne and clinked her glass against his. Simon could not hear her laugh, but he knew the sound, like the throaty purr of a cat—irritating, but arousing, too.

"Lord, but she's a pretty child!"

Turning his head slightly, he discovered that Lord Torcaster and Miss Rogers had followed him. Torcaster had spoken.

"I remember the first time I saw her," he went on. "She was Shylock's daughter in *The Merchant of Venice*. This would have been before your time, my dear," he added, patting Miss Rogers's hand.

"Not at all. I was Portia," she coolly replied.

"Really? Then you know her?"

Selina lifted a shoulder. "Slightly."

"She had a scene in the play where she elopes with her Christian lover," Torcaster said, returning to his narrative. "When St. Lys went down the ladder backwards in those breeches, there was not a man in the house who did not sit up and take notice. For weeks, I searched in vain for that raven-haired Jewess. Months later, I found her: Cordelia in *King Lear*. Blond, by God, and a Christian!"

"Dreadful production," Miss Rogers said, shaking her head.

"Worst *Lear* I ever saw!" Torcaster said with feeling. "What can they have been thinking? Edmund Kean was fine in the role, but they *killed* Cordelia! It's as though they'd never read the play. Cordelia marries Edgar. Lear regains his throne, and Cordelia marries Edgar. Everybody knows that. Her death made a tragedy of the whole thing, and that *cannot* be what the Bard intended."

Selina laughed. "But that is exactly what the Bard intended. They changed it in the seventeenth century. Mr. Kean thought it might be fun to change it back again."

"Fun! I don't go to the theatre to see beautiful girls murdered."

Simon smiled faintly. "The first time I ever saw St. Lys was in the role of Desdemona."

Selina sniffed. "That part should have gone to me. St. Lys is more suited to comedy, don't you think? I don't say she is a *bad* actress, only that some roles are just too big for her."

"It was the role that made her famous," said Simon, shrugging.

"Only because you men came back from the war hungry for blue-eyed blondes," she said. "All you men were in love with her in the summer of 'fourteen. Dark girls like me didn't stand a chance in those days. She still has a certain fondness for a red coat," she added, glancing across the room.

"She's always had the most deplorable taste in men," said Torcaster. "Lord Palmerston had her first, of course. Then there was that demmed Frenchy—"

"Oh! The Marquis de Brissac, as he called himself," sneered Selina.

Torcaster grunted. "Got himself killed in a duel, didn't he?"

"No, my lord. You remember. When Napoleon escaped from Elba, he rushed back to France to stand with his king and got himself killed. Anyone would have thought she was his widow the way she carried on!"

"She seems to have recovered from her grief," Simon observed.

"Yes," Selina agreed, laughing.

Torcaster shook his head. "Poor thing," he murmured. "She could have had me."

Chapter 4

"No, Clare; I beseech you," Celia protested weakly even as she took her third glass of champagne from the young man's hand. "You promised. One glass."

"There's no such thing as one glass of champagne," he replied. "Look! They made it pink just for you."

Awestruck, Celia held up her glass. "How did they do that?"

"By adding three drops of claret."

Celia laughed, and touched her glass to his.

"What are we drinking to?"

"To Mr. West, of course," she said, looking down at the Honorable Thomas West, upon whose strong young back she was seated. Looking down made her feel slightly dizzy. "Are you all right, Tom?"

"Tom's all right," Fitzclarence assured her carelessly, and seated himself beside her. Tom grunted in surprise, but his back held up nicely. Fitzclarence leaned closer to Celia to murmur in her ear. "You'll never guess who is here."

"You are right," she said, laughing. "I shall never guess, so you had better tell me."

Fitzclarence half rose and glanced over his shoulder, then hastily ducked back down. "Oh no! He's coming this way."

There was only one person, she thought, who could have such an extraordinary effect on her friend. "Your father," she guessed, giggling.

"Worse!"

"Who?" Celia was on her feet. She saw him at once: Colonel Lord Simon Ascot, commander of the Royal Horse Guards. He was looking right at her with those frigid green eyes. As she stared at him, shocked, he made her a slight bow. He had never done *that* before.

She sat back down, ducking her head, her heart pounding. Picking up a mother-of-pearl marker, she tossed it onto the green baize table.

"I'm sorry, Miss St. Lys," the attendant apologized. "The wheel is in motion. No more bets."

Flustered, Celia took it back. "Lord! What is *he* doing here?" she whispered anxiously to Fitzclarence.

"Who, Miss St. Lys?" asked Tom West. Half-hidden by her skirts, he could see nothing but the lower half of the room.

Celia gave the young man a rap on the rump with her fan. "We discussed this already, Mr. West. If you want to be my garden bench, you must remain perfectly quiet."

"Beg pardon, Miss St. Lys!"

"Hush!" cried Celia, watching the turn of the roulette wheel as avidly as those who had placed bets. As the croupier announced "Zero," which was the house's pocket, and swept away all the chips in play, Celia sighed in sympathy with all those who had gambled and lost. She would have lost, too, if Lord Simon had not distracted her.

She glanced over at him again. He had not been coming toward her before, but now he was. "He *is* coming this way. What can he want with me?"

"I owe him fifty pounds."

"Have you got it?"

"Of course I haven't got it."

"Let's just stay calm. Don't look at him, for heaven's sake! He might go away if you don't look at him. They say it works on lions."

Fitzclarence could not help looking. "No; still coming. He looks *very* determined."

"That's just his face. It's made of granite, you know," Celia said bravely, but a slight quickening of breath gave her away. Few people on earth had the power to discompose St. Lys, and no one could do it so thoroughly as Lord Simon. Her hand shook as she placed her last chip on number five, but then, in a fit of indecision, she withdrew it from play before the croupier set the ball on the track.

"He's looking at you." Fitzclarence sounded relieved.

"He can have nothing to say to me," she declared, watching the wheel spin. "I'm not the one who owes him money."

As she spoke, she could feel the crowd separating to make way behind her back—Lord Simon was just the sort of man, she thought sullenly, that weaklings always felt compelled to give way to. She could feel her legs trembling, and was very glad not to have to stand on them. *He's only a man*, she reminded herself, watching the little ivory ball bounce from pocket to pocket, as if her very life depended on it. *He cannot eat me, after all.*

Recalling the adage about flies and honey, Simon had every intention of being polite to St. Lys. That was before he saw what she was sitting on, or rather whom. He could not see the boy's face, but he recognized the uniform. His temper frayed at the sight, and it was all he could do not to kick the young idiot in the buttocks.

"Captain Fitzclarence!" he said sharply. "Is this one of your men?"

"No, my lord," replied the craven Fitzclarence. "I've

never seen him before. You will excuse me, Lord Simon," he added, bowing quickly. "I must fetch more champagne."

Simon let him go; he had not come to quarrel with young Fitzclarence, after all.

Celia was vexed, but said nothing. She had expected Fitzclarence to abandon her. Indeed, everyone seemed to have abandoned her. A moment before, she had been surrounded by a warm wall of friends. Now she could feel a cold draft at her back. He stood next to her.

Now that the danger was actually upon her, she felt quite calm, as she did when she stepped onto the stage. She was Celia St. Lys, and people were watching. She would not, on any account, allow Lord Simon to get the better of her—certainly not in public.

"Good evening, Miss St. Lys."

She took her cue from him—he wished to be civil; therefore, she would be rude. She waved her hand twice, as if to brush away a gnat, but did not otherwise respond.

"Madam, I would speak to you," he said, an edge to his voice.

This time Celia favored him with a sidelong glance that did not rise above his waist. "Move along, young man!" she said crisply. "The great and powerful Lord Simon has declared this place off limits to the little children of the Royal Horse Guards. You may not fear your colonel's wrath, but I assure you, he quite terrifies me."

No one at the table dared to laugh, but there were smiles, especially from her friends in the Life Guards. Simon was all too aware that any public quarrel with St. Lys was likely to attract the notice of the whole room, and probably would find its way into the gossip columns as well. "Don't let's play games, madam," he urged her in a low voice.

"Don't play games," she repeated loudly, laughing.

"Don't let Mr. Crockford hear you say that in his establishment! This is a house of games, you know."

This time there was laughter, scattered about the room.

"Dammit, Celia," Simon muttered. "Must you—" He bit back his words.

Celia tilted back her head to see his face. "Why, Lord Simon!" she cried, affecting astonishment. "It *is* you, after all. Did we not agree, sir, to divide London between us? You were to have the *miserable* half. It's not fair of you to try to make *my* half miserable, you know. You would not want me to make *your* half happy. Of course, you are never happy unless you are making someone else miserable."

He let her babble. "Get up," he said curtly.

Her eyes flashed. "You cannot give me orders, Lord Simon. I am not one of your men."

"I was talking to your—what did you call him? Your garden bench?"

"Are you acquainted with my garden bench?" she asked.

"What's your name, boy?"

"You may answer," said Celia sweetly.

"Have you no self-respect, Mr. West?" Simon demanded when the boy had given his name.

"We're just having a little fun with him," said Celia. "Tom is new to the regiment—"

"Breaking him in, are you?" he sneered. "By God, if he were one of mine—"

"But he's not."

Simon's lip curled. "No. He's one of *yours*."

Celia laughed lightly. "Is this true, Tom? Are you one of mine?"

Tom West did not hesitate. "Yes, Miss St. Lys!" he cried. "Thank you, Miss St. Lys. I'm so happy," he added in a burst of spontaneity. "I was never so happy in my life."

It was now almost necessary for Simon to kick the boy, but he restrained himself.

Celia smiled sweetly. "There, you see, Lord Simon! He is happy."

"He is a bloody fool and a disgrace."

"That is your opinion."

"And you, madam, are drunk."

Celia looked swiftly around the table. Everyone had heard, but they pretended they had not. They were all afraid of him. She lifted her chin and glared at Simon, her eyes blazing. "How dare you," she gasped.

"Did he insult you, Miss St. Lys?" cried Tom West. "If I were not on my knees at present, I would defend you."

"It is very rude to eavesdrop, Mr. West," she told him, rapping him smartly on the buttocks with her fan.

"Sorry, Miss St. Lys!"

"I only want to talk to you," Simon said.

"You can go to blazes," she hissed at him.

"Don't be a fool, Celia," he advised her. "It is in your best interest to hear what I have to say. Take a turn about the room with me and hear me out. Then you can go back to ruining yourself and everyone around you."

"I don't wish to take a turn about the room with you," she declared, her voice a little unsteady. "I don't wish to know you, or see you, or hear you, or *smell* you. If you persist in bothering me, I shall have no choice but to appeal to the management for relief. Since there are no *men* here to defend my honor," she added fiercely, glaring around the table.

"But Miss St. Lys—"

"Shut up, Tom!" she snapped. To Simon she said coldly, "*Rouge ou noir, monsieur?*"

"I beg your pardon?"

"Choose," she said, holding up her last marker. "Red or

black? If you win, I will take a turn about the room with you. Lose, and you must go away. That's fair, isn't it?"

"Black."

"Of course." She placed her chip on the board. As the ivory ball dropped onto the track, she gazed up at him steadily.

"Twenty-seven," the croupier announced presently. "Red."

Bursting into immoderate laughter, she clapped her hands in delight. She had not won much money, to be sure, but she had won her freedom from an odious man, and that was not an inconsiderable prize.

"Did you win?" asked Fitzclarence, returning to the table at that moment with champagne.

"Yes, I did," said Celia, snatching the glass from his hand. "Good-bye, Lord Simon," she added, fluttering her fingers at him. "Parting is such sweet—"

She broke off abruptly, gasping. "Juliet!" she cried, jumping to her feet. "Dear God—the play! Oh, I must get home at once! Oh, Clare! You *promised.*"

"I will take you," Simon said neatly. "We can talk on the way."

"You lost, my lord," she reminded him.

"I said I'd go. We can go together."

Celia frowned at him, but before she could speak, a small, thin creature in yellow satin darted forward to seize Simon by the sleeve.

"Fine gen'leman you are!" bawled the creature, a Cockney under a cloud of bushy black hair. "I done what you wanted. Now *pie* me what you owes me!"

Laughter erupted around the room, but Celia could only stare in mute astonishment.

"And you call yourself a gen'leman," Lord Simon's friend grumbled, drawing more laughter from onlookers.

"'Ere, what are you laughing at?" she demanded angrily. "I earned that money, I did!"

They only laughed harder.

"Do you know this person, Lord Simon?" Celia asked incredulously.

"Certainly not," he said coldly.

"She certainly seems to know *you*," Celia observed. "For shame, my lord! Why, she's hardly more than a child!"

Simon glared at Eliza. "I told you to wait outside, girl. Here—take your money and go, before I lose my temper." So saying, he flung a handful of coins at her.

With a howl, the girl fell to her knees to retrieve the money. Some others, thinking it a good joke, began to toss coins at the girl, too, to her delight. Celia thought it a disgusting spectacle. "Stop it!" she said angrily. "That's quite enough."

Eliza went on picking up coins until Celia made her stop. "Come, my dear," she said gently, helping her to her feet.

"Friend of yours?" Simon said coolly.

"I stand friend to any member of my sex who is mistreated by one of yours," Celia replied. "Come, child. We'll take you home. We'll look after you now, won't we, Clare?"

"We will?" said Fitzclarence, much surprised. "Yes, of course we will," he added swiftly, as Celia gave him a look. Gallantly, he offered the creature his arm. "Yes, my dear. You are quite safe now. Come."

The crowd parted to let them through. Simon did not pursue them. The lady had won the first battle, but she would not win the war.

"Wait!" cried Tom West, bumping into him. He had gone to fetch St. Lys's fur-lined cloak; it was draped over his arm. Simon halted him with a hand. Holding the boy at arm's length, he surveyed him dispassionately. He could not have been more than seventeen. Thick golden curls tumbled into his guileless blue eyes. As he looked up at Simon, who was the taller, he tossed his head like a young colt to clear his vision.

"I know you, don't I?" Simon said, frowning. "Your father is Lord Ambersey, is he not?"

"Yes, my lord." The boy looked past Simon anxiously. "Should I—should I not go after them?" he asked.

"I wouldn't bother," Simon replied.

"But—won't Miss St. Lys wonder what has become of me?"

Simon laughed shortly. "Trust me, boy. Miss St. Lys has already forgotten that you exist."

As the hackney coach rumbled away into the night, Fitzclarence looked doubtfully at the creature in yellow satin, who was seated opposite, petting the cushions. "What on earth are you going to *do* with her?" he whispered to Celia, who was seated beside him.

Celia did not answer because she did not know. "What's your name, child?" she asked the girl very gently.

The girl looked at her, as if surprised by the question. "Who, me? I'm Eliza. Eliza London."

"How do you do, Miss London? I am Celia St. Lys."

Eliza giggled. "Oh, I know you are, Miss St. Lys! Everybody knows you. And you, too, Capting Fitzclarence," she added coyly.

Fitzclarence raised his brows. "You think you know me, child?" he said coolly.

"Oh yes!" she cried. "You're the king's grandson."

Fitzclarence was pleased. He liked people to know that royal blood flowed in his veins. But he said, modestly, "Unfortunately, I was born on the wrong side of the blanket, so it's of little consequence. I never think of it."

"Nothing wrong with being a bastard, is there?" Eliza said quickly. "I'm a bastard myself, you know. That's 'ow I got the name o' London. My father could 'ave been any man in London walking about on two legs."

"Really? Celia's a bastard, too," Fitzclarence said.

Celia stiffened with indignation. "You have no proof that I'm a bastard," she said coldly. "The only thing that can be said for certain is that I'm a *foundling*, like Tom Jones."

Eliza gasped. "I know 'im! Ain't 'e the flashman at the Cocoa Tree?"

"Celia here was left in a church when she was but a few days old," Fitzclarence told Eliza. "All tucked up in a dirty blanket, she was, and there was nothing with her but a handkerchief and two little locks of hair tied up in a pink ribbon."

"I *beg* your pardon," Celia said. "'Twas a clean blanket."

"How romantic!" cried Eliza. "Oh, it's just like a princess in a story, ain't it? Then what happened?"

"I don't know; I never asked," Celia answered repressively. "*You* shouldn't ask, either," she added as Eliza opened her mouth again.

"Sorry, Miss St. Lys."

Celia shrugged. "Where do you live, Miss Eliza?" she asked. "We'll take you home."

"Oh, you can just set me down anywhere," Eliza said cheerfully. "I got plenty of money now." She jangled her coins in her hands happily.

"It's nearly three in the morning, child," Celia protested. "Set you down anywhere? I *don't* think so. Why, with all that money, you might end up in the Thames with your throat cut," she added, only half in jest. "And then your friend would blame *me* for your untimely demise."

Eliza stared at her. "My what?"

"Your friend Lord Simon," Celia said. "Tall? Black hair? Green eyes?"

"Oh, was that his name?"

Celia shook her head. "He didn't even tell you his *name*? How rude!"

"I didn't even know 'e was a lord."

"He's the younger son of a duke."

Eliza was impressed. "Blimey!"

"How is it you happened to meet him?" asked Celia. "Is it a regular thing, or what?"

"If you don't mind her asking," Fitzclarence said dryly.

"Forgive me, my dear, but you are not exactly the sort of female I would have thought *he* preferred," said Celia. "Not that you don't deserve him, of course—I am sure that you do—but Lord Simon is the sort of man who thinks very well of himself. Just to give you an idea, his last mistress was Miss Selina Rogers of Covent Garden. You've heard of her, I suppose? That last play of hers was utter trash, I'm sorry to say, but she made her entrance by hot air balloon, so that's something, I suppose."

Eliza stared at her wide-eyed. "Mistress!" she said faintly. "Blimey! I ain't 'is mistress."

"No, I didn't think you were."

"I only just met 'im tonight—hafter the ply."

"The ply?" Celia repeated, puzzled. "Oh, the *play*. What play?"

"Your ply, Miss St. Lys."

"*My* play?" Celia was astonished. "Do you mean to tell me that Lord Simon dragged you all the way from Drury Lane to St. James's Street? Why on earth would he do that?"

"And then he forgot to 'pie' her," Fitzclarence put in.

Eliza looked at them in confusion. "Well, 'e was looking for you, wasn't 'e?"

"You mean looking for him?" said Celia, meaning Fitzclarence.

"You mean looking for her?" said Fitzclarence, meaning Celia.

"I mean looking for you, Miss St. Lys."

"Looking for me?" said Celia, taken aback. "Lord Simon was looking for me? Should I be flattered or terrified?" She forced out a shaky laugh.

"Terrified," Fitzclarence said ominously. "Most definitely. People have been known to disappear when Lord Simon looks for them. A visit from Lord Simon is rather like a visit from the Angel of Death."

Eliza gasped.

"Oh, he doesn't kill people," Fitzclarence assured her. "He merely frightens them to death."

"Don't exaggerate," Celia said crossly. "Did he say *why* he was looking for me?" she asked Eliza.

"No, Miss St. Lys. You're not angry with me, are you?" Eliza asked anxiously, as Celia sat chewing at her bottom lip. "'E said 'e'd give me 'alf a crown if I told 'im where you'd gone. That's a lot of money."

Again she shook the coins in her hands. She seemed to like the sound they made.

"Why should I be angry with you, child?" Celia said absently. "I'm sure it's nothing." Impulsively she opened her reticule and gave the girl her handkerchief. "Here; tie up your money in this, if you like."

While Eliza was thus engaged, Celia turned to Fitzclarence and whispered, "What do you suppose he wants with me?"

Fitzclarence shrugged. "How should I know?"

Celia shivered. "I didn't realize he was *hunting* me. I know he cannot resist attacking me whenever we happen to meet, but I had no reason to suppose that he was *looking* for me."

"Have you ruined any of his men lately?"

"Certainly not. His officers have learned not to come near me anymore, and I scrupulously avoid them."

"Perhaps you should have taken a turn about the room with him when you had the chance," Fitzclarence drawled. "You could have asked him then."

"That is hardly helpful, Clare," she said, frowning at him. "He did not say *anything* to you, Miss Eliza? Nothing at all?"

Eliza shook her head. Her money, now securely tied up, was thrust down the front of her dress, between her small breasts. "I didn't know 'e was the Angel of Death. I thought 'e was a friend of yours."

"Did he say he was my friend?"

"No, Miss St. Lys."

"Then why did you think he *was*?" Celia demanded.

"Because 'e was looking for you," Eliza explained.

"Did he seem friendly?"

"Well, no."

"The monster has been drawn from his lair. I should like to know why."

"You *did* meet his brother this evening," Fitzclarence broke in. "Could that be it?"

Celia thought about it for a moment. "You're right, of course," she said, beginning to smile. "That *must* be it. He thinks I am a bad woman. He would not want me anywhere *near* his precious brother. He means to frighten me off."

"Well, in all fairness, you are a bad woman," said Fitzclarence.

Ignoring him, Celia rested against the seat cushions. "First, he'll try to bully me," she murmured, smiling to herself. "Then he'll offer me money, some paltry amount. I'd be a fool to let the Duke of Berkshire go for less than . . . say . . . ten thousand pounds."

Fitzclarence snorted. "Ten thousand pounds? You're dreaming. You only just met the man. Besides, why should Lord Simon care if you become his brother's mistress?"

Celia's face was aglow with greedy excitement. "He wouldn't, of course. But if his brother wanted to marry me—! Well, that would be a very different matter."

"Marry you! Don't be silly."

Celia frowned at him. "You said he could not keep his eyes off of me," she reminded him. "You said I could make him marry me. Lord Simon must think so, too."

Fitzclarence had the grace to look ashamed. "I was only joking you, I'm afraid. The Duke of Berkshire isn't going to marry you, Celia. Men like that don't marry girls like you."

"The Duke of Bolton married an actress," she said stubbornly. "Lord Derby married Miss Farren. Lord Craven married Miss Brunton. For heaven's sake, Lord Berwick married that—that courtesan, Harriette Wilson's own sister. At least I am not a woman of *that* kind."

Fitzclarence merely shook his head. "Flying mighty high, Lady Icarus."

"I don't want him to marry me. I just want him to propose. Then his family will have to 'pie' me," she added, laughing.

"He may propose to you, my dear, but it won't be an offer of marriage."

"Well, he must have said *something* to alarm his family," she insisted. "Why else would Lord Simon want to buy me off?"

"He hasn't actually *offered* to buy you off."

Her face was glowing with greed and excitement. "Not yet, but he will. If I play my cards right, I might get as much as *twenty* thousand. Oh, Clare!" She caught her breath. "Twenty thousand pounds! I'd never have to work another day in my life. And, best of all, I'd still be *free*. No husband. No lord and master. No horrid old dowager shooting me nasty looks down the length of the breakfast table. Just me, and all that lovely, lovely money."

"You don't mean to say that if *the Duke of Berkshire* asked you to *marry* him, you'd say no?" cried Fitzclarence.

"Of course not. I'd say yes. Once the engagement is announced formally, I can name my price. His mother will pay anything to be rid of me. Then, when I have got my money, I shall jilt him."

"That's wicked!" cried Eliza London, staring at her.

"No, it isn't," said Celia. "It's business. If they want to get rid of me, they'll have to pay. It doesn't do for girls like us, Miss Eliza, to feel sorry for *them*. We live with their boots on our necks every day of our lives. I'm just getting my own back."

"I don't live with nobody's boot on my neck," Eliza said indignantly. "Not since I left the Temple of Venus."

"Were you at the Temple of Venus, Miss Eliza?" Fitzclarence said in astonishment. The Temple of Venus was a brothel that catered to the very rich.

"I was," she said. "For ten years. You wouldn't recognize me, though. My hair was bright red in them days. People used to say, 'Don't look now, dearie, but your 'ead's on fire!' I got so sick of it."

"Ten *years*?" said Celia, taken aback. "Why, you can't be more than seventeen!"

Eliza nodded. "That's about right, I suppose."

Celia was shocked, but as Eliza herself seemed quite unconcerned, she quickly changed the subject. "And where do you live now that you have left the Temple of Venus?" she asked. "In rooms over some dismal shop, I suppose?"

"Rooms over a shop?" said Eliza. "Wouldn't that be lovely! I suppose *you* live in rooms over a shop, Miss St. Lys?"

"Not bloody likely," Celia said scornfully. "I have a house in Curzon Street."

Eliza glanced at Fitzclarence. "Of course. I should 'ave known 'e'd keep you in a 'ouse like a gen'leman."

"Keep me?" Celia said indignantly. "Nobody keeps me, child. I am my own mistress. It's not a very large house, but it's mine. I bought it with my own money, and no one can ever take it away from me."

Eliza's eyes were round. "Nobody keeps you? But what about the Capting?"

Celia and Fitzclarence exchanged a glance and laughed.

"If anything, she keeps me," said Fitzclarence.

"We're not lovers, Miss Eliza," Celia said quickly.

"She's much too old for me," Fitzclarence explained. "You see, Miss Eliza, when you are as famous as St. Lys, you can't go anywhere without a gentleman escort."

"You mean—"

"He means," Celia said dryly, "that I 'pie' him."

Chapter 5

"Blimey," said Eliza, staring. "You must be very rich indeed, Miss St. Lys!"

"I do all right," Celia admitted.

"Must be nice," Eliza ventured, "being an hactress."

Celia lifted her brows. "Oh? You think it's easy, do you?" she said coldly.

"Well . . ." said Eliza, not sure what she had said wrong.

"She only meant that you make it look easy," Fitzclarence said soothingly.

Celia did not wish to be soothed. "People always think it's so easy, but actually it's a lot of hard work. Can you act, Miss Eliza? Can you sing? Dance?"

"I can sing," Eliza said in a small voice.

"Of course you can sing," said Fitzclarence. "Anyone with a voice can sing. Come! Let us hear you. Do you know 'Hot Codlins'?"

He started it for her, but Eliza quickly joined in, very loudly and off-key, making Celia wince.

"There was a little woman, as I've been told,
Who was not very young, nor yet very old;
Now this little woman, 'er living she got
By selling codlins, 'ot, 'ot, 'ot!"

"Now I'll be thinking of them 'ot codlins all night," Eliza complained, rubbing her rumbling stomach. "Well?" she asked them brightly. "What did you think?"

They had arrived in Curzon Street. At that moment, the hackney carriage rolled to a stop and the jarvey gave a shout. Fitzclarence quickly opened the door and climbed out.

"That was extremely *interesting*, Miss Eliza," Celia told her. Opening her reticule, she took out a card. It was pale pink with her name printed in gold. "Come to the theatre tomorrow, and we'll find something for you to do."

Eliza cradled the card in her cupped hands. "Oh, Miss St. Lys!"

Taking Fitzclarence's hand, Celia climbed out of the hack.

"What the devil am *I* supposed to do with her?" he wanted to know.

"Well, she can't stay with *me*," Celia replied. "I have my reputation to think of. Get her a room somewhere, and something to eat. Some hot codlins, perhaps."

"Well, she did sing for her supper," he said grudgingly, as Celia took out her purse and handed him a single gold sovereign. He kept his palm open until she gave two more. During the silent negotiation, Fitzclarence had become aware that they were being observed.

"Don't look now," he said as he escorted her up the steps to her door, "but there's that nosy neighbor of yours. What's his name, Dickory? That spaniel of his must have a bladder the size of a pea. He always seems to be out walking it in the middle of the night."

"Good evening, Mr. Dickson," Celia called out pleasantly.

The gentleman with the spaniel whirled around, apparently startled at the sound of her voice, even though he must have heard the hackney arriving. A middle-aged man with a pleasant, if bland face, he squinted at them through thick spectacles in the flickering light provided by the street lamps. "Miss St. Lys! Is that you? I—I was just walking Queenie."

"Hello, Queenie!" Celia called out sweetly. The spaniel instantly broke free of its master and bounded toward her.

Fitzclarence recoiled in disgust as Queenie sniffed his boots. "For God's sake, why do you indulge these people?" he muttered angrily to Celia.

"*These people* have made me rich," she replied softly. "An actress is nothing without the affection of her public." Bending down, she patted the spaniel's head. "What a good doggie! You must be so proud of her, Mr. Dickson."

For a moment, Mr. Dickson stared at the beautiful actress, but then he seemed to gather his courage. "You shall have a puppy from the next litter, Miss St. Lys!" he blurted out.

"Oh," said Celia, a little taken aback. "That is very good of you, Mr. Dickson, but I—I am so seldom at home. It wouldn't be fair—to the puppy, I mean."

Behind her, the door of her house opened, and the huge hulk of Tonecho, her Spanish manservant, filled the doorway, a branch of candles in his fist. Formerly a sparring partner to Mendoza, the famed boxer, Tonecho clearly was not a man to be trifled with. "Good evening, Doña Celia," he growled.

Mr. Dickson shrank noticeably. Braver than her master, Queenie gave a low, warning growl.

"It's all right, Queenie," Celia assured the spaniel. "That's only Tonecho. His bark is worse than his bite."

"Come, Celia," Fitzclarence commanded. Quite out of patience with her insipid conversation with this nobody and his dog, he caught her by the elbow. "Remember, you have lines to study for tomorrow."

Mr. Dickson gasped in delight. "Do you play tomorrow, Miss St. Lys?" he asked eagerly. "I had no idea! There was nothing about it in the *Theatrical Inquisitor*, was there, Queenie? I read the theatrical pages to her every morning."

"I'll leave a *billet d'entrée* for you at the door, Mr. Dickson," Celia promised as Fitzclarence pushed her up the steps. "But now I really must go. Good night! Good night, Queenie!"

"If I *were* your lover, I'd find a way to make that man disappear," Fitzclarence muttered. "What a bloody pest!"

"He's a very nice man," she said. Her next breath was a gasp of dismay. "Oh no! He's looking in the hack! You'd better be quick, Clare—before he sees that wretched girl!"

Hastily, she closed the door in his face. Leaving Tonecho to lock up and bar the door, she made her way past the tall porcelain Chinaman on the hall table. A mandarin, no less, he seemed to nod sagely to her as she paused to light her bedroom taper.

Five minutes later, she was curled up in bed with a well-worn copy of *Romeo and Juliet*. Resolutely, she opened it to the first page. Notes she had written at the margins three years before were undecipherable now. With a sigh, she reached for the tiny gold spectacles on her bedside table. She really ought not to have had that last glass of champagne.

Dorian, Duke of Berkshire, could not sleep. The events of the evening had upset him greatly. Whenever he closed his eyes, he saw Miss Tinsley, her face contorted with jealous rage, striking the beautiful Miss St. Lys across the face. Finally, he stopped closing his eyes.

Slipping on his dressing gown and slippers, he made his way to the stairs. Berkshire House was dark and quiet. As if across a great distance, he heard the quarter chime of the clock in his mother's boudoir. Downstairs, in the library, he found his mother seated at the massive mahogany desk that had been his father's. Dressed for bed, a cap over her gray hair, she was writing busily and did not hear him come in.

"Mama?" he called to her softly, holding up the bedroom taper he had brought with him.

"Dorian!" she exclaimed, glancing up. "You should be in bed."

"So should you be," he said.

"I couldn't sleep."

"Neither could I."

The duchess set down her pen. "Do you want to talk about it?" she asked.

Dorian walked over to the fire and added a log from the box. "I keep turning it over and over in my mind," he said bleakly. "Poor Miss St. Lys! I ought to have done something. I ought to have stopped it."

"What could you have done, my darling? It is not your fault. I am sure Miss St. Lys does not blame *us* for Miss Tinsley's shocking behavior."

"It never should have happened. We should never have gone to the Green Room at all."

"You're quite right, of course," she said. "It was very wrong of Miss Tinsley to insist upon going backstage after the play. I was quite shocked. But then, blood will tell."

Dorian looked at her incredulously. "If you knew she was wrong, madam, why did you indulge her? It is clear, I trust, that I shall not be making Miss Tinsley an offer of marriage."

"No indeed," she agreed very readily. "I have already struck her from the list."

"You have a list?" he asked, momentarily distracted.

"Of course I have a list," she replied. "Miss Tinsley is no longer on it. You need never see her again. I have been writing to the other patronesses," she went on. "Miss Tinsley's vouchers to Almack's are to be revoked at once. As of tonight, she is no longer welcome in the first circle of society. She will find her level, I daresay. With a dowry of three hundred thousand, *someone* will marry her, but it will not be anyone *we* know."

"Fortunately, the Duke of Berkshire has no need to marry for money," Dorian said coldly.

"No indeed," she said. "But I did think I ought to just let her *try*. However, it's clearly no good. We must cut our losses and move on."

Dorian stretched out in one of the chairs beside the fire. "Who is next on the list?"

"Lady Rowena West. Pretty girl, just seventeen, quiet and pretty-behaved. Her father is the Earl of Ambersey. Her fortune is but twenty thousand pounds, but I understand there is a grandmother who might do something for her if she marries well."

"Do you not think, Mama, that it would be better if I— if I were to choose my own wife this time?" he said.

"Dorian! You do not know what you are saying," she protested. "Choose your own wife! My dear! That is how mistakes are made."

"You chose my first wife," he said quietly.

She bristled. "That was not my fault. Her family concealed from me the fact that she was sickly. If I had known she enjoyed poor health—"

Dorian held up his hand. "It's no one's fault, Mama. I don't blame you. I simply want the freedom to choose my own wife in my own time. I would never marry to disoblige you, if that is what you fear. You want a daughter-in-law of large fortune and good breeding. *I* want delicacy of mind and sweetness of temper. I want good health and—and laughter. I want conversation. I want a companion, not—"

"A moment, please," she said, stopping him while she took out a clean sheet of paper. "You were saying?" she prompted, her pen poised over the page.

Dorian sighed.

She set down her pen. "You are tired, my darling. Go to bed. Tomorrow we will begin again. We'll call on Lady Rowena, shall we? I'll send a note to her mama in the morning to make certain she is kept home for you in the afternoon."

Dorian grimaced. "Seventeen? What have I to say to a child of that age? Don't any of these girls have elder sisters?"

The duchess recoiled. "Elder sister!" she repeated indignantly. "We need not settle for that. My dear Dorian, if a girl is not snapped up by the end of her first season, then there is something wrong with her. If you do not find someone soon, and fix your interest, all the good ones will be taken."

Dorian rubbed his eyes wearily.

"Of course we need not call on Lady Rowena tomorrow, if you do not wish to," she said hastily. "I can arrange for you to meet her at Lady Torcaster's ball on Saturday, if you prefer. I am sure she has been invited. If not, I can arrange that, too."

He shrugged. "Frankly, I'd rather be down at Ashlands for the foaling."

His mother looked at him for a moment. "You are tired," she said gently. "Perhaps we have been concentrating too hard on the business of finding you a wife. You are a bundle of raw nerves. You need to relax. A man must think of *pleasure* as well as duty, after all. Why don't you ask Miss St. Lys to dine with you tomorrow night?"

Dorian started in his chair. "Mama!" he said, blinking at her in astonishment.

"What?" she replied, looking back at him frankly. "You have to see her tomorrow, anyway, to give her the ten pounds I promised to her for her foundlings."

"I thought I would send it."

"Send it! Don't be silly. She expects you to bring it to her. She wants you to. If she didn't, she wouldn't have given us her direction. Eighty-one Curzon Street."

"Eight-four," he corrected her unthinkingly.

She smiled triumphantly. "There! I knew you liked her. Indeed, who would not like her? She is beautiful, charming, spirited . . . In a perfect world, she would be the heiress with three hundred thousands. Ask her to dine with you. I'll make the arrangements for you, if you like. The squab at the Pulteney Hotel is simply breathtaking."

"I shall do no such thing," he said. "After what happened tonight, I'm sure she never wants to see me again."

"Nonsense. I could tell she was attracted to you. And she is *exactly* the sort of woman whom the Duke of Berkshire *ought* to have in keeping."

"Good God!" Dorian said, acutely embarrassed.

"You would be the envy of every man in London," his mother went on, unperturbed by her son's discomfort, "which is precisely what you ought to be. Your father would not have hesitated."

Dorian left his chair and poked the fire again. "You forget, Mama. Miss St. Lys has a protector already."

She laughed aloud. "I hope you do not mean Captain Fitzclarence! He is no rival for *you*, my love. He may be the king's grandson, but he's still a bastard, and he is poor."

"What does that matter, if she loves him?" Dorian said sharply.

"Even beautiful actresses must have something to live on," replied the duchess. "Houses in Curzon Street do not pay for themselves, after all. I wonder who pays her rent? I shall have to inquire. It can't be Fitzclarence; he hasn't a penny to scratch himself with. You could buy him off, I daresay, for a few hundred pounds."

"Mama!"

She took up her pen. "You are right, of course. It is *St. Lys* we are talking about. I had better offer him a thousand."

"If he lets her go for a thousand pounds, then he is not worthy of her," said Dorian.

"No indeed," she agreed. "All the more reason *you* should take her. *You* would not give her up for a thousand pounds."

"No. Never!"

She smiled complacently. "Then it's all settled. I'll send Captain Fitzclarence his money, and you shall dine with Miss St. Lys tomorrow night with a clear conscience. I'll have Cartwright draw up the papers."

"Papers?"

"Yes, dear boy," she told him firmly. "If she is going to be your mistress, we must do the thing properly. We must have a contract. It is as much for her protection as yours," she went on quickly, as he began to protest. "A thousand pounds per annum, I think, would be a fair offer."

"I cannot offer her money!" he protested. "We have only just met. She probably hates me."

"Nonsense. You are the Duke of Berkshire. She'd be a fool not to jump at the chance. She will be expecting you to make her an offer. If you don't, she will think you do not find her desirable. Her feelings would be hurt. You *do* find her desirable, don't you?"

"Naturally, I—Look here, madam, I do not wish to discuss such matters with my mother!" he said angrily.

"There's no need to be embarrassed. Your feelings are perfectly natural. Offer her two thousand per annum, if it makes you feel better. We would not want her to think you hold her cheap. Oh, I have no doubt that Miss St. Lys will make you an excellent mistress. And what beautiful children you will have. I shall never see them, of course, but when the time comes, I shall find husbands for all the girls, who are sure to be pretty, and government posts for the boys, who are certain to be clever. But I do not think you should keep her in Curzon Street. For one thing, it is much too close to *us*, and for another, she should have nothing but what you give her. The house in Duke Street would be better. I'll evict the tenants tomorrow."

"You think of everything," he murmured, rather dismayed by her efficiency.

"Madam!"

It was morning. Celia's bedroom was flooded with light, and Flood was calling out to her. With a groan of weak, inarticulate fury, Celia thrust her head under the pillow.

"Madam, you must get up," Flood cried, shaking her.

"Why?" Celia whined, burrowing under the covers. "What time is it?"

"Half past seven, madam!"

"What!" Celia was so surprised, she sat up and rubbed her eyes. "Half past seven?" she repeated stupidly, her heart pounding. "Half past *seven*?"

Leaping out of bed, she ran to her dressing closet, howling, "How could you let me sleep so late, you stupid cow? I've missed rehearsals! I shall be late for the curtain!"

"'Tis half past seven in the *morning*, madam," Flood told her.

"Morning?" said Celia, as if she had never heard of this word, *morning*. "Yes; that would explain the morning light pouring in at the windows. But . . . I don't understand, Flood. How could you let me sleep so long—all day and all night? They will think I missed Mr. Palmer's benefit on purpose! Well? What do you have to say for yourself?"

"'Tis *Wednesday* morning, madam," Flood told her patiently. "You've not missed Mr. Palmer's benefit. 'Tis hours away, that."

"Wednesday morning?" Celia turned slowly, her eyes closed against the sunlight. "No. That can't be right. That would mean that yesterday was *Tuesday*, and yesterday could not possibly have been Tuesday."

"Yesterday *was* Tuesday, madam."

"You're quite wrong."

"No, madam."

Celia barely opened her eyes. "Am I to understand, Mrs. Flood, that you have awakened me at half past seven on *Wednesday* morning?" she said thinly. "Why have you done this terrible thing to me? Haven't I always been good to you? I am not expected at the theatre until one o'clock."

"There's a gentleman here to see you," Flood explained.

"Is that all?" cried Celia. "Go away, you vile creature, before I turn you off without a character. And close the bloody curtains!" she added, stumbling back to her bed.

"What do I tell the gentleman?" asked Flood, hurrying to the window and yanking the two curtains together.

"Tell him to jump in the Thames," Celia suggested. Turning her pillow over to the cool side, she thrust it under her cheek. "Or you may tell him to go to Halifax. I really don't care."

"I can't tell the Duke of Berkshire to jump in the Thames," Flood protested.

Celia's eyes opened wide. "The Duke of Berkshire?" she cried, jumping out of bed. "You did not say it was the Duke of Berkshire!" Hurrying to her dressing table, she consulted the mirror. She certainly was not in her best looks. Who is, at half past seven? Her face was pink and puffy. Her eyes were seamed with sand. Her pillowcase had left deep, livid creases in her cheek. Her hair was tangled around her face. "What does he mean, coming here at half past seven? The Beau got it wrong. He is not Lord Granville without his smirk. He's Lord Granville without his *watch*."

Still grumbling, she filled the washbasin. Then, bending quickly at the waist, she plunged her whole face into the ice-cold water. Coming up again, she cursed through chattering teeth, "Bloody hell!"

Flood handed her a warm towel.

"He would not call on a *lady* so early in the morning," Celia grumbled, patting her face dry. "He is eager, I daresay, but that is no excuse for such rudeness. Well, I certainly can't let him see me like *this*," she added, looking at herself in the mirror with despair. "I look like I've been put through the mangle. Did you tell him I was still asleep?"

"I told him nothing."

Celia thought quickly. "Well, I can't see him with my eyes all puffy. He'd go away and never come back. Tell him I'm—tell him I'm in the middle of a costume fitting, and I cannot see him now. Ask him to return in an hour or so. No! No, he might be offended. Ask him to wait," she said decisively. "Tell him I won't be long. And send the girl up with some bloody coffee," she added, picking up her hairbrush.

Three quarters of an hour later, she was ready. More than ready; she was perfect. Her eyes sparkled like sapphires. Her skin looked flawless, her cheeks were rosy, and her lips were like cherries. She had dressed herself very carefully, with minute attention to detail. She took one last look in the mirror, craning her neck to get a good look at her bottom, then went down to the drawing room on the first floor with a light and confident step.

Opening the door, she went quietly into the room.

The Duke of Berkshire was standing at one of the two tall, narrow windows overlooking the street below. His back was to her.

"Your Grace," she said. "How very nice of you to come and see me!"

Dorian turned at the sound of her voice. As she moved toward him, her hand extended, his hazel eyes widened in disbelief, and his handsome face slowly turned crimson.

"Miss St. Lys?" he exclaimed, quite stunned by her appearance. Though he took her hand, he knew not whether to shake it or kiss it. "Is that you?"

Celia grinned proudly. She could not have been more pleased by his reaction. She had chosen her costume well. The superbly tailored scarlet dolman, heavily adorned with gold, fit her like a glove, while from the waist down her long, shapely legs were encased in skintight breeches of glazed white leather and polished black top-boots. A tall shako, gilded and lacquered, with a white plume, covered her head. There was even a sword, a needlelike rapier in a black and gold sheath, buckled at her side.

Holding his hand, she made a slow pirouette before him, like something from a dance, affording him an excellent view of her exquisitely molded rear end. "What do you think, Your Grace?" she asked when they were face-to-face. "Am I a good boy?"

Her magnificent blue eyes twinkled up at him, full with mischief.

"If I knocked on your door and offered you my services,

would you take me on?" she asked. "As your servant, I mean."

"I'm afraid I don't quite understand," he murmured apologetically. "Why should you do such a thing?"

"That's what happens in the play," she explained, smiling. "The heroine disguises herself as a boy, and the Duke of Illyria takes her on as his servant. The whole play hangs on it, if you see what I mean. So! If *I* came to your door—completely out of the blue, mind—and offered myself to you, would you take me on? Or would you send me away?"

Dorian seemed a little short of breath. "I most certainly would not send you away," he said, plucking at his neckcloth, which suddenly seemed too tight.

"I am *very* glad to hear that, Your Grace," she said, laughing. Releasing his hand, she stepped away and unbuckled the chin strap of the shako. Removing it, she shook out her golden curls. "If the duke rejects me in the first act, it will be a very short play indeed!" she added, placing the shako on the little desk that stood between the two windows.

"You have nothing to worry about, Miss St. Lys," he said. "I think I can safely say that you shall not be rejected in the first act."

She glanced at the clock on the mantelpiece. "I hope you have not been waiting long."

"No, not at all," he assured her.

She winced. "Oh dear. As long as that? I am sorry. But, you see, I never know how long these fittings are going to take. Do you forgive me?"

"My dear Miss St. Lys, there is nothing to forgive," he protested.

"But you were so angry when I came in. You were scowling."

"Was I?" he said. He had not been scowling, of course,

though he had been a little annoyed. He was not, after all, accustomed to being kept waiting. "I beg your pardon."

She smiled. "Of course, if I had *known* you were coming to see me this morning . . ."

"Oh, how thoughtless of me," he said quickly. "And so early, too."

"It's not important," she said. "I'm just sorry you had to wait. Your Grace is looking very countrymanlike this morning," she went on, looking over his rust-red coat, doeskin breeches, and boots with obvious approval. "I suppose you have been riding? Which park?"

Her house was convenient to both Hyde Park and Green Park.

"I do like a good gallop in the morning," he said. "I rode all the way to Kensington Palace and back again. I was so close to you that I thought I would just stop and see how you were doing. I can see that your face did not bruise. I was so afraid—"

"Let us not speak of it," she said quickly. "I was insolent, perhaps, and deserved it. Would you be good enough to apologize to Miss Tinsley for me? Truly, I meant no harm."

He stared at her. "You want me to apologize to her? My dear girl, she should be on her knees begging your forgiveness! What she did to you was unforgivable."

"No," she said demurely. "She was just jealous, poor thing. If you were mine, I might be jealous, too," she added softly.

She actually heard him catch his breath. It was very gratifying. "What do you mean?" he stammered. "I am not—I do not belong to Miss Tinsley!"

She lifted startled eyes to his face. "But . . . are you not engaged to marry her?"

"Certainly not!"

"Oh, I see. I beg your pardon," she said, looking away quickly, as if in confusion. "Do please forgive me. I misunderstood."

"There is nothing to forgive," he said. "My mother invited Miss Tinsley and her father to the play, not I. Needless to say, I shall never see them again."

"Then you will not be able to apologize to her for me?" she said slowly.

"I'm afraid not."

She looked up at him with shining eyes. "In that case," she said softly, "won't you sit down?"

Chapter 6

"You have a very pretty room here, Miss St. Lys," Dorian complimented his hostess as she was pouring out the tea sometime later.

"Do you like it, Your Grace?" she said, with a proud glance around the room. "It suits me, I think."

The room was sparsely furnished, its walls lined in pink silk, but everything in it had been chosen with exquisite taste. A suite of French furniture consisting of a sofa and two deep armchairs formed an attractive cluster around the fireplace. There was no rug upon the parquet floor. The only pictures in the room were of the actress herself, prints of St. Lys in her various roles: Desdemona looking back on Venice, Juliet on her balcony, Ophelia drowned. Over the fireplace was a large oil painting depicting Celia as Peggy, the heroine of *The Country Girl*. She sat at her desk, a letter in her hand, looking back over her shoulder. Judging by the expression on her lovely face, the letter could only have been from her lover.

"I should not tell you this, perhaps," he said presently. "You may laugh."

She was already smiling. "I may; for I dearly love to laugh."

He smiled back at her. "I shall risk your derision, and

tell you that I did a little amateur acting when I was at Eton."

She did laugh, but kindly. "Let's have it, then," she invited him.

"'A mote it is to trouble the mind's eye,'" he declaimed, rising from the sofa. "'In the most high and palmy state of Rome, a little ere the mightiest Julius fell, the graves stood tenantless, and the sheeted dead did squeak and gibber in the Roman streets.'"

Celia frowned, puzzled. "*Julius Caesar*?" she guessed.

"You have been led astray by false clues, Miss St. Lys," Dorian told her, clearly delighted that she had gotten it wrong. "Those lines are not from *Julius Caesar*. They are from *Hamlet*."

Celia groaned. "Yes, of course. Polonius, is it not? I should have known; I've played Ophelia often enough."

"Ophelia? I wish I had seen you."

"Oh, I *love* going mad!" Celia said eagerly. "I just wish they'd let me drown myself onstage. It's absolutely no fun to die in the wings, I can tell you. I much prefer to die onstage—and so I shall tonight," she added, "when I play Juliet."

Dorian was taken aback. "You play tonight?"

She nodded. "In Mr. Palmer's benefit. Mrs. Copeland was to have the part, but she has been taken ill. In truth, she has fallen pregnant and his lordship has taken her off the stage. I could not say no to Mr. Palmer. He has five children, and they must have something to live on in the summer months when the theatre is closed."

"It is most unfortunate," he murmured. "I was going to ask you to dine with me tonight."

"I should love to!" she said quickly. "I can never eat a bite *before* I play—butterflies in my stomach—so I'm always starving afterward. I should be delighted to dine with you after the play. You need not attend the performance, of course—you might just send your carriage for me."

"Not attend?" he exclaimed. "And miss the chance to see your Juliet?"

"It may be your last chance," she said. "I am getting a bit long in the tooth to play Juliet. Why, I've not played as Juliet these four years at least! I was up all night looking over my lines. 'Give me my Romeo, and when he shall die, take him and cut him out in little stars, and he will make the face of heaven so fine, that all the world will be in love with night, and pay no worship to the garish sun.' Why, I do believe I got it right that time!" she added, pleased with herself. "Though I daresay I shall make a perfect mangle of it onstage tonight! I shall have to fudge and slur my way through it somehow."

"You will be too tired, perhaps, after the play," he said anxiously.

"Too tired for what, Your Grace?" she asked, smiling innocently.

"To dine with me, of course."

She laughed. "Too tired to lift a fork? Too tired to raise a glass? Never!"

"Then I shall not fail to collect you," he said warmly. "And the night after?"

"Back to Mr. Goldsmith, I'm afraid," she said. "But next week, on Thursday night—touch wood—we begin *Twelfth Night*. Oh, I do hope we run more than twelve nights!"

He wrinkled his forehead in concentration. "*Twelfth Night*. Is that the one about the two gentlemen from Verona?"

"No, Your Grace," Celia answered, laughing. "That's *The Two Gentlemen of Verona*, oddly enough. *Twelfth Night* begins with a shipwreck. Viola's twin brother is lost at sea. She washes up on the shores of Illyria. Disguising herself as a boy, she goes into service to Duke Orsino. Viola falls in love with the duke; he is in love already with Countess Olivia. Olivia falls in love with Viola in disguise—" She broke off, laughing. "It's . . . complicated."

"And you are to play in this costume?" he asked. "In breeches?"

"Oh yes," she assured him. "My public love me in breeches. I have been practicing the art of manly behavior. I must bow instead of curtsy. I must walk with my chest puffed out. I must stroke my chin manfully when deep in thought. I must curse, and smoke, and drink, and stomp. And break women's hearts. You men really are quite awful, you know!"

"My dear Miss St. Lys," he murmured, blushing.

The clock on the mantel began striking ten o'clock, and at once Celia set down her cup and rose from the sofa. As if connected to her by a string, Dorian jumped up, too. "Oh dear! Here I am, going on and on with my nonsense, and you have been longing to get away!" she said merrily. "You must have so many things to do. I shan't keep you an instant longer."

"I have nothing to do," Dorian assured her. "I can stay all day if you like."

"Nonsense," she said quickly. "I know how busy you are, even if *you* do not. An important man like you? Really, I could not in good conscience detain you another moment."

"No, really," he insisted. "I've absolutely nothing to do. I'm free as the air."

"But I am not, Your Grace," she confessed. "Monsieur Alexandre will be here at any moment to do something with my hair, and then I must dash to rehearsal."

Dorian was mortified that he had not gotten the hint

before. "Of course *you* are busy, Miss St. Lys. How very stupid of me."

"Not at all, Your Grace."

Dorian bent over her hand, but before he could go, the doors of the drawing room were thrown open, and Lord Simon, one hand upon the hilt of his sword, strode into the room. His eyes burned holes into Celia, who had jumped behind a chair for protection.

"I hope you are satisfied, madam!"

With these words, he flung a folded newspaper at her. It landed on the tea table, knocking over one of her delicate pink cups.

"Simon!" cried Dorian, more astonished than angry. "What do you mean bursting in here shouting at Miss St. Lys? Have you taken leave of your senses?"

Simon, brought up short at the sight of his brother, was for a moment robbed of speech.

"Dorian," he said stupidly.

Celia had composed herself. "How nice to see you again, Lord Simon," she murmured coolly. "I believe you know your elder brother already, but if you don't, I should be very glad to present you."

Simon ignored her. "What are you doing here, Dorian?"

"I might ask you the same question, sir!" Dorian said indignantly.

"I have some business to discuss with Miss St. Lys," Simon said at the same time.

Dorian retrieved the newspaper from the table. "Something to do with this?" he asked, scanning the columns until something caught his eye. "Venus defies Mars," he read. "Why, this is about you, Simon," he exclaimed, glancing up in surprise. "No names are given, of course, but it *is* you, is it not? You are 'Mars' and—and Miss St. Lys, you are 'Venus.'"

"Oh, thank you, Your Grace," Celia said, resuming her seat. "May I see that, please?"

"Of course," Dorian said courteously, handing it across to her while he remained standing. "Really, Simon, you cannot hold Miss St. Lys responsible for the latest *on dit*."

"'Venus defies Mars!'" Celia exclaimed softly as she read. "'Venus *defeats* Mars' would have been better, but at least they give me top billing. That's something, anyway."

With a light laugh, she tossed the newspaper back onto the table.

"Oh, you *are* enjoying yourself," Simon said, eyeing her with cold contempt. "St. Lys is a heroine!" Simon said scathingly. "And where's the girl now, may one ask? I daresay you left her to die with her fleas on the nearest street corner."

She frowned. "You've come for the girl?"

"That guttersnipe? Certainly not. I don't care three straws about her!"

"Then why are you so angry?" she asked reasonably. Smiling when he made no answer, she climbed to her feet. "I am sorry I don't have more time for you today, my lord . . . Your Grace. I wish I did. It has been fascinating. But I'm afraid I'm frightfully busy today. I hope you will come again very soon—when I have more time," she added firmly as neither man showed any sign of moving.

"Come, Simon," Dorian said at once. "Miss St. Lys has much to do before she plays tonight. You can't blame her for the newspapers. She can have no control over the press. Nobody reads that stuff, anyway."

Simon frowned at Celia. "I didn't know you were playing tonight, madam."

"I didn't know I needed your permission, my lord," she returned, still smiling.

"I must speak to you. I shan't require more than five minutes of your time."

"So sorry. Really, I've no time to spare!"

Without another word, Simon bowed curtly, turned on his heel, and left the room. A moment later, they heard the front door open, then close very firmly.

"You must forgive my brother," Dorian said. "He was packed off to the army when he was but fifteen, and he has been fighting the whole world ever since. I fear he is ill-qualified for the demands of a polite society. Peace is not his metier."

"Clearly," she agreed. "Until tonight, Your Grace," she said, holding out her hand.

He kissed her hand and left.

Celia stood at the window to watch the duke leave the house. When he looked up, as she knew he would, she kissed her fingertips to him. He got on his horse and, accompanied by his groom, rode off in the direction of Hyde Park. No sooner had the duke disappeared from her sight than the drawing room door opened and Simon was upon her again.

Celia stared at him in astonishment as he closed the door behind him. "How did you get in?" she demanded.

"I never left," he explained.

"But we heard the door—"

"Yes. I pretended to go out."

"I see. Did you hide in the linen closet?" she asked politely.

"Book room," he replied, naming his hiding place.

"I have a book room?" she exclaimed in surprise.

"You have a room with book*shelves*," he replied dryly. "It is located behind the servants' staircase on the ground floor."

"Ah! The shelf room. It's where I keep all my shelves. It's quite handy having them all in one place."

He strode toward her, his left hand, as always, on the pommel of his sword.

"If you've come back to murder me," she said, remaining at the window, in full view of the street, "let me just warn you that I have some very inquisitive neighbors. Mr. Dickson, in the house opposite, is particularly attentive. If he were to look out of his window and see you slicing off my head with your saber, he might be tempted to—"

"Applaud?" Simon suggested, moving past her to the mantelpiece. He coldly glanced up at the painting of Celia. Not for the first time, he wished she was not so bloody beautiful.

Celia gave a silvery laugh. "*Raise the alarm*, I was going to say. Applaud! I'd forgotten how amusing you can be when you try, young man. *Quite* the rattle!"

Simon bit back an angry retort. "I have not come to murder you," he said. "Not today." Withdrawing his eyes from her image, he forced them to look upon the original. He glanced over her regimentals with disdain; though, as a man, he could not help but notice and appreciate the firm yet feminine contours of her legs and haunches. "I see you've joined the regiment at last. Did Meyer make those breeches for you?"

"Of course," she replied. "The blouse is by Schweitzer. I mentioned your name, and the staff were most attentive. They measured me so carefully. I may be the most measured woman in London. I do believe every man in Savile Row has had a turn at my inside leg. Have you come here to discuss breeches with me?"

"No."

"Am I supposed to guess, then?" She laughed. "Very well! I shall guess. You have come here to ask me—nay, to *demand* that I give up your brother. You think me unworthy of him."

"I am not my brother's keeper," he replied.

She frowned slightly. "You have not come here to rescue Dorian from me?"

"I expect his own good judgment to come into play at some point," Simon replied. "He will discover, as I did three years ago, that you are a lying, cheating baggage. Then, of course, there will be no need for anyone to rescue him. He will run away from you as fast as he can."

"As you did?"

He made no reply, merely looked at her. "You look tired," he said. "You look older."

She flinched. "I *am* tired," she said coldly. "I *am* older."

He smiled unpleasantly. "You are still very beautiful, Celia. What will you do, I wonder, when your looks have gone?"

"I hadn't really thought about it," she said, shrugging. "I never think of the future. I live in the present. Some man will look after me, I expect."

He shook his head. "I wouldn't count on it, if I were you. You have nothing to offer but your beauty. When that is gone, no one will want you."

"In that case, I shall throw myself into the Thames," she said, laughing. "Drown myself like poor Ophelia. Or perhaps I shall plunge a dagger into my breast, like poor Juliet! Yes . . . when my looks are gone, I shall certainly kill myself."

"Oh, for God's sake," he said impatiently. "You are not on the stage now, madam. Must you always be so bloody dramatic?"

"You said you had some business to discuss with me," she reminded him. "Won't you sit down?" She crossed the room and took one of the armchairs, crossing her legs like a man, one knee over the other.

He remained where he stood, looking down at her. "You are acquainted, I think, with Sir Lucas Tinsley?"

She blinked, startled, but recovered quickly. "Am I?"

Simon frowned down at her. "You met him at Lawrence's studio."

"Did I?"

"You seduced him."

"How did I do that?" she wondered.

"You invited him to come and see you," he said, biting back his annoyance.

She laughed. "Is that all it takes to seduce one of you men? The sterner sex, my foot. You are the silly sex! Don't you know, young man, that I invite *everyone* to come and see me? Young and old, tall and small, rich and poor, male and female. Bums in seats, Lord Simon. It's how I make my living."

"You were posing for Lawrence. He saw you every day for three weeks."

"You mean those meetings were not coincidental? He came there to see me?"

"You were posing in the nude, I believe."

"Yes. Sir Thomas is painting the *Judgment of Paris*. I am Venus, of course, being awarded the golden apple. Well, I couldn't let him put my face on an inferior body, now, could I? It's not a crime, Lord Simon. It is art. Sir Thomas is paying me quite handsomely."

"I don't doubt it," he said dryly. "Sir Lucas became infatuated with you. He sent you a diamond necklace."

She shook her head, bewildered. "What did you say his name was?"

"Sir Lucas Tinsley."

"Old King Coal! Why didn't you say so? Yes, of course. I met him at Lawrence's studio. What an old sweetie. I quite liked him. We got on so well. We have so much in common."

"Such as?" he said, taken aback.

"We were both born into poverty and obscurity."

"One of you shall return to it."

"This will astonish you, I know, Lord Simon, but not all of us were born with silver spoons in our mouths. Some of us have had to work for what we have."

"You call that working, do you? Strutting on the stage like a peacock? Displaying your naked body for all the world to see?"

"If I wanted to hear a sermon, young man, I'd go to church. Is there a point to all this?"

Simon focused on a point behind her head and drew a sharp breath. "Sir Lucas wants his diamond necklace back. I am come to collect it."

She raised her beautifully groomed brows in cool disdain. "Why?" she asked.

"Why? You dare ask? You failed to keep your end of the bargain, madam."

"What bargain is that?"

"You promised you would grant him your favors. In return, he advanced you the necklace. You must either keep your promise or give the necklace back. Those are your choices."

She stared at him. "Are you quite mad?"

"*Don't* play the innocent, Celia. Not with me. I know you too well."

"If *this* is what you think, you do not know me at all," she said angrily. "Do you really think I would sell myself for a diamond necklace? I am Celia St. Lys! If I want diamonds, all I have to do is snap my fingers. I don't even wear jewels."

It was true. Offstage at least, she never wore jewelry. She might wear flowers, ribbons, bits of lace, feathers—but never jewels. When asked about it, she reportedly had said, "I can't afford diamonds, and I refuse to wear paste."

"Then you won't mind giving it back."

She glared at him. "Why are you here? What business is it of yours, anyway?" she demanded. "I thought you served the Prince of Wales. Are you now dogsbody to Sir Lucas Tinsley as well?"

"I stand friend to any member of my sex who is mistreated by one of yours," he replied, throwing her own words back at her.

Her eyes glinted. "Indeed? Your reputation precedes you. But you won't find *me* as easily bullocked as poor Mrs. Cleghorn."

"I have respect for Mrs. Cleghorn. She kept her word."

"Prinny kept his word, too, and gave her his IOU. Only you robbed her of it afterward. Poor woman! When you left her, she was so frightened she could not speak. They say her hair turned positively white with terror. But I am not afraid of you, Lord Simon. You will not intimidate me. The necklace was a gift. I never promised him anything in return."

"You must have promised him something. Why else would he have given you a necklace valued at three thousand pounds?"

"Three thousands? He paid too much."

"Give it back," he said. "Give it back, or you will never be rid of me, Celia St. Lys. I will make it my business in life to ruin you."

She laughed. "I have already agreed to kill myself when my looks are gone. Don't you know when you've won, young man?"

"The necklace, madam."

"No. Anyway, I don't have it anymore. I sent it back."

"When?" he said sharply.

"Oh, I don't know," she replied carelessly. "Let one think! Yesterday? The day before? One's life is such a whirlwind! I hardly know if I'm coming or going!"

"Sir Lucas has not received it."

"Well, no. I didn't send it back to *him*. Is that what you thought I meant? No no. I sent it back to the jeweler. It *scratched* my neck when I tried it on. Mr. Grey is going to line it with velvet for me. I should have it back soon. I mean to wear it onstage."

Simon was now out of patience. "Either return the necklace or take Sir Lucas to bed," he snapped. "Which is it to be? Choose carefully."

"What are you going to do to me, sir? Drag me to the man's bed, strip me naked, and hold me down while he enjoys me? That *would* be disagreeable."

"Don't be ridiculous," he said coldly. "We both know I can make things very difficult for you. You are hoping to become my brother's mistress, are you not?"

She shrugged. "If you say so."

"Return the necklace, and I won't stand in your way."

"Won't you?"

"Refuse, and I will tell my brother . . . about us."

"You mean you haven't told him already?" she exclaimed.

"Believe me, madam. He would not be interested in you if he knew."

"About our night together? What fun we had! Haven't you told him, really?"

"I never told a soul."

"You *are* discreet. Here I thought you had *recommended* me."

"Not bloody likely!" he said roughly. "Loving you was the worst mistake I ever made."

"Loving me!" she exclaimed softly. "Did you *love* me, young man?"

"I thought so," he answered. "I thought I'd found heaven on earth."

She smiled complacently. "I know! I still have the letters you sent me when you were camped at Brighton. 'Darling, when are you coming?'"

He stared at her. "You kept my letters?"

She laughed. "You wrote me every day faithfully for three whole weeks. Don't think I wasn't tempted. Rooms over a shop! Horseback riding in Marine Parade or whatever. I even went to Schweitzer to have a proper riding habit made—blue and white and gold like your uniform. You said a cavalryman's woman should have a good seat, and I wanted to be a credit to you. But before the month was out, I . . . I *did* hear that you'd found heaven on earth with someone else."

"I waited for you as long as I could," he said stiffly.

"Three weeks!" She laughed. "Such fidelity!"

"Fidelity!" he said, red with anger. "You're a fine one to speak of fidelity. You were Lord Palmerston's mistress when I had you."

"Oh yes. What can I say? I disgraced myself. You were so very attractive. It was the summer of 'fourteen. The war had just ended, and no one thought it would start up again so soon. There were so many balls and parties. And you . . . you were so attractive. You even used to smile in those days. I could not resist you."

"You swore you would leave Palmerston—and you did—for that Frenchy."

"Armand, yes. Shall I tell you why I chose him over you?"

"Don't imagine that I care, madam!"

"I didn't say you cared. I'm sure you don't. I thought you might be curious, that's all. He offered me marriage."

Simon stared at her incredulously.

"Yes, I thought he was mad, too," she said. "But he asked me to marry him. If Bonaparte had not escaped from Elba, I might be the Marquise de Brissac. I might have been happy with you at Brighton for a while, but you would never have married me."

He looked at her, not sure whether he believed her. "If this is true, why did you not tell me? You never answered my letters. Did you think I would not understand?"

"Of course I never answered your letters; I was engaged to be married. I could not be so disloyal to my future husband. I was honored by his proposal. It was—as Juliet might say—'an honor I dreamed not of'! I wasn't going to see you or write to you behind his back."

"You didn't mind cheating on Palmerston," he reminded her.

"Henry was not my husband," she said simply. "I would have left Henry for you, if not for Armand. That is the truth."

"But you kept my letters," he said slowly. "Was that not disloyal of you?"

"I am an actress," she replied. "I suppose I could not bring myself to burn such rave reviews! They were good letters," she added. "We had our time together. But don't pretend you loved me, young man. Don't pretend I broke your heart. You wanted me at Brighton for a trophy, nothing more. You cannot blame me for choosing marriage. Anyway, it hardly matters now. Only I . . ."

"Yes?"

"I never wanted you for an enemy," she said. "I know we cannot be friends . . ."

"No," he said quickly and curtly. "We shall never be friends. But we need not be enemies. Give me the necklace, and you will never see me again. Refuse and—"

"Yes, yes! You need not repeat your threats. I know when I am beaten. I know better than to throw myself on your mercy. I surrender."

"Good. Write me a note for the jeweler. Mr. Grey, was it? I'll collect the necklace and that will be the end of it."

She nodded. Getting up, she went to her writing desk and sat down. Drawing a sheet of pink paper toward her, she took up her pen. "In such cases, I believe it is best to submit to one's fate cheerfully," she went on as she began to write. "I shall find a way to turn this little setback to some advantage. See if I don't."

He watched in silence as Celia finished her letter. Calmly, she folded it and sealed it with a wafer, pressing her seal, a fleur-de-lis, into the wax. Without rising from her seat or looking at him, she handed it to him.

"What is this?" Simon demanded angrily, as he saw the direction. "What are you playing at? You were supposed to write to the jeweler."

"I decided," she said, "to write to Sir Lucas instead. That's all right, isn't it?" Looking up at him, she smiled. "You said I must either return the necklace or grant Sir Lucas my favors. I have no intention of returning that necklace, so . . ."

Simon stared at her, aghast. "What are you saying?"

Chapter 7

"Those were the choices you gave me, were they not?" Celia said. "What's the matter? You look as though you've been kicked! Do you need to sit down?"

"Don't be a fool, Celia," he snapped. "No one expects you to go to bed with the man." Angrily, he threw the letter back at her.

"But you *said*—"

"Never mind what I said," he snapped. "Anyway, he doesn't want *you*. Not anymore. He just wants the necklace back."

She laughed. "Of course he wants me! He wouldn't have sent me diamonds in the first place if he didn't want me. Some men send jewels. Some men send roses. You, of course, sent me wildflowers. Bluebells. Was I supposed to believe you went out and picked them yourself?"

"My valet," he said coldly.

"Of course. I should have known. I should have taken your valet to bed instead of you."

"I wish you had."

Rising from her chair, she put the letter in his hand. "Take it. When Sir Lucas reads this, he'll forget all about his diamonds, I promise you. If I am wrong, I'll give you the damn necklace. But I am not wrong."

Simon regarded her impassively, his face like roughly hewn stone. Then he shrugged. "Fine. I don't really care."

"It shows," she told him.

"Damn you," he said softly.

"I meant it as a compliment," she protested.

The door opened and her manservant brought her a card. "Ah!" she said, smiling. "Send him up."

Hardly had the words left her mouth before Tom West came bounding into the room like an eager puppy. He had brought St. Lys her cloak. "Oh! I beg your pardon," he said, stopping short as Lord Simon, his face black with fury, turned to look at him.

"It's quite all right, Tom," Celia said warmly. "Lord Simon was just leaving."

Without another word, Simon left the room. This time, when she heard the front door bang shut, she knew he was really gone. She had given him no reason to stay, after all.

From Curzon Street, Simon walked to his club in Charles Street, the Guards Club, where he had left his horse. From there, he rode straight to Sir Lucas Tinsley's red brick town-house in fashionable South Audley Street. An austere butler showed Simon upstairs to the library.

Sir Lucas stood at the window overlooking the street, his hands clasped behind his back. "Well?" he said, without turning around. "Do you have the necklace?"

Simon silently drew Celia's letter from his coat. The lady's paper was distinctive: pale pink, embossed with a border of a gold fleur-de-lis. She had folded the page so that it formed its own envelope and sealed it with a wafer of white wax. Caught under the wax—Simon had not noticed it before, but he saw it now—was a strand of golden hair.

For a moment, Sir Lucas simply stared at the missive. Then he took it up with a most unconvincing show of indifference. His hand shook as he broke the white seal. Simon looked out of the window as the other man read what Celia had written in peacock-blue ink. Behind him, Sir Lucas sat down like a man whose knees had suddenly given way. "*She* wrote this?" he asked, his voice shaking with strong emotion. "With her own hand?"

"I watched her do so."

"I am to dine with her tonight at Grillon's Hotel in Albemarle Street. A private room!"

"Congratulations," Simon said coldly.

"I was to escort Lucasta to a ball tonight, but no matter," Sir Lucas murmured to himself. "I shall make my excuses. Her chaperone can take her. God knows I pay the creature enough. You are to collect Miss St. Lys at the Theatre Royal after her performance tonight."

Simon discovered, much to his surprise, that this last line had been addressed to himself. "I beg your pardon?" he said, turning from the window with a sharp frown.

"Miss St. Lys cannot arrive at the hotel unescorted. I cannot fetch her. I have my reputation to think of. How would such a thing appear?"

"I daresay they are used to that sort of thing at the Grillon," Simon said dryly.

"How dare you, sir!" said Sir Lucas, rising from his chair. His left eye circled its socket rapidly, like a cat chasing its own tail. "You will mind what you say about that lady, Lord Simon. When you see her tonight, you will treat her with the respect she deserves. She will tell me if you do not."

"I shall treat St. Lys exactly as she deserves," Simon replied. "If she chooses to make a commodity of herself, it is no concern of mine. But you must find someone else to collect your prize for you, Sir Lucas. I fear I must decline the honor of escorting her to you. I am not a panderer."

"Then I shall not cancel the annuity." Quickly, he unlocked one of the drawers of his massive mahogany desk and took out the document. "His Royal Highness shall continue to pay me ten thousand pounds per annum until he is dead. If he does not, I shall take the matter to the courts."

Simon smiled thinly. "Fine," he said. "I'll take her to you. Shall I undress her for you as well?"

"Do not be insolent, sir," said Sir Lucas, putting away the annuity and locking the drawer. "I expect you to be discreet, as well. If Miss St. Lys complains of anything, you shall not have the annuity. Do I make myself clear?"

"I understand." With a curt bow, Simon left the room.

Forty-five minutes later, he presented himself to the prince regent at Carlton House. The prince received him in his dressing gown, as he had just come out of his bath. At fifty-four, His Royal Highness was unquestionably fat, but there still remained about his person some of that manly beauty that had marked his youth. "Well?" he asked hopefully.

"Sir Lucas has agreed to cancel the annuity. There are just one or two details to be worked out. I believe I shall have some very good news for Your Highness tomorrow."

"Excellent, dear boy! How many does that make?"

"This will be the seventh annuity I have retrieved for Your Highness," said Simon.

"You must be saving me close upon a hundred thousand per annum," said the prince. "I thank you, sir, from the bottom of my heart, for all your hard work. I know it cannot be pleasant for you. People hate you, I expect."

"To be hated for my sovereign's sake is no hardship," Simon replied.

The regent clapped Simon on the shoulder. "You are

right, of course. Still, one is grateful. How did you get Sir Lucas to agree? He seemed unassailable."

"We all have our weaknesses, sir."

"Oh yes. And what is his?"

"It would be better, perhaps, if Your Highness were to remain in ignorance of it."

The prince winced. "As bad as that? Well, perhaps you are right. Perhaps one had rather not know. Best you keep it to yourself, then. But you are a miracle worker, sir!" he went on jovially. "Indeed you are. What am I going to do without you?"

"What do you mean, sir? Do without me?"

"Yes, I know you will be very sorry to leave me. I shall be very sorry to see you go. But we must make up the numbers somehow."

"The numbers, sir? I don't understand."

"We are down three seats in the House of Lords," said the prince. "I can't think of anyone more deserving than you, dear boy. I've decided to create you Earl of Sutton."

"It has a nice ring to it," said Simon.

"I know I've threatened you with a peerage before, but this time I mean it. You shall take the oath next Friday, if that is convenient."

"Friday would be most convenient. Thursday would be slightly better, however."

The prince chuckled. "Thursday is quite out of the question, I'm afraid. One is invited to the theatre next Thursday. Miss St. Lys has a new play! Captain Fitzclarence tells me she means to play in breeches. She is using him for a role model, I daresay. For the pleasure of seeing Miss St. Lys in breeches, I am prepared to hear a lot of boring speeches," he added, laughing at his own wit.

"Indeed, sir."

"I have not seen her onstage since the summer of

'fourteen. Do you remember? She was Desdemona in a nightgown. Prince von Blücher was our guest that night. He said it was all he could do not to storm the stage and rescue her from Othello! She was so charming when we met her after the play."

"I remember."

"Blücher fell in love with her on the spot! 'Is it true what they say about Prussians?' she asked him. 'That they are not born of woman, but hatched from cannonballs!' How we all laughed. If she were a man, I would knight her."

"Sir?"

"Never underestimate the power of charm, Lord Simon. Why do you suppose that Blücher and his Prussians came to relieve us at Waterloo? For love of *Wellington*? This nation owes a debt to St. Lys. She charmed the old warrior and he never forgot it."

"Sir!" Simon protested. "With all due respect, that is . . ."

The prince raised his brows.

"An interesting theory, Your Royal Highness."

"Oh, it's not a theory," the regent insisted. "It's amazing what we men will do for the approbation of a beautiful woman. Speaking of which, I may have encountered a spot of bother with Lady Conyngham, if you see what I mean. I don't suppose you could smooth things over with her husband? I'd be most grateful."

"Of course, sir."

Prinny sighed. "Charm, Lord Simon! Never underestimate a woman with charm."

"No, sir."

"Good evening, Dorian."

The Duke of Berkshire, seated alone, without even a footman in attendance, started in surprise as his brother entered his stage box that night. Then he motioned to Simon to be quiet. Celia St. Lys was onstage. Slipping into the chair next to his brother, Simon watched as "Juliet" prepared, with much hand-wringing and speechifying, to drink Friar Lawrence's potion. Finally she drank the vial, collapsing on her bed in a deathlike coma, leaving the audience in tears. The curtain came down to thunderous applause.

Dorian wiped his streaming eyes with his handkerchief. "What on earth are you doing here, Simon?" he asked.

"What are *you* doing here?" Simon returned. "It's Wednesday. Shouldn't you be at Almack's looking for a wife? You can't spend all your time in the theatre. Your mother is sure to regard this as a dereliction of duty."

"I am taking a break," Dorian informed him.

"So I see. May I remind you of your duty to marry and produce an heir? You cannot spend all your time gawping at actresses. Miss St. Lys is beautiful and charming, but she will never be a duchess."

Dorian was taken aback by his brother's contemptuous, angry tone. "Simon, I know you hate Miss St. Lys, but you *are* in the minority, you know. The rest of us worship the ground she treads on. You should have seen her at the balcony."

"Indeed, she is a national treasure. I have just been informed that she is responsible for winning the Battle of Waterloo!"

"You're in an odd humor," Dorian observed. "What has she to do with the war?"

"Her charm is more powerful than the might of armies. She would make slaves of us all."

"Do you really dislike her so much?" Dorian asked.

"Yes," Simon replied. "I really do. More than I can possibly say."

"Good," Dorian murmured. "I am hoping to make her my mistress, you see, and I would not like it if my brother were secretly in love with her. But, since you don't like her . . ."

"For God's sake, Dorian. Are you so eager to join the throng? She's had more lovers than you have years. Doesn't that bother you?"

"It would be a strange thing indeed if I were the only man who had ever desired Miss St. Lys," Dorian replied. "Naturally, she has had lovers. Poor thing! She has never had the opportunity to marry. Nor is she likely to."

Simon bit his lip. "By all means, make her your mistress. Just don't expect her to be faithful to you."

Dorian frowned. "What do you mean?" he said sharply.

"Ask Lord Palmerston," Simon replied.

"No," said Dorian, "I don't think I will ask Lord Palmerston. I'm a grown man, Simon. I can look after myself."

"You are determined to have her, then?"

"I am determined to make her an offer," Dorian replied.

"An offer?" Simon repeated sharply. "An offer of what, may I ask?"

Dorian glanced at him. "I am going to ask her to be my mistress, of course. What did you think I meant?"

"That is what I thought you meant," Simon said. "I don't suppose I can talk you out of it?"

"No."

"And when do you mean to make her this offer? Soon, I daresay?"

"Tonight. After the play."

"Tonight!" Simon exclaimed. "Quite out of the question, I'm afraid. Tonight she dines with Sir Lucas Tinsley."

"What are you talking of?" Dorian said angrily. "Tonight she dines with me."

Simon shook his head. "I'm afraid it's all been arranged.

Sir Lucas wants her, and she has agreed to . . . to sell herself to him."

"What!"

"I'm sorry. I am to escort her to him. Believe me, it's the only reason I'm here."

Dorian was frowning. "You arranged this?"

"Ten years ago, the regent borrowed a hundred thousand pounds from Sir Lucas. He's been paying an annuity of ten thousand pounds ever since. Sir Lucas has agreed to cancel the annuity in exchange for—"

"In exchange for Miss St. Lys?"

"I am sorry to pain you, Dorian, but it's perfectly true. She agreed to it."

"I do not believe you," said Dorian, thrusting out his jaw. "Miss St. Lys? Celia St. Lys? No! No, I don't believe you."

"I am sorry, Dorian," Simon said again. "Sorrier than I can say."

"It isn't true," Dorian whispered.

After the interval, the play went on, the two brothers watching in silence. In the final act, Juliet awakened in the tomb. Finding her Romeo dead, she took her own life, plunging a dagger into her breast. Aided by her delicate beauty, Celia gave a heart-wrenching performance. The audience wept like babies.

"I cannot believe it," Dorian whispered stubbornly. "Simon, you will not make me think ill of her. She is lovely! She would not sell herself."

"I see. You think she will agree to become your mistress for love? You were not thinking of offering her some reward for services rendered?"

Dorian glared at him. "That is different."

"How so? A mistress is a mistress."

"She would not sell herself to Sir Lucas Tinsley."

"She has already done so," Simon told him. "It gives me

no pleasure to be the one to tell you. Indeed, I wish it were not so. I'm your brother. I would not lie to you, Dorian."

Still shaking his head, Dorian left the box.

Simon sat for a moment. He was not wrong, he was sure. Someone had to put a stop to St. Lys's reign of terror. The Marquis de Brissac, he reflected, had been fortunate in death. Had he lived, he would have been obliged to marry St. Lys, and she certainly would have brought him to misery. Even in France, a faithless wife could bring ruin and disgrace to her husband. The marquis, Simon decided, must have been mad even to think of such a thing.

Rather surprised that St. Lys did not return to the stage for any calls, he left the box and joined the throng of men on their way to the Green Room. An excitable bunch, they seemed to have but one wish—to catch a glimpse of St. Lys. In a few weeks, Simon thought coldly, they would all be able to go to the exhibition at the Royal Academy and see their idol six feet high and perfectly nude, as Venus in the *Judgment of Paris*.

St. Lys was not to be found in the Green Room, but Simon thought he saw her slipping down the steps toward the tiring rooms. Pushing his way through the crowd, he descended into the maze of corridors. Catching up to her, he caught her by the arm.

"Where do you think you're going, my girl?" he said.

In her final scene, Juliet had been attired in a drape of filmy white muslin—someone's idea of a burial shroud. That, combined with her unbound golden ringlets, made her quite a distinctive figure. Or so he thought. But the girl who cried out in surprise and turned to look up at him was not Celia. She wore an excellent golden wig and a costume identical to Celia's. She was young and pretty, but she certainly was not the Saintly One.

"Who the devil are you?" he demanded, scowling at her.

"I beg your pardon, sir!" she gasped, frightened.

"Who put you up to this? St. Lys?"

The girl cowered beneath his fierce gaze and tried to stammer some reply. "I'm sure I don't know what you mean, sir!"

Belatedly he realized she was hardly more than a child. He had been duped, to be sure, but surely Celia St. Lys was responsible for that, not this infant. Ashamed of himself, he released her. "I beg your pardon, child," he murmured less brusquely. "I thought you were St. Lys."

"But I'm Belinda," she stammered, looking up at him with huge brown eyes.

With a bow, he left her. Pushing his way against the crowd, he slipped into the passageway that led to the actresses' tiring rooms. Celia's was not difficult to find. A brass plate engraved with her name marked her door. And if that were not indication enough, a man was on his knees peering into the keyhole.

"You there!" Simon called angrily. "What do you think you're doing?"

Startled, the man leaped to his feet. "N-nothing!" he stammered, staring helplessly as Simon bore down on him, looking incredibly warlike in his uniform, one hand on the hilt of his sword. By contrast, the other man was small and bland, a nonentity. "I-I-I dropped my spectacles, that's all. Can't see past the nose on my face without them."

"They're on top of your head," Simon told him dryly.

"Oh! Thank you, sir," the man said gratefully.

"You're a bloody Peeping Tom is what you are," said Simon. "Go on! Get out of here."

He did not have to tell the man twice. He ran away as fast as his legs could carry him. When he was quite out of sight, Simon knelt down and put his own eye to the keyhole. The room was either completely dark, or St. Lys had a keyhole cover.

At that moment, as he was in that position, the door opened. "Is it yourself, Lord Simon?"

Simon looked up into Flood's lean, leathery face. "Good evening," he said, climbing to his feet. "Miss St. Lys is expecting me, I believe."

"On your knees?"

"Is she ready?"

"She is not," said Flood. "I'm afraid you'll have to wait, my lord."

"She has ten minutes."

Flood inclined her head at a regal angle and closed the door in his face.

Chapter 8

Some fifteen minutes later by Simon's watch, St. Lys still had not come out. Simon was quite annoyed, but before he could rap on the door, a girl came hurrying down the corridor. "Oh!" she said, stopping in confusion before him. "It's you."

Simon looked down at her, belatedly recognizing the little actress whom he had mistaken for Celia a while before. Now dressed demurely for the street in a carriage dress of brown bombazine, she had shed her golden wig and scrubbed her face. Her own natural hair was chestnut brown, and neatly pinned in a twist at the base of her slender neck. She was prettier than he had thought before, with delicate features and the huge, frightened eyes of a fawn.

"We meet again," said Simon gently. He still had not found a suitable mistress to replace Miss Rogers, and he was regretting his earlier rudeness to the girl. He hoped to make up for it now. "Belinda, is it not?"

She nodded.

"What a pretty name," he said, hoping for a smile. "Were you named for the heroine of Mr. Pope's poem?"

"No, sir," she said, looking down in confusion. "For Miss Edgeworth's heroine."

Simon was taken aback. "You must be very young."

"Yes, sir, I am not sixteen," she replied.

Fifteen! Simon was not interested. His tastes did not run in the direction of inexperienced young girls.

Belinda raised her hand to knock upon the door, but hesitated. "Were you waiting for Miss St. Lys, sir?" she asked. "I was just coming to return her wig." She had it in her hands, a rich display of gold coils, like stacks of guineas, attached to a flesh-colored cap. "It is made of her own hair, and she is very particular about it."

Flood, at that moment, opened the door of her mistress's dressing room. "About time, too, you whey-faced hussy!" Snatching the wig from Belinda's hands, she inspected it thoroughly while the girl stood wringing her hands.

"What is this?" Flood demanded, rounding on Belinda furiously. Some flaw, apparently, had been discovered.

Belinda burst into tears. "I'm sorry, Mrs. Flood! I didn't think you would notice."

"Didn't think I'd notice!" Flood cried, red in the face. "You've butchered it altogether, Miss Archer."

"Indeed, Mrs. Flood, it wasn't my fault!" Belinda protested. "It was a gentleman. He wanted a lock of the Saintly One's hair. He cut it with a penknife before I knew what was what. He must have thought I was Miss St. Lys."

"You?" Flood sneered. "Mistaken for my mistress? Was the gentleman blind?"

"No, Mrs. Flood," Belinda said miserably.

"Wait until my mistress finds out!" said Flood, shaking her fist at Belinda.

The door slammed.

"Miss St. Lys is going to *kill* me," Belinda whimpered. "That is her favorite wig."

"Dry your eyes, girl," Simon told her, offering her a clean handkerchief. "It's only a bit of hair; it'll grow back."

Belinda did not understand that he was joking. "Grow back, sir? How can it? It is a wig."

"Never mind," he said quickly. "What did you need it for, anyway? I don't recall a scene with two Juliets."

"Do you remember the scene when Juliet's body was carried to the tomb?" she asked him. "Well, I was the corpse."

"*You* were the corpse?" Simon repeated, surprised. "Where was St. Lys?"

"In her dressing room, preparing for her final scene. I was at the Capulets' ball, too," she added. "I was one of the dancers. I was dressed in green."

A voice made for the stage suddenly rent the air. "Belinda! Belinda, my love!"

Sybil Archer, still costumed as Dame Capulet, had caught sight of her real-life daughter with the tall officer and was barreling down the hall to put a stop to anything that might need stopping. Though well past her prime, and perhaps a little stout, Mrs. Archer had not lost all of her beauty. She certainly had not lost any personality. "What are you doing here, child?" she asked Belinda, glancing over at Lord Simon suspiciously. "And who are you, sir?" she demanded, before her daughter could answer.

Simon recognized her from the stage. "Good evening, Mrs. Archer," he said, bowing politely. "I am Lord Simon."

"Lord Simon!" cried Mrs. Archer, her eyes widening. "Of course you are! Do forgive me. I ought to have recognized you. Belinda, this gentleman serves the Prince of Wales. He has sent for us at last! Go and put on your green dress, my love! Quickly! We mustn't keep the prince waiting!"

"His Royal Highness?" Belinda gasped. "Oh no, Mama! Why should the prince want to see *me*?"

"Because, my darling, you are charming," replied her mother. "Now run along and do as you are told. Do not argue with your mother!"

Belinda did as she was told.

"Poor child," said Mrs. Archer, reaching for Simon's arm. "She knows nothing."

Simon eluded her grasp. "I'm afraid there has been some mistake, Mrs. Archer. You seem to think that His Royal Highness has sent for you. It is not so."

She blinked at him. "He doesn't want to see Belinda?"

"No. Why should he?"

"Because she is his daughter, of course!"

Simon smiled disdainfully. "I would advise you, madam, not to say such things."

"But it's true!" she insisted. "You have only to look at her to see her noble father! She is the image of Princess Charlotte—everyone says so. Her father is George, the Prince of Wales."

"Is she?" said Simon, unimpressed.

"Indeed she is. Twenty years ago, I was a beautiful young actress and he was a handsome young prince. We were madly in love."

"*Twenty* years ago?" Simon echoed. "But your daughter is *fifteen*. She told me so herself."

"Belinda," Mrs. Archer said firmly, "is nineteen."

"Surely, madam," said Simon, frowning, "there can be no reason for Miss Archer to lie about her age."

"That is my fault, Lord Simon," Mrs. Archer said quickly. "I ask Belinda to say she is fifteen. Well, you cannot expect me to own that I am forty-nine!" she added defensively. "*Forty-five* is quite bad enough. I was thirty when Belinda was born. I have letters to prove what I say."

"You have letters?" Simon said sharply.

"I was his Perdita and he was my Florizel. You know the play? *The Winter's Tale* by William Shakespeare? Florizel is a prince. He falls in love with Perdita and wants to marry her. His father objects because she is not of royal blood."

"I see," said Simon. "Florizel proposes to Perdita?"

Mrs. Archer smiled. "Of course I would never, ever *dream* of using those letters to embarrass His Royal Highness."

"I am very glad to hear that, madam."

"I want only what is best for Belinda, you understand. I am glad her father means to acknowledge her at long last. Indeed, he can hardly deny her, the resemblance is so striking. He will know her and love her the moment he sets eyes on her, I am sure."

"But he is not going to set eyes on her," said Simon.

"Isn't he?" she said, blinking at him. "But isn't that why you are here, Lord Simon?"

"No, madam. You have taken me by surprise completely."

"Oh, I see. He does not wish to see her. I understand. But he has sent you to make us a handsome settlement, so I shall not be angry."

Simon lifted his brows. "Settlement?"

"He will want to make his daughter a most generous provision, I am sure. I understand he gave Mrs. Cleghorn ten thousand pounds, and *she* is not even the mother of his child! He'll do more for his own flesh and blood, I am certain."

The door to St. Lys's dressing room opened, and Flood stepped into the hall, keys in hand.

"I should be very glad to discuss the matter with you, Mrs. Archer," Simon murmured, "another time, perhaps."

"But we are both here now," she said. "Why don't we take Belinda home and put her to bed. Then you and I can talk, Lord Simon. I'm sure we can come to an agreement."

Simon hardly heard her. "Where is your mistress?" he demanded of Flood, who was locking the door.

"Were you waiting for St. Lys, Lord Simon?" Mrs.

Archer said, considerably surprised. "Don't tell me the prince has succumbed to *her* charms!"

"No indeed," Simon said.

"*You*, my lord?" Mrs. Archer shook her head sadly. "If you were hoping to see her tonight, then I'm afraid you have been duped. She has been gone these thirty minutes at least. The moment the curtain went down, she was off like a rocket."

"What?" said Simon, glaring at Flood. "Is this true?"

"Aye," Flood said proudly.

His eyes narrowed to slits. Taking the keys from her, he pushed open the door. The room was black as pitch. St. Lys had indeed given him the slip. "Where did she go?" he shouted, turning on Flood furiously.

"She didn't say," Flood replied.

Simon knew it would be useless to question her further. He let her go, saying, "Your mistress will rue the day she crossed me." As Flood made her escape, he turned to Mrs. Archer. "Did *you* see where she went, madam?" he asked, checking his temper.

"No," said Mrs. Archer. "I assumed she had gone off with one of her friends in the Life Guards. She has so many beaux, one cannot keep them straight. Anyway, you are well rid of her. She is not worthy of you, Lord Simon. You could do much better. You are the younger son of a duke, after all. What is she? She came to us from the gutter, and her kind is always two steps from the street. Ah! Here is my Belinda now. Isn't she lovely?"

Miss Archer was indeed hurrying up the corridor, having changed from brown bombazine into sea-green silk. She looked charming.

"Is she not an angel, Lord Simon?" her mother enthused. "She would be a credit to you, sir. She would be a credit to anyone. She has beauty, talent, and modesty. A rare combination. I say it though I am her mother. She should have been Juliet tonight, you know."

"No, I did not know," said Simon, looking at Belinda.

"Oh yes. She was understudy to Mrs. Copeland. But St. Lys, of course, *insisted* on taking the part, even though she is much too old to make a convincing Juliet. Belinda would have been *so* much better, and St. Lys knows it. She has always been jealous of my Belinda. Now that Mrs. Copeland is gone, my daughter is her only competition. Belinda is younger and prettier, and St. Lys can't stand it!"

Belinda heard her mother and blushed. "Mama, you mustn't say such things."

"Stand up straight, child," said her mother. "Shoulders back! Let his lordship look at you. There, my lord! Is she not the image of Princess Charlotte?"

Simon saw little, if any, resemblance. In any case, he hadn't the time to pursue the matter further. "Please excuse me now," he said, giving them a bow. "It was very nice meeting you both."

"Oh!" said Belinda, raising her eyes to Simon's. "Then . . . you have not come to take us to the prince?" she asked timidly.

"No, Miss Archer," Simon told her. "I'm afraid that was a mistake."

"I am so glad!" she said with obvious relief. "I'm sure I would have died of fright!"

"Lord Simon was waiting for St. Lys," said Mrs. Archer, with a touch of bitterness. "But she has let him down. She has run off with someone else."

"Oh no," murmured Belinda kindly. "How wicked of her!"

"You are much better off with us, Lord Simon," said Mrs. Archer. "Belinda would never treat you so ill. She is a good girl."

"Mama!" the girl protested, blushing rosily.

"I pray you will excuse me," Simon murmured. "I really must be going now."

"But we have so much to discuss, Lord Simon!" Mrs. Archer protested. "Belinda—His Royal Highness—the settlement! What about the settlement, my lord?"

Simon paused, remembering her talk of letters. She might not really have them, of course. But then again, she might. "Perhaps," he said, "you might do me the honor of dining with me tomorrow, Mrs. Archer? I should be very glad to discuss it with you then."

"Did you hear that, Belinda?" said Mrs. Archer. "Lord Simon wants to take us to supper! We would be delighted, my lord. You may collect us after the play, if you like. Belinda is to take the part of Constance Neville tomorrow. So it is to be a very big night for her."

"Until tomorrow then," Simon said, hastening away.

"Well, child," said Mrs. Archer, left alone with her daughter. "What did you think of him?"

Belinda blinked at her. "What did I think of who, Mama? Of Lord Simon?"

"Yes, child. Is he not a handsome man? And he was quite taken with you, my love. I shouldn't be a bit surprised if he—But I get ahead of myself."

"Was he not waiting for Miss St. Lys, Mama?"

"That is what he said," replied her mother. "But that was only an excuse to meet you, my love, I am sure."

"Why should Lord Simon want to meet me?"

"He has heard the rumors. I suppose he wanted to see you for himself."

"Rumors? What rumors?" Belinda asked, quite bewildered.

"About your father, of course."

"My father!"

"Oh, my dear," said her mother, taking her hands. "I suppose it is time you found out. Your father was not Mr. Archer."

"What!" cried Belinda, staggered.

"Your father, my love, is none other than the Prince of Wales!"

This was too much for Belinda. Her eyes crossed. She fainted, crumpling to the ground, where she lay still.

"The Duke of Berkshire's carriage stops the way!"

Pale and composed, Dorian made his way through the crowded crush room to the open doors. The air outside was so wonderfully clear and cold that he almost wanted to dismiss the carriage and walk home. He had ordered it in the expectation that he would take Miss St. Lys to supper after the performance. Otherwise, he would have walked to the theatre—if, indeed, he had decided to go to the theatre at all that night, which did not seem very likely. If not for St. Lys, he would have gone to Almack's that night, as usual. One always went to Almack's on a Wednesday during the season.

But the carriage was already here, and he might as well use it. He climbed up. The footman folded the steps and closed the door. For some reason, the carriage lamps had not been lit, and it took his eyes a moment to adjust to the darkened interior.

"Good evening, Your Grace," said Celia from the opposite side of the carriage.

Startled, Dorian jumped at the sound of her voice. "Miss St. Lys!" he exclaimed, squinting at her in the gloom. "What are you doing here?"

Celia lowered the hood of her cloak and her golden hair spilled around her shoulders. "We are going to supper, are we not, Your Grace?" she said. "You have not forgotten me, surely?"

"No," he said, recovering his composure. "I have not forgotten. But I thought—"

He broke off, confused.

"You thought what, Your Grace?" she asked as the carriage whisked off into the night.

"My brother gave me to understand that you—that he—Well, it doesn't bear repeating."

"He told you I had come to terms with Sir Lucas Tinsley," said Celia calmly. "That I had agreed to a rendezvous with that gentleman? It's quite true, I'm afraid. I did not want to agree to it, of course, but your brother told me I had to. He made threats. I was never so frightened in all my life!"

"Simon threatened you? I cannot believe it."

"I could hardly believe it myself," she said. "I did not dare say no to him. I would have agreed to anything to make him go away. Of course," she went on virtuously, "I never had the least intention of going through with it. The rendezvous, I mean. I knew that you would protect me, Your Grace. I have been hiding in your carriage since the end of the play, terrified that your brother would find me. You must think me a dreadful coward," she added, trembling. "I *am* a dreadful coward! But I did not know what else to do."

"I do not know what to think," Dorian said frankly. "My brother is a gentleman. He would never use a lady so ill."

"But I am not a lady, Your Grace," she told him sadly. "I am merely an actress, and of little consequence."

"You are Celia St. Lys!" he protested.

"Thank you, Your Grace," she murmured. "But Sir Lucas is so very rich and powerful. Men of that kind may take what they want."

"I am shocked!" said Dorian. "What has my brother to do with any of this? He serves the Prince of Wales, not Sir Lucas Tinsley."

"I am but a pawn between these great men," said Celia. "The prince must want something from Sir Lucas. In return, it seems that Sir Lucas wants something from *me*. Your brother is the facilitator of these black bargains." She shivered eloquently. "What chance do I have when such forces are arrayed against me? I must either submit, or throw myself in the Thames!"

"Throw yourself in the Thames!" he cried, alarmed. "No no! You mustn't do that."

"Then I must submit to him," she said, beginning to cry. "I must give him what he wants, though my soul dies within me!"

"No! That is not what I meant." Quickly, he took out his handkerchief and gave it to her. "Dry your eyes, Miss St. Lys. The situation is far from hopeless."

"I am sure you are right, Your Grace," she said bravely, through her tears. "I mustn't give up hope. You must not worry about me. I shall be quite all right. I'll be just fine! Just set me down anywhere, and forget you ever saw me. That is all I ask of you. I should never have gotten you involved in this. Do please forgive me."

She attempted to return his handkerchief, but instead of taking it, he shortened the distance between them and took both her hands in his. Half kneeling, half seated next to her, he kissed the backs of her hands, crying, "Set you down? Forget you? Never!"

Celia looked at him hopefully. "Your Grace?"

"From this moment, my dear," Dorian said resolutely, "you are under my protection. I shall never let any harm come to you."

"But Sir Lucas! Lord Simon!" she protested.

"I am the Duke of Berkshire," he said simply. "Believe me, you are quite safe. I'll never let anyone hurt you."

"Do you promise?" she said.

"I promise. I shall always keep you safe."

"Thank you, Your Grace."

Releasing her hands, he returned to his seat. "Now then," he said briskly. "You said you would be hungry after the play. Shall we dine at the Pulteney? Unless, of course, you would rather go home and go straight to bed," he said quickly. "I'm sure I wouldn't blame you."

"Your Grace!" she said, scandalized.

"Oh no!" he said, blushing. "You would go to bed alone, of course. I didn't mean *that*. I just thought you might be tired, that's all."

"I'm very tired," she said. "But I am also very hungry."

"You will like the Pulteney," he said. "Have you ever dined there?"

"No, Your Grace. Could we not go to Monsieur Grillon's hotel?"

"Grillon's?"

"They know me there," she said. "It's like a home away from home for me. The chef is a particular friend of mine, and Monsieur Grillon always looks after me so well when I am there. I often stay there when I feel the need to be absolutely alone. No servants, no visitors. It's like a little country retreat for me, right in the heart of London."

He smiled pleasantly. "Very well, then! We shall dine there, if you prefer."

"Thank you, Your Grace," she said sweetly, and he knocked on the window to tell the coachman.

In Albemarle Street, Monsieur Grillon himself came out to greet them at the door of his elegant hotel. To Dorian's surprise, the Frenchman kissed Celia on both cheeks as if she were his long-lost daughter. They spoke in French. Dorian could not help feeling a little neglected; he was used to being fawned over wherever he went. But he stood, smiling and good-natured until Celia, at last, presented the hotelier to him.

Smiling, Monsieur Grillon conducted Mademoiselle St. Lys and *monsieur le duc* to a private room. Though by no means a small chamber, it boasted but a single table, set for two.

When he had seated Miss St. Lys, Monsieur Grillon clapped his hands and a flurry of waiters brought iced champagne, smoked oysters, and caviar. Much French was spoken. At last, monsieur clapped his hands again, and suddenly Dorian had Celia all to himself again.

"You seem to be feeling much better," he remarked.

"Why not? I am among friends now."

"So I noticed. Do you ever think of returning to your native land?" he asked her.

Celia helped herself to some caviar. "My native land? What do you mean?"

"Well, France, of course. Are you not French?"

"Lord, no!" she said, laughing. "I'm as English as you are. At least, I hope I am. I don't really know. I was a foundling, Your Grace," she explained in response to his questioning look. "My parents could have been French, I suppose."

"Oh, I see," he said gravely. "You've done very well for yourself, my dear."

"Considering my humble origins? Yes, Your Grace. I have done well for myself. But I never forget where I came from. I often visit the Foundling Hospital, and it is my privilege to help raise money for the children there.

The ten pounds your gracious mother promised would do much good."

"Oh, good heavens," he murmured in dismay. "What you must think of me! I meant to give it to you yesterday—with a contribution of my own."

"It would be better if Your Grace gave it to the Foundling Hospital in person," she said. "I could arrange a tour, if you like. I'll show you where I used to card wool."

"You are a credit to the place," he said. "Did they teach you to speak French there?"

"No, Your Grace," she said. "I had the good fortune to be adopted by a rich lady. She had two sons, but no daughter. I suppose she singled me out because I was pretty. She dressed me up like a little doll. She quite doted on me. I grew up with the best of everything. I even had a French governess."

"So did I." He laughed. "But she never did me much good, I'm afraid."

"Oh, but I was a very eager pupil," she said, smiling. "I lived in fear that I would be sent back to the Foundling Hospital. I would have done anything to please my benefactress. I learned to sing and dance. I would perform dramatic readings in the drawing room for the whole family."

"You were destined for the stage then," he said warmly.

"Certainly I was not cut out for obscurity," she replied. "Obscurity tried to claim me once, but I fought my way back."

"And now you are the most famous woman in London!"

"Fame is a two-edged sword," she said. "Most people are good. But every now and then I meet a Sir Lucas."

His face darkened, but as the waiters had come into the room bearing the first course before them on silver trays, he said nothing. "Do not think of him," he said softly. "You are under my protection now. I shall look after you, Miss St. Lys, always."

She laughed. "Forgive me," she said, still laughing, "but I have heard *that* before."

He frowned. "Not from me, you haven't," he said firmly.

"Yes, actually, I have," she said, startling him. "I have heard it from you, Dorian. I never thought I would hear it again. But then . . . I never thought I would *see* you again."

He blinked at her. "I beg your pardon?"

"You don't recognize me, do you?"

"Of course I recognize you," he said faintly. "You are Celia St. Lys."

"Yes, I am," she said. "In spite of you!"

"I'm sure I don't know what you mean, Miss St. Lys," he stammered. "Have we—? Are you saying we have met before?"

"Of course you would not remember *me*," she said bitterly, and he was both appalled and fascinated to see that there were tears standing proud in her beautiful eyes. "Why should you, after all?"

"I am sorry," he said slowly. "I honestly do not know what you are talking about."

"I used to dream of this moment," she went on. "I never thought it would happen, but here we are. You talk of protection! You think I don't know what that means? You want me in your bed! You are the same as Sir Lucas! You think you are better than he, but you are not. In fact, you are worse! You think, after all you have done, that I should be glad, even grateful for the chance to be your plaything!"

"No, of course not. I don't—Look here! What do you mean, after all I have done? I haven't done anything."

"You *would* see it that way!" she cried. "Let me tell you something, Dorian Ascot! I would not consent to be your mistress if I were *starving* to death and you were the bloody butcher! The thought of you *touching* me makes me feel quite ill, in fact. I would rather abandon myself to a whole camp full of soldiers than suffer *one* kiss of yours. That, sir, is how much I hate you!"

Dorian stared at her, stunned. He was certain that no one had ever hated him in his life, and even more certain that he had done nothing to deserve it.

"I do not understand this hostility," he protested in confusion. "Why should you hate *me*? What have I ever done to you?"

"What indeed!"

"Well, whatever it is you think I have done," he said, growing angry, "it was yourself who brought me here to this point. Did you not encourage me to offer you my protection?"

"If I did, believe me, it was only for the pleasure of throwing your disgusting offer back in your face!" she returned.

As the door opened, Dorian shouted the waiters out of the room. When they had withdrawn, he said, tight-lipped with anger, "Are you mad? Or just distempered? *What*, I pray, has the Duke of Berkshire ever done to you? We have not met above thrice, and on all occasions, I believe I have behaved with *perfect* decorum!"

She stared at him. "Are you going to sit there, really, and *pretend* that you don't know me?"

"Of course I *know* you," he said, quite baffled. "Everybody knows you. You are Celia St. Lys!"

"I wasn't always," she said. "I was once a frightened little girl, and you—Look at me, Dorian!" she commanded. "Take a good, long look! Are you *quite* sure you don't know me? Do I not look at all familiar to you?"

"My dear girl!" he protested, falling back. "Of course

you look familiar. Your face is in every shop window in London."

"Think back!" she snapped, shaking her head impatiently. "The first time you saw me—the first time you saw *Celia St. Lys*, I mean—did you not think to yourself, *I know that face! I have seen that face before—somewhere*."

"No," he answered. "I'm sure I would have remembered."

Tears pricked her eyes. "Have I really changed so much?" she asked, sinking down onto her chair.

"It seems you have, I'm afraid," he told her.

"You are exactly the same as I remember you," she said sadly.

"I wish you would tell me what I've done," he said quietly. "I am sure it must be some mistake . . . But if I *have* done wrong, I promise you, I will put it right if I can."

"You cannot put it right!" she said, searching his face. Tears stood in her eyes. "How could you put it right? I see now just how little I meant to you. And I am told I have a face no one could ever forget."

"I can see you are very upset," he said. "But, my dear, whoever it was who hurt you—it was not me. Could it have been Lord Granville?" he asked suddenly. "There is said to be some slight resemblance between me and that bounder—though I never saw—"

"It was *you*, Dorian," she said, choking back a sob. "I was called Sarah then. I'm *Sarah*. Surely you remember!"

Dorian shook his head slowly. "I—I'm sorry, my dear."

"But you've got to," she insisted. "I used to sit on your knee, and you would tell me I was the prettiest girl in the whole world."

"No, my dear," he said, holding up his hands. "*That* I would remember."

"Did I imagine it, then?" she said angrily. "You used to tell me if I didn't want a husband, I could always go to

London and make my fortune treading the boards at Drury Lane. Where do you think I got the idea?"

"I don't know, madam! Look here! I don't know what game you're playing at, but I know I don't like it. I am leaving." Rising from the table, Dorian flung down his napkin.

"Go then," she said angrily. "You are dead to me anyway. I shall never forgive you as long as I live!"

He shook his head. "You are confused, madam. Your mind is unbalanced. I am sorry for you, but I cannot help you."

"For my seventh birthday," she said loudly, arresting his progress to the door, "your father gave me a gold locket in the shape of a heart. It had an S on it, picked out in diamonds. I want it back, if you please."

Dorian stopped dead with his hand on the door handle. "A locket?" he repeated, turning to look at her, his face suddenly quite pale. "In the shape of a heart?"

"You had no right to take it from me," she said, her voice shaking.

"Good God!" he cried out softly. In the next moment, he was on his knees beside her chair. "Sally?" he said, seizing her hands. "Is it you? Is it really you?"

Chapter 9

Celia pushed him away. "*Sarah*, if you please," she said coldly. "My name is Sarah Hartley. Yes, Dorian. It is I. I lived with you at Ashlands for six years, after your mother took me in. I should have thought you'd remember me, but no! Neither of you did. I was actually nervous to meet you again after all these years, though I do believe I hid it rather well. You looked right at me, didn't you? But all you saw was Celia St. Lys, potential mistress. Do you remember me now, Your Grace?"

"Of course I remember you," he said, staring at her. "You were nicknamed Sally. I just didn't—I didn't *recognize* you, that's all. I have not seen you in—in ten years."

"Have I changed so much?"

"Yes, my dear, you have," he said softly. "You are a woman now. My God! Little Sally! How can this be? What in God's name happened to you?"

He would have taken her hands, but she snatched them away.

"What do you mean, what happened to me?" she cried. "You know damn well what happened to me! When I was eight years old, your mother brought me home with her as a pet—a charity case, if you prefer. I'd never seen anything like

Ashlands! Suddenly I was a fairy princess in a fairyland. You called me your cousin Sally. You were my cousin Dorian, and your mother was my aunt Fanny! I suppose you meant well when you took me in. I was happy. But you made me believe I was one of the family. That was cruel. You promised to take care of me always, and I believed that, too. But you lied, Dorian. You lied!"

"No, Sally. It was not a lie."

"Of course it was a lie!" she cried. "The truth is, your mother was bored. I was a pretty little thing. I amused her for a time. She took pleasure in bestowing her bounty upon me. Her drawing room was my first stage. You were my first audience, and how I strove to please you all! Lord! I thought I'd died and gone to heaven. When it was all taken away from me—"

She broke off, trembling helplessly as she blinked back fresh tears. "When it was all taken away from me," she began again, in a steadier voice, "I could not understand what *I* had done wrong. Why didn't Aunt Fanny love me anymore? Why did Cousin Dorian send me away?"

"Send you away?" he repeated, gray around the mouth. "Good God! How could you think that? I would never have sent you away! Never! We were all so fond of you, Sally."

"But you *did* send me away, Dorian," she said.

"No," he said. "Of course I didn't."

Celia stared at him. "Am I to believe you did not know?" she exclaimed.

"I swear it. I have no idea what you are talking about!"

"Did you not notice that I was gone?" she cried.

"Of course I did—we all did! We felt the loss very keenly, but—"

"Out of sight, out of mind!"

"That is not how it was at all," he said sharply. "My wife fell ill. I took her to Bath to take the waters. When Joanna and I returned to Ashlands, you—you were gone, Sally, my dear."

"And you never wondered what happened to your little *cousin*? Did you never try to find me?"

"No," he said. "I never wondered about you. I never looked for you. Because you were dead, Sally."

She blinked at him, unable to understand. "What?"

"My mother told us you were dead, that you had died while we were away at Bath. All this time, Sally," he went on gently, "I have believed you to be dead and buried in the churchyard at Ashland Heath."

She stared at him, stunned. "Dead and buried?" she echoed. "I—I don't understand."

"Nor do I. We grieved for you. We mourned you. We all did. But there was no reason to *wonder* what had become of you. We thought we knew."

"If I am dead, how did I die?" she said. "Answer me that, if you can."

"You took a fall from your pony and broke your neck. You died instantly."

"Your mother told you that?"

"Yes, she did."

"At least I didn't suffer," she said tartly. "*Where* did you say I was buried?"

"In the churchyard at Ashland Heath. There's a very nice stone, and the grave is kept very neat and tidy, I do assure you. I do not understand any of this, my dear, but I am very glad to see you. I wish you were glad to see me," he added.

Tears slid down her cheeks. "But, Dorian! Your mother sent me away. Your father would never have allowed it when he was alive, but she said . . . Oh, Dorian! She told me it was what you wanted. You and Cousin Joanna."

"Joanna was as fond of you as I," he said. "We were both quite shocked to learn of your death. If my mother told you that . . ." He shook his head. "Why would she do such a thing?"

"You really didn't know she had sent me away?" said Celia.

"Of course not," he said, frowning. "If I'd known, I would have found you and brought you back to Ashlands, where you belonged."

"Do you mean that, Dorian?"

"Yes," he said simply.

"Then it was *she*," Celia said. "It was she and she alone who did this to me. Oh, Dorian! All this time . . . I have hated you—you *and* Joanna."

"My dear Sally!" he murmured. "What happened?"

"I don't know," she said. "I suppose she just got tired of having me around. She buried me, all right, but not in the churchyard at Ashland Heath. She sent me to Ireland."

"Ireland!" he exclaimed. "We have no acquaintance there."

"Nor did I. It was a cold, gray, barren place where I was."

He shuddered. "Well, but you had someone to look after you, at least, I hope," he said. "Surely you were not alone?"

Her lips twisted into a travesty of a smile. "No, I was not alone."

"Were they good people at least? Were they kind to you?"

"No, Dorian," she said, shaking her head. "They were *not* kind to me. *He* was not kind to me at all!"

"He?"

"My husband," she said simply.

"Husband!" Dorian exclaimed.

"Not only did she send me away, she arranged for me to be married. I thought it was what *you* wanted for me, Dorian."

"But you were only fourteen," he whispered. "How could she—"

"I was fifteen on my wedding day, if that makes you feel any better."

"No, it doesn't!" he said grimly.

"Fortunately, he was quite old. He only lived to torment me for five years. I am grateful it was no longer. When he died, I wept tears of joy. He left me some money. Not much, but enough. Enough to get me to London, which was all I wanted."

A waiter tentatively poked his head in the room, but Dorian waved him off. "I think you should come home with me to Berkshire House," he said decisively. "We'll confront my mother together. Her cruelty shall be exposed. She must answer for what she has done."

"I don't want that," said Celia. "You cannot expose her without exposing me. I am not Sarah Hartley anymore. I am Celia St. Lys. I've worked very hard to get where I am. No one can ever know that I was—that I was ever her pet, her plaything, her charity project. Do you think I want people to know about my brute of a husband? You would only expose me to ridicule, or worse—pity! Swear to me, Dorian, on your life, that you will not say a word about this to anyone. No good could ever come of it. We cannot change what happened. I would be humiliated if people knew. If you ever cared for me at all, say nothing. Tell no one. Not your mother, not your brother. Oh, certainly not your brother."

"He played no part in this business, at least," said Dorian.

"No," she said quickly. "He'd already been packed off into the army when I came to live with you. How he would gloat if he knew! Please, Dorian, if you ever cared for me at all, say nothing to your brother. Say nothing to anyone."

"Of course you have my promise, if that is your wish."

"Do you swear?"

"I swear I shall not tell a soul," he said gravely. "If that truly is what you want."

"That is what I want," she assured him. She smiled faintly. "How I have hated you all these years! Do please forgive me! I should have known you would not use me so ill. Not my dear, sweet cousin Dorian. I brought you here tonight with no other purpose than to hurt you. I was going to make you fall in love with me. I was going to make your mother pay me to go away. Then I was going to break your heart. Somehow, I couldn't go through with it. I had to tell you who I was."

"I am very glad you did."

She smiled faintly. "So am I. I have missed my cousin Dorian."

"I have missed you, too, Sally," he said. "Why did you not come to me sooner?"

"How could I? I thought you had thrown me away. I had to wait for you to come to me."

"Shall we finish our supper?" he asked gently, for the waiters were again hovering.

Celia shook her head. "I'm not hungry anymore. I think I'd like to be alone now, if I may."

"Of course," he said, studying her strained face. "I'll take you home now."

"No," she said. "Suddenly, I'm quite exhausted. I just want to sleep. Would you be good enough to arrange a private room for me? My maid can come in the morning to attend me," she added, as he looked rather doubtfully at her. "We will talk again, Your Grace, very soon."

"No, you must never call me that again," he said. "You must call me Dorian, as you used to, when we first met. When my father was still alive, and you were the prettiest little girl in Berkshire."

He left briefly, to make the arrangements for her.

* * *

Simon searched for St. Lys all over London. Finally he gave up and made his way to Grillon's Hotel, where, though it was nearly four in the morning, Sir Lucas still waited.

The hours had not been kind to Sir Lucas. His clothes were rumpled, his cravat quite ruined. He had been drinking and his eyes were bloodshot. His wig was askew.

"Lord Simon! At last!" he said angrily as he admitted the other man into the private room he had engaged for himself and St. Lys. "I have been waiting for you this age."

Simon took in the scene at a glance. A table had been set for two near the fire. The napkins were still folded in neat, upstanding triangles, but the tablecloth was stained with claret. The doors to the next room—presumably a bedchamber—stood closed.

"My patience has worn thin, sir! Where is she?"

Like Sir Lucas, Simon was out of humor. "I cannot tell you," he replied. "She slipped away from me at the theatre."

Sir Lucas's left eye skittered in its socket. "*You let her go?*" he cried.

Simon lifted his brows. "Certainly I let her go. What would you have me do? Abduct her? She is free to move about as she pleases."

"But I have her letter," Sir Lucas cried. "She *promised* to meet me."

Simon shrugged. "It seems the lady has changed her mind, Sir Lucas. A woman's prerogative, I believe."

"This is intolerable, Lord Simon! You must find her. She must be made to keep her promise to me. I will not be made a fool of by an actress."

Simon frowned. "I will get your necklace back for you, Sir Lucas. Further than that I cannot go," he said sharply.

Sir Lucas frowned. "I am not asking you to assist me in

a rape, sir," he protested. "She agreed to meet me. She must keep her word."

Simon smiled coldly. "In a civilized society such as ours, I fear there is but one way of forcing a female to keep her word, Sir Lucas."

"Indeed, my lord! And what is that?"

"Marry her, of course," Simon said curtly.

Sir Lucas recoiled in disgust. "Marry her! Don't be ridiculous! I? Marry an actress? What would Lucasta say if I presented her with such a woman as a replacement for her sainted mother?"

"I really don't know, Sir Lucas," Simon said impatiently.

"Marry St. Lys! I am not such a fool as that, I assure you."

"It was not a serious suggestion, Sir Lucas," Simon said thinly. "I was merely pointing out that you cannot force a woman to do anything unless she is your wife. Miss St. Lys has changed her mind. That is her right. I cannot assist you any further."

"This is your fault," Sir Lucas declared. "If you had brought her to me directly as you promised, she would have had no opportunity to change her mind. Instead, I have sat in this room all night like a bloody fool! Needless to say, I shall not be canceling your royal master's annuity, after all. You did not keep your end of the bargain."

"The lady is unwilling, Sir Lucas. There is nothing more to be done."

"I have her letter," said Sir Lucas. "If she does not keep her word to me, I shall publish it. I shall drag her name through the mud."

Simon frowned. "And your own, Sir Lucas."

"Oh, I shall keep *my* name out of it, of course."

"Give me more time," Simon said, after a pause. "I may be able to persuade her to give up the necklace. I'll buy it back from her, if I must."

"What do I care about the necklace?" said Sir Lucas. "I don't want it back; I never did. It is the *principle* of the matter, Lord Simon. She made me a promise, and now she must keep it. I demand that she keep her promise. If she refuses, I shall ruin her. You may tell her that!"

Simon bowed. "I will leave you to your reflections, Sir Lucas."

Walking quickly, he made his way back to the stairs. To his surprise, Monsieur Grillon was waiting for him on the landing. "Yes?" he said impatiently.

The Frenchman bowed politely. "The lady will see you now," he said, gesturing. "This way, if you please, my lord."

Simon stared at him. "Lady? What lady?"

"Mademoiselle St. Lys," replied M. Grillon, smiling calmly. "She wishes to see you now. Please to come this way."

"She is here? St. Lys is here?" Simon said in disbelief.

"*Mais oui, monsieur*. She has been waiting for you for quite some time."

Bemused, Simon followed him.

Celia had taken the suite identical to Sir Lucas's on the opposite side of the hotel. She did not answer the door right away. When she did, it was evident that she had been roused from a deep slumber. "You're very late, my lord," she complained, pulling her dressing gown tight around her shoulders and yawning.

"I wonder why," he said tightly.

She stood aside to let him in. "Would you like a drink? There's some very good cognac here."

"No," he snapped. "I would not like a drink, madam. I would like an explanation."

"Oh dear!" she murmured, closing the door. "You don't look at all pleased to see me. Rough night?"

Simon strode into the room, taking it in at a glance. As in Sir Lucas's suite, the door to the bedroom was closed.

She spoke briefly in French to the hotelier, then closed the outer door. They were alone. Celia sat down in one of the chairs beside the fire.

Simon took a position at the mantelpiece. "I have been looking for you all night, madam. I trust you have been amused."

"Were you looking for me, my lord? What for?" she asked innocently.

"You know damn well what for," he snarled. "You had an appointment, madam, with Sir Lucas Tinsley!"

Her eyes widened. "What? Good heavens! Was that tonight?"

"You know damn well it was tonight," he said, glaring at her.

She groaned. "Lord, I'm such a half-wit! I'd forget my own head if it weren't attached to my body. Really, I've the most dreadful memory."

"That must make it difficult to learn your lines, Miss St. Lys," he observed.

"Lines?" She laughed, throwing back her head. "I don't have to learn lines, Lord Simon. I have golden hair and perfect breasts. Or hadn't you noticed."

Simon swore under his breath.

"You little devil!" he said. "You knew this was the last place I would ever think to look! I almost feel sorry for Sir Lucas! The damn fool has been eating his heart out all night, and you were here the whole time, laughing at him, no doubt."

"Actually, I haven't given him a single thought."

Simon shook his head. "I shall never understand you! Why let him think he could have you when he could not? That was cruel, Celia, even for you. And why let me think—" He broke off and raked his fingers through his hair. "You never had any intention of meeting him tonight, did you?"

"No," she answered. "But I had every intention of meeting you, my lord! I ought to slap your face! You, feel sorry for Sir Lucas? Don't. He thought he could buy me! Now he knows better. So do you, perhaps. Celia St. Lys is not for sale."

"You have made him angry."

"Good. Imagine how I felt when *you* showed up at my house accusing me of God knows what and demanding that I grant the man my favors. You, of all people! God knows I have my faults, my lord, but I am not a harlot. The necklace was a gift. I did not ask for it. I certainly never agreed to do tricks for it! Do we understand each other now?"

"He has your letter, Celia," said Simon. "He means to hand it over to your friends in Grub Street."

She only smiled. "You wouldn't let him do that to me, surely," she said. "The only reason I wrote that letter is because you made me."

"I certainly did not," he said angrily. "I only wanted you to return the bloody necklace!"

"But you never told me why," she remarked. "If I had to guess, I would say that your master, the prince regent, wanted to borrow some money from Sir Lucas. And Sir Lucas would only agree to it if you brought me to him as a sacrifice."

"He asked me to get the necklace back," Simon said. "That is all. I would never have agreed to anything else. It was not my idea to bring you here," he reminded her, "but yours."

"But you knew he wanted me."

"Naturally. But I never dreamed you would offer yourself."

"Was I right about the money?" she asked.

"You know I cannot discuss that."

She sighed. "I could not give you the necklace, even if

I wanted to," she said. "It's to be auctioned off at the end of the season. The proceeds are to go to the Foundling Hospital. I've given them my word. I shan't go back on it."

"I would not ask you to," he said. "Good night, Celia. Good morning, I should say. I'll leave you to enjoy your triumph."

"Wait," she said, rising from her seat. "I never said I wouldn't help you."

Going to the writing table at the back of the room, she found paper and pen.

"He doesn't want a letter, Celia," Simon said impatiently. "He wants you in his bed."

"No, he doesn't," she replied, writing quickly. "That's just what he *thinks* he wants. Like before, when he thought he wanted the necklace. It seems complicated, I know." She laughed. "If it were simple, I could make you understand it."

"Very funny."

"Have faith, young man! He liked my first letter, didn't he?"

"Oh yes," he admitted. "He practically danced a jig."

She chuckled. "This one," she said, bringing him the finished letter, "will have him turning cartwheels."

She was quite wrong. Sir Lucas did not attempt any cartwheels. He was too drunk even to leave his hotel room, let alone attempt such exercise. "What is this?" he demanded groggily, as Simon dragged him out of bed.

"A letter from St. Lys," Simon told him, putting Celia's latest into the man's hands.

"It's not pink," Sir Lucas slurred, pushing it away.

"No, Sir Lucas. She wrote it here at the hotel. See the letterhead?"

Sir Lucas squinted up at him in confusion. "She was here? Miss St. Lys was here?"

"Yes."

Rousing himself, Sir Lucas opened the letter. Upon reading it, he threw up his massive head and glared balefully at Simon. "You brute!" he spat, shaking his fist. "Did you think Miss St. Lys would not tell me how you treated her? How you insulted and terrorized her? You *forced* her to agree to meet me. You frightened my poor girl out of her wits. You villain!"

Simon scowled. "What! Let me see that!"

Sir Lucas moved with surprising speed. "You shall not see her letters! No one shall!" he cried, flinging Celia's letter into the fire. Taking her first letter from his inside coat pocket, he added it to the flames. "Here! Take the annuity, too. I do not want it. Take it!"

Simon took it, glancing over it.

"Now she is quite safe from you, Lord Simon!" Sir Lucas said. "You shall never see her again. You are out of our lives. We are rid of you forever! We are free! Free!"

"Thank you, Sir Lucas," said Simon, pocketing the annuity.

"I should like to make you suffer as you have made her suffer," said Sir Lucas, striding to the door. "I should like to challenge you to a duel! But I would not add to Miss St. Lys's distress."

He tore the door open. "You, my lord, are a scoundrel! One day, you will get what you deserve."

"I certainly hope so," said Simon. "Good night, Sir Lucas. It has been a pleasure doing business with you."

"You should be boiled in oil!" Sir Lucas shouted after him, and slammed the door.

Chapter 10

Simon ran lightly down the stairs, crossed the landing, and climbed the stairs on the other side of the hotel. Passing down the corridor, he found Celia's door and knocked. This time she did not keep him waiting.

"Well?" she said, opening the door a few inches. "Did he give you what you wanted?"

She stepped back to admit him into the room, but he merely bowed, preferring to remain in the hall. "Yes," he said, adding after a slight pause, "thanks to you."

"I'm always happy to help," she said, not moving from the doorway.

"And he burned your letters, too."

"Naturally," she replied. "I asked him to. I told him I was afraid of what might happen if they fell into the wrong hands."

"*My* hands, I suppose."

"No, my lord. His," she replied. "I hope the prince will be pleased."

"I should think so."

"I am hoping he will come to my play on Thursday next," she said. "I don't suppose you would be good enough to mention it."

"Why don't I come in," he murmured. "We'll discuss it. I would very much like that drink, if the offer still stands."

She smiled. "Hadn't you better be getting back to Carlton House? Aren't you on duty? What if His Royal Highness should fall out of bed? Who will pick him up if you are not there?"

"Lady Conyngham, I should think."

Her eyes widened. "Really?" she said eagerly. "Is it a one-off or is Lady Hertford out altogether? And what does Lord Conyngham have to say about it?"

He smiled. "Let me in and I'll tell you all about it."

Celia considered it for a moment. "No, I don't think so," she decided. "If I let you in, you're going to kiss me. And if you kiss me, how am I to resist what you do next? As much as I love palace gossip, I think I'd better keep myself to myself tonight."

He frowned. "You are teasing," he said. "Let me in. You know you want me. Why else have you been here all night in this room waiting for me?"

"Oh, I see!" she said, laughing. "You think I did all this for you?"

"Yes, and now I am here," he murmured, leaning against the door.

"No, young man," she insisted, pushing against the door he was holding open. "I gave myself to you once, much too quickly, and you have held me cheap ever since. I've learned my lesson."

"I never held you cheap, Celia."

She merely shook her head. "It's very late, my lord, and I am tired. Please go."

"Very well, then," he said. "Good night."

She did not answer, but closed the door softly.

* * *

That afternoon, Captain Fitzclarence brought Miss Eliza London to the Theatre Royal.

"How are the rehearsals going?" he asked Celia as she returned to her dressing room from the stage. Celia was in half costume, with Kate Hardcastle's panniers tied over her own skirts.

"Surprisingly well," she replied, as Flood hurried to remove the troublesome hoops. "Miss Archer is not as bad as I feared. In fact, she's much, much better than I ever dared to hope. I think we just might survive the night. Where did those come from?" she asked Flood, catching sight of some flowers partially wrapped in silver tissue. In the room were several handsome vases filled with pink roses, but these were wildflowers: bluebells, wild lupine, snowdrops, and golden asphodel intertwined.

Flood brought her mistress the card. It said only *Tonight*.

"Not even a question mark," she murmured, smiling to herself.

"Are those from the Duke of Berkshire?" Fitzclarence asked.

"I'll never tell," she replied, turning her attention to the smartly dressed young woman seated next to the officer on the pink sofa. "Who is your pretty friend?" she asked.

The young woman burst out laughing. "Go on with you, Miss St. Lys!" she cried, in unabashed Cockney.

Celia gave her another look. "Good heavens, Miss Eliza!" she exclaimed.

A bath and clean clothes had worked wonders for Miss London. Her gown of sprigged muslin was in the very latest style, as were her green velvet gloves and bonnet. Her hair had been washed, cut, and styled by an expert. Glossy black ringlets framed her unusual little face. Her wide-set gray eyes sparkled. Her full lips, emphasized with a little rouge, looked positively bee-stung. Even her teeth were good. Though she was still too thin, she looked very well; not quite a beauty, but certainly alluring.

Fitzclarence was grinning. "I told you she wouldn't recognize you, Lizzie!" he said.

Eliza jumped to her feet to give Celia a top-to-toe view of her transformation. "Don't I look a treat?" she cried, preening.

"You look lovely, my dear," Celia said sincerely.

"Lovely!" Fitzclarence said indignantly. "She looks good enough to eat! I'll say this for Lord Simon: he knows how to spot a diamond in the rough."

"Pshaw! I ain't no diamond," Eliza cried, blushing.

"I think you are, Miss Eliza," said Celia.

"Even her teeth are good," said Fitzclarence, clearly proud of his new acquisition.

"A man once offered me ten shillings for me chompers," said Eliza. "'Ow do you think I'd look without them, Miss St. Lys?" Opening her mouth, she drew her lips over her teeth at the same time, making an outrageous face. "Like an old woman, eh?"

The girl was so droll that Celia could not help laughing.

"Oh, Miss St. Lys!" Eliza went on. "You've been so good to me! I don't know 'ow I'll hever be hable to thank you for hall you've done."

"Thank me, child? Whatever for?"

"For me new dress," said Eliza, holding up her skirt. "For me new 'air," she said, touching her curls. "For me new everything!" she cried, spinning in a circle.

"But surely, Captain Fitzclarence did all that."

He laughed. "Naturally, I did—with your money, Auntie Celia."

"Oh, I see," said Celia, her hands on her hips. "How much did all this cost me?"

"Never mind the cost," Fitzclarence said impatiently.

"Look at her! It had to be done. The poor girl was in rags! Besides, you won't get the bills for weeks and weeks. By then you will be rolling in it."

"Rolling in it?" Celia repeated in distaste. "Rolling in what?"

"Money, of course. Did you not dine last night with the Duke of Berkshire?"

"I did."

"And did he not make you a handsome offer?"

"He did offer me his protection," she admitted.

"My dear Celia! Congratulations," cried Fitzclarence. "I'm sure you deserve it! I'm sure you shall be very happy. He seems like a dull, plodding, dependable sort of man—just what you need. He'll look after you properly. Make sure you get it in writing, however, and don't let him slip any conditions into the contract when you're not looking. My father promised my mother four thousand a year, but he cut her off when she went back to the stage. She was ruined, as he must have known she would be. Anyway, it was in the settlement, though I doubt she bothered to read it."

"Don't worry," Celia told him. "Nothing like that is going to happen to me. The Duke of Berkshire is nothing like your father, I'm happy to say."

"Indeed! How much is he offering you?"

"None of your business," she said primly.

"Perhaps it isn't. But you certainly can afford a few hundred pounds for Miss Eliza!"

"A few hundred pounds!" Celia exclaimed. "What did you do, take her to Madame Lanchester?"

"Of course," he said. "Could I do anything less for your protégée? The protégée of Miss Celia St. Lys must cut a dashing figure. I knew you would want Miss Eliza to have the best of everything. Now she is a credit to you."

Eliza clasped her hands together. "And I'll work as 'ard

as hanything for you, Miss St. Lys. I'll pay back hevery farthing of what I owes you, I swear I will!"

"First of all, my dear," said Celia. "My name is pronounced *Sin-Lee*, not *Sighnt-Lee*. You must learn to speak properly, and mind where you put your H's and where you don't."

"Yes, Miss Sigh—Miss St. Lys. I'll be sure to mind my aitches."

"Good. Now then! What sort of work can you do, my dear?" Celia asked kindly.

"Can you sew?" Flood broke in to ask.

"Mrs. Flood!" Fitzclarence said sternly. "Let us be clear on one thing! Miss London is not here to assist you in your menial labors. Miss London is to be an actress. She is to grace the stage with Miss St. Lys."

Celia gave a startled laugh. "Indeed? Well, perhaps when she has learned to speak."

"No, tonight," he insisted. "I want her in the play tonight. I have been boasting to all my friends that my new mistress is to take the stage tonight—with my old mistress."

"I am not your mistress," Celia said coldly. "Old or otherwise."

"They don't know that. Come on, Celia. All you have to do is snap your fingers, and she's in."

"No, Clare. She's not ready."

"I shall look a fool if you don't," he said, frowning. "Come, Celia! You owe me. I want you to put her in the play tonight."

"I do not owe you anything, Captain Fitzclarence," she said sharply. "In any case, what part do you imagine her playing?"

"She'll be the maid, of course," he said, as Eliza sat mutely begging with her huge gray eyes. "Poor child! She can't talk well enough for anything else—yet," he added, squeezing Eliza's hand. "What do you care anyway? Does it really matter who plays the maid? It's only one scene, half a dozen lines at the most."

"Mr. Grimaldi was going to do it for a lark, *en travesti*," said Celia.

"Good old Joe!" said Fitzclarence. "He won't mind. He's the last person to stand in the way of a hopeful young talent."

Celia looked thoughtfully at Eliza. "You'll have to learn a few lines."

"I'm a fast learner," cried Eliza. "Indeed, I am!"

"Where would you be now, Celia, if no one had ever given you a chance?" said Fitzclarence persuasively.

"Oh, all right!" Celia said crossly. "After nuncheon I'll try her out."

"Oh, Miss St. Lys! Do you mean it?"

"I'll have to talk to Mr. Rourke, of course," she added, raising her voice to be heard over Eliza's squealing. "I can't promise you anything."

Fitzclarence grinned. "Oh, Rourke won't say no to you. No one can say no to Celia St. Lys—you keep them all in business, my dear. I knew I could count on you," he added, climbing to his feet. "Didn't I tell you, Lizzie? Didn't I say it would be all right?"

"You did, Clare, you did!" Eliza cried, flinging her arms around him and covering his face with kisses.

"There, there," he said, extricating himself from her enthusiastic embrace. "Let me go, there's a good girl."

"Yes, Clare," she murmured meekly, composing herself.

"I must be off now, or I shall be late," he said. "Lizzie, you stay here with Auntie Celia, and do what she tells you."

"For the last bloody time, I am not your auntie!" Celia said indignantly.

Eliza clung to Fitzclarence as he started for the door. "Aren't you going to stay and watch me, Clare?"

"I wish I could, little one, but I can't," he told her. "You know I can't. I'm taking Miss Tinsley for a ride in the park this afternoon. I mustn't be late."

"What?" cried Celia. "How did that come about?"

He smiled, pleased with himself. "I met her last night at Almack's. At the doors of Almack's, I should say, for her vouchers have been revoked."

"No!" said Celia, laughing. "Have they really?"

"Yes, my dear. The Duchess of Berkshire had her vouchers revoked, and she could not get in, for all her three hundred thousand pounds. Miss Tinsley was beside herself. 'Do you know who I am?' she fairly shrieked at the poor attendant, who, naturally, had no idea who she was. Nor did he care. Her little chaperone was in tears. I quite felt sorry for them."

Celia laughed. "I'm sure you did."

"Naturally, I could not leave them there weeping. So I took them to the opera. I told Miss Tinsley you had broken my heart, Celia—that you had thrown me over for the Duke of Berkshire and his forty thousand a year. Heartless baggage! I made her promise that she would never see her faithless Berkshire again. She made me promise that I would never see *you* again. And now," he finished, smiling, "we are the best of friends, Miss Tinsley and I."

"So you are taking her for a ride," said Celia, "in more ways than one."

He laughed. "And don't forget you promised to make me a present of a thousand pounds on my wedding day."

"Wedding day!" Eliza cried in dismay.

"Now, don't be jealous, Lizzie," he told her firmly. "We discussed all this. *You* have my heart, but Miss Tinsley is to have my name. I am sorry for it, but there it is. I am obliged by my circumstances to marry an heiress. One must have money, after all. You don't have to like it, but you must accept it."

"Yes, Clare," Eliza said meekly, hanging her head. "I know. It's just . . . 'earing you sigh 'wedding dye' like that. It 'urts me 'eart."

Taking her in his arms, he kissed her in the doorway. "If you had a fortune, my Lizzie, I'd marry you tomorrow," he told her warmly.

Eliza brightened immediately. "Oh, Clare! Would you, really?"

"Of course I would," he assured her. "But, as it is, I shall marry Miss Tinsley."

"Shall I wait up for you, Clare?" she asked. "Or go to bed?"

"Both, you silly goose," he replied, laughing.

Then he was gone.

"Did you 'ear that, Miss St. Lys?" Eliza cried, hugging herself. "If I 'ad a fortune, 'e'd *marry* me!"

Flood snorted. "Sure he'd marry *me* if I had a fortune, the low-down dirty buccaneer."

"That," Eliza cried in shock, "is no way to speak of the king's grandson!"

"Come, Miss Eliza," Celia said quickly, stretching out her hand to the girl. "Come and meet everyone."

The cast and crew had assembled in the Green Room to partake of a cold repast before going on with rehearsals. They all sat comfortably together at one long, cloth-covered trestle table, chattering and arguing and laughing like an extended family. Celia found a place for herself and Eliza on either side of Joseph Grimaldi, the famed pantomime clown.

"Miss St. Lys!" he exclaimed in mock awe. "To what do I owe this great honor?"

"This is my friend, Miss Eliza London. I'd like her to

try for the maid's part tonight. If she can do it, you needn't bother."

"Heavens! I am betrayed," he cried.

"I thought you might work her into one of your harlequinades," said Celia. "You should hear her sing 'Hot Codlins.' It's really quite amusing."

"'Hot Codlins'!" he protested, bristling with mock fury. "That's *my* song, darlings! I own it outright! Nobody ever heard of 'Hot Codlins' before Joe Grimaldi."

"And nobody ever heard of Joe Grimaldi before 'Hot Codlins,'" Celia replied, laughing. "Come, sir, won't you let her sing it? We just want to borrow it—isn't that right, Miss Eliza? We'll give you a kiss for it," she added.

Joe Grimaldi pretended to be quite shocked. "Oh! For shame!" he cried, making everyone within hearing laugh at the line he had uttered so often onstage.

"It's only one scene, Mr. Grimaldi," Celia pleaded prettily, "and it would mean so much to the girl. When I first came to the theatre, you helped me. You and Mrs. Jordan. No one else had a kind word for me. When I went onstage, they'd all line up in the wings and make faces at me, and show me their arses, too! Anything to break my concentration. But you were always kind to me."

"And now you want to help this girl?"

"If we don't, Mr. Grimaldi, who will?"

There was no softer touch in the London theatre than Joe Grimaldi. "Oh, all right!" he said gruffly. "She can have the part, steal my song, and leave me broken and bleeding on the floor—just like every other woman in my life."

"Thank you, Mr. Grimaldi!" said Celia, kissing his left cheek.

"Thank you, Mr. Grimaldi!" said Eliza, kissing his right cheek.

"Yes, yes," he said, waving them off like an impatient father. "Run along now."

Simon arrived at the theatre that evening well before the curtain was slated to rise. Upon entering his brother's box, he was surprised to find his brother there.

"What are you doing here, Dorian?" he asked, taking the seat next to his brother. "Surely the queen is expecting you to attend her drawing room tonight. If not," he added, "your mother certainly is. You cannot spend all your nights in the theatre."

Dorian seemed out of humor. "I have no intention of going to St. James's Palace tonight," he said coldly. "I may never go there again. Did our mother send you here to find me?"

"No," said Simon, puzzled. "I have not seen our mother for two days; not since we were all here together on Tuesday, playing happy family. Why should she send me to find you? Have you run away from home, Dorian?" he asked, chuckling.

"Certainly not," Dorian snapped. "But I have removed from Berkshire House for the time being. I shall be at my club."

"Removed from Berkshire House?" Simon repeated, startled. "Why should you do that?"

"I have my reasons," Dorian muttered. "I would not stay another night under the same roof with that woman."

"Well, I certainly can't blame you for *that*," said Simon dryly. "But what did Her Majesty ever do to you? She will be expecting to see you at court. Do you really mean to disappoint her because you have had a disagreement with your mother?"

"I have not had a disagreement with my mother," Dorian

replied. "I have not spoken to her since breakfast yesterday morning."

"She still wants you to marry Miss Tinsley and her three hundred thousands, I take it?"

Dorian glanced at him, startled. "No. Oh no! On that, at least, we are agreed."

"Then what?" Simon asked. "What has she done that would make you leave your home in the middle of the season and hole up in your club like a fox run to ground?"

Dorian shrugged uncomfortably. "I need not explain myself to you, surely," he said. "I promised Miss St. Lys I would attend the play tonight. We are to dine together afterward."

"What?" Simon said sharply. "You are to dine with St. Lys?"

"With Miss St. Lys, yes."

"And when did you make her this promise?" Simon demanded.

"I don't see what business it is of yours," said Dorian. "And I certainly hope you have not come here tonight to browbeat her again about Sir Lucas Tinsley," he added.

"Browbeat! Is that what she told you?"

"Yes. She told me all about it last night."

"Last night! When did you see her last night?"

Dorian looked at him, shaking his head. "You should be ashamed of yourself, Simon. When I left the theatre, there she was. I found her hiding in my carriage, frightened to death."

"Frightened to death," Simon scoffed. "Frightened of what?"

"Of you, of course. She only agreed to do what—what you asked of her—out of fear. But of course she couldn't go through with it. You owe her an apology."

"So she was with you last night," Simon murmured

coldly. "I might have known! You took her to the Grillon, I suppose?"

"I had the honor of escorting Miss St. Lys to Monsieur Grillon's establishment, yes. They know her there."

"They certainly do!"

Dorian flushed with anger. "What is that supposed to mean?" he demanded.

"I think you know what I mean, sir," said his brother, also red with anger.

"Miss St. Lys and I dined together, nothing more. I respect her."

Simon snorted. "Ah . . . but does *she* respect *you*?"

"Simon, I am warning you," Dorian said stiffly. "That lady is under my protection. If you go on like this, we shall quarrel. I do not want to quarrel with you," he added. "Apologize, if you please, and we'll say no more about it."

"Perhaps I should apologize to *her* as well!" said Simon.

"Indeed you should," said Dorian. "I hoped, in fact, that that was why you were here."

"No," Simon replied. "I have a much more agreeable reason for being here. Like you, I am come to the theatre seeking a mistress."

"Miss St. Lys is not my mistress," Dorian said firmly.

"No, of course not," said Simon. "You respect her."

Dorian hastily changed the subject. "Tell me, Simon, which lady has caught your eye? Old Mrs. Archer? I did not think you liked older women."

"I have my eye on Mrs. Archer's daughter, as a matter of fact."

Dorian consulted his playbill. "Ah yes! Miss Archer plays in the role of Miss Neville tonight. I suppose she's pretty?"

"You suppose correctly," said Simon. "More than that, she is sweet and unspoiled. Quite unlike *your* treasure.

And," he went on, as Dorian scowled, "there is a distinct possibility that she is the natural daughter of the Prince of Wales."

"Distinct possibility?" Dorian repeated. "What, pray, does *that* mean?"

Simon shrugged. "As you know, His Royal Highness has a strict policy against acknowledging any of his by-blows. When confronted by a rumor, he neither confirms nor denies the child. But when I mentioned Mrs. Archer to him, there was a definite gleam in his eye, and he did say that he would like to see Miss Archer, if she ever took the stage like her mother."

Dorian frowned. "And that is why you take an interest in the girl? Because she may be the regent's natural daughter."

"No," said Simon. "I like her for herself alone, naturally. I hear that she is quite an accomplished actress. She was to have played Juliet last night, in fact, but St. Lys became jealous and took the part herself."

"And she was exquisite in the role."

"I am glad you liked her performance," said Simon. "It will probably be the last time she is ever seen in the role."

"Why do you say that?"

"St. Lys is almost thirty, I should think. Juliet is but fifteen."

"Sally is but twenty-four," Dorian said coldly. "And Juliet is not yet fourteen in Shakespeare's play—though her age is given as sixteen in some earlier sources."

"Sally?" Simon repeated in astonishment.

"Miss St. Lys, I should have said," Dorian murmured. "I suppose you will be taking Miss Archer to supper after the play?" he went on quickly.

"Yes. Why not?" said Simon. "And you will be dining with St. Lys. Perhaps we might all go together. What could be more wholesome? Two actresses out on the town with their . . . protectors."

"I shouldn't think so," said Dorian.

"Of course. I understand. You'll want to be alone with Sally . . . the better to respect her."

"Miss St. Lys and I have a great deal to discuss, as it happens," said Dorian. "Anyway, you will be making love to Miss Archer. We would only get in the way."

"Then I shall take my girl to the Pulteney," said Simon.

"And I shall take Miss St. Lys to the Grillon."

"Again?"

"I shall take her wherever she wishes to go," Dorian snapped.

"Naturally," said Simon. "But . . . what have you done with Fitzclarence?"

Dorian looked startled.

"Has she broken with him? Have you bought him off, or what? Or is she to keep two strings to her bow?"

"You are right," Dorian murmured. "I shall have to deal with Fitzclarence."

"You cannot both protect her, after all," said Simon. "What if she loves him? It would be cruel to take her away from him. Like King David stealing the wife of Uriah."

"She is not his wife," said Dorian. "She may love him, but he is not worthy of her. In any case, he does not *love* her. If he did, he would have made her his wife."

"Made her his wife? A half-pay captain and an actress! There's a match made in heaven," Simon said with a short, dry laugh. "You think her suited to the domestic life, do you? Dorian, you've only just met her. You don't know about her."

"I know a great deal about her, as it happens," said Dorian.

"Oh yes? Where does she come from? Who are her people?"

"She comes from Berkshire," Dorian replied.

"From Berkshire? You amaze me, Dorian. Did she tell

you she was from Berkshire? Your own, sweet county? If you were the Duke of Durham, she would have been from Durham, I promise you. You are too naive."

"She was not born in Berkshire, perhaps, but she was brought up there. I know this for a fact. You see, I met her before. Years ago. She was just a girl then."

Simon frowned. "What do you mean?" he asked, after a long pause. "You knew her before? You knew her when?"

Dorian shrugged. Remembering his promise to Celia, he had no intention of saying anything more. Indeed, he was sorry he had said so much. "What does it matter? *Obviously* there was nothing between us in those days. She was only a child then, and I was a married man."

"But *I* did not know her."

"No. No, you were in India when she—at that time. It was a slight acquaintance, nothing more."

"What was she? Village maiden? Farmer's daughter?"

"I have given her my word to say nothing more of her— her past. She has worked very hard to escape it."

"I see. Was it as bad as that?"

"Yes, Simon," Dorian said quietly. "I rather think it was as bad as that."

Simon was silent. He'd never given much thought to what Celia's life might have been like before she had become an actress. "Surely," he said, "things could not have been so bad, not in Berkshire."

"No," said Dorian. "I believe she was happy there. It was that brute she married. He was the source of her unhappiness."

For a moment, Simon could not speak. Finally he was able to choke out three words: "Celia is married?"

"Widowed," said Dorian. "Oh, I should not have told you this. I gave Sally my word. Simon, she told me in confidence."

"And now you are telling me in confidence," said Simon. "Don't worry, Dorian. I shan't say a word to anyone."

At that moment, the curtain went up and they were distracted by the opening of the play.

Miss St. Lys made her entrance. Tonight her throat was bare, but as she lifted her skirts a little, she showed the audience slim ankles encased in stockings of pink silk. Her friends in the pit roared with approval. Celia clearly enjoyed the attention. She simpered and twirled, shamelessly displaying herself. The play came to a complete standstill.

Only then could the actors go on.

Simon could not help but steal a glance at his brother's face. Rather to his surprise, Dorian looked dismayed. Clearly, he did not care to see his "Sally" as the object of such open gallantry. "St. Lys is in fine form tonight," he murmured.

Dorian sighed. "I do wish she would not—not—"

"Egg them on?" Simon finished his thought.

"Yes," said Dorian, watching Celia with despair. "She should not encourage them like this. It will make them too bold."

"But she loves the attention. She basks in it like a snake sunning itself on a rock. She'd freeze to death without the approbation of the crowds."

"You mean to imply, of course, that she is a cold-blooded creature," said Dorian. "She is not. She just wants to be loved. *This* is not love, though she may think it is. This is merely blind adoration. These people do not know her. They will never know her."

"You sound rather as though you mean to take her off the stage," said Simon, raising his brows. "That will only make you the most hated man in London, I fear."

"They'll find someone to take her place," Dorian said softly.

Simon looked at him, frowning. "You are serious! You mean to take her off the stage."

Dorian made no reply.

On the stage, golden in the light of the foot lamps, St. Lys put her fingers to her lips, effectively silencing the whole theatre. The play resumed, and the brothers did not speak again until Dorian suddenly nudged Simon in the ribs. "Here is your pretty friend," he murmured.

Miss Archer had indeed blundered upon the scene. She came out a little early, before Celia had finished her speech, and was obliged to stand there, looking foolish, until it was over. Fortunately, hardly anyone in the audience noticed her faux pas, as all their attention was upon the ravishing figure of St. Lys. Then Celia turned to her and, stretching out her hand, said, "'I'm glad you're come, Neville, my dear. Tell me, Constance, how do I look this evening? Is there anything whimsical about me? Is it one of my well-looking days? Am I in face today?'"

As Miss Hardcastle asked these questions of Miss Neville, she seemed to appeal more to the audience than to her friend. The young men in the pit answered her loudly and with enthusiasm: "Yes, Miss St. Lys!"

St. Lys was not satisfied. "I said: Am I in face today?" she repeated.

"Yes, Miss St. Lys!" bayed her pack of hounds, louder still.

Celia gurgled with laughter and gave them all a fond wink.

Now it was Miss Archer's turn to deliver her lines. Frightened by the noise of the crowd, she found she could barely speak. When she did, she stammered and whispered, her voice so faint that even Miss St. Lys seemed to have difficulty hearing her.

"We can't hear you!" someone called from the gallery.

Cries of encouragement erupted from the pit: "Speak

up, love!" and "Don't be nervous!" But this only seemed to frighten her more. Hanging her pretty head, Belinda whispered more lines, turning her red face away from the audience. Finally, her lips moved no more. She stood, petrified, and almost in tears. She turned as if to run from the stage.

"She is shy, poor thing," Dorian murmured to Simon. "Most unfortunate for an actress."

St. Lys did not miss a beat. Grabbing Belinda's arm, she threw back her head, laughing gaily. "What's that you say, my dear Constance?" she said, linking arms with the other actress. "'Sure no accident has happened among the canary birds or the goldfishes? Has my brother or the cat been meddling? Or has the last novel been too moving?'"

These were the lines Belinda ought to have delivered.

"'No; nothing of all this,'" Celia went on, giving her own lines. "'I have been threatened—I can scarce get it out—I have been threatened with a lover!'"

The scene continued with Celia, in effect, playing both parts. Belinda went on whispering her lines to Celia, and Celia went on blithely repeating them with a merry "What's that you say?" to the audience. Then she would speak her own lines.

The audience applauded wildly, always ready to approve of their idol. Belinda was rescued, and so was the scene. "Well done, Celia," Simon murmured under his breath.

"If this keeps up, Miss St. Lys will be hoarse by the end of the night!" Dorian complained as the curtain went down on the first scene.

Fortunately, Miss Archer seemed less nervous as the play went on. She even improved a little. She was at her best in those scenes she shared with her mother, and at her worst when being made love to by Richard Dabney, the actor in the role of Hastings. Still, she was not very good.

Dorian tried to be tactful. "She's very pretty," he told his brother. "I can see why you like her."

"She's a little nervous."

"Nervous! She would have been laughed off the stage if Miss St. Lys had not come to her rescue," said Dorian. "What jokester told you Miss St. Lys was jealous of her talent?"

"Her mother," Simon admitted.

Dorian laughed, and Simon, after a moment, joined in.

Eliza's moment came in the third act, right after the interval. As the scene began, people were still returning to their seats. Miss Hardcastle's maid entered stage right and, with the stage to herself, began straightening up her mistress's room, humming "Hot Codlins" as she did so. The audience, of course, knew the song made famous by Grimaldi the clown, and some of them gamely began to hum along with the pretty little maid. Encouraged in her mischief, the maid found her mistress's best dress and slipped it over her head—backwards, which made the audience laugh.

"Who is this?" Dorian asked, consulting his playbill. But the maid's part was such a small one that it was uncredited. "Whoever she is, she has a natural gift for comedy."

In her borrowed finery, the maid pretended she was at a ball, simpering and flirting with imaginary admirers, coldly rejecting others. Finally, fluttering her eyelashes seductively, she offered her hand to the air. With a slightly wobbly curtsy, she began clumsily to dance with her pretended partner, while the orchestra, softly at first, began to play a waltz under the stage.

But what began as a facsimile of an elegant waltz soon deteriorated into a wild jig. The audience, led by the unruly young men in the pit, shouted encouragement and began to clap their hands in time.

By the time Miss Hardcastle appeared, the maid was careening about the room like a whirling dervish. Startled, the little maid froze for a moment in the most unlikely of positions—both arms and one leg flung up—as her mistress strolled past her, lost in her own thoughts. Without seeming to notice anything amiss, Miss Hardcastle began to speak. The maid quickly disembarrassed herself of her mistress's dress, and by the time Miss Hardcastle turned around, all was innocence. The audience roared with laughter.

When Miss St. Lys came out for her first curtain call at the end of the play, flanked by Mrs. Archer and Miss Archer, the audience had not forgotten the little maid. Since no one knew her name, they called her to the stage by singing her song, "Hot Codlins."

"Did somebody call for me?" cried Grimaldi the clown, sailing from the wings.

"No!" they cried.

But he began singing his song anyway, getting through two verses before they could persuade him it was the girl they wanted.

"What?" he cried, feigning injury. "You don't want me?"

Pouting, he left the stage.

The entire cast came out and stood onstage, seemingly perplexed. "Who do they want?" they all asked themselves. "Who can it be? There's nobody else!"

Then Eliza came shuffling out, lugging a mop and bucket as if she meant to mop the stage, and was greeted with tumultuous applause. She stared at them all in surprise.

"Wot's all this?" she wanted to know.

Then everybody sang "Hot Codlins," and the play was officially over.

Chapter 11

St. Lys, still in costume, was holding court in the Green Room, something she did not do often, but tonight she was bringing out a protégée. By the time Simon and Dorian made their way backstage, she was knee-deep in Life Guards, a glass of pink champagne in her hand. Eliza was with her patroness, half-hidden by the officers crowded around them. Fitzclarence was not among the throng of admirers, but nearly a dozen of his fellow officers were dancing attendance on the two actresses, veteran and novice alike.

Simon held back, watching his brother as the latter plunged into the crowd. His eyes narrowed as he watched Celia greet the Duke of Berkshire with a dazzling smile. He could not hear what they were saying, but Dorian turned and beckoned for him to come. Reluctantly, Simon made his way to them.

"I believe my brother owes you an apology," said Dorian, but Celia laughed.

"No indeed!" she said quickly. "That was all just a silly misunderstanding, was it not, Lord Simon? Best we forget it altogether. Indeed, I have already forgotten it."

"And so have I," Simon said with a cold bow.

Celia beckoned to Eliza. "Your Grace, may I introduce my friend Miss London to you?"

"How do you do, my dear?" said Dorian, shouting over the noise. "You were wonderful!"

Eliza seized on him. "Would you believe they pies me to do it?" she shrieked in his ear.

While they were conversing, Celia caught Simon's arm. "Tonight," she murmured in a low voice.

"I beg your pardon?" he said sharply.

She gurgled with laughter. "Did you really think it would be so easy? That all you had to do was send me a handful of bluebells and I would fall at your feet? I have not spent the last three years building a throne for you in my heart, Lord Simon, as you seem to think. You will have to try harder, I'm afraid."

"I'm sure I don't know what you mean, Celia," he said, watching his brother fetch champagne for the new girl.

"Did you not send me wildflowers? And did the card not say, with rudest simplicity, *Tonight*?"

"There must be some mistake," he said. "I did send some flowers, but not to you. I am very sorry if you were inconvenienced. They ought to have gone to Miss Archer."

"To Belinda? You cannot be serious!" She laughed.

He glanced at her. "I assure you, I am quite serious."

"*Tonight*?" she said, lifting her brows.

"I am taking Miss Archer to supper tonight."

"How sweet! Hot codlins and pork pies from a street vendor, I suppose?"

He glared at her. "Private room at the Pulteney Hotel," he snapped.

Celia burst out laughing. "I'm afraid you're going to be very disappointed, Lord Simon." Turning away from him, she seized hold of the nearest man. "You remember Mr. West, of course. Tom, this is Lord Simon. Lord Simon is the devoted admirer of Miss Belinda Archer. Tom knows Miss Archer very well, don't you, Tom?"

"I wouldn't say that I know her well, Miss St. Lys," the young man answered in confusion.

"But, Tom! You have been making love to her!"

"Miss St. Lys!" protested the young man, blushing. "I have been doing no such thing!"

"Yes, you have, Tom," she insisted. "You were making love to her for hours and hours this afternoon. I saw you."

"That simply isn't true," he said, frowning. "I was not making love to her. *She* was making love to *me.*"

Celia threw back her head and laughed. "So she was! And not doing a very good job of it, I'm afraid."

Tom sighed. "It's true she is not very good. *You* are much better, Miss St. Lys."

"I ought to be; I have been at it longer. But I have given her the benefit of my experience. I have showed her over and over again how to make love to you, but she just doesn't seem to have the knack! Oh! If I weren't your sister, Tom, what I might do to you!"

"I collect Mr. West has been helping you with the new play," Simon said coldly, tired of her nonsense.

Celia blinked at him in amazement. "Yes, of course! Why? What did you think I was talking about? I hope you did not think I was impugning the good name of your fair friend? Tom has been standing in as Sebastian at rehearsals. Sebastian is Viola's twin brother; I am Viola. Don't you think we look alike?"

"No."

Celia sighed. "I'm afraid rehearsals are not going very well, are they, Tom?"

"I'm sure it's my fault, Miss St. Lys. I told you, I'm no actor."

"Oh, you mustn't blame yourself, Tom," she told him

sweetly. "Poor Belinda is no better at making love to *me* than she is at making love to *you*."

"Miss Archer was endowed by her maker with natural feminine delicacy," said Simon. "Being a modest female, she is loath to put herself on display. It is true, she may be ill-suited for the profession, Miss St. Lys, in which you excel, but that is to her credit, not her shame."

Her eyes narrowed with anger. "Perhaps you would be good enough to make her your mistress, then, and take her off the stage. I'm sure we'd all be most grateful—especially the audience."

"Perhaps I will," he said.

"*Tonight*?" she said, smiling.

Simon made no answer. Bowing, he left her to her friends. Celia stared after him, frowning, but as Dorian made his way to her, she gave him a dazzling smile. "What do you think of Eliza, Your Grace?"

"Very amusing," he murmured.

"She needs polish," Celia admitted, "but she has a certain something about her, and she's quite fearless on the stage. That's half the battle, you know, overcoming one's nerves."

"My dear," Dorian said, breaking in, "it's becoming very hot and crowded and noisy. Shall I escort you to your room to change your dress?"

She laughed. "But I like it hot and crowded and noisy! That is how it should be. *Life* is hot and crowded and noisy. Or hadn't you noticed? But of course you haven't! You live in an ivory tower."

Dorian seemed taken aback. "I do not live in an ivory tower."

"No; a marble mansion in Mayfair! It might as well be an ivory tower—or the dark side of the moon, for that matter—'tis so cold and remote!"

"I am sorry you think so, my dear," he murmured. "Still, I do think it is time to go."

He tried to take her elbow, but Celia pulled away from him. "No! I cannot leave now," she protested, stealing a glass of champagne from one of the officers. "Tonight we are celebrating the debut of a great new talent. I mean to stay up all night! Gentlemen!" she cried, stumbling a little as she attempted, rather unwisely, to climb up on a crate at the back of the room. Two officers of the Life Guard came to her rescue and lifted her up. "A toast!" she cried, lifting her glass. "To Miss London!"

"But, my dear!" Dorian protested as the company erupted into cheers. "I had hoped to have a quiet dinner with you this evening. We must have a serious talk, you know, about your future."

Celia glanced down at him crossly. "No no no, Your Grace! Of all things, I hate a serious talk. I am much too young for a serious talk, I am sure! I want to sing and laugh and dance the night away. And I shall! Everyone! I'm giving a party, and you are all invited!"

"Who's giving a party?" someone shouted from the back of the room. "I love a party!"

"*I* am," cried Celia. "In honor of my friend Miss London! You are all invited to my little house to celebrate her first appearance at Drury Lane. The first of many, I hope."

"When? When?"

"Now, of course!" she answered. "Is there ever a better time?"

"My dear," Dorian said gravely, helping her down from the box. "Is this wise, do you think? All these people . . . in your house?"

"Of course it's not *wise*," she returned recklessly. "In fact, it's a very bad idea—worst idea I ever had! But if I wanted to be wise, Your Grace, I'd grow a beard and read law. You needn't come to my party, if you don't wish," she added primly.

"But of course I shall come, Sally," he said, frowning.

"Are you sure? Because it's going to be hot and crowded and noisy, and I know how you hate that. You might think it beneath your dignity."

"Not at all, my dear," he assured her. "I shall be delighted to attend your party."

"Good," she said. "How would you like to be in charge of the food and drink?"

"My lord!" Mrs. Archer welcomed Simon to the dressing room she shared with her daughter. She was dressed to go out in a low-cut gown of blue satin trimmed with ermine. A purple turban crowned her head. Pinned between her continuously jiggling breasts was a jeweled and enameled badge in the form of three white feathers encircled by a golden belt, the emblem of the Prince of Wales. In his youth His Royal Highness, Simon knew, had been in the habit of offering such tokens to his favorites. "How good of you to come and see us again so soon," said the woman, inviting him to sit. "May I offer you some sherry? Belinda is dressing, but she will not be long."

Like St. Lys's dressing room, Mrs. Archer's was divided into two sections, but the curtain that divided them was of crimson velvet, not flimsy muslin. Simon could hear Belinda sniffling behind the curtain, but of her he could see nothing.

He despised sherry but accepted the glass. When she had filled her own glass, he proposed the toast. "To Miss Archer."

"To Belinda!" Beaming, Mrs. Archer sat too close to

him on the sofa. "Now then, my lord. Have you come with an offer?"

"You must understand, madam, that the matter is delicate," Simon began. "If Belinda is, in fact, the natural daughter of the regent—"

"If!" she said indignantly.

"If," Simon said firmly, "it is so, why have you waited so long to come forward?"

"But I have not waited, my lord. When Belinda was born, His Royal Highness made me a present of five thousand pounds."

"Most generous."

"That is only what he did for me," she said. "He promised to look after Belinda. He promised to make her a handsome settlement upon her marriage."

"Upon her marriage?" Simon repeated politely. "I see. And is Miss Archer engaged?"

"She is not engaged at present," Mrs. Archer admitted. "And, without a fortune in hand, I do not suppose she will be engaged anytime soon. If we only knew what we could expect by way of a dowry . . . His Royal Highness's letter was not specific as to the amount of the settlement. He only said it was to be handsome. *Handsome*. That was the exact word he used."

"May I see the letter?" Simon asked.

She smiled. "Oh, I couldn't possibly do that, my lord! His Royal Highness has used me very ill, it is true, but as long as I have a heart, I could never bring myself to betray him. The letter is very precious to me. Not even Belinda has seen it. Indeed, it is the sort of thing a mother might show only to, say, a future son-in-law."

"I see," said Simon.

"Well, it would not be right to keep Belinda's husband in ignorance," she said. "He should know that his wife is of royal blood, and that her father has promised her a handsome settlement. I, of course, would never pursue the matter, but *he* might."

"Then it is your intention for Belinda to marry."

"Certainly," said Mrs. Archer, bristling. "It's true she has grown up in the theatre, but I have guarded her virtue most carefully, my lord. She is as pure as the day she was born. All that is lacking is a fortune. But with a dowry of ten thousand pounds, I see no reason why I might not one day address my daughter as 'my lady.'"

"Ten thousand pounds?" said Simon. "I shouldn't call that handsome. I should call it fantastical."

"Ten thousand is nothing to him," she said indignantly. "He gave as much to Mrs. Cleghorn for the pleasures of one night. I should think he would do that much at least for his own daughter. If she cannot marry, what will become of her? She will be passed from man to man. Is that what he wants for his child?"

"But surely, Miss Archer is destined for the stage," Simon said. "Like her mother before her."

"It seems she has not inherited my talent," said Mrs. Archer darkly. "She is well enough in rehearsals, but on-stage she loses her nerve completely. You saw her tonight, my lord. She let the St. Lys woman steal her lines and talk all over her!"

"She seemed a little nervous at first," said Simon. "But she got better."

"Oh, the pit was in a frenzy when she came on. But then, St. Lys had riled them all up, winking at them and showing a bit of leg—the hussy! Poor Belinda must have thought they were going to eat her. She is too timid for the stage. She may get a little better, but she will never be good enough for London. I am no longer young, Lord Simon," she went on. "The parts are drying up for me.

When I die, I shall have nothing to leave my daughter but debts. Debts . . . and His Royal Highness's letter. I would see Belinda married soon."

"She is charming enough to attract a husband even without a dowry."

"Yes, but of what kind?" said Mrs. Archer. "I would not see her marry anything less than a gentleman. But so far, I have received offers only of the most disreputable kind. Gentlemen do not see her as marriageable. They think she is like the other actresses. I would not see her become a rich man's mistress, Lord Simon. I would see her married."

"That is certainly to your credit."

"But . . . one has debts, you see. Terrible, crushing debts. Shall I speak plainly, my lord?"

"Please do."

"If His Royal Highness does not keep his promise—if Belinda cannot marry—I fear she must be brought out by some gentleman or other as a woman of the town! Though it breaks my heart to say it," she added, with a sidelong glance.

At that moment, Belinda herself emerged from behind the velvet curtain, looking younger than her nineteen years in a simple gown of sprigged muslin. "Oh!" she said. "Forgive me, Mama! I did not know you were entertaining a gentleman!"

Rising from the sofa, Simon bowed to her. "Good evening, Miss Archer. Your mama has been telling me all about you. Shall we go to supper?"

"Don't just stand there! Get your cloak, child! Hurry! We mustn't keep Lord Simon waiting. You must forgive her, Lord Simon—she's never dined with a gentleman before."

"Yes, I have, Mama," the girl protested. "This month alone, we have dined nine times with nine different gentlemen. It's been very jolly."

"But I am *always* there to chaperone," said her mother quickly. "I give you my word, Lord Simon, she is never out of my sight."

"That's true," said Belinda. "I would not go with them if Mama was not with me. I do not like how they look at me. They frighten me."

"You are not frightened of me, I hope."

She stared at him. "No," she said, after a moment. "I do not think I am frightened of you, sir. You do not look at me the way they do."

"And how do they look at you, child?" Simon asked.

She shivered. "Like hungry wolves at a lamb, sir. Like heartless, hungry wolves."

"You must say *my lord*, child," said her mother severely, "not *sir*. Lord Simon is the younger son of a duke. You must show him proper respect."

On impulse, Simon offered the girl his arm. "Miss Archer may call me Simon, if she wishes," he said. "That is what my friends call me."

"Oh, I couldn't, sir—my lord!" the girl stammered.

"Do not argue with Lord Simon, child," said Mrs. Archer. "One does not argue with the younger son of a duke."

"I'm sure I did not mean to argue with you, sir—my lord!"

"Simon," he said, quietly and firmly, taking her hand.

"Simon." She forced the word out as a whisper.

"Shall we?"

They left the theatre by the stage door, and Simon put them in a hackney carriage. Soon they were installed in the dining room of the Pulteney Hotel.

"I have been remiss, Miss Archer," Simon said, when the dinner had been ordered. "I have not yet complimented you on your performance this evening, my dear."

She hung her head. "I don't know what happened to

me," she mumbled. "I was so good in the rehearsal—even Miss St. Lys said I was good in the rehearsal! But when I went out on the stage, my voice—it just wouldn't come!"

Simon patted her arm. "Not everyone is cut out to be an actress, you know."

"Miss London is, it seems," said Belinda. "How I envy her! She had never set foot on a stage before today, but she was not nervous at all."

Mrs. Archer snorted. "She was only the maid. In my opinion, they destroyed the scene."

"The audience seemed to like it," Simon said mildly.

Mrs. Archer bristled. "What do *they* know? Philistines! Barbarians! I have no opinion of the audience."

"No, nor do I," said Belinda. "The audience frighten me to death. Sometimes I could *swear* they were looking right at me! It was most disconcerting. If Miss St. Lys had not been with me in my first scene, I don't know *what* I would have done. Oh! If only I could play to an empty house, I'm sure I would like it much better."

"Of course you would, my dear, because you are a true artist!" crooned her mother. "You think of the play first. St. Lys thinks of nothing but the audience. She winks at them. She blows them kisses! She'd crawl around on all fours if she thought it would please them. Do not seek to emulate St. Lys."

"As though I could!" cried Belinda.

"Acting is sacrifice. One must give oneself completely to the role. When I am Cleopatra, I cease to exist. I annihilate myself! But St. Lys is always St. Lys! She is not an actress," sniffed Mrs. Archer. "She is a *performer*. No formal training at all. Four years ago, she was nothing more than the kept mistress of Lord Palmerston. *She* wanted to go onstage, and *he* wanted to indulge her. He paid Rourke ten pounds to put her on. That was how she got her start."

"And before Palmerston?"

Mrs. Archer shrugged. "God knows where he found her! Some brothel, I should think."

"Mama!" cried Belinda. "You mustn't say such things about Miss St. Lys."

The waiters came in and Mrs. Archer greedily served herself from the silver dish. "I must speak as I find, child," she chattered on. "St. Lys did not earn her place in the theatre, whatever she may pretend now. Her place, such as it is, was bought for her by her lover, Lord Palmerston. I daresay his lordship only meant it for a lark. He must have been quite dismayed when his little mistress made such a hit as Jessica, of all things, in *The Merchant of Venice*. It wasn't long before she began to see other men. Then she took up with that Frenchy. The Marquis de Brissac, as he called himself."

"They were *very* much in love," Belinda said eagerly, her face aglow. "He wanted to marry her."

Mrs. Archer snorted. "That is what she *said*."

"You have reason to doubt it?" asked Simon.

"I have every reason to doubt it!" said Mrs. Archer. "He promised her marriage, to be sure, but he never intended to make her his wife. She actually thought he was going to make her his marquise, poor thing."

The last two words were spoken without any sympathy whatsoever. "He deceived her, then," said Simon. "He promised her marriage so that she would leave Palmerston."

"That is dreadful," Belinda said softly. "Poor Miss St. Lys!"

"I heard," Simon said, after a pause, "that she was married before she came to London."

Mrs. Archer's eyes lit up. "Do tell!" she cried. "Oh! I had not heard *that*. I suppose Lord Palmerston persuaded her to leave her husband and run off with him?

How deliciously sordid! And she so piously swears she does not approve of adultery! Her name has never been linked to that of any married man. And, all the while, she was a married woman!"

"She is a widow, I believe," Simon said quickly, now sorry he had said anything.

"A widow!" Mrs. Archer made a face. "Too bad. There's nothing sordid about a widow. Unless, of course, she murdered him. How did he die?"

"I have no idea," said Simon.

"I bet he was a soldier," said Belinda. "She's always had a soft spot for a soldier. One almost never sees her without she is surrounded by red coats."

"Aye," said Mrs. Archer. "It was the soldiers coming home from war that made her famous. I suppose they were tired of all those swarthy Spanish ladies. They were in the mood for something blond. She certainly gave herself to them most freely—and still does, I daresay. I forget what the play was that summer, when the regent had his jubilee."

"*Othello*," Simon said coldly.

"Oh yes! She was Desdemona to Mr. Kean's Othello—dreadful, overrated monkey of a man! She *would* come out for her death scene practically naked. She *dampened* that nightgown, too, you know, so that it would cling to every curve of her body. *Nothing,* my dear sir, was ever left to the imagination."

"Didn't *you* dampen your muslins, Mama, when you played Cleopatra?" Belinda asked.

"Eat your squab, my love," her mother told her sharply. "Belinda loves squab, my lord," she went on, forcing a laugh. "She never eats anything else. I have heard that Princess Charlotte is very fond of squab. Is that true?"

"I cannot tell you," Simon answered distractedly. Looking up, he saw a young officer of the Life Guards making his way toward them.

"My lord," said Tom West, making him a bow. "Ladies. I do beg your pardon. Terribly sorry to interrupt and all that sort of thing."

"Good gracious!" squawked Mrs. Archer. "Has the Corsican escaped from Saint Helena? Has the war started up again?"

"No, ma'am," he hastily assured her. "That is, not that I know of," he added, with a confused look.

"That is reassuring, Mr. West," Simon said dryly. "Why are you here?"

"It's your brother, my lord," the young man told him. "The Duke of Berkshire is taken ill. Miss St. Lys sent me to fetch you. She says you are to come at once to her house."

"What?" cried Simon, rising from the table so quickly that he overturned his chair. "What's the matter with him?" he demanded roughly. "What's happened?"

"I hardly know!" cried West. "One moment, His Grace was juggling oranges with Joe Grimaldi, and the next thing we knew . . ." He shrugged helplessly. "He just sort of fell over!"

"My brother was juggling oranges?" Simon said incredulously.

"Yes, my lord. Then he just sort of slipped down and never got up again. We tried to wake him, but . . ." He shrugged helplessly. "Will you come, my lord?"

"Yes, of course!" Simon started for the door, then paused. "Perhaps you would be good enough to see these two ladies home. I should be most grateful to you, Mr. West."

"I should be delighted, of course," West replied, after only the slightest hesitation. "Miss Archer. Mrs. Archer."

"Much obliged to you, sir."

With a curt bow to the ladies, Simon quit the room, walking briskly out of the hotel into the noise and traffic of Piccadilly.

White-faced, Celia met Simon at the door of her town house. She had changed from her costume into one of her simple pink dresses. She looked a little rumpled, and there were smudges of lampblack under her eyes, but she did not seem drunk, only frightened.

"He is in my room," she said from the doorway. "Tom and I put him to bed. My servant is with him now."

Two floors up, he found his brother snoring on Celia's bed, on top of the quilted coverlet, with Mrs. Flood watching over him. His shoes had been removed and his cravat loosened, but otherwise he was fully clothed.

"I didn't know what else to do," she murmured.

Going quickly to the bed, he established that his brother had a strong pulse. Dorian smelled strongly of liquor. "What the devil happened?" Simon asked, rounding on Celia angrily. Celia seemed close to tears. "I don't know!" she answered, pulling her pink shawl tightly around her shoulders. "After the play, I invited everyone back to my house. We were all having a lovely time."

"Was my brother having a lovely time? Juggling oranges, was he?"

"I really don't know what he was doing when—when it happened. I wasn't in the room at the time. I'd gone upstairs with Captain Harris."

"Oh yes?" he sneered.

She glared at him. "He was showing us his sword exercises," she said, "and he accidentally cut his hand. I was tending to his wound, when . . . when Dorian fell down.

There was an awful lot of blood—when Robbie cut his hand, I mean, not when Dorian fell," she added quickly.

"I see."

She frowned. "I am sorry I had to send for you, my lord, but I—I did not know what else to do. Is—is your brother *prone* to such strange fits?"

"Certainly not," Simon told her curtly. "What had he to eat and drink?"

"We all ate the same supper, my lord."

"Yes, but where did it come from? Your kitchen?"

She scowled. "I'm not sure where it all came from. No, not my kitchen, certainly," she added sourly. "There wasn't a thing in the house when I got home. Suddenly there were hampers of food, and bottles. I suppose they must have come from some coffee house or hotel. I don't really know. But you cannot think he was *poisoned*, surely?"

"No," he said. "Merely drunk."

She looked astonished. "Drunk!"

"Very drunk. I shall take him home and put him to bed. He'll have a bad head when he wakes tomorrow, but he'll survive."

"But he can't be drunk," Celia protested. "I tell you, he drank nothing but punch!"

"Oh yes? Tell me about this punch of yours. Who made it?"

"Tom West made it," she said. "But you can't blame him. He's the younger son of Lord Ambersey."

"What has *that* to say to anything?"

"Only that it wasn't anyone from the theatre, if that was what you were thinking. Anyway, there was nothing at all in the punch but brandy, whiskey, scotch, and gin. Oh! and lemon, of course. Could it have been the lemons, do you suppose?"

Simon looked at her incredulously. "It's a bloody wonder he's not dead!"

"Nobody else got sick."

"Did *you* drink any of that unholy muck?" he demanded.

"Well, no," she admitted. "I only drink champagne."

"I remember. Where are the rest of your guests? Scattered to the four winds, I daresay?"

"What do you mean?"

"You said you invited *everyone*," he reminded her. "Where is *everyone*? Where did they all go?"

Celia blushed with embarrassment. "I suppose they all went home when—when—"

"When the Duke of Berkshire keeled over?" he suggested. "I'll just bet they did! Poor Celia! Did no one stand by you in your time of need?"

"Tom stayed with me," she said. "I sent him to fetch you."

"He's braver than I thought."

"Where *is* Tom?" she demanded. "Did you eat him?"

"No," he answered. "I had already dined. I asked him to escort Mrs. Archer and her daughter home."

Her brows rose. "Mrs. Archer *and* her daughter? How cozy for you! I didn't know you liked that sort of thing."

"There's a lot you don't know about me."

"Clearly! Which did you enjoy more, the mutton or the lamb?"

"Neither. We had the squab."

"So it was a foursome, then?" She sniffed. "How cozy!"

"Did you summon a physician?" he inquired.

"No. Should I have done?" she asked, frowning. "I thought *you* would know best what to do."

"Sending for me is the only thing you did right, my girl," he told her. "Where are his footmen? Did they run away, too?"

"No. Your brother dismissed them when he got here, along with his carriage," she replied. "Shall I—shall I send for my manservant to help you carry him down the stairs?"

Simon smiled thinly. "If it isn't too much trouble," he said coldly.

Chapter 12

In the hackney coach, Dorian roused himself briefly, but only, as it turned out, to vomit, spattering Simon's boots and narrowly missing Simon's lap. Fortunately, Berkshire House stood at no great distance from Celia's house. Dorian's mother, roused from her bed by the servants, came down the stairs behind the butler, who had armed himself with an ancient blunderbuss.

Dorian had never been carried home drunk before, and at first Her Grace refused to believe that her son was intoxicated. She insisted on sending for the family physician.

While the doctor was with the patient, she paced up and down the hall outside the duke's bedroom. Her iron-gray hair, though as tightly curled as ever, was mostly hidden under an enormous lace cap, and her small body seemed almost lost in the voluminous shawl in which her maid had wrapped it.

"Well?" she cried, when at last the doctor emerged from the room.

"His Grace is perfectly well, madam," the physician assured her. "A little foxed, perhaps."

"Foxed? What do you mean, foxed?"

"Your son is a trifle disguised, Your Grace."

"A trifle *disguised*? I don't understand."

"The Duke of Berkshire is drunk, madam," Simon explained, and, with a gentle cough, the doctor confirmed it.

"How could this have happened?" demanded the duchess. "My son never touches strong drink."

"He never touches it, perhaps," Simon murmured, "but it would seem that he drinks it."

She turned on him furiously. "You did this to him," she accused. "You plied him with drink! You got him drunk as a—as a—"

"Lord?" Simon suggested lightly. "No indeed, madam. It was not I. I was only called to the scene *after* the damage was done."

"What scene?" she demanded, furious. "Where *was* he tonight? Who called you? Who did this to him? I am his mother; I have a right to know."

"I rather think he did it to himself," Simon replied.

"Nonsense!"

Simon shrugged. "If you want to know more, you must ask Dorian, I'm afraid. I am certainly not going to tell you. But if you are wise, madam, you won't say a word to him about it. You must trust, as I do, that he has learned his lesson. I, of course, plan to tease him mercilessly, but *you* should not. You should remain silent on the subject forever."

"I must go to him," she said resolutely. "He needs me now."

"I fear His Grace seems a little agitated at present," said the physician, with an apologetic look. "It would perhaps be best not to upset him, Your Grace. What he needs most now is sleep. 'Sleep that knits up the raveled sleeve of care,'" he added, a touch whimsically.

But the duchess was not at all the whimsical sort. "You

dare to imply that *I* would upset my own son?" she trilled. "Upset him how? Stand aside, you fool!"

She would have darted past the man if Simon had not restrained her. "The doctor has given his best advice, madam. *You* would be a fool not to heed him."

"Thank you, my lord," said the physician. "His Grace has been asking to see you . . . alone."

"But I am his mother!" the duchess protested.

"And he wouldn't want to worry you," said Simon. "You will see him in the morning, when he is feeling better. He won't want you to see him like this."

"That is like him," she said, smiling tremulously. "Dorian is always thinking of other people. Well, don't just stand there, Simon—go to him. He calls you. Tell him . . . tell him that I forgive him. Tell him Mama loves him."

Simon slipped into the room. Dorian was actually sitting up in the huge four-poster bed, looking pale and quite cross. His lips were gray, his eyes were far from clear, and his chestnut hair was sticking up in all directions. "Why did you bring me *here*?" he asked irritably as Simon stood at the bedside.

"It is your home," Simon pointed out mildly. "It seemed best."

"You should have taken me to Brooks's," Dorian grumbled, "not here. I told you I was staying at my club, did I not?"

Suddenly, he was not so certain. "I'm sorry," said Simon. "I forgot you told me you were staying at your club."

"Help me out of bed!" Dorian commanded weakly. "I refuse to sleep under the same roof with that woman."

"I think you'd better stay where you are, old man—at least until the effects of the punch have worn off," Simon replied. "You've already cast up all your accounts in a carriage once tonight. Are you so eager to do it again?"

Dorian sank back against the pillows, his energy expended.

Simon chuckled. "You'll have a bloody head in the morning, I daresay."

"I've got a bloody head now," Dorian moaned. "Sally!" he called out suddenly. "What must she be thinking of me!"

"Sally? You mean St. Lys, I suppose? She did seem rather anxious to be rid of you, and I'm sure I don't blame her. You frightened away all her lovers."

"I am glad to hear that, at least," Dorian murmured. "I couldn't let her go home with all the officers—not by herself. I say!" He suddenly opened his eyes wide. "You didn't tell your mother where I was tonight, did you?"

"Of course not," said Simon. "What do you take me for—a spy?"

"That's all right, then," said Dorian, sighing as he closed his eyes. "Oh, but you should have seen me juggling those oranges, Simon."

"You should have stuck to your juggling," Simon told him. "The punch sounded positively lethal."

Dorian shuddered. "It was. But they were all drinking it, and I didn't want to be rude. Mr. West said it was nothing to the punch he used to make in Buckinghamshire. He said a baby could drink it! They must have stomachs lined in copper, is all I can say. Sally must have been so frightened. How is it you were there, Simon? I thought you were dining with that girl—what's-her-name? The one who can't act?"

"St. Lys sent for me," Simon explained, "when you fell ill."

"Was she very frightened?"

"She was concerned, certainly."

"She must think me a damned bloody fool."

"Very likely."

"She may be worried still. I must go to her at once." Dorian actually started up as if he meant to leave his bed, but before he could do so, nausea overwhelmed him, and he fell back, moaning. "Simon, you must go to her at once."

Simon lifted his brows. "I don't think that is a good idea."

"She may be worried. I'm sure she is worried. I would go to her myself, if I could, but as it is . . . you must go in my place. Tell her I shall call on her tomorrow—though not—not too early, perhaps. Tell her I am very sorry for ruining her party. It was great, good fun, and she mustn't blame herself for my foolishness. I ought to have conducted myself better."

"Write her a bloody letter, why don't you," Simon muttered. "I'm not telling her all *that*. All right, I'll go. But only because her house is convenient to my club in Charles Street. Otherwise I shouldn't bother."

"Thanks, old man," said a faint voice, followed by a loud snore.

The dowager duchess pounced on her younger son the moment he came out of the room. "Your brother was with St. Lys tonight?" she hissed. "Why did you not tell me?"

"For God's sake, woman," Simon said angrily. "Were you *listening* at the door?"

"Yes, of course I was," she returned without remorse. "I couldn't hear everything, but I heard enough to know that that woman is responsible for his present condition."

"No wonder he prefers to stay at Brooks's!" Simon remarked. "He has no privacy here! Do you have the servants spy on him as well, madam? Or do you do it all yourself?"

"If you were his mother, you would understand. But

never mind all that," she said impatiently. "What are we going to do about St. Lys?"

"We are not going to do anything about St. Lys," Simon said firmly.

"Well, we must do something. She obviously is a bad influence. And she seemed so charming when I met her. A little mischievous, perhaps, but I did not think she would hurt him."

"What did you think she would do?"

"We mustn't let this get out of hand, Simon. I knew he was with her *last* night, but tonight, too? He should have been at the palace with me tonight."

"Her Majesty, though an excellent woman in her way, is not as charming as St. Lys," Simon said dryly. "Wait a minute! You *knew* Dorian was with her last night? How? Do you have him followed?"

"Don't be ridiculous," she said. "Why should I have my own son followed?"

"Then how do you know he dined with her last night?"

"It was my idea," she told him. "I thought an evening of pleasure would be good for your brother. She seemed absolutely perfect for the position."

"What position?"

"Well, I thought she would make him an excellent mistress," said his mother. "It seems I was mistaken."

"You thought St. Lys would make Dorian an excellent mistress?" Simon repeated sharply. "St. Lys? You were indeed mistaken, madam."

"I admit it," she said. "She is beautiful and charming, but much too wild for my dear boy. Hopefully, Dorian will realize that before it is too late. Perhaps he has realized it already?"

"Perhaps," Simon replied. "I wouldn't count on it, however."

"What do you mean?" she anxiously inquired.

"St. Lys can be very charming indeed," Simon told her. "For example, did you know she was responsible for our victory at Waterloo?"

Celia was not alone when Simon reached her house. He had not expected her to be. Her choice of companion, however, did strike him as rather strange. His clothes proclaimed him to be a tradesman of some sort, and he and the actress were engaged in a heated argument.

"My good fellow," St. Lys was saying as Simon entered her drawing room. "Do you know who I am? Have you any idea whom you are addressing?"

"I know you owes me money, missus!"

"Missus!" she cried, outraged. "How dare you! I do not owe a penny! I did not order the food. I did not order the drink."

"This is the direction. Eighty-four Curzon Street," he shouted, red in the face, waving a piece of paper in her face. "Plain as the day is long, missus."

"I don't care what you have there, my good man."

Simon coughed gently. "Perhaps I can be of assistance?"

Celia whirled around to face him. "Who the devil let you in?" she demanded angrily.

"No one. Your door was standing open," he replied. "I closed it for you. What seems to be the trouble?"

They both began talking at once, but Celia subsided first, throwing up her hands.

Simon chuckled. "Suddenly there were hampers," he murmured. "Where did you think they had come from— heaven?"

"I didn't order the food. I don't know who did."

"Someone has to pay for it, Celia. You do realize that?"

She glowered at him. "Naturally. But why should I pay for something I did not order?"

"You may send the bill to me at Carlton House," Simon told the tradesman curtly. "I am Lord Simon." To Celia's annoyance, the man bowed at once and scurried out of the room.

"He must be the only man in London who doesn't know my face," she said, looking at him resentfully.

"My dear, have you seen your face recently? You are not looking your best."

"What?" Snatching up the candlestick, she ran into the hall and looked in the glass hanging there. "Why did no one tell me?" she cried. Moistening her fingertips with her tongue, she rubbed at the smudges under her eyes.

"Dorian asked me to call on you," Simon replied.

"He is awake, then? That is a good sign."

"He thought you might be worried," Simon said.

She frowned at him. "You told me he was only drunk. Naturally, I believed you. Were you wrong?"

"No. I was not wrong."

"No, of course not. You're never wrong, are you?" she murmured. "Wait here for a moment, if you please."

Leaving him, she went up the stairs to her bedroom. A few minutes later she returned, having washed her face properly and tidied her hair. She gave him a ten-pound note. "That should cover the man's bill, I should think. If it doesn't, you know where to find me, I think."

"If you had the money," he said, exasperated, "why did you not simply pay the man?"

"I wouldn't expect you to understand. It's the principle of the thing. He was trying to bully me because I am a woman. I shouldn't have to pay—"

"Because you are a woman?"

"I should not have to pay for food I did not order," she

said, frowning. "It's intolerable that *you* should pay for it, however. And besides, I wouldn't want a man like that to know I keep money in the house. He might come back and rob me. I'm fairly certain *you* won't come back and rob me. Come, I'll show you out." She started to move past him, from the landing to the stairs, but he stood in her way.

"What's your hurry? Have you got a lover waiting for you upstairs?"

"Naturally," she said. "You're welcome to join us if you like," she added. "Unless, of course, you are too exhausted from your exertions with Mrs. Archer and her lovely daughter."

Leaning forward, he murmured in her ear. "You're jealous."

She laughed. "I? Jealous of Mrs. Archer? You must be joking."

"You know very well I am talking of Belinda."

"Oh, her. I feel sorry for her, that's all."

"You're so jealous you can hardly see."

"Why should I be jealous of Belinda Archer?" she wondered. "You're the one who's jealous! I suppose Dorian told you I dined with him last night?"

"Among other things," he said coldly. "How long have you known him? Was he your first lover?"

"Who? Dorian?" She seemed genuinely shocked. "Of course not! How could you think such a thing?"

"Is he your lover now? Are you his mistress?"

"Certainly not. We dined together, that is all. You don't really think that I would be so crass as to take him to my bed after—after everything that has passed between us?" she cried.

"What exactly has passed between us?" he wanted to know. "Three years ago, when I held you in my arms, I thought I was the most fortunate man in the world."

"I am sorry!" she said. "I chose marriage over love. Whether you believe it or not, I have regretted it ever since. I have suffered for it. I know that you will never forgive me."

"I'm sure you did regret it, my dear," he said curtly. "I'm sure you regretted it very much. When did you find out that he never meant to marry you?"

She bit her lip. "Who told you that?"

"It must have been quite a blow to your pride."

"Yes, if you must know," she said crossly. "When the war ended, Armand thought he would be restored immediately to all those honors and privileges formerly enjoyed by his family before the Revolution. But it was not so. His lands had been confiscated, sold more than once. He petitioned the French king, of course, but there were legal and bureaucratic hurdles to be got over. All that costs money, you know."

"That's why you never left the stage."

She nodded. "I had to keep working; he needed the money. As it turns out, a French marquis can be rather expensive."

"How expensive?" he asked, not without sympathy.

"When he died, I had nothing left but this house and my name," she said. "I've only just cleared all his debts. But I shall be all right. You needn't feel sorry for me."

"I don't. In some ways, I actually admire you."

She smiled faintly. "You admire me? And yet, you chose to spend the evening with Miss Archer."

"And who is waiting for you upstairs?" he returned.

"Wouldn't you like to know?" she said, laughing.

To her surprise, he suddenly pushed past her, vaulting up the stairs. On the next floor up, he found her bedroom, and threw open the door. The room was quiet. The light from the fire in the hearth allowed him to see that the bed was unoccupied, though Dorian's brief rest there had left wrinkles in the coverlet. As Celia came into the room with her candle, he was rifling through the wardrobe. Crossing the room, she placed the candle next to the bed and watched, amused, as he looked under it. "Do you really think I could love a man who would be so craven as to hide under my bed?" she asked softly.

Still down on one knee, Simon watched as she sat down on the edge of the bed. The bed-curtains, of pretty, flowered chintz, hung loose on either side of her, framing her like a picture. "Your taste in men is baffling, to say the least. Palmerston! De Brissac! Fitzclarence!"

"I chose *you*," she retorted.

"You seemed to regret it afterward," he said.

"No," she said. "I never regretted it. Did you?"

He made no answer.

"The war had just ended—or so we all thought," she said, her voice soft yet filling the room. "London was full of men. Real men—fighting men—and they all wanted to make love to me. They all wanted me to leave Henry and run off with them. I was besieged on all fronts! I could have named my price. But I chose you."

"Why?" he asked her. "Why did you choose me?"

"I thought you were the finest man in London," she answered, closing her eyes briefly, as if to summon the memory from the depths of her consciousness. "And you wanted me so much; more than the others, I thought. When I told you I would meet you in Brighton when the theatre closed, I meant it. I would have gone. I planned to go. But . . ."

"But you got a better offer. I understand."

"I don't think you *do* understand," she said, laying her hand on his arm. "If you did, you wouldn't be looking under my bed or behind the curtains. If you understood me at all, you would not be jealous. You would know there's no one else."

He looked down at the hand on his arm but did not shake it off.

"I did betray you," she went on. "I chose de Brissac over you. But, believe me, I am sorry for it now." Her other hand crept to his face, and to her amazement and joy, he actually allowed her to caress his cheek. "I never loved anyone but you."

He seized her hand, pressing it to his face. "I wish I could believe you, Celia."

"You need not believe me," she said, "to take what I am offering."

He could bear no more. Taking her in his arms roughly, he pressed her close to him, kissing her hungrily. Almost maddened with desire, he surged onto the bed, lifting her out of her shoes and dragging her with him.

"Wait!" she cried, laughing as she fumbled at his sword belt. "You won't be needing this to slay any dragons tonight."

Impatiently, he unbuckled the sword and let it hit the floor. Weaponless, he took her in his arms, and again their mouths melted together as if there had been no interruption.

"I thought I'd never feel your arms around me again," Celia murmured a long time later, resting her head against his chest to listen to the hard and fast rhythm of his heartbeat.

His arms tightened around her. "I've been a fool," he said harshly. "For three years, I've been an absolute fool. I've tried to hate you. I even thought I had succeeded."

"What could I do but pretend to hate you, too?"

"Why did you not tell me the Frenchman had offered you marriage?" he asked.

"What would you have done? Matched his offer with one of your own?"

"No," he admitted. "I could not have done that."

"No," she said, pulling away from him. "Of course not. You would have given me up."

"I would not give you up now," he said fiercely.

"You don't have to."

Sitting up, she loosened the laces at the back of her dress. Reaching out to her, he pulled her to him, easing the gown down from her shoulders and trailing his lips over her skin as her breasts were revealed. Celia wriggled out of her muslin slip, impatiently kicking it to the foot of the bed. Then she was naked in his arms.

What she offered was irresistible. Her body was slim, her breasts small but perfectly formed. Naked, she seemed more angel than Venus, an angel sculpted of shimmering white porcelain, but he knew there was nothing fragile or angelic about Celia. She was quite surprisingly athletic when aroused. With her head arched back, she murmured encouragement as he kissed and caressed her breasts. Her nipples formed tight pink buds in response as he suckled gently. It was she who pushed his hand lower down, she who placed his hand at the soft joining of her thighs, she who arched her back in silent demand. For a moment, he was startled to find that all the soft golden hair had been removed. The pudenda gleamed like pearls.

"What the devil—?" he murmured. "What have you done to yourself?"

"Do you like it?" she asked, displaying herself to him shamelessly. "I think I look like a statue. It's for the painting," she explained. "Sir Thomas wanted me to look like a classical statue. Do you not like it?"

"It will take some getting used to," he murmured. "I have thought often of your golden triangle these last three years."

"It will grow back," she assured him. "Is it really so dreadful?"

"I suppose I can bear it."

Actually, it fascinated him. He had never seen a woman so unclothed. Her sex was tiny and perfect, the neatest he had ever seen. If he didn't know better, he would have thought it was the innocent, untouched girlhood of a virgin. The soft pink lips seemed to pout as he stroked them gently with his finger. She wanted his mouth, and told him so. No stranger to pleasure, she gave herself up entirely to his probing tongue, her legs falling naturally over his strong shoulders. The warmth of his mouth alone was almost enough to send her into spasms, and it did not take him long to wring fierce cries of joy from her throat.

All this he remembered. She was wanton, and yet there was a sweetness in her surrender. When she gave herself, she gave completely. As she lay recovering, he slipped from the bed to undress. Celia watched with half-closed eyes, not bothering to cover herself, but as he pulled his shirt over his head, she suddenly cried out in dismay. Kneeling up on the bed, she ran her hands across the crisp black hairs on his chest. "What is this?" she demanded, finding the ugly, thick seam of a scar slanting from his navel almost to his armpit.

He caressed her cheek as her mouth moved over the old injury. "Did you memorize all my cuts and scrapes?"

"I know every inch of this body," she said. "I thought I did, anyway. I heard you were wounded at Waterloo. My poor darling. It must have hurt a great deal. You must have been in agony."

"I am in agony now, madam," he said, laughing.

"What?" she cried, then laughed as she guessed his meaning. Climbing out of bed, she helped him out of his boots and breeches. His sex fell neatly into her hands, pleasingly large and so rigid that it was hardly necessary for her to take its velvet tip in her mouth, but she did so anyway, kneeling at his feet to luxuriate in the taste and scent of his manhood.

He had neither asked for nor expected this service on their first meeting, but she had seemed so eager . . . Afterward, she had explained that the maneuver served a practical purpose; she did not want a child. The first spending was more dangerous than the second, and once she had taken him in her mouth, he could then enjoy her as he willed.

She would have suckled him in earnest now, but Simon suddenly drew her to her feet and, gripping her in his arms, fell with her onto the bed. Celia made no protest, but clasped him joyfully with her arms and legs. He took her then almost violently. It was over too quickly for her to find pleasure again, but Simon, shattered by his crisis, collapsed in her arms, his back shiny and slick with sweat.

Celia lay with him uncomplaining, knowing that he would soon rise again. After a moment, he threw himself down on his back beside her.

"I heard that you captured a French general at Waterloo," she said, touching his wound again. "Is that when you were wounded?"

"Hmm?" he murmured sleepily. "That old story."

A smile touched her lips. "You mean it's not true? You didn't capture a French general at Waterloo?"

He chuckled. "I'm sorry to disappoint you. 'Twas one of my officers who captured the general. He has since sold out. I turned my back on him for one minute, and the damn fool catches sight of the *maréchal* and off he goes! Brains of goose, he had."

She frowned, disappointed. "So *he* captured the general?"

"Having pulled the *maréchal* across his saddle like a

sack of flour, the young idiot suddenly found himself surrounded by cuirassiers."

"What happened?" she asked, her chin on his chest.

"Somebody had to go save him from his own idiocy, and I was his commanding officer."

She laughed. "So you *did* capture the *maréchal* after all."

"No indeed. Musgrove captured him. I merely captured Musgrove. Damned if the *maréchal* wasn't still draped across his saddle when we got back to the line!"

"And that is when you were struck?" she murmured, running her hands across his scarred torso. "I wish I had been there to look after you," she whispered, dipping her head to kiss the tip of the scar.

He half smiled. "What? Celia St. Lys, a woman of the camps? Never!"

She grinned. "I would have made an excellent soldier's doxy!"

"Lord Simon's doxy," he corrected her. "You would have had pride of place among all the women of the camp."

"I would have scrubbed your shirts in the river with the rest of them," she said gamely. "Cooked your dinner over a campfire, and delivered your bastards in a tent."

"Don't be silly," he said. "You would have been quite safe in a hotel in Brussels with servants to look after you."

"In rooms over a shop, no doubt!" she said, laughing. "How droll! And if you had fallen in battle, the other officers of the regiment would all have drawn lots for me."

He took her hand and kissed it. "I am not rich, as you know, but I think I can manage something a little better than rooms over a shop. You shall have a house of your own."

"I have a house of my own already, young man," she said, laughing. "You are in it. What did you think this was, a nutshell?"

He paid no attention to her raillery. "You cannot stay here. I shall find you new lodgings, first thing."

"What?" she said, shaking her head in puzzlement. "I don't need lodgings."

"Who pays for this house?" he asked, frowning.

"I do," she said, affronted. "That is to say, I did pay for it. I own it. It is mine. I like it, and I have no intention of leaving it to please you or anyone else."

"You own this house?"

"You do not believe me?"

"Very well; you may own it. But who bought it for you?" he demanded. "One of your lovers, no doubt. Lord Palmerston?"

Celia sat up. Finding her slip at the foot of the bed, she pulled it over her head angrily. "Ten minutes in my bed, and the man thinks he owns me!" she cried. "For your information, my lord, *I* bought this house. It's mine, and I do not mean to give it up. And even if Lord Palmerston had given it to me—what a joke! But even if he had, it would still be mine, and why shouldn't I keep it? Would you have me give everything back?"

"Yes," he said immediately.

"Oh, I see!" she said, leaping out of the bed. "I am to have nothing but what I receive from your hand."

"I certainly won't allow you to keep any presents from other men," he snapped. "The diamond collar must go back to Sir Lucas."

"Is *that* what this was about?" she cried, turning pale. "You're still after that bloody necklace? Is that why you took me to bed?"

"No," he said savagely, springing out of bed, "of course not. But if you are to be my mistress, you must learn to respect my wishes."

"What makes you think I want to be your mistress?" she demanded. "That would not suit me at all! Oh, you're well enough for a tumble here and there, I grant you that!" she added, taking a step back as he lunged at her. "You are a tyrant!" she complained. "You want a slave, not a mistress. Why should I give up my house for you? Why should I give up my diamonds? Would you have me give up the stage, as well?"

"When the children come, yes," he said. "We were not so careful this time. There might be a child."

"I pray not," she said violently. "You want to take me off the stage. You want me breeding and dependent on you for everything! You don't want to love me. You want to own me. I am such a fool."

"If there is a child, you will never be rid of me."

"If there is a child, I shall go abroad," she declared. "I should give the babe to gypsies, and you would never see it!"

Simon's eyes narrowed. "I would hunt you to the ends of the earth, madam."

She laughed bitterly. "Now I see the attraction of Miss Archer! Yes! Little Belinda will serve you well. She is too stupid and timid to think for herself. She will be very happy to exist solely for your pleasure. You can train her as you would one of your dogs."

"I did find her manners very pleasing," he said, beginning to dress. "She will make me a fine companion. You, on the other hand, are only good for one thing. You do satisfy my man's body, I'll grant you that."

Her eyes flashed angrily. "Go! Get out! Go back to your virgin! And when you are quite bored with her, don't even think of coming back here to me. I'd only laugh in your face."

He finished dressing and left without another word. She did not seek to detain him but jumped as she heard the front door slam. After taking a moment to compose herself, she took up her bedroom taper and hurried downstairs to lock the door and bolt it.

Chapter 13

Dorian awoke in his bed at Berkshire House with a violent headache and only the vaguest memories of the night before. Almost before his eyes were open, his mother, who had passed the night in a chair at his bedside, was upon him. "Dorian!" she cried, launching herself onto the bed to seize his hand. "Thank God! You naughty boy! What a scare you gave your mama."

Dorian struggled to sit up. Still groggy, he was too slow to prevent his mother's attack on his person, but he did manage to prevent her from fluffing the pillows. "Give over, woman," he snarled. "I'm not a boy; I am the bloody Duke of Berkshire. Send Hill to me at once," he added, in a weakening tone. "My head is very bad, and I seem to have broken a nail."

"I am not surprised," his mother said severely as she withdrew from the bed. "You were brought home drunk, sir—very drunk indeed!"

Dorian covered his ears with his hands. "I cannot hear you, madam," he told her. "You are wasting your breath. I want Hill!"

"Your valet is not here, Dorian," she informed him. He had never noticed it before, but she had a voice rather like a

French horn. "You left him at Brooks's. Don't you remember? I daresay Hamilton can be prevailed upon to look after you. You do need looking after," she added with a motherly tenderness that grated his nerves.

Dorian scowled at her. "Why did Simon have to bring me *here*? I was perfectly all right where I was."

The duchess sniffed disdainfully. "Apparently *that woman* did not agree. She threw you out into the street, I believe."

With a swiftness born of anger, Dorian threw off the bedclothes and jumped to his feet. "That woman!" he cried. "You dare call her that? You, of all people?"

She stared, flabbergasted by his rage. "How dare you shout at me," she whimpered. Taking out her handkerchief she pressed it to dry eyes. "Your own mother! I realize 'twas my idea for you to take a mistress, but really, Dorian! I do not think Miss St. Lys has been at all good for you. There! I said it! She should not have given you so much to drink. Even your brother was shocked by your behavior, and as you know, nothing shocks *him*."

Dorian staggered a little, but by gripping the table, managed to remain upright. "Are you suggesting that I discard Miss St. Lys?" he demanded, thrusting out his jaw. "Believe me, madam, I would sooner discard *you*!"

Shocked, she fell into a chair. "Dorian, you cannot mean that!" she gasped.

"I do mean it," he assured her. "Have a care what you say about Miss St. Lys, madam, or you may find yourself persona non grata here at Berkshire House. As it is, you are definitely persona non grata in my bedroom. Get out! Get out and send Hill to me or Hamilton or whoever. Just get out!" he shouted, a vein throbbing in his temple.

"Dorian!" she cried, choking back a sob. "I do not deserve this!"

"I have yet to decide what you deserve," he said coldly. His energy spent, he sagged against the bedpost. "Is there nothing that weighs on your conscience, madam?"

"Of course not," she answered, bewildered.

He looked at her, shaking his head. "Out of respect for my father, I shan't turn you out," he said. "I shall remove to Brooks's for the rest of the season. After that . . . after *that*, madam, we shall see. But I cannot live with you; that much is certain. Now, for God's sake, leave me!"

To no avail the duchess pleaded and protested. Dorian would neither relent nor explain his anger. Forced to quit the room, she hastened to the morning room. Three quarters of an hour later, she observed from the window that Dorian had summoned his cabriolet. His groom slowly walked the perfectly matched bays up and down the street, keeping them warm for the duke.

As she stood fretting, her maid burst into the room. "Madam! His Grace has gone mad!"

This was no more than the duchess's own private fear, but she turned on her servant savagely. "Nonsense, Alcott!"

The maid stood her ground. "He is in your dressing room, madam! He has broken open your jewel chest!"

"What!" cried the duchess. Picking up her skirts, she ran upstairs as quickly as a young girl. Upon entering her dressing room, she stood stunned, unable to believe her eyes. Dorian had indeed broken open her jewel chest, and was pawing through the contents like the most brazen of thieves. "My God! What are you doing?" she whispered, aghast.

Dorian held up a fistful of diamonds and emeralds. "These are mine, I believe," he said, shoving the jewels into his pocket. "That is to say, they belong to the estate— to me."

"They are the Ascot emeralds," she stammered.

"And the ring on your finger," he said, holding out his hand. "Unless I am mistaken, that belongs to me as well."

"My engagement ring!"

"Give it to me," he said implacably. "Give it to me, or I shall tear it from your finger."

Mute with fear, she drew the huge, glittering green stone from her finger and dropped it in his hand.

"Thank you." His gaze was frigid as he walked past her to the door. "I seem to have broken your jewelry box," he added as he went out of the room. "Get yourself a new one—have them send me the bill at Brooks's."

"Good God, Dorian! What is the matter with you?" she cried, her face ashen; but the duke was already gone.

He drove himself to Celia's house. She was with Flood in the back room on the first floor up. They were working, sorting through Celia's vast collection of theatrical costumes. She had not decided what she would wear in the very first scene of the new play, the scene where Viola washed up on the shores of Illyria after the shipwreck. As he came into the room, she was on her pedestal in a flowing white garment of almost Grecian aspect, her head tilted to one side as she studied the effect in the long mirrors that lined all four walls. Even the back of the door was mirrored.

Dorian knew the room; he had collapsed in it the night before.

"My dear sir," she greeted him, climbing down from the pedestal, much to the annoyance of Flood, who was on her knees before her mistress, her mouth full of pins. "I do hope you feel better than you look!" Celia added, laughing as she held out her hands to him.

"What a fright I must have given you," he murmured, embarrassed.

"I was a little worried," she admitted, "but your brother assured me you would be all right."

"I am glad you sent for him. I know how much you dislike one another."

"Indeed, your brother and I will never be friends," she answered. "But he is your brother, and I know that he loves you."

"He was not rude to you, I hope?"

She laughed. "I can never see your brother without I feel sorry for his men. What they must endure! Fortunately, I am not one of his men. He can't have me flogged, however much he may wish to."

"I wish you could be friends, Sally," Dorian said sadly. "Simon is the best man I know, and if you are ever in difficulty, you could not do better than to apply to him for assistance. I wish you would let me tell him of your connection to the family," he went on hopefully. "Then he would treat you with more respect."

"I doubt it. He might pity me, but he certainly would not respect me. That I could not bear! To be pitied by Lord Simon! I would rather he hate me."

"Of course I shan't tell him, if that is what you wish," he assured her. "Though it seems a pity. You always admired him so much."

"Admired him!" she exclaimed, astonished. "What do you mean?"

He smiled at her. "You know what I mean, Miss Sally! Many is the time I found you at the top of the stairs at Ashlands, staring up at his portrait with an adoring gaze."

She frowned. "I was only a child then," she said crossly. "I didn't even know it was a picture of a real person, let alone a living creature, until your father told me one day."

Dorian chuckled. "Caught you looking at his favorite son, did he? Yes, Simon was his favorite," he went on in answer to her look of surprise. "He was a rough-and-tumble boy. A hell-born babe, as they say. My father liked that. He was but fifteen when that portrait was painted but, alas, already old in sin."

"Oh yes?" said Celia. "And what were the sins of his youth?"

He chuckled. "Women, of course! That is why he was packed off to the army. An affair with some girl or other when he was at Eton."

"What sort of girl was she?"

"The sort that persuaded my father to send him to India. We did not see him again for nearly eight years."

"By then, *I* had been packed off to Ireland."

Dorian shuddered. This is what he had come to talk to her about, and he had been dreading having to bring it up. "Was it very bad for you, my dear?"

She took his hand. "Let us not speak of it," she said firmly. "It would only cause you pain. There was a time," she added, bringing his hand to her cheek, "when I wanted very much to cause you pain."

"And now?"

She smiled. "Now I am glad to see my cousin Dorian again. Shall we go sit in the drawing room?"

She led the way, and the maidservant brought the tea. Celia presided over the teapot with real pleasure. "I used to do this at Ashlands, do you remember? Your mother taught me the art. Yes, Cousin Dorian; there is an art to making tea, an art to being a good hostess."

"You were happy at Ashlands."

"It was like paradise to me. The first year I was with you I was black-and-blue from pinching myself. I'd have the most dreadful nightmares. I lived in fear that I'd be sent back to the Foundling Hospital. Your father did not like me at first," she added, "so my fears were not unfounded."

"You soon won him over," he remembered. "He came to adore you."

"I made it my business to win him over," she replied. "I did not want to be cast out of paradise, after all."

"Within six months, he was living in your pocket. We all were."

"After a year, I stopped pinching myself. I had never known such happiness, such security. I was never happier than when I was with you at Ashlands."

"And to Ashlands you must return," he said eagerly. "As my guest. This summer, when the theatres close, what else have you to do? Come to Ashlands and stay as long as you like."

Celia was shaking her head. "Impossible! The servants might recognize me. Servants are much more observant than their masters, you know. They must be, if they are to keep their places."

"The servants!" he exclaimed suddenly, drawing in a shaking breath. "I had not thought of them. Why, all these years, they must have known the truth! Not all of them, perhaps, but some of them had to know you were alive. They could not *all* have been in ignorance. Who knew? Who amongst them knew you had been sent away?"

"No one would dare question your mother," said Celia. "She would have given them orders. They would have had no choice but to obey. Indeed, you shall not blame the servants."

"Why should I not blame them?" he returned. "If they had orders, they were not *my* orders. I am master at Ashlands, not my mother. All these years, they have deceived me!"

"I beg you, do not think of punishing your servants!" she said, alarmed. "Not for my sake. They were always kind to me. It is not their fault I fell out of favor with the mistress."

"And the vicar!" he went on, as if he had not heard her. "Whom did he think he was burying? *Was* there really a funeral? The stonemason who carved your headstone—did *he* know 'twas for an empty grave? At least, one assumes it was an empty grave. At this point, I wouldn't put anything past my mother! She could very easily have slaughtered a village girl and tossed *her* body in the coffin."

Celia laughed shakily. "Don't be ridiculous, Dorian."

"Did they pack you a trunk, at least? You had your things about you?"

"I had my clothes, some of them. I wasn't allowed to keep any books or letters. I could have nothing to show where I'd come from. The little presents I'd received over the years—those were taken from me. My dolls. My silver hairbrushes. My locket with my parents' hair inside. She did let me keep my handkerchief, though."

He looked puzzled. "Your handkerchief?"

"The one that was with me when I was found as an infant. It was accounted quite without value, and I was allowed to keep it."

"May I see it?" he asked, surprising her.

"Why?"

"Will you not indulge an old friend?"

Celia looked rather doubtful, but after a moment, she left the room, returning a short time later with a small box inlaid with ivory. Opening it, she removed a small bundle, which she unwrapped. Now slightly yellow with age, the handkerchief had been folded to show the embroidery at one corner. Two initials, an S and an L, had been joined inside a crudely stitched heart. Celia held it out in her palms like a wounded bird. "They named me at the Foundling Hospital. S for Sarah. The heart and the L became Hartley, I suppose."

"And you changed the S and the L to St. Lys," he said.

"Yes. When I escaped from Ireland, I wanted a new start and new name to go with it. Sally was too common. And Sarah much too plain. Celia suits me, I think."

"This is not an inexpensive handkerchief," Dorian went

on, examining the fragile cambric. "Whoever she was, your mother was not poor."

"She might have gotten it secondhand, you know." Celia laughed at his blank expression. "No, I don't suppose you *do* know. I don't suppose the Duke of Berkshire has ever gotten anything secondhand!"

"Only my houses, my lands, my titles, and my jewels," he said, making her laugh.

"Touché!"

"I still say your mother must have been a gentle-woman," he pursued. "Only a gentlewoman would think to ruin a perfectly good handkerchief with such indifferent needlework."

"And if my mother was a gentlewoman, then my father *must* have been a gentleman," she said, laughing. "At least, *you* will have it so."

"What if we could find them now?" he said. "Your parents, I mean."

"My parents?" she said, blinking in surprise. "Lord, they'd be old and gray by now, if they are still alive."

"We might make inquiries," he suggested, ignoring her attempt at humor.

"After all this time? Who would even remember?"

"Indeed, some memories might have faded," he admitted. "But consider this: the passage of time might have made people more willing to speak. What may have been a scandalous secret twenty-four years ago might not seem so very important now."

Celia shrugged impatiently. "Whoever they were, Dorian, my parents did not want me."

"You don't know that. You might have been stolen from them."

"Yes; obviously I am a stolen princess. I am the lost queen of Byzantium. It was the villainous vizier who dropped me in the streets." Impatiently, she took back the handkerchief and restored it to its box.

"You were not dropped in the streets. They left you at a church, Sally. That's something. They knew you would be cared for."

She shook her head. "What difference can it possibly make now? Frankly, at this point in my life, I'd rather not know."

He was silent for a moment. "I looked for your locket at Berkshire House. I shall keep looking."

"My locket—if it still exists—could be anywhere," she said. "I doubt your mother kept it. Why would she?"

"Now I think of it," he said, frowning, "it must be in your grave."

"In my grave, sir?" she said, shivering. "It's not my grave, if you please. I have no grave. I am still very much alive."

"*The* grave, shall we say? I'm almost positive that my mother told Joanna the locket had been buried with you. You were not buried, of course, but the locket may have been. It is but thirty miles to Ashlands; we can be there by nightfall."

She grimaced. "*We*? As delightful as it may sound, I can't just go scampering off with you to Berkshire to dig up a grave! I have a play tonight."

"But you don't have to bother with all that anymore," he said. "I'll look after you. All that sort of thing is beneath you, anyway."

She stared at him in surprise. "Beneath me? What do you mean? It's how I earn my living, Dorian. It's honest work."

"But you should not have to *earn* your living at all," he said, the words bursting from his lips as if he had long contained them. "You were brought up to be a lady. You were brought up in my father's house, as my cousin."

"But I am *not* your cousin," she replied. "I'm a nameless

nobody from the Foundling Hospital. Or, at least, I was. Now, of course, I am Celia St. Lys. There is nothing wrong with being Celia St. Lys, I hope. I quite like it."

"I have no wish to offend you, Sally. But you must see that I am right. Had my father lived, your life would have been very different."

"Your father was afraid I might have 'bad blood.' But your mother assured him I was much too attractive a child to have 'bad blood.'"

Dorian pursed his lips. "My father did have some rather odd ideas. But that was before he knew you. He soon came to love you as a daughter. He would never have permitted you to set foot on a stage. The very idea would have offended him."

"True," she admitted. "My life would have been different had he lived. But he did not live. Your mother—alas!— did not love me as a daughter. She did not choose to keep me in her house, not even as a servant. She got rid of me, and it was her right to do so. All things considered, I think I've done all right for myself, Dorian."

Dorian rested his fist on the mantelpiece. "Naturally, I do not blame you for the life you have been leading," he began.

"Thank you!" she said tartly.

"I do not judge you."

"No indeed."

"But, Sally," he said slowly, "you must quit the stage now. Surely you see that."

"Quit the stage!" she said, becoming angry. "Why should I do that?"

He blinked at her. "Obviously, you cannot go on like this. I cannot permit it. My conscience simply won't allow it."

"I beg your pardon!"

"I propose this: that you become my ward."

"You want to adopt me?" she said incredulously.

"I would be your guardian, yes. I would look after you. You would want for nothing."

Celia was on her feet. "Ward! I am twenty-four years old! I can look after myself. I have been doing so for quite some time now. I need no guardian. I work for my living—proudly. You are not going to make me ashamed of myself!"

Dorian was horrified. "That is not my intention, dear girl. I would not for the world make you unhappy. You would be cared for and respected as you should be. I would grant you a handsome annuity. How does three thousand pounds a year sound? You would never have to work another day in your life."

She stared at him. "Dorian! Are you . . . are you asking me to be your *mistress*?"

"Of course not," he said, genuinely shocked.

"You just want to *give* me three thousand a year?" she said. "No strings attached?"

"You would have to leave the stage, of course. But that is all I would ask of you."

"Oh, is that all? What would I do all day if I left the stage?"

"Whatever you liked."

"I like being on the stage!" she cried.

"But, my dear, does it not distress you to be so much . . . so much on *display*?" he asked. "Surely you don't *like* being ogled by all those men in the pit?"

Celia laughed. "Don't I? That's the best part of it. When they *stop* ogling me I shall be very sad indeed."

"I know you cannot be serious, my dear."

"But I am. I love my life, Dorian, just as it is. I am never happier than when I am onstage. You cannot take that away from me."

"I shall replace it with something better—the life you ought to have had."

"What? You mean to send me back to Foundling Hospital?"

"If you had remained with us at Ashlands," he went on doggedly, "if my mother had not done this terrible thing to you, you would have been brought out into society. You would have been presented at court like any carefully brought up young lady."

"Celia St. Lys at the Court of St. James! Fancy that!"

"Miss Sarah Hartley of Ashlands, ward of the Duke of Berkshire, at the Court of St. James," he countered. "You would have been invited to balls and parties."

"Oh, but I *am* invited to balls and parties," she said archly.

"Yes! Disreputable balls and parties."

"Is there a better kind?" She sighed. "I know you mean well, Dorian. But I'm afraid it's too late for me to become a proper young lady. I've been on the stage for years. I've had lovers. I'll never be respectable."

"I don't know what to do," he confessed.

"Can you not be my friend?" she said. "I would like that very much."

"I am your friend, of course."

She laughed. "Good! That's settled, then."

"But nothing is settled," he protested. "You must let me do something for you. You must let me make amends somehow."

"You may drive me to the theatre if you like," she said. "I must leave now, or I shall be late for rehearsal."

He waited while she went to change her dress, then they set off together in his cabriolet. Celia had dressed to please him, and looked demure and ladylike in her pink carriage dress and pink velvet bonnet. Their progress down Piccadilly did not go unremarked.

"People will think you are my mistress," he fretted, observing the stares directed at them.

She laughed. "But of course they will! I don't mind, if you don't."

"The truth is, I've never really had a mistress."

"You've never had a mistress?" she repeated incredulously. "I don't believe you! What, never? Never, ever?" As his face slowly turned bright red, she began to laugh.

"You must understand," he murmured. "I married young. And Joanna was always ill. It wouldn't have been right to deceive her. She would have been so hurt. And, of course, we were always trying to have a child. I did not think it right to—to waste my substance with other women, if you see what I mean. Imagine if a *mistress* had borne me a son! No, I could never have done that to her. She was a good girl."

"Do forgive my silliness," Celia said softly. "I know you loved her very much."

"No," he said. "You don't understand. I never loved Joanna."

"What?"

"I did not love my wife. I cared for her, of course. I was as kind to her as I possibly could be, but I . . . I never loved her. I've never been in love."

Celia stared at him. "But you were so devoted to each other. Yours was the perfect marriage, I thought."

"The marriage was arranged. We made the best of it; what else could we do?"

"We are becoming maudlin again," she observed. "Let us have no more serious talk today, I beg you. The day is too fine, and I have always wanted to be driven about town by a handsome young duke."

At that moment, her name rang out as she was recognized by someone on the street, and she smiled and waved to her devotee.

"Impudent wretch!" Dorian muttered.

"Not at all," she laughed. "How I should like to be seen driving with you in Hyde Park in Rotten Row with all the beau monde looking on enviously!" she cried, her eyes sparkling.

"Would you like that, indeed?" he said rather doubtfully.

"I should like it above all things!" she cried. "Could we not go tomorrow? 'Tis Sunday. The theatre will be closed. Or we might ride, if you could lend me a horse. I'm a tolerable horsewoman, you know."

"I know. I taught you myself," he said.

"Shall we do it, then? Shall we take them by storm? It won't do your reputation any harm to be seen with me, and it could only do me good. People are tired of seeing me with Fitzclarence. They'll be very glad to see me with you. I might even make you fashionable."

He smiled faintly. "Why not? I had thought to leave for Ashlands this afternoon, but I suppose I can put it off until Monday."

"Are you so eager to dig up my grave?" she teased. "Let it wait until Monday. Let us spend all Sunday together."

He laughed. "Very well, my dear. Your resurrection is hereby postponed until Monday. Shall I collect you in the morning for Sunday services? Then, afterward, we might have our ride—and I'll arrange a picnic, too."

"Sunday services?" she said rather blankly. "Oh! You mean *church*. Lord, I haven't set foot in a church since my wedding day. I'll say this for Sir Terence—he wasn't much of a God-botherer."

"But, Sally!" he said, shocked. "We used to go to church every Sunday."

"I remember." She laughed suddenly. "Of course I'll go to church with you. It'll be great fun. I can hardly wait to see the looks on all their faces when the Duke of Berkshire brings his mistress to church! We'll have the whole town talking. 'St. Lys is converted!' I may have to organize a revival of *The Fair Penitent*."

Dorian's face fell. "Oh dear," he murmured in dismay.

"What shall I wear? One simply *must* have something sensational to wear to church, don't you agree? I don't suppose you could lend me the Ascot emeralds?"

He smiled. "Why not?"

She laughed. "I was only teasing you," she said quickly. "Why, if you took me to church and I was wearing the Ascot emeralds, people naturally would assume that—that—"

"That what, Sally? That we are engaged?"

"Well, yes."

"Would that be so terrible?" he asked quietly.

Celia laughed lightly. "Your mother would go off like Mount Tambora!"

To her relief, he laughed, too. For a moment, she had feared he might be serious.

Chapter 14

Dorian did not mean to stay long at the Theatre Royal, but he was so warmly received by Celia's colleagues that he found he could not get away. With good grace he accepted the mocking cheers and applause from those who had witnessed his collapse the night before. Everyone was very glad to see the Duke of Berkshire so well recovered, and everyone wanted to shake his hand. Before he quite knew what was happening, Mr. Grimaldi had persuaded him to make a handsome contribution to the Drury Lane Theatrical Fund, and Mr. Rourke had invited him to stay and give them the benefit of his opinion on the first dress rehearsal of the new play.

"Oh, I don't know," Dorian said uncertainly. "I'm sure I'd only be in the way."

"We are players," Celia assured him. "We love an audience! Of course, you need not stay if you don't wish . . . I know how it pains you to see me on the stage."

"Oh?" said Mr. Grimaldi. "I don't think she's as bad as all that, Your Grace. Though, between ourselves, she's not as good as she thinks she is. She tries, of course."

"I do try," said Celia. "I rehearse all day and I play all night. But I never seem to get any better."

"You work too hard," said Dorian. "You exhaust yourself. You should not rehearse and play on the same day—it's too much. We never did so at Eton."

"At Eton, Your Grace?"

"Did I not tell you?" cried Celia. "His Grace is an actor, too. He did Shakespeare when he was at Eton. He was Polonius in *Hamlet.*"

"Hardly worth mentioning," said Dorian, blushing. "I was also Aufidius in *Coriolanus.* And Brutus in *Julius Caesar.* Mind you, it was nothing like all this. We only did it for fun."

Celia laughed. "*Coriolanus? Julius Caesar?* That's your idea of fun, is it?"

"As I was saying, my dear, you work too hard," said Dorian. "Why don't I buy out the play tonight? Then you and everyone could have the night off, couldn't you? I'll take you to supper. I'll take you to Vauxhall Gardens. Anything you like."

"Thank you, Your Grace!" exclaimed Joe Grimaldi appreciatively.

"Your Grace is not serious," Celia said severely. "Are you, sir?"

"I most certainly am," said Dorian, missing the import of her tone. "What would it cost to buy out the theatre tonight, Mr. Rourke?" he asked, calling out to the actor-manager. "A thousand pounds?"

"No one wants your money here," Celia said indignantly.

"Speak for yourself," said Joe Grimaldi. "I want his money. What's more, I'd love to go to supper and Vauxhall Gardens. So would Mrs. Grimaldi."

"A thousand pounds would be more than adequate, Your Grace," said Rourke.

"A *hundred* pounds would more than cover the house,

Mr. Rourke," Celia said coldly, "and you know it. How dare you try to take advantage of him!"

Dorian was surprised. "A hundred pounds? As little as that? I'll double it, Mr. Rourke. Oh, what the hell! Shall we say, an even five hundred pounds?"

"Your Grace!"

"Dorian!" Celia said sharply. "What do you think you are doing? You can't just come here and buy the house and shut down the play."

"Of course he can," said Mr. Grimaldi.

"No, he can't," said Celia. "People have already bought tickets. I won't have them disappointed."

"They'll get over it," said Joe Grimaldi. "They'll get their money back."

"They'll say you did it for me, Your Grace," said Celia quietly. "They'll say that I let everybody down just so that I could go off on a binge of pleasure with you, the Duke of Berkshire. My public simply won't stand for it. I did not get to be where I am by forgetting all the little people who put me here. If they are kind enough to take the time to come and see us, we are going to give them a show."

Dorian looked into her eyes and saw that she meant it. "Very well, my dear," he said, after a moment. "Forgive my interference. It was kindly meant."

Joe Grimaldi sighed.

"Are we going to have a rehearsal today or not?" cried Sybil Archer, sailing from the wings, fully made up and in costume for the part of Maria, waiting woman to the Countess Olivia. "Belinda and I have been waiting an age! Ah!" she sniffed, catching sight of Celia. "I see St. Lys has decided to grace us with her presence, after all. *Now*, perhaps, we can begin."

"You might have started without me, dear," said Celia. "After all, I'm not the one who needs the practice."

"How dare you! Belinda is stepping into a new role on very short notice."

"Indeed she is," said Rourke unctuously, "and we're all most grateful—"

Mrs. Archer glared at him. "What do you mean you're *almost* grateful? You should be completely grateful!"

"No, Mrs. Archer," he said quickly. "What I meant to say is that we are all *most* grateful," he repeated slowly, minding his diction and enunciating each word. "Aren't we, Celia darling?"

"Yes indeed," said Celia. "We are almost grateful."

"I see you have brought a man with you," said Mrs. Archer.

"Actually, he brought me," said Celia. "May I present His Grace, the Duke of Berkshire. The *ninth* Duke of Berkshire."

"The eleventh," said Dorian. "Dear madam," he went on, addressing Mrs. Archer, "if Miss St. Lys is late, you must not blame her. It is entirely my fault. I delayed her."

Mrs. Archer stared at him. "Your Grace!" she exclaimed, with a simpering smile. "You honor us with your presence. May I present my daughter, Miss Belinda Archer? Belinda! Belinda! Dash it all—where is that girl?"

"Here, Mama," said Belinda, stepping out from behind her mother. As the Countess Olivia, she wore full mourning for a dead brother, and a heavy black veil framed her enchanting little face. She executed a wobbly curtsy.

Dorian bowed to her. "I believe I owe *you* an apology, Miss Archer," he told her. "You and your mama."

Belinda's soft brown eyes widened. She looked, Celia thought rather sourly, like a frightened fawn. Some men, she supposed, found that helpless sort of female quite appealing. "An apology, Your Grace?" Belinda whispered, bewildered. "Whatever for?"

"You dined last night with my brother. Your evening was interrupted because of me, I believe. I—I fell ill quite suddenly. Do please forgive me."

"I'm sure there is nothing to forgive, Your Grace," Belinda told him prettily. "You could not help that you were ill."

"No indeed," put in Mr. Grimaldi. "It happens to the best of us."

"I owe you an apology as well, Miss Archer," said Celia.

"Y-you do?"

"Yes. It seems that Lord Simon sent you some flowers yesterday, but they were brought to my room by mistake. They were only wildflowers, so I'm afraid they didn't keep very well."

"*Wildflowers*, Miss St. Lys?" said Mrs. Archer scornfully. "Are you sure? Surely a gentleman like Lord Simon would not send a girl wildflowers. He would send roses or lilies."

Dorian laughed. "Oh, that's Simon, all right. When he likes a girl, he sends his valet down to the country to pick wildflowers for her. He says that anybody can get hothouse blooms, but wildflowers, you know, come from the heart."

"Really?" Celia said coolly. "I thought they came from the dirt."

Belinda frowned. "You mean he doesn't even pick them himself?" she cried indignantly. "He makes his valet do it?"

"I'm sure he tried picking them himself, dear," said Celia. "But, you see, everything Lord Simon touches withers and dies."

"Oh!" said Belinda, her eyes round. "Oh, I see."

"Miss St. Lys is only joking you, of course," Dorian told her.

"Oh!" said the girl brightly. "Then he *does* pick them himself?"

"Er . . . no," said the duke. "The part about the valet is true. Miss St. Lys was joking about the withering and the dying."

"Of course I was," said Celia.

"I'm glad!" said Belinda earnestly. "He has asked to take me riding in the park tomorrow, and Mama says I must go. I should be very sorry to see anything wither and die."

"I hope you are a good horsewoman, Miss Archer," said Dorian. "You'll have to be able to keep up with my brother, I'm afraid."

"No," said Belinda. "I've never even sat on a horse. But Mama has furnished me with a very pretty green riding habit. And Mama says that Lord Simon will teach me."

Dorian looked rather doubtful, but Celia said firmly, "Yes, of course he will. Just make sure he knows it's your first time, and I'm certain he'll be patient and gentle with you."

"Yes, Miss St. Lys. I'll be sure to do that."

Clapping his hands, Rourke called the actors gathered on the stage to order. Joe Grimaldi, who was to play the Countess Olivia's clown, showed Dorian to a seat at the front of the pit, and the rehearsal began with Rourke proclaiming rather grandly, as the Duke Orsino, "'If music be the food of love . . . play on!'"

The first scene was so fully realized that Dorian applauded at its conclusion. "Oh, thank you, Your Grace," said Rourke, coming to the proscenium. "I thought perhaps my timing was a little off . . . ?"

"Oh!" said Dorian, not realizing that the actor was only fishing for compliments. "Perhaps a little. Shall you try it again?"

The next scene, in which Celia made her first appearance as the shipwrecked Viola, was hardly more than a sketch. The actress ran through her lines with the captain, and did not even bother with the long speech at the end. Dorian was flabbergasted, but no one else seemed discomfited in the least. "You're—you're not going to do it like that, are you?" he called out as Celia was leaving the stage.

Celia laughed. "Of course not, Your Grace. I shall be drenched from head to toe in the white gown I showed you earlier."

"W-white gown?" he repeated. "Drenched? But won't that make it rather more—"

"Rather more what, Your Grace?"

"Well! Rather more transparent than not, if you see what I mean."

"I can't help that," she replied. "There's been a shipwreck. I've been lost at sea. Naturally, I am going to be wet."

"But must you wear a *white* gown?"

"Well, you see, Your Grace . . . First of all, I am a virgin—" Naturally, someone coughed, though Dorian could not tell who. "That is to say, *Viola* is a virgin," Celia corrected herself. "And virgins wear white, don't they? Besides, Your Grace, it's important for the audience to see that I am actually a woman, because for the rest of the play, I'm dressed as a man."

"Oh, I see," said Dorian, faintly. "Carry on, then."

"Thank you, Your Grace."

The scene shifted to the Countess Olivia's house, and Joe Grimaldi mounted the stage.

All was well until Celia and Belinda's first scene together. Nothing seemed to work for Miss Archer. Even with allowances made for the fact that she was stepping into the role of Olivia on short notice, it was clear she was drowning in the part.

"I am so sorry, Miss St. Lys," she cried, bursting into tears after flubbing her lines for the tenth time. "I just get so nervous when you look at me like that, and you say those things to me."

"I am not wooing you for myself, child," Celia explained impatiently. "I am wooing you on behalf of the duke. I don't even like you. In fact, I hate you, because the duke is in love with you, and I am in love with the duke."

"The duke is in love with me?"

"No, idiot! Mr. Rourke is in love—aargh! *Orsino* is in love with Olivia. Viola is in love with Orsino. We are rivals for the same man, Miss Archer."

"I understand all that, Miss St. Lys. It's just the part where I am supposed to—to *like* you—Viola—Cesario, I mean. I know I'm supposed to think you are a man, but I'm afraid . . . well . . . all I see is Miss St. Lys in breeches! I'm sorry, Miss St. Lys—but I simply *cannot* make love to you! It's unnatural, if you see what I mean."

Celia quickly became exasperated. Dressed in her sky-blue dolman, white leather breeches, and top boots, with her hair tied back ruthlessly, she looked as masculine as she possibly could. "Would it help if I put on the mustache?" she offered.

"We could try," Belinda said doubtfully.

Celia at once glued on a false mustache, but all that did was make Belinda giggle.

"Poor child! She's just not very good," Dorian murmured to Joe Grimaldi, who was watching the scene with him. "Why does no one tell her?"

"No need, Your Grace," Grimaldi replied. "She knows she's not very good. That's the better part of her trouble."

"She was much better in her scene with you."

"Naturally," Grimaldi said. "She doesn't have to make love to *me*."

"She knows her lines," said Dorian. "She just can't seem

to deliver them properly. She simply can't make love to Miss St. Lys."

"It is rather a daunting prospect," said Grimaldi. "*I* couldn't do it myself."

"Is there no one else who can play the part of Olivia?"

"And learn it by Thursday?" Grimaldi shook his head. "It's Belinda or nothing, I'm afraid."

"Who was to play the part originally?"

"Peggy Copeland, of course."

"Whatever happened to her?" Dorian inquired. "She was rather good."

"Lord Torcaster has forbidden her the stage. His lordship swears he will take her child from her and cut her off without a penny if she defies him. She was very sorry to leave us in the lurch, but what could she do? If Belinda cannot perform," he added, "I'm afraid we shall have no choice but to cancel the play."

"We shall *not* cancel the play," Celia declared, jumping down from the stage, looking quite dashing in her glistening, snow-white breeches. "This is mutiny, Mr. Grimaldi! I won't have that kind of talk in my house."

"But, my dear," Dorian protested mildly, keeping his voice low, "she really *is* no good. She drags everything down. She has no vivacity—no spark!"

Celia drew her sword, a slender fencing blade with a button on the end of it for safety, and lifted the duke's chin with the end of it. "I *said* I won't have that kind of talk in my house and I meant it," she said with mock severity. "We have nearly a week to get her ready. That's plenty of time."

"God help us," Grimaldi murmured.

Dorian moved the blade away with one finger. "I daresay you are right, Sally," he said dryly. "All Miss Archer needs is a little more rehearsal, I am sure."

Celia put up her sword, looking at him thoughtfully.

"Perhaps what she needs is a different kind of rehearsal," she said slowly. "She was better yesterday with Tom."

"Tom?"

"Mr. West," said Celia. "I've been using him for my role model, you see. He was helping us yesterday, but he could not be here today. Belinda seemed to find it easier to play the scene opposite a real man. How would you like to step in, Your Grace?"

"Who, me? Certainly not," Dorian protested, growing red in the face.

"Oh please," she begged. "If you could stand in for me in this scene, it might make all the difference for Belinda."

"You want me to stand in for you—for Viola—in this scene?"

"Viola, disguised as the young man, Cesario," Celia swiftly explained.

"I suppose," said Dorian, "if you think it will help, I can read the lines with Miss Archer. But . . . won't she eventually have to play with *you*, Sally, in, you know, the actual play?"

"Yes, of course she will have to make love to *me* in the actual play," said Celia. "There's no getting around that, I'm afraid. This is just rehearsal; she can make love to you instead. Then, when the time comes for the actual play, she can imagine that I am you or Tom or whoever."

"That's a bit mad, don't you think?"

"I don't care if it's mad," Celia replied. "If it works, it works. She can pretend she's making love to Dick Whittington's cat, as long as the right words come out her mouth."

"All right," he said, unbuttoning his coat. "I'll do it. I should warn you, though, it has been years since I played. Script?"

Celia promptly handed him a copy of the play. "Off you go."

"I'll just need a few moments," said the duke gravely, "to warm up my vocal cords."

Whereupon he burst into song.

Belinda, when she was informed that the Duke of Berkshire would be playing the next scene with her, promptly fainted.

"We are doomed," Mr. Grimaldi murmured to Rourke.

After rehearsal, Celia felt uncommonly depressed. "I'm sorry I wasn't much help," Dorian apologized as he drove her back to Curzon Street.

Someone on the street called out excitedly, "St. Lys! There is Celia St. Lys!" But instead of smiling and waving, Celia just sank lower in her seat, hiding her face behind her hand. "I'm not sure anyone can help us," she said gloomily.

"Are you quite sure you don't want me to buy out tonight's performance?"

"Quite sure. I'll get through it somehow."

"And you have tomorrow to look forward to," he reminded her.

"Oh yes," she murmured wearily. "Riding in the park with the fashionable world."

"And a picnic, don't forget."

"Suddenly I don't think I could stick it," she said. "Suddenly I'm sick to death of London! I'd rather go to Ashlands with you, and dig up my own grave!" She laughed. "What do you say, Your Grace? Shall we picnic in the churchyard of Ashland Heath?"

He frowned. "You don't mean that, surely."

"Well, no," she said. "I've never been too keen on picnics. I like my food served by waiters and without too many ants in it! But I *would* like to go to Ashlands with you, if I may. I want nothing more than to be away from London—

far away from everything. You can bring me back on Monday without any trouble, can't you?"

"Of course," he said immediately. "I should be delighted to take you to Ashlands! It is your home, you know," he added, squeezing her hand, "and always shall be, as long as I am Duke of Berkshire."

Celia blinked back sudden tears. "Thank you, Dorian."

"My dear, you are crying!"

"It's nothing," she said quickly. "I'm just happy, that's all. Happy to be going back to Ashlands after all this time. You can have no idea what it means to me."

"I have some idea," he replied, taking out his handkerchief and giving it to her. "I love the place, too, you know. The bluebells will be just beginning, I shouldn't wonder."

"Oh! The bluebells!" she said, with a heart-wrenching sigh. "If your brother's valet hasn't picked them all for Miss Archer."

He chuckled. "We'll leave first thing in the morning."

Celia was wiping her eyes. She shook her head violently. "I don't want to wait. Let's leave tonight—directly after the play! I want to see the sunrise at Ashlands. Please, Dorian! I know it's silly, but won't you indulge an old friend?"

He smiled at her. "All right then, my dear. We'll leave tonight, directly after the play. I'll collect you from your dressing room."

"We'll have to be cleverer than that, I'm afraid," she said, beginning to smile, "if we are to avoid detection. Just imagine the gossip if you whisk me away from the theatre into the night! People will think we've eloped! I shouldn't mind that too much, but they might come after us—and *that* I would mind."

"So would I," Dorian said fervently. "But what do you suggest?"

"Let's go to my house and cudgel our brains. Dr. Aziz is

coming over with his amazing, magical fingers to give me an all-over body shampoo. It's an ancient Eastern technique. It's really the thing for revitalizing the tissues. Have you ever had an all-over body shampoo?"

The Duke of Berkshire admitted that he had not.

"Then you shall have one now!" she cried.

Upon returning to his barrack room at Horse Guards that evening, Simon was none too pleased to find his mother waiting for him.

"Simon! At last! Where have you been all day?" cried the duchess, springing to her feet. "Did you not receive my urgent message?"

Simon had just come from parade. Calmly he removed his helmet and handed it to Hawkins, his valet. "Hawkins, did we receive an urgent message from Her Grace?"

"No, my lord," Hawkins replied.

"But you must have received it," the duchess insisted. "I sent it to your rooms at the Albany."

"Ah," said Simon, enlightened. "Perhaps you are not aware that we have removed from the Albany. His Royal Highness has honored me with rooms at Carlton House."

The duchess grimaced in disgust. "That can't be convenient!"

"It is very convenient for His Royal Highness," Simon replied. As he spoke, he unbuckled his gold-embellished steel cuirass. Having disposed of his master's helmet, Hawkins returned for the cuirass, which the valet deftly removed and took away. "What was so urgent?"

"I am worried about Dorian," she replied. "Have you seen him today?"

"Should I have done?"

"You might have had the decency to look in on him this morning," she said. "After last night—"

"Dorian drank too much last night," Simon told her. "I doubt he'll ever do that again. He must have had a devil of a head this morning," he added, laughing.

The duchess stared at him. "I see nothing funny about it!"

"No—but *I* do!" Simon retorted.

"This is your brother's life we are talking about! You don't seem very concerned, I must say."

"Quite the opposite," he agreed, taking off his blue coat. "But I haven't told you yet what he's done."

"I am waiting," he said dryly, as Hawkins helped him into another coat. This one was not to be worn under a cuirass and was highly ornamented with gold oak leaves.

"Your brother," she cried, "has *stripped* me of my jewels!"

"He did what?" Simon said sharply. For the first time, he looked interested in his mother's babble.

"He has taken the Ascot emeralds!"

"When?"

"This morning. He was like a madman. He *broke* my jewel box and frightened my abigail out of her wits."

"Well, technically your emeralds do belong to him," Simon said.

"He even took my engagement ring. Look!" Stripping the glove from her left hand, she showed him her bare fingers. "He practically *tore* it from my finger. That ring had not left my hand since your father placed it there. Why should Dorian do that unless he is contemplating marriage?"

"Don't you want him to contemplate marriage? He needs an heir, after all. You can't have your cake and eat it, too."

"Of course I want him to marry," she snapped. "But

whom? Not Miss Tinsley, certainly. The only female in whom he has displayed the slightest bit of interest is—"

"Do not say it!" Simon said harshly.

"St. Lys!"

"Dorian would not be so foolish."

"I used to think so," said his mother, "but you did not see him this morning. He was like a man possessed. The woman is very beautiful. Your brother may be more susceptible than I ever realized. Who knows what the woman may have persuaded him to do with her arts and allurements? An actress!"

"She would not *dare*!"

"Depend on it—if *he* is foolish enough to offer her marriage, *she* will not be so foolish as to *refuse* him. What are we to *do*, Simon? We cannot stand by while your brother makes the biggest mistake of his life! They were seen driving together in Piccadilly today. They might be on their way to Scotland as we speak!"

"Calm yourself. He wouldn't take her to Scotland. He'd marry her by special license, and that cannot be accomplished overnight. We have time."

"But what are we to do?"

"It would be better for you not to know," he replied. "My methods might be described as somewhat ruthless."

"Good!" she said. "Make sure you punish her for her impudence."

"Believe me, madam, I shall."

Chapter 15

Toward the end of the second act, Celia hurried to her dressing room to change out of Miss Hardcastle's silk gown. In the next scene Marlow was to mistake her for a quaint country barmaid, having already mistaken Mr. Hardcastle's house for a quaint country inn.

"Damnation!" she cried savagely, slamming the door. "Did you *see* that, Flood?" She sat down on the settee to examine her shoe. "Charley Palmer trod on my foot in the scene! He *kicked* my heel—I'm quite certain he broke it. I know he's supposed to be a bit awkward, but—damnation! It's not my fault I'm taller than he! Look! It's all wobbly!"

Holding up her left shoe, she demonstrated that the heel had indeed come loose.

But it was not Flood who came through the muslin curtain to look.

"Ah! Here is the real Celia St. Lys," said Simon. Stepping from the alcove, he mocked her with slow applause. His eyes mocked her, too, even as he noted that she looked gloriously beautiful even though she was cross. He noted, too, that a collar of pink diamonds glittered at her throat. "No one who ever saw you onstage would ever guess what a foul-mouthed shrew you really are."

Celia glowered at him. "What do you want? As if I didn't know," she added with a sneer. "You want what all men want. Well, you'll have to be quick about it, I'm afraid. I've a costume change—and I need the jakes, too."

"Don't flatter yourself, madam. I have not come here to repeat the mistakes of last night."

She smiled sweetly. "Oh, that's right. I forgot! You prefer virgins now. I'm afraid Miss Archer is onstage at the moment—and she's the only virgin we've got at the moment."

"They do seem to be scarce as hen's teeth in this place."

Kicking off her other shoe, she climbed to her feet and walked in her stockings past the muslin curtain. There was no sign of her faithful Flood in the alcove.

"I see you are wearing Sir Lucas's necklace."

"No, my lord. I am wearing *my* necklace. Where the devil is my bloody dresser?" she went on angrily. "What have you done with her, you brute?"

"I'm here, madam!" cried Flood, coming in through the outer door. "I've brought you the other mules. And sure Charley Palmer will be getting an earful from me, for he done that on purpose!" The Irishwoman stopped short as she saw Lord Simon. "What's he doing here?" she asked warily, as she darted into the alcove.

"Pay no attention to him, Flood," Celia called to her gaily. "Just come and help me change. What do you want, my lord? I'm sure it *must* be important. Lord Simon is a very important man, you know. Everything he says and does is of the utmost importance. Just ask him! He serves the Prince of Wales, you know."

Glaring at Simon, Flood quickly drew the curtain. "I don't care who he serves. He's no business in your dressing room, madam."

"But a girl such as I must make way for these great men," said Celia. "We must take great care not to offend them, lest they ruin us poor girls. Whom do you fetch me for tonight, Lord Simon?" she called. "Last time, it was only a coal merchant, which vexed me greatly. Why, I wouldn't lie down for anything less than a viscount."

Simon could hear the rustle of silk as Flood began unlacing her mistress's gown. "I am looking for my brother, Miss St. Lys," he said, holding his temper in check. "Have you seen him today?"

"In *my* dressing room?" Celia cried. "For shame, Lord Simon!"

"He is not in his box tonight," Simon replied, "but you know that already."

"I do hate to see an empty box," Celia admitted, "even though his subscription is paid up. He might at least have lent it to a friend for the evening!"

"Did you *expect* to see him tonight?" Simon pursued. "Had you made plans?"

"Oh, I'm *always* making plans," she responded with maddening gaiety. "I never leave anything to chance, if I can help it. Life is rather like going to war, isn't it? It's important to marshal your forces and choose your ground. It's the high ground that's most desirable, isn't it?"

"Do you know where Dorian is?" Simon demanded roughly.

"How would I know? He's your brother, not mine."

"Have you seen him today?"

"What if I did?"

"*Did* you see him?" Simon shouted.

"There's no need to shout," she said primly. "I am not deaf. Yes! I saw him earlier today."

"When? Where?"

"I don't know *when*," she said crossly. "I don't live with an eye on the clock, you know. What do you take me for, a bank clerk? His Grace came to my house to apologize for his conduct last night. I don't suppose *you* have any intention of apologizing for *yours*?"

"And you have not seen my brother since?"

"Since . . . ?" She sounded confused.

"Since he apologized to you!"

"You're shouting again," she complained. "He drove me to the theatre in his cabriolet. He watched some of the rehearsal for the new play. Then he left."

"Where did he go?"

"He took me home."

"Then what?"

"Then he left. Before you ask, I don't know where he was going. He didn't say."

He looked at her intently. "Were you not curious?"

"I'm always curious, Lord Simon," she replied, "but never inquisitive. Unlike yourself."

Celia stepped from behind the muslin curtain. She had removed her bonnet and was now plainly dressed in a modestly cut gown of brown bombazine, ready to be mistaken for the barmaid. "No, wait! I tell a lie! Now that I think of it," she said slowly, as if recalling a distant memory, "he did say something about a ball."

Simon frowned. "Ball? What sort of ball?"

"I think we can safely assume that it wasn't a *cannon*ball."

"Which ball?" he said, flushing with anger. "I mean, whose? It's the height of the season. There must be five balls going on tonight."

"How should I know whose ball?" she snapped. "*I* wasn't invited!"

Simon smiled thinly. "Poor Celia!" he murmured. "Out in the cold again. I could have told you Dorian was not for you. He wants a wife, not a mistress."

She smiled slowly. "Oh! Did you think he was going to ask me to marry him?"

"Certainly not."

"Yes, you did," she said, her smile growing wider. "That's why you are here, looking for him so frantically. Don't worry! I haven't the slightest yearning to become a duchess. All those secret pregnancies, and she gets murdered in the end, anyway—strangled by her brothers."

"What are you talking about?"

"*The Duchess of Malfi*, of course. What are *you* talking about?" She laughed. "Don't you worry about me, young man. I'll be just fine out here in the cold. Something will turn up for me. Something always does."

There was a knock on the door. "Five minutes, Miss St. Lys!" the call boy cried through the door.

"If you don't mind," said Celia, pointing to the door. "Time is short, and I still need to visit Mr. Jakes behind the screen."

Simon at once made his way to the door. "I must be going, anyway," he said. "I am on duty at Carlton House tonight."

"Miss Archer will be so sorry she missed you," said Celia. "I'd be happy to convey a message to her for you."

"No message. I look forward to taking her riding in Hyde Park tomorrow afternoon."

Celia smiled. "On her unicorn?"

He opened the door but paused with his hand on the knob. "Perhaps we will have the pleasure of seeing *you* there, Miss St. Lys, mounted on your dragon."

"I shouldn't think so. I've better things to do."

"But you ride every Sunday in Hyde Park with Fitzclarence," he taunted her.

"Not *every* Sunday," she said coldly.

Simon clucked his tongue. "Do forgive me! I did hear that Fitzclarence had broken with you. His new mistress is in the play, is she not? That must be hard for you."

"Not at all. I've already replaced him—with Tom West."

He laughed. "Tom West! Your garden bench? Oh, you *are* scraping the bottom of the barrel, aren't you?"

"You have your virgin, and I have mine," she said. "That's fair, isn't it?"

Simon bit his lip to contain his fury. "You forgot to remove your necklace," he informed her. "You'll never be mistaken for a barmaid with a collar of pink diamonds at your throat—not until you open your mouth, that is."

As Celia's hands flew to her throat, he went out without another word, slamming the door behind him.

"Good God!" exclaimed the duchess when she saw her younger son's face. She had been waiting in her carriage outside the theatre for three quarters of an hour and her nerves had gotten the better of her sense. "You've seen him!" she squawked. "They are married!"

"Don't talk nonsense," he said roughly. "Of course they are not married."

"Then why do you look like that?" she cried. "I vow, you are *ashen*."

"Sometimes I think I could cheerfully murder that woman," Simon muttered.

The duchess shuddered. "Oh, I do hope it doesn't come to that!"

"I shouldn't think so," said Simon, regaining his composure. "You have nothing to worry about."

"Nothing to worry about! Where is Dorian? Where is my son?"

Simon chuckled. "Dorian," he replied, "is at a ball."

"A ball?" she repeated in disbelief. "What sort of ball?"

"I think, madam," he replied, "we can safely assume it is not a *cannon*ball."

* * *

Dorian was indeed at a ball, for he had his instructions. In fact, he went to five separate balls that night, staying at each one just long enough to make his presence felt before moving on to the next. A little after two in the morning, he made his way to Grillon's Hotel, where Celia was waiting for him, bundled in furs in a plain, hired chaise-and-four. While waiting for the duke, she had enjoyed a light supper and a refreshing nap in a private room of the hotel.

"Sorry I'm a bit late, Sally," he said as he settled into the seat opposite her.

Celia yawned comfortably as the carriage rolled out of the drive onto the street. "I assume you were having a good time?"

"Yes," said Dorian, sounding surprised. "I did rather enjoy it."

"First time without your mother?"

"Yes, as a matter of fact."

"I guessed as much. Did you dance?"

"I had my orders, didn't I?" he replied, grinning. "At each venue, I marched right up to the prettiest girl and asked her to dance."

"And did any of these fair maidens think it a good idea?"

"Yes; all of them," he replied modestly. "I made quite a splash."

Celia laughed. "Well done, Casanova! And how many balls did the Duke of Berkshire grace with his presence?"

"Four—nay, five! At the fifth, I did not dance, for upon arriving I heard that my mother was there—looking for *me*, no doubt! I felt it best to move on."

"Your brother was at the theatre this evening," she told him.

"Looking for me?"

She shrugged. "I daresay he was there to see Miss Archer. But he *did* inquire about you. I told him you had gone to a ball. I believe I was able to convince him that you and I had quarreled about it. Anyway, I'm sure he suspects nothing."

"You'll never guess who I met at one of these balls," Dorian said brightly, after a pause. "Lady Torcaster's, I think. Yes; I believe it was hers, for I also saw Fitzclarence there. I'm sorry to have to tell you this, but he was making love to the heiress, Miss Tinsley."

"Never mind all that," she said impatiently. "Who was it you met?"

"Your friend Mr. West has a sister."

"Eligible?"

"Unmarried, if that is what you mean."

"Yes, of course. Did you dance with her?"

"I did," he answered. "You said I should find the prettiest girl in the room and bother her conspicuously. Lady Rowena—that is her name—is very handsome. She looks a bit like you, Sally, at least from a distance, anyway. Up close, her hair has more red in it. Her eyes are not as blue. You are certainly taller. And she has freckles on her nose."

"Other than that, we could be twins! Did you like her?"

Dorian shrugged uncomfortably. "She's too young. And hot-tempered! I paid her a compliment, and she practically snapped my nose off."

"What was the compliment?"

"I asked her if anyone had ever told her she looked an awful lot like Celia St. Lys."

"You didn't really say that to her, did you?" Celia laughed.

"She ought to have been flattered. Instead, she seemed to take offense."

Celia cast her eyes up to heaven. "Oh, you are hopeless!

You go to a ball. You walk up to a pretty girl—and you say, 'Pardon me! But has anyone ever told you you look an awful lot like *my mistress*?"

"You are not my mistress," he protested.

"But that is what everyone thinks. You're lucky all she snapped off was your nose!"

"I haven't told you the best part! She said, 'No, Your Grace. Has anyone ever told you you look like Lord Granville?'"

Celia laughed. "You do look like Lord Granville."

"I do not."

"Do too. Right down to his webbed feet."

"I do not have webbed feet."

"He denies it, too."

"Anyway, I returned her ladyship to her mama after we danced. I got out of there and went on to the next one."

"Good," said Celia. "And finally, you went to your club?"

"Yes, and dismissed the carriage and both footmen," he answered. "I came here to you in a hackney. It wasn't as nasty as I thought it would be, the hackney carriage. There was straw on the floor, but it seemed to be clean."

"The first time is always the hardest," Celia told him. "And you told your valet to send flowers to all your victims? I mean, to all your dance partners? It will be expected."

"I couldn't quite remember the name of the last girl," Dorian confessed. "But Hill assured me it would be in the morning paper, or else he'd get it from the servants' grapevine. He's a very resourceful man, Hill. What shall I do without him? I've never been anywhere without my valet before."

"Exactly," said Celia. "If you took him with you, the bloodhounds would *know* you had left town. Do you think I like going away without Flood?"

"Someone will look after you at Ashlands," he assured.

"And you," she told him, laughing. "Hotchkiss will do the honors himself, I'm sure."

"And who will you have?" he asked, smiling. "Mrs. Stampley?"

"Heavens, no!" said Celia, remembering Mrs. Stampley as the rather forbidding housekeeper at Ashlands who ruled the servants with an iron hand. "I should like one of the little housemaids. They will think it a treat to look after me. Mrs. Stampley, I am persuaded, would regard it as an insult."

"Very likely," he agreed, laughing.

"I wonder if any of them will know me when they see me," Celia said, no longer laughing. "Mrs. Stampley had an especially sharp eye. One never dared put a foot wrong when she was about. I could feel her eyes upon me, cold and suspicious. She always seemed to know when I was going to *break* something."

"If anyone recognizes you, it will be Hotchkiss," Dorian declared. "Nothing ever escaped his notice." He frowned. "He certainly must have known you were not dead, Sally. Which means he has lied to me all these years. And Mrs. Stampley, too. I'll put up with a lot, God knows, but I won't put up with that."

"You mustn't be too hard on them, Dorian," Celia said quietly. "Your mother had all the power. They had to do as they were told or risk their livelihoods."

"I shall never forgive my mother," he said. "I know you do not want her crimes exposed, my dear—"

"No, I don't," she said fiercely. "And you have given me your word."

"Yes," he agreed. "I have given you my word."

She smiled at him. "I just want my locket back—and to see the bluebells."

"We'll be there before the sun comes up," he promised.

The sky was streaked scarlet and gray as the hired chaise drew near Ashlands, the ancestral seat of the dukes of Berkshire. Celia had not slept at all, but Dorian slumbered on the opposite seat, his head on his chest. She let him sleep until they reached the lodge gates. Then she reached out and touched his knee.

He opened his eyes and smiled at her. "Sally! Are we home at last?"

"Not quite, Your Grace," she replied. "The gates are closed. You must show yourself, or we'll never get in."

"Yes, of course," he said, stifling a yawn. "I always send my man ahead of me to smooth the way. No one is expecting me today—and most especially *not* in a hired chaise."

"A duke in a post chaise . . . What *is* the world coming to?" Celia murmured.

"I should warn you, too, that I've never brought a woman home before. The servants are bound to think . . . well, you know."

"You'll just have to swear them all to secrecy," she answered with a shrug. "No one will ever know that I was here."

A shadow passed across his face. "Yes," he murmured. "My servants have been keeping secrets *from* me for the last ten years. They can bloody well keep a few secrets *for* me. If not, they must seek employment elsewhere. I've a mind to turn them all out as it is."

Opening the door, he leaned out, shouting, "It's all right, Mrs. Ruddle! It is I, Berkshire. Tell your husband he can open the gate."

Looking out the window, Celia beheld a woman in a nightcap at the lodge window.

"Is that you, Your Grace?" cried the woman.

"I am come home," Dorian said simply, closing the carriage door.

Chapter 16

As they waited, the sky continued to lighten.

"You remember Mrs. Ruddle, don't you?"

"I remember a Mrs. Ruddle," Celia replied. "However, mine was considerably older ten years ago. I know that time stands still here at Ashlands, but I didn't think it went backwards."

"Why, that's right!" he said. "Old Mrs. Ruddle died—oh, it must be six years ago now. This is New Mrs. Ruddle. She married Old Mrs. Ruddle's son, Bert."

"Oh yes. When I knew her, she was called Mrs. Bert."

"She'll send young Peter up to the house on the pony to let them know the master has come unexpectedly. I don't think I've ever come home unexpectedly. It will be interesting to see how they rise to the occasion."

"Young Peter!" Celia exclaimed. "I remember him—Peter at the Pearly Gates of Heaven. He was such a pretty little baby! I quite adored him. And so clever! He could blow bubbles the day he was born. I used to come and tickle him in his cradle. He seemed to like it."

"I daresay."

"I liked Old Mrs. Ruddle," Celia said sadly. "I'm sorry she's no longer with us. She made the best plum cake in the

entire world. I used to come and help her wind her wool
sometimes, and she'd pay me in cake. I don't suppose New
Mrs. Ruddle—"

"I'm afraid not," Dorian told her, grimacing. "She does
her best, poor soul, but I'm afraid Old Mrs. Ruddle took the
secret of her plum cake with her to the grave. We shall
never see its like again."

The creaking of the cast-iron gates distracted him.
"Those hinges want an oiling," he said, frowning as the
carriage passed through the open gates into the passage
carved into the stone lodge. Dorian ordered the driver to
stop. As Celia watched, amused, it took him a moment to
lower the steps. As he climbed out of the carriage unas-
sisted, she rewarded his efforts with a burst of applause.

"If only Hill could see you now, Your Grace! He'd burst
with pride."

"Nonsense," Dorian replied cheerfully. "Hill would
never approve. I'll just be a moment—I want a word with
Ruddle about the noise. I won't have my gates *creaking*."

By now, Ruddle was closing the gates behind the chaise.
Celia heard Dorian's boots crunching on the gravel as he
went to have a word with his servant. On impulse, she left
the carriage herself. Finding the door of the lodge standing
open, she went in.

The Ruddles' big, warm kitchen was just as she remembered, though the woman putting a kettle onto the hob over
the kitchen fire was not the same woman, and the baby
gurgling in the wooden cradle was not the same baby. "I
beg your pardon, Mrs. Bert," Celia called softly and gently,
but the woman at the fire jumped as if she had shouted.

New Mrs. Ruddle had dressed in a hurry, throwing her
apron and work dress over her nightgown, by the look of it.
Upon seeing Celia, she hastily sketched a curtsy. "Bless
you, madam!" she cried, her face red from the fire. Her

eyes looked Celia up and down, and Celia could just guess what the other woman was thinking. *Who are you?*

"I'm Miss St. Lys," Celia told her.

"*Miss* St. Lys," Mrs. Ruddle repeated, with unpleasant emphasis on *Miss*. Her lips pursed in strong disapproval. Obviously, she thought Celia was no better than she should be. "You've come down with His Grace, then, have you, miss?"

Celia tried again. "Yes. I'm Miss *Celia* St. Lys, from London."

Mrs. Ruddle's eyes hardened. "London, is it?" she said coldly. "Figures."

"I'm an actress at the Theatre Royal in Drury Lane," said Celia, struggling to keep her countenance. "Perhaps you've heard of me, Mrs. Bert?"

"No, miss," Mrs. Ruddle said shortly. "And it's Mrs. Ruddle, thank you kindly. Was you wanting the privy?"

"Privy?" Celia raised her brows in surprise. Ten years ago, the lodge had boasted no such luxury, though the Ruddles, like the good lodge-keepers they were, always had a clean chamber pot at the ready for a weary traveler. It was more than a mile from the lodge to the great house, and not everyone had been blessed with a strong bladder.

"Oh, *we* never use it *ourselves*," New Mrs. Ruddle told her, misunderstanding Celia's hesitation. "'Tis for the use and enjoyment of His Grace and His Grace's friends—such as yourself, miss. You'll find it sparkling clean."

"I'm sure," Celia murmured. "You're very kind, Mrs. Ruddle. But I would not want to inconvenience you."

"You won't find a better one nor a cleaner one at the great house," Mrs. Ruddle said belligerently, "if that's what you think!"

Celia was taken aback by the woman's vehemence.

"Thank you, Mrs. Ruddle," she said gently. "I should be delighted to use your privy."

"So I should think," said Mrs. Ruddle, grumbling. Still grumbling, she led Celia to the surprisingly modern convenience at the back of the house.

"There! You see!" Mrs. Ruddle said proudly, setting a candle on the washstand beside the privy chair. "Sparkling clean! The last person to sit there was Her Grace, the Dowager Duchess of Berkshire. On Christmas day, it was. Her Grace was returning from church when nature called. 'Ruddle!' said she, 'never have I seen a privy so clean. Keep up the good work.' It will do for *you*, miss, I daresay," she added with a sniff.

"It is indeed very clean, Mrs. Bert," said Celia. "Er— Mrs. Ruddle, I mean," she hastily corrected herself as the woman drew herself up indignantly.

"I suppose you know what to do?" Mrs. Ruddle asked suspiciously.

Celia hid a smile. "Yes, thank you, Mrs. Ruddle!"

Mrs. Ruddle nodded. "I thought you might!" she said, her lips pursed in disapproval. "I'll leave you to it, then."

When Celia returned to the kitchen, she found Dorian seated at the deal table with a tankard of ale, and Mrs. Ruddle was frying streaky rashers over the fire. "I'm afraid we've been asked to breakfast," the duke told her rather sheepishly. "I hope that's all right."

"Of course," said Celia, going over to the cradle to look at the baby. She was delighted to find the child awake. "Boy or girl, Mrs. Ruddle?" she asked.

"Girl." The woman and her husband exchanged a nervous glance as Celia played with their baby. It was as though they feared the child might catch the London disease.

"What is her name?" Celia persisted.

"Hilda," Mrs. Ruddle answered shortly.

"Ah!" said Celia, looking down at the infant benevolently. "May I?" she asked the babe's mother, and Mrs. Ruddle made no protest but watched anxiously as Celia lifted Hilda from the cradle. "You were named for your grandmother, weren't you, little Hilda?" she crooned to the babe, who looked up at her with round blue eyes. "Or should I call you New Hilda?"

"Was you acquainted with my old mother, miss?" cried Bert Ruddle in astonishment.

"I was," said Celia. "But that was before I went to London to make my fortune."

"You don't say!" cried Bert Ruddle.

"I used to come here quite often," Celia said. "I'd sit on the stool at your mother's feet and help her with her spinning. In return, she'd give me a slice of her famous plum cake."

"I've not had proper cake since Mother died," Bert Ruddle lamented.

"I know how she made it," said Celia. "I ought to know; I sat and watched her do it often enough. I'll show you, Mrs. Ruddle, if you like."

"Did you know my mother well?" Bert Ruddle asked her slowly.

Celia laughed, bouncing the baby in her arms. "Don't you know me, Bert Ruddle?"

Mrs. Ruddle forgot to tend the bacon. "Mr. Ruddle! What's she ever talking about?"

"Hell's bells!" said Bert Ruddle, staring at Celia. "If I didn't know better, I'd think you was—"

Swallowing hard, he shook his head.

"Who, Bert?" Celia said eagerly. "Pretend you *don't* know any better. Who am I?"

She wanted so badly to be remembered that tears filled her eyes.

"Your Grace!" Bert Ruddle cried, appealing to the other man. "Look at her! Look at her, Mrs. Ruddle! Is she not the spit and image of—of Miss Sarah what died at so young an age?"

"Why, it can't be!" cried Mrs. Ruddle, staring. "It couldn't be."

Celia smiled at her. "Tell me, Mrs. Bert, did little Hilda blow bubbles the day she was born, too? Is she as clever as her big brother, Peter?"

Mrs. Ruddle's mouth fell open. "Oh, my stars and garters! It *is* you, Miss Sarah! But how—You're not a ghost, are you?"

"No, Mrs. Ruddle," said Dorian. "She's not a ghost. Miss Sarah has come home."

Mrs. Ruddle hurried back to the bacon. "Mind you," she said darkly, tossing the words over her shoulder, "I always said it wasn't done proper, didn't I, Mr. Ruddle?"

"Aye, so you did, Mrs. Ruddle," her husband confirmed.

"What wasn't done right?" asked Dorian.

Mrs. Ruddle began bringing the food to the table. "The doctor never came, did he, Your Grace? And my brother Frank, what works in the stables, said it was a mighty strange thing, Miss Sarah taking a fall like that, when he was certain her pony had never left the stall all that morning! And the way the poor child was put in the ground! With no one there to mourn her except Her Grace and the two footmen what carried the coffin. I said it then, and I say it now—it wasn't done right!"

"And I told *you*," said Bert Ruddle, getting in on the act, "that I saw Miss Shrimpton leave two days before the accident, and Miss Sarah was in the landau with her! So it couldn't have been Miss Sarah in the coffin. But you said I was drunk."

"And so you were, Albert Ruddle," said his wife primly. "Not what he's a drinker, Your Grace," she added hastily, taking the baby from Celia.

"No," Dorian said gravely.

Celia joined Dorian at the table. "Well, you were both right," she said diplomatically. "I *did* leave Ashlands with Miss Shrimpton before the 'accident,' and, no, it wasn't handled proper."

"Did you ever tell anyone what you saw, Ruddle?" Dorian asked. "Besides Mrs. Ruddle, I mean."

"No, Your Grace," Ruddle confessed. "If my own wife didn't believe me, what chance did I have? Anyway, I thought—Well, when we heard Miss Sarah had *died*, I realized I couldn't have seen her leaving. I decided I must have been mistaken in what I saw. And I haven't touched a drop of drink since the day."

"That's too bad," said Dorian. "I could use a drink right about now."

"So could I," said Celia.

"Who do you suppose is in the grave if it ain't Miss Sarah?" asked Mrs. Ruddle, wrinkling her brow. "One of them gypsies, I daresay, though I wouldn't have thought any of them fair enough to be mistaken for our Miss Sarah."

"Good God, I hope not," Celia cried. "Dorian! Is it possible?"

"We'll find out soon enough," he said. "We shall have to open the grave. There's nothing else for it."

"Never on a Sunday, Your Grace!" cried Mrs. Ruddle, scandalized.

"Yes, I'm afraid so, Mrs. Ruddle. Don't worry, my dear," he added, glancing across the table at Celia, who looked decidedly nauseous. "You'll be spared all of *that*. I'll set you down at the house and go on to see the vicar myself."

"But where did you go, Miss Sarah?" asked Mrs. Ruddle. "Why did you leave us? Where have you been all these years?"

"That's not important, Mrs. Ruddle," Dorian said quickly. "What's important is that Miss Sarah has come back to us. She is home where she belongs."

"For a little while, anyway," said Celia, smiling.

After breakfast, she returned to the hackney carriage with Dorian and they completed the drive up to the house. The sun was now up, and the sight of the lime avenue, gilded by the dawn, brought tears to Celia's eyes. "I never thought I would see it again," she murmured, drying her eyes. "It's even more beautiful than I remember. The lodge, too. What a happy place. And wasn't it good of the Ruddles to remember me?"

"I thought you wanted to keep your identity a secret, my dear."

"Yes, I thought so, too," Celia replied. "But no, I want to be remembered. Besides, it was rather obvious that Mrs. Ruddle thought I was your fancy woman. That sort of thing is all right in London, of course, but not in the country! I didn't want her to think ill of me."

He laughed.

"I don't care so much what people think of *me*," she added quickly. "But I should hate for your servants to think that *you* have gone shameless! That sort of thing will earn you a visit from the vicar. Did you ever hear of the country gentleman who kept a mistress? Reproved by the parson of the parish, and styled a whoremonger, he asked the parson whether he had a cheese in his house, and being answered yes, says to him, 'Pray, does that make you a cheesemonger?'"

She laughed, but Dorian did not. "I wish you would not make such jokes, my dear."

Celia sighed. "I'm sorry. I shall try to be more ladylike, for your sake, Dorian."

"Thank you. I shan't wait for the vicar to pay me a visit. I shall go to him presently. I wonder, did he know then that he was presiding over an empty grave?"

"If it *is* empty," said Celia, shivering.

As they rode along in silence, a herd of red deer suddenly careened across the lawn, startling the horses. The driver was obliged to stop. "Good heavens!" cried Celia, thrusting her head out the window to look. "Where did they come from?"

"I've enclosed the park and hired a first-rate gamekeeper," he told her proudly. "The population is coming along quite nicely, I think."

"Yes," she agreed. "Splendid!"

"At Christmas, I hold a penny lottery, and one lucky family is awarded a month's supply of venison."

Celia laughed. "Ah, the country life!"

"They are very glad to get it," he said indignantly, "and the money goes to the church."

"Admit it," she said. "You're not a true aristocrat! In your heart, you're nothing but a country booby squire! In fact, I think you'd be perfectly happy living in the gatehouse lodge with the Ruddles. You certainly looked comfortable sitting at the kitchen table."

"So did you," he retorted. "Miss Sarah."

"A deer park!" she remarked as the herd disappeared and the chaise resumed its course up the long drive. "What other improvements have you made? I must say, I rather enjoyed the privy at the lodge. Mrs. Ruddle is very proud of it, and with good reason."

"I believe she is proud of it," said Dorian. "I've put three in at the main house. One for the servants. One for my guests. And one for family. Other than that, the house is pretty much the same."

As he spoke, the vehicle moved past a screen of trees and the house came into view, a baroque masterpiece in yellow stone. With the early morning sun sitting upon its gables and turrets, it gleamed like gold. Celia caught her breath.

"I've dreamed of this moment," she whispered, tears slipping down her cheeks. "I never thought it would come to pass. This is home. I've never really felt that I belonged anywhere else."

He smiled. "That's because you do belong here, Sally."

By now the servants had been alerted of the duke's return, and Hotchkiss himself, the dignified if rather antiquated butler, came out to greet his master. If Hotchkiss was at all surprised to see His Grace emerge from the yellow cab of a hackney chaise, he did not show it.

"Welcome home, Your Grace."

Dorian escorted Celia into the house, the butler following. Inside, Celia broke from Dorian and danced around the black-and-white marble floor of the vast entrance hall. "It's just as I remembered!" she cried, gazing up at the white marble statues set in the niches on both sides of the room. "Except . . ."

She came to a stop, her brow furrowed with concern. "Why is Apollo wearing a fig leaf?"

"That was my mother's idea," Dorian confessed sheepishly. "She hired a plasterer without telling me. I was at a shooting party in Scotland, and when I returned, I was presented with a fait accompli."

"In my experience, fig leaves do not make for comfortable garments," she said, laughing. "I once posed for an artist, dressed as Eve. The next day, I woke up with the most *embarrassing* rash—and so did poor Adam. You might say that we also were presented with a fait accompli."

"Sally!" Dorian admonished her, quite scandalized.

Celia clapped her hand over her mouth. "Sorry, Your Grace," she whispered contritely.

Hotchkiss cleared his throat gently.

"Hotchkiss, this is Miss St. Lys," Dorian told him.

"Hello, Hotchkiss," said Celia, presenting herself for inspection.

The butler hardly glanced at her. He was annoyed, though not with her, and certainly not with his master. Rather, he was annoyed with the boy Peter, who had brought the news from the gatehouse of the duke's return, but had made no mention of His Grace's female companion. "Welcome to Ashlands, Miss St. Lys," he said, offering her a slight bow. "I trust you will find everything here to your satisfaction."

"Oh dear," said Celia, disappointed. "He talks at me as if I were a person of great importance! Do you not know me, Hotchkiss?"

He blinked at her. "I beg your pardon, miss?" he murmured.

"It is I, Hotchkiss! Sarah Hartley! I have come home! His Grace has brought me home. Are you not glad to see me?"

The old man stared, his creased face turning pale. "Miss Sarah? Is it really you?"

"Well, I am not a ghost," she replied.

"As you can see, Hotchkiss, Miss Sarah is not dead, after all," Dorian said sternly. "But then, you knew that already, didn't you?"

"Your G-grace," the butler stammered. "Forgive me! I—I do not understand."

"Nor do I," said Dorian. "Shall we discuss it in the drawing room?"

The drawing room was cold, the fire unlit, the curtains drawn. The furniture had been covered in brown holland cloth while the family was away. Even the chandeliers were wrapped in cloth. Celia went at once to the windows and opened the curtains.

"Well, Hotchkiss?" said Dorian, standing with his hands clasped behind his back. "I believe you owe me an explanation. You've known all along that Sally—that Miss Sarah—is not dead. But you kept it to yourself all these years. You deceived me. Why?"

"Deceived you, Your Grace! Was it not what you wanted, Your Grace?" Hotchkiss asked plaintively. "Was it not Your Grace's wish that Miss Sarah leave this house and never be mentioned again?"

"What?" Dorian exclaimed. "Who told you that?"

"Her Grace the dowager."

It was the answer Dorian had expected. Still, anger flared in his eyes. "She told you that, and you believed her. That is what you think of me? That is what you have—what you all have thought of me all this time."

Hotchkiss hung his head. "I did wonder at it, Your Grace, but the dowager duchess said—It is not for me to doubt her word."

"Please don't be angry with Hotchkiss, Your Grace," Celia said quietly. She had placed herself in the window seat, and looked small with the large window behind her. "It's the same thing your mother told me, more or less. She told me you wanted me gone, and . . . like Hotchkiss, I believed her. I begged her to tell me how I had offended you, but she would not say."

"Good God! How could you have offended anyone? You were but a child."

"I did break one of the Chinese vases," she reminded him.

"Oh, Sally! Nobody cared about that."

"Begging your pardon, Your Grace," said Hotchkiss. "But I believe it may have had something to do with your late father's will."

Dorian frowned. "What are you saying, Hotchkiss? My father left Sally no legacy that I am aware of. His will was frightfully out-of-date, as a matter of fact. When it was read out, we found he had left money to people who had been dead as much as ten years."

"Yes, Your Grace," said Hotchkiss. "The day before His Grace, your father, died, a Mr. Crutchley from the village was summoned to the house. He was with your father for nearly an hour. Her Grace—your mother—was very angry about it, I remember. The very next day, your father passed away in his sleep."

"What of it? Who is this Crutchley person? I never heard of him."

"No, Your Grace. He is an attorney in the village of Ashland Heath," Hotchkiss replied. "He lives there still."

Dorian frowned. "Are you saying that my father changed his will before he died? Impossible. Such an event could not have been kept a secret."

"I cannot be certain, Your Grace," said Hotchkiss. "But I believe he did change it—or at least, he wanted to."

"Surely," said Celia, "the estate was entailed upon his eldest son."

"The bulk of it was entailed, to be sure," said Dorian. "But my father did have *some* personal property, to dispose of as he pleased. He left you a few pounds, Hotchkiss, did he not?"

"His Grace was most generous," said Hotchkiss. "I believe he was thinking of Miss Sarah when he sent for Mr. Crutchley."

"Of me?" said Celia, surprised.

"You think my father altered his will in Sarah's favor?"

Hotchkiss hesitated. "Perhaps it is not my place to say, Your Grace."

"Spit it out, man," Dorian said impatiently. "Tell me what you know. Let us have no more secrets in this house."

"The day your father died, I happened to see Her Grace in the drawing—in this very room. She was burning something in the fireplace. It looked . . . important."

"Important?" Dorian said sharply. "Such as a new will, perhaps? Speak up, Hotchkiss!"

"I do not accuse Her Grace of anything," Hotchkiss said quickly. "Only, it did seem odd that she should be burning something on that day, and just a few minutes after Mr. Crutchley had left the house. A few months later, when Your Grace was at Bath, Miss Sarah was packed up and sent away. The dowager duchess told us it was your wish, and that we were to say she had died. I always wondered if the two things might be connected. We never knew what became of Miss Sarah, but she was missed. You were very much missed, Miss Sarah," he went on, lifting his eyes to look at Celia. "You were the light of this house. We all loved you."

"Thank you, Hotchkiss."

"I think," said Dorian, "that I must pay this Crutchley fellow a call. Will you be all right here, Sally? On your own, I mean?"

"Of course I shall be all right," said Celia. "I won't be on my own. The servants will look after me."

"We'll take very good care of her, Your Grace," said Hotchkiss.

"Really?" the duke said coldly. "You didn't do such a good job of it before! You are very fortunate that Miss Sarah has asked me to be merciful. Otherwise, you would be dismissed from my service."

"Yes, Your Grace," Hotchkiss murmured.

"Don't just stand there," Dorian snapped. "Miss Sarah is tired from her journey. Find a maid to look after her."

"Yes, certainly, Your Grace."

Celia rose from her seat. "No need to show me the way, Hotchkiss," she said. "I'm sure I can remember. If I get lost, I'll ring for help."

She did not see Dorian again until late that evening, when he returned from the village. Having spent the day going over the house, room by room, she had dined from a tray in the music room and afterward had fallen asleep on the huge, comfortable sofa. Someone had covered her with a soft quilt as she lay sleeping. Dorian woke her gently.

"How have they been treating you?"

"Like a princess," she answered, smiling as she sat up. "Cook made me my favorite tea, and Mrs. Stampley has let me have the Rose Room. My old room was very well for a girl of fourteen, but it's nothing to the Rose Room. I hope that is all right?"

"Of course," he said. "How did you end up here? I never come in this room anymore."

"I was just wandering about. I came across the piano, and thought I might just try playing something. How I used to practice! There was that piece, do you remember? Eight sharps in a row! I used to do it beautifully. But I've gotten so lazy in my old age. Oh, you do look exhausted!" she exclaimed, catching sight of his face. "Do sit down! Shall I ring for some tea?"

"No, thank you." He rang the bell himself and when Hotchkiss appeared, asked for brandy.

"I suppose your day was not as pleasant as mine," Celia said softly. "I am sorry."

"It wasn't all bad," he told her, forcing a smile. "I can

say with absolute certainty that there is no unfortunate gypsy child in your grave. In fact, there's no one at all in your grave."

"The coffin was empty! Oh, I'm so glad."

"Not *quite* empty," he told her, setting a small box on the table beside the sofa.

Celia looked at it uneasily. "What is it? Did that come from the grave?"

"Open it," he said. "It's perfectly safe," he added. "No worms or beetles."

Cautiously, she opened it. "My locket!" she cried, retrieving the heart-shaped gold pendant and chain from the box. "And the locks of hair? Are they still within?"

"You must see for yourself," he told her. "I have not opened it."

Slowly, she pried the two halves of the heart apart.

"Well?" he asked.

She could only nod, being too overwhelmed by emotion to speak.

"I'm glad," he said. "I know how much it means to you. There's more, too. I was able to see Crutchley."

Hotchkiss brought in the brandy, and paused. "Will there be anything else, Your Grace?"

"No, Hotchkiss. I must speak to Miss Sarah alone. Perhaps you would be good enough to wait for me in my dressing room. I've left Hill in town. I'm afraid you'll have to do the honors."

"Very good, Your Grace."

Celia had clasped the chain around her neck. "Don't keep me in suspense," she said, as the butler withdrew. "What did Mr. Crutchley say? Was there a new will?"

"My father did change his will," said Dorian. "I have it here," he added, taking out an unprepossessing sheet of paper covered with a heavy scrawl.

She smiled. "Did he leave me something? How kind of him to think of me! I should be very glad to have something to remember him by. I always liked that little picture in the summer breakfast parlor. The one with the cows. I don't suppose he left me that?"

"No. He made but two significant changes to his original will. First, he made me my brother's guardian. When my father died, Simon was still in India, and just a few months shy of his twenty-first birthday. According to the old will, my mother was made his guardian. She was given control over Simon's fortune. She has used that power to keep his inheritance from him ever since."

Celia stared at him. "What do you mean? How can she keep his fortune from him?"

"The old will gave her the power. The new will stripped her of it."

"And that is why she burned it?" cried Celia. "How wicked! But, hold a minute! If she burned the will, what is it you have there in your hand?"

"I have in my hand the original, written by my father. I cannot be certain, of course, but I believe it was a copy my mother burned."

"How awful."

"I have not told you the rest. Let me do so now. My father also named me *your* guardian, Sally, with the stipulation that I place the sum of twenty-five thousand pounds in trust for you."

"What!"

"You were to receive your fortune—both principle and compounded interest—on your twenty-first birthday. That, I believe, is why my mother decided to get rid of you."

Celia stared at him. "Twenty-five *thousand* pounds?" she cried, shocked and horrified.

"Yes, Sally."

She shook her head. "It's too much," she protested weakly. "Twenty-five *hundred* pounds would have been too much, let alone twenty-five thousands! No wonder . . . No wonder your mother was furious with me! I'm surprised she didn't k-kill me!"

"There are limits to what even she will do."

"I don't know what to say! I am so surprised! Your father . . . He seemed so stern. He didn't even want me to come here in the first place."

"No, not at first," Dorian admitted.

"I'm sure I don't blame him. I was such a little guttersnipe."

"Hotchkiss is right: you were the light of the house. My father obviously adored you. He wanted you to have this money, Sally. He wanted you to have a real chance in life."

"Twenty-five thousand pounds!" Celia shook her head. "It's too much, Dorian. I could not accept even half so much. This is madness!"

"My father was not a madman," he said quietly.

"No! Of course that is not what I meant," she said quickly. "But surely you agree it is too much. I am not his daughter, after all."

"It is not for me to say what is too much or too little. My father had every right to leave his property as he wished. He wrote down his wishes here even before he sent for Crutchley. Crutchley was to have his clerk make a fair copy of the document. You know what my father's handwriting was like."

She smiled. "He often said it was so bad no one could ever hope to forge it."

"Indeed. This is no forgery. Crutchley was to return the following day to have the new will properly signed and witnessed. Before he could do that, my father died."

Celia breathed a sigh of relief. "Then the will is not valid? We have been bothering ourselves over nothing."

"The will may not be legal," said Dorian. "But I consider it to be quite binding. My father was ill when he wrote this. He was dying. He knew he was dying, and he made out his will. *This* will. I don't care what the courts may say about it. I know my father's hand. I know without a doubt what he wanted. I am his son and heir. It would be a very strange thing if I did not feel bound to honor his wishes."

"But, Dorian, if the will is not legally valid—" she began.

"I don't care three straws for the law! My father made his wishes clear, and I shall honor them."

"But I cannot accept so much money! I'd feel as though I were robbing you of your inheritance, taking advantage of your good nature."

"Most of my father's estate was entailed upon me," Dorian said. "But he was perfectly entitled to dispose of the residue as he saw fit."

"Residue!" she exclaimed. "You would call twenty-five thousand pounds a residue?"

"Yes, I would," he said simply. "My own fortune is quite substantial, you know."

"But what about your brother's fortune?" she said. "He might like having twenty-five thousand pounds. He has far more right to it than I."

"Simon's fortune has been held in trust for him since the day he was born," said Dorian. "It comes to him from our grandfather, Lord Kenelm. 'Twas all spelled out in the settlement, when my father married my mother. Your little bequest is a pittance to his."

"Is it?" she said faintly.

"Simon will get his fortune, and you will get yours. I shall not rest until it is so."

"I'm sure it was very kind of your father to remember me, Dorian," she said. "I am truly touched by the gesture, but I am not his flesh and blood. Only trouble can come of this. Your brother won't like it. And your mother—she'll fight you tooth and nail."

"She cannot stop me," said Dorian. "Not now. If I wish to settle thirty-five thousand pounds upon my ward—or, indeed, upon a perfect stranger—what has she to say about it?"

"*Thirty*-five thousand!" she exclaimed. "I thought you said *twenty*-five thousand!"

"Yes," he replied. "I was to place twenty-five thousand pounds in trust for you ten years ago. In the four percents, over ten years, that would amount to at least an additional ten thousand in interest. And then there is the matter of damages."

"Damages!" she said weakly. "For heaven's sake, Dorian!"

"She took you away from your home, sent you to live with a stranger, forced you into wedlock at the tender age of fifteen! Yes, my dear," Dorian said grimly, "I'd say you are entitled to damages."

"No," Celia said firmly. "I would not take a penny from her—or you."

"But this is from my father. You have been cheated all these years, and my brother, too! She has kept him dancing to her tune long enough, I think. Do you know she makes him collect his allowance in person? Once a month, like a servant being paid out his wages!"

"How he must hate that."

"And all along, she knew! She *knew* my father had changed his will. If I had known about this, Simon would have come into his fortune when he came of age. I would have insisted upon it. I shall insist upon it now. I shall meet with my attorneys the very instant we return to London."

Celia shivered. "She'll fight you, Dorian."

"I don't care if she does!" he said sharply. "I almost hope she will," he added coldly, "but somehow I doubt it. She won't want any of this to come to light. She'll never let it go to court, certainly. A widow burning her husband's will before he is cold? Even if it is not a legal document, surely she had no right to burn it. She had no right to keep it from me."

"She must have known how you would see it—as a mandate from your father."

"I daresay! Is there any other way to see it?"

"You mean to confront her, then," Celia said nervously. "I suppose it cannot be avoided now. Will you have to tell her who I am? She tried to destroy me once. She very nearly succeeded."

"You need not be afraid of her," he said. "Not anymore. I shall have to confront her about the will, of course, for Simon's sake."

"I understand."

"But I shan't have to tell her anything about you," he added. "When we get back to London, I shall arrange with my attorneys to set up a trust for you. The matter will be kept completely private. My mother need never know anything about it."

"A trust? Oh, I wish you would not, Dorian. You've given me so much. It wouldn't feel right to take your money, too."

"It's not my money," he replied firmly. "Don't you understand? It never was."

Chapter 17

The following morning, after breakfast, Celia bid farewell to Ashlands. Dorian found her on the landing of the grand staircase, pulling on her gloves. For propriety's sake, the duke had slept in the west wing, leaving the entirety of the east wing, including the Rose Room, to his guest. Celia was both reluctant to leave her childhood home and anxious to get back to London to work on the new play.

"Simon will be pleased," Dorian said, looking up at the portrait of his brother. It had been painted the year Simon had joined the army, and showed a lean, cocky, fresh-faced cornet, leaning against his horse. The young lord's green eyes looked out on the world with absolute aristocratic arrogance. Life-sized, the portrait hung at the landing on the east wall.

Startled, Celia glanced up and, following the direction of his gaze, smiled briefly. "I expect he *will* be pleased," she said, "if your mother proves to be as amenable as you say. But if she chooses to fight you—No, he won't be pleased."

"She will not fight me," Dorian said with quiet confidence. "It is a fight she cannot win. She cannot prevent

Simon from claiming his birthright. If she dares to try, she will lose everything. I will expose her. What do you suppose the other patronesses of the ton might think of her behavior? She'd be ostracized."

"What has she done, really? She burned a piece of paper, an invalid will."

"If it was so invalid, why burn it? Why not show it to me? No; she was wrong and she knows it. She will do as I tell her, or she will suffer."

Celia was still looking up at Simon's portrait. "He will be rich then. Good."

"He will be very rich. I'll say this for my mother: she has husbanded his accounts well."

"I'm glad. He was such a bold, beautiful boy," Celia murmured. "I wish I could have known him then. But he has not aged well, I am bound to say. His face has gone all mean and craggy. His mouth is cold and hard, rather like his heart."

Dorian chuckled. "It is as well he never saw *you* in those days, Sally. No pretty girl was safe from him. He was the terror of the housemaids."

"You mean he wasn't faithful to the master's daughter at Eton? Shocking!"

"When the scandal broke, there was talk of marriage, as I recall. Well, they were a goodish sort of family, but in the end, my father decided they were not worthy of the honor."

Celia flashed a look of surprise. "Did he love her, do you suppose?"

"Simon? Oh, I shouldn't think so," Dorian replied. "He seemed more upset at the prospect of leaving Ashlands than Eton. He told me once there was nothing at Eton he would ever regret. Shall we, my dear?" he added, offering her his arm.

"I can well understand not wanting to leave Ashlands,"

Celia said, as he led her down the stairs. "It *is* the most beautiful place in all the world."

"You need not leave if you don't wish, Sally," he told her seriously. "You can stay forever, if you like. It is your home."

Celia sighed. "I should like nothing better than to stay, but no! No, I must go back. I can't let everyone down. The new play is in a shambles. Something will have to be done about Belinda. Don't tempt me!"

"But I mean it," he said. "You are welcome to stay here forever. Let someone else worry about the play, and Belinda, and all the rest of it. Let me look after you."

"Dorian, you are very kind. But . . . I have no place here. I must go back."

Suddenly he seized her hands. "Marry me, Sally! Then you would have a place. You would be mistress here. All this would be yours—ours. We would grow old here together. You would be Duchess of Berkshire."

"Good heavens," she murmured, very much taken aback. "My dear sir, this is too much all at once. First, you insist on making me an heiress—now you would make me a duchess. Mistress of Ashlands! If I didn't know better, I'd say you were a devil sent to tempt me!"

She gave a shaky laugh.

"Then you are tempted, at least?"

"Of course I am tempted! I'm only human. But, Dorian, you must know that I cannot marry you," she added quickly, pulling her hands away. "I'm in love with your *house*, not you. I don't love you, not as you deserve. Not as a wife should love her husband."

"But—"

She shook her head firmly. "I am sorry to be so blunt, but you have caught me in surprise. I hardly know what to say. I should be thanking you for the honor of your proposals. Indeed, I am grateful—"

"Never mind all that," he said. "I have been thinking of asking you, ever since we dined together at Grillon's Hotel. Ever since I learned of the terrible wrong that had been done to you. I want to make it right."

"Then you do not love me?" she said.

"My dear, of course I do," he protested.

"But not, I think, as a husband should love his wife," she said. "My dear Dorian, if the master's daughter at Eton was not good enough for Lord Simon, how could I ever hope to merit his elder brother? Sally Hartley, a duchess? Don't be silly. You cannot marry an actress."

"It is not unheard of. The Duke of Bolton married an actress. The Earl of Derby married Miss Farren. Why, only ten years ago, Lord Craven married Miss Brunton."

She only laughed. "And you seek to flatter these gentlemen by imitation? You forget, sir, they were all violently in love with their ladies. There can be no other possible excuse for such unequal marriages."

Dorian sighed. "But you must admit it would be an excellent revenge," he said. "You would take the place of the one who wronged you."

"An excellent reason to marry!" she said lightly. "I shall need a better one to put my head in the noose again. Please, let us say no more about it."

"I would not by any means distress you."

"I am not distressed," she said, taking his arm. "It was very kind of you to ask me. I wish I did love you. Then it would all be so easy."

"I'm generally thought to be quite a catch."

She laughed. "But I was brought up to think of you almost as an uncle."

He winced. "Uncle!"

"It was your brother I loved," she said, as he led her down the stairs to the grand hall.

"Simon? You didn't even know him," he protested.

She laughed. "And that explains how I was able to love him! No, it was his portrait I loved. When I met the original I was cured of my childish affliction. But in those days, I used to gaze up at his portrait, my pulse racing, my heart on fire—"

"It's the regimentals," said Dorian. "You girls cannot help yourselves."

"Yes. The effect of regimentals on the female pulse is well documented," she agreed. "But it was a little more than that. I used to read his letters out to your father in the evenings—"

"All three of his letters!" Dorian said dryly.

"He was not a very prolific correspondent," she allowed. "I used to imagine I was with him in India, riding elephants with maharajahs, and shooting at tigers. Naturally, I was disappointed when I met him in the flesh. I expected too much of him, I suppose."

"Where did you meet him?"

"Where did I meet Lord Simon? The Green Room, of course. He was making love to all the girls after the play. When he met me, he naturally swore they meant nothing to him. I was the only woman in the world. 'Do you always make love to girls who mean nothing to you?' I asked him. And he said, 'Naturally, I prefer the other kind, but one meets them so seldom. They might as well be rare as comets.'"

"Oh, that is crass!" Dorian said, shaking his head. "Even for my brother. How could he say such a thing to you? I suppose you gave him the tongue-lashing he deserved?"

"Among other things," she said, hiding a smile.

They went out to the chaise waiting on the gravel drive. It was the hired chaise that had carried them from London, but two of Dorian's footmen now stood behind the cab.

Hotchkiss presented Celia with a huge bouquet of bluebells from the meadow.

"From all of us, Miss Sarah," he said, indicating the rest of the staff, who had come to see them off.

"Thank you," she said, taking the flowers from him. "Thank you, everyone! You've been most kind."

And, from force of habit, the actress curtsied. "Thank you! Thank you all so much!"

"Come, Sally!" said the duke, with a touch of exasperation.

"Well, my dear! What are you going to do now that you are rich?" Dorian asked her on the journey back to London.

"I don't know. I haven't had time to think about it, have I?"

"You'll leave the stage, of course?"

A frown passed over her face. "Must I?"

"I place no condition upon your inheritance," he told her quickly. "Your fortune is yours, whatever you decide to do. My father did not forbid you the stage, after all. He would not have thought it necessary."

"He would never have approved of the way I live," Celia said gloomily.

"He would never have permitted it! Perhaps," Dorian added, "you will think about what my father would have wanted for you when you make up your mind."

"Of course I shall think of him," she said, "but I can't quit now. I play Miss Hardcastle tonight! There will be a riot in London if I don't appear as advertised!" she added, half joking. "At least, I *hope* there would be a riot! Oh God! What if they merely yawn? It's mortifying to think I might not be missed."

"I am sure you would be missed, my dear."

"Not tonight, I won't be. Of course I must go on. And we

begin a new play on Thursday. I can't just leave. What would they do without me?"

"It's up to you, of course, but don't you think that it would be rather selfish of you to stay?"

"Selfish! You have no idea."

"But surely they can find someone to replace you. The world is full of actresses."

"You think me so easily replaced?" she asked, nettled.

"No, of course not. But you are rich now, my dear," he told her. "You don't need to earn your living. Let someone else have a chance. For some of these girls, it could mean the difference between life and death. It could mean the difference between an honest living and the poverty and misery of the streets."

Celia at once thought of Eliza London and girls like her. "You are right," she said. "There must be a hundred girls ready to take my place. I shall miss the theatre more than the theatre misses me. But what shall I do without it? I feel lost already."

She drew a deep breath. "I certainly have got a lot to think about, don't I?"

"Yes, my dear."

"What am I going to tell people? How am I to explain the fact that I am suddenly so rich that I can quit the theatre without a backward glance?"

He shrugged. "Someone died and left you a fortune. You need say nothing more."

"Uncle Cuthbert," Celia said decisively. "My poor, dear old uncle Cuthbert! Who would have thought the old man had so much money? And he left it all to me! But then I *am* his only living relation. What did he die of? Brain fever, of course. People are always dying of brain fever in Antigua, aren't they?"

"Is that where he is from? Antigua?"

"I think so. Isn't that where rich uncles usually come from?"

It was with mixed feelings that Celia met Miss Julia Vane that afternoon. Not only had the new actress turned up for Monday's rehearsal with deplorable punctuality, but in Celia's absence, she gamely had stepped into the role of Viola. Celia found her onstage with Belinda. Rourke and some of the rest of the cast were watching from the pit.

"Hello, everyone! Sorry I'm late. What have I missed?" Celia asked, stepping onto the stage with a smile that fooled absolutely no one. "I see you've been muddling through without me," she added, glancing over the new girl coldly.

Rourke made the introductions. Miss Vane simpered and smiled and curtsied as if Celia were the queen of England. "This *is* an honor, Miss St. Lys." She gushed like a schoolgirl, though her polished accent was that of a gentlewoman. "Possibly the greatest honor of my life. You are the reason I became an actress."

"Oh dear," Celia murmured coolly. "Can you ever forgive me?"

Miss Vane laughed lightly.

"I see you have taken my place, Miss Vane," Celia remarked. "I wouldn't want to get in the way. Shall I leave you all to it, then?"

"Of course not, Celia darling," cried Rourke. "Belinda was just getting in a little practice while we were waiting for you."

"Oh, I do humbly beg your pardon, Miss St. Lys," Miss Vane cried. "I was just going over some lines with Miss Archer. I didn't mean to step on your toes. You don't mind, do you?"

"No indeed," Celia said, smiling magnanimously. "I am obliged to you, I'm sure. There is nothing so tedious as going over lines with Miss Archer, as I'm sure you have discovered."

Belinda, dressed in mourning, started up from her chair, a black veil flung back from her face. Celia had not noticed it before, but her left arm was in a sling. "I am trying my best, Miss St. Lys!" she quavered, almost in tears. "Really I am."

"What happened to your arm?" Celia asked, feeling slightly ashamed of her impatience with the girl—but only slightly.

"I fell, if you must know," said Belinda. "Lord Simon took me riding in the park, and I—I fell. It was not my fault," she added. "It was the horse's. *I* wanted it to be still, but it *would* keep moving, no matter what."

"*That* is Lord Simon's fault," said Celia. "If he had looked after you properly, you would never have taken a fall from your horse."

"Oh, but I didn't fall off the horse, Miss St. Lys," said Belinda. "I never actually got *on* the horse, you see. I fell off the mounting block."

"I see," said Celia, fighting the urge to laugh. "I wish I had been there to see it. I mean, I would have given Lord Simon a proper scolding!"

"I wish you *had* been there," said Belinda. "He wasn't very nice to me at all. And he used the most shocking language I have ever heard."

"Really? What did he say?"

Belinda's eyes widened. "I could never repeat what he said, Miss St. Lys! I told you it was shocking."

"Well, my dear," said Celia, "he *is* a soldier."

"Mr. West is a soldier, and *he* never uses rough language like that! He is a gentleman."

"I'm sure you're right," said Celia. "I'm sorry you had such an unpleasant time yesterday. Are you quite sure you are well enough to go on with rehearsal? You do seem to be a little hoarse. Are you coming down with a cold?"

"I don't think so," said Belinda, her hand at her throat.

"Are you sure, my dear?" Celia said solicitously. "You do sound *very* hoarse."

"It was rather cold in the park yesterday," said Belinda, now with both hands at her throat. "Now you mention it, I do feel a little . . . a little . . . congestion." She coughed.

"There! I knew it. You must take the rest of the day, and rest your voice, or you will have laryngitis by tonight. Go on, child. Do as I say."

"Might I really be excused, Mr. Rourke?" Belinda asked weakly, coughing.

"I really do think we need her to rest her voice," Celia said firmly. "Don't you, Mr. Rourke? I can stand in for Miss Archer, and Miss Vane can rehearse with me."

"Oh, thank you, Miss St. Lys!"

"No talking, dear," Celia commanded. "Run along. Have a nice, long rest."

Belinda scampered off, leaving Celia alone on the stage with Miss Vane. "You come to us from Bath, I believe, Miss Vane?" Celia began politely, moving in a slow circle around the other actress. "What did you do there?"

"I was Lydia Languish in *The Rivals*," said Miss Vane, turning to face her inquisitor. "I was Dorinda in *The Beaux Stratagem*. Lady Townley in *The Provoked Husband*. Donna Olivia in *A Bold Stroke for a Husband*. Marianne in *The Mysterious Husband*. Lady Teazle in *The School for Scandal*. Angelina in *Love Makes a Man*. Harriet in *The Jealous Wife*. Rosaria in *She Would and She Would Not*. Julia in *The School of Reform*."

Miss Vane ticked them off on her fingers until she ran

out of fingers. Celia stopped in front of her, and they stood face-to-face.

"Is that all?" Celia asked, unimpressed.

Miss Vane was not as tall as Miss St. Lys. She lifted her chin defiantly. "No, Miss St. Lys. I was Marian in *The School for Prejudice*. I was Volante in *The Honeymoon*. And I was Leonora in *The Revenge*. I'm only seventeen!" she added.

Celia shrugged. "I *was* hoping you might have done a *little* Shakespeare."

"I was Beatrice in *Much Ado About Nothing*. Miranda in *The Tempest*. And . . . I was Juliet in *Romeo and Juliet*."

"Oh?" said Celia. "That's something, anyway. Shall we just take up where you left off with Miss Archer?"

Miss Vane looked around, confusion in her large, expressive eyes, which were neither blue nor green nor gray, but all three at once. "But, Miss St. Lys, Miss Archer and I were practicing one of the scenes she has with *you*, not with me."

"Yes, I know," said Celia. "Shall we begin with—what is it? 'Give me my veil; come, throw it o'er my face.' Somebody get a veil."

"Really, Miss St. Lys," Miss Vane protested. "I wasn't trying to take your part! I don't want to be Viola. I'm perfectly happy in the role of Sebastian."

"Really?" said Celia. "You wouldn't want to be Olivia?"

"I—I don't know what you mean, Miss St. Lys," said Miss Vane. "I was hired to play Sebastian."

"Not in *those* breeches, my dear," said Celia dryly. "I don't know how things are done in Bath, but here in London, we're rather particular about our breeches, I'm afraid."

"I beg your pardon!" said Miss Vane. "Mr. Rourke! Are you going to let her talk to me like that?"

"Now just a moment, Celia darling," Rourke protested, though rather weakly.

"Go on!" Celia invited him. "Defend these breeches, if you can."

Miss Vane stamped her foot. "Nobody talks to me like that! I don't care if you *are* Celia St. Lys!"

Celia yawned. "Look here, child! Can you play Olivia, or not? Because it is obvious to me that Miss Archer *cannot*. Unless, of course, by some miracle she has suddenly become an actress? No? I didn't think so!"

The stagehand brought Celia the veil she had called for, but Miss Vane would have none of it. She tossed her blond curls. "If you think that *I* am the sort of person who would stoop so low as to steal a role from another actress—"

"Save it for *The Inquisitor*," Celia said impatiently. "You won't have to steal anything. It's being offered to you on a silver platter. Now, can you do it or not?"

"Of course I can do it," said Miss Vane.

"We'll see," said Celia. "Your hair will have to go back to being brown or whatever it was before you went blond, of course. Olivia and Viola can't both be blond."

"I beg your pardon!"

"You keep saying that," Celia observed. "I can't imagine why."

"What about Sebastian?" asked Rourke.

"I shall play both parts," Celia announced. "Sebastian *and* Viola. They *are* meant to be twins, after all. They are never onstage together, except the last scene. Belinda will have to do that. It's only a few lines. Surely she can manage it."

"I should think so," Rourke agreed. "Yes! It could work."

"I shall have to study the part," said Miss Vane, who had, by this time, taken the veil.

"I'd rather you *learned* it, dear, if you don't mind," Celia said sweetly. "You have three days—plenty of time. Shall we just run through it now? Someone fetch Miss Vane a script."

"May I have ten minutes?" cried Miss Vane.

"This is *London*, my darling," Celia told her. "You may take five."

Six hours later, Celia took the stage as Kate Hardcastle. After the play, Rourke knocked on her dressing room door. "Celia darling! Are you decent?" he called.

"Come in," Celia called, so pleasantly that it almost frightened him out of his wits.

"Are you all right?" he asked nervously, remaining in the doorway.

"Of course, Davey! What can I do for you?"

Rourke decided to risk it. "The thing is, Celia my love, Miss Vane's asking for more money, now that she is to play Olivia, and so I was wondering . . ."

"You were wondering if you might take a little from my share to pay her?"

"Well, it *was* your idea, Celia darling, to give her the part of Olivia."

Celia emerged, smiling, from the alcove, in a pink and white ensemble. "It's perfectly all right, Davey," she said. "She's good. She's worth it. You should pay her whatever she wants."

He stared at her in amazement.

"I feel as though a great weight has been lifted from my shoulders," Celia went on. "Have you told Miss Archer yet that she's been replaced?"

"It's her mother I'm worried about."

"Well, I can't help you there, old friend," she said, looking at him almost tenderly. "We've been together a long,

long time, haven't we, Davey? You've always been good to me."

To his horror, tears began to trickle down her cheeks. Not once in four years had he ever seen her cry, except on-stage. "Good God, what is the matter?" he asked, deeply shaken.

"Oh, Davey! Something's happened. I've come into some money. Rather a lot, I'm very sorry to say."

"Well, that would make anybody sad, wouldn't it?"

"I am leaving you at the end of the season. I haven't told anyone else yet. I shall finish out *Twelfth Night*, of course," she assured him. "I wouldn't leave you in the lurch. But then I must go."

"You will be missed," he said simply.

Celia frowned. "No," she said. "This is the part where you beg me to stay. There will be blood in the streets if I go. The theatre will go dark, and nothing will ever be the same. For about five minutes," she added bitterly. "Then I shall be quite forgotten—like Mrs. Siddons and Mrs. Jordan."

"You will never be forgotten, Celia darling," he told her. "You'll live forever, just as they do, in our hearts. Don't forget us."

"No, of course not," she said. "I shall always be with you in spirit."

"Please, God, no!" he said, making a face. "Drury Lane has ghosts enough without you haunting the place."

A little later, Dorian came to collect her. His carriage was waiting at the stage door. "Shall we go to supper?" he asked.

Celia felt strangely energized, as she always did after a performance, but she could see that he was tired. "Not tonight, I beg of you," she said, using a thin voice. "I don't know why, but I'm simply exhausted. Would you mind terribly just taking me home?"

He smiled. "Of course. I'm rather tired myself, and I still have much to do."

"What can you have to do at this hour that cannot wait until tomorrow?" she protested.

"I have been with my attorneys all day. They have the papers ready for my mother to sign. I see no reason to put it off."

"Do it tomorrow," she advised. "You're tired."

"I shall sleep better knowing the thing is done," he said. "I've asked Simon to come to Berkshire House in the morning. I want to present him with his inheritance, not an argument with his mother. The thing will be done tonight."

Celia shivered. "I am glad it falls to you and not to me."

Chapter 18

Her manservant opened the door to her, a branch of candles in his massive fist. "*Buenas noches*, Doña Celia," he said, as she stood waving good-bye to the duke's carriage.

"*Buenas noches*," she replied, throwing off her cloak and jerking off her gloves. "I don't suppose you could find me something to eat?" she asked him prettily, clasping her hands together, behaving rather more like a damsel in distress than the mistress of the house.

"*Claro que sí*, Doña Celia," he replied. "*Enseguida*. And this letter, she came for you yesterday," he added, indicating the pearl-gray envelope on the tray on the hall table. "Did you not see it?"

"By hand or by post?" Celia asked, with a terrible sinking feeling.

His eyes widened in surprise. "*Por cierto, a mano*, Doña Celia," he said, and Celia was happy again. Of course the letter had been hand delivered; if it had come in the post, it would have been in a bag with dozens of others.

She picked it up, broke the seal, and read it, recognizing Simon's scrawl immediately. "I am at my club. Send word to me when you get this, and I will come to you."

He hadn't even signed it! "Of all the arrogant, *insufferable*, crass—"

"Doña Celia?" Tonecho was locking the door. He turned to her with a look of concern. "*Es una mala noticia?*"

"No, it's not bad news," she quickly assured him, tossing the note back onto the tray. "It's . . . it's nothing of importance. You may go to bed, Tonecho. I'll find something to eat in the kitchen. No, really, I'll manage," she insisted, overriding his protests. "I'm not completely helpless, you know. Good night! *Buenas noches! Adelante!*" She herded him down the hall to the servants' staircase.

In the kitchen, she found bread and cheese and beer—and Captain Fitzclarence. Startled, Celia almost dropped the beer jug as the latter emerged from the scullery. She scarcely recognized him, for he was out of uniform. Rather, he was attired in a black evening coat with a snow-white waistcoat, black jersey breeches, silk stockings, and buckled shoes. His cravat was a work of art. "Clare!" she said angrily. "You frightened me out of my wits!"

"Yes, I can see that," he said, taking the beer from her and setting it on the table. "I don't know why you're surprised. Didn't you get my note?"

"*Your* note?" she cried, staring at him. "*That* was from you? But I thought—"

"Never mind what you thought," he said impatiently. "I am in a hurry, in case you hadn't noticed."

"On your way to St. James's Palace, by the look of you," she said, laughing.

"Look here!" he said plaintively. "Don't you know a desperate man when you see one? Can you lend me the money or not?"

"What money?" she asked, frowning. For a moment, she forgot she was an heiress, and felt very protective of her little savings.

"You told me if I married Miss Tinsley you'd give me a thousand pounds."

Celia gasped. "Clare!" she breathed, sitting down at the table. "You haven't done it!"

"Well, not yet," he admitted. "But she has agreed to marry me. I'm just going to fetch her now. I need that money, Celia!" he added rather violently.

"Well, I don't have it, young man," Celia said tartly. "I know it's remiss of me, but I don't happen to *keep* thousands of pounds lying about the house just in case you should show up in the middle of the night asking for it!"

"I don't need all of it," he said crossly. "Just fifty pounds or so, for the post chaise?"

"Fifty pounds," she repeated, laughing. "It will take a good deal more than that to get to Scotland. It's quite three hundred miles. Even if I had enough money, you'd never make it. Her father *will* send the Bow Street runners after you, you know. If that matters!"

"For your information," he said coldly, "I am not taking her to Gretna Green. I'm to be married from Bushy House this morning."

Bushy House, as Celia knew, was the residence of His Royal Highness the Duke of Clarence. It stood some thirteen miles from London.

"Oh," she said, considerably relieved. "Then you are not *eloping* with Miss Tinsley, per se? You have your father's consent. She has her father's consent, I suppose?"

"Of course. Do you take me for a fool?" he snapped. "Look here, Celia! I need money for the post chaise, and money to pay the parson. She may be an heiress with a dowry of three hundred thousand pounds, but she ain't *made* of money. Will you help me?"

Celia rose immediately from the table. "Of course I'll help you, you silly boy," she said. "Wait here."

Taking up the candle, she went upstairs. When she returned a few minutes later with the money, Fitzclarence was no longer alone. He was seated at the table with a huge figure standing over him.

Celia stared in dismay. "What are *you* doing here?" she demanded angrily.

"Busy night?" Simon coldly inquired. He looked like a giant in his uniform. She could almost swear the top of his head touched the ceiling.

"No more than usual, my lord," she answered, recovering some of her poise, if not all of her composure. "May I offer you some bread and cheese?"

"Do I look like a mouse to you?"

Fitzclarence got up from the table. "Is that for me?" he asked quickly, reaching for the banknotes in Celia's hand.

"Why is she paying *you*?" Simon wanted to know. "Shouldn't it be the other way around?"

"How dare you," Celia gasped, glaring at him. "Clare!"

"Hmm?" Fitzclarence had counted the money and was tucking it away.

"Are you going to let him talk to me like that?"

"Like what?"

"But I wasn't talking to you, Celia," said Simon. "I was talking to your pretty boy. I asked you a question, Captain Fitzclarence. Why is she paying you? Are you her kept boy?"

"No, my lord," Fitzclarence replied, frowning. He wanted to be going; he wanted no altercation with the big dragoon, but Lord Simon stood between him and the door. "It's a wedding present, that's all," he answered civilly.

Simon's eyes widened. "You're *married*?" he said, with a catch in his voice.

"Not yet," said Fitzclarence. "But it *is* my wedding day. I'd like to collect my bride now, if you don't mind."

Simon did not move. "I don't believe it," he said, looking from one face to the other.

"I can scarcely believe it myself," said Fitzclarence nervously. "Well, aren't you going to congratulate me, Lord Simon? It is customary."

"No," said Simon, looking hard at Celia. "I do *not* congratulate you. I do not wish you joy. I wish you hanged. I wish you at the devil. I wish you a lifetime of pain and misery beyond all human imagining. I hope you and your *wife* know nothing but darkness all the days of your lives. All the joy shall be mine as I watch you suffer."

Fitzclarence giggled nervously. "That's . . . not very nice," he observed.

"I'm not a very nice man," Simon told him.

"I couldn't agree more," Fitzclarence murmured under his breath.

"What is the matter with you?" Celia's eyes flashed angrily at Simon. "Why can't you just offer him your best wishes like a normal person?"

"Those *were* my best wishes."

"Oh, you are impossible," she said bitterly. "I suppose you have come here to put a stop to it! Why? What business is it of yours? Why can't you just let the boy be happy? What gives you the right to interfere in his life?"

His eyes blazed with terrible fury. "*You* ask me that?" he roared. "You *dare* ask me that, madam? My God, I could throttle you! Do you expect me to be glad for you? Do you expect me to stand aside while you make the worst mistake of your life? Does he know I was in your bed only three nights ago?"

"I rather think he knows it now!" Celia said furiously, her face turning pink.

"You gave yourself to me so sweetly, so wildly," he went on, much to Celia's dismay. "You were a tigress in my arms, but I tamed you. You cried out for mercy when the pleasure would have torn you in two. You wept like a child at the beauty of it."

"Oh, hush!" she pleaded, covering her eyes with both hands.

Fitzclarence, too, seemed more embarrassed than interested—but Simon was still between him and the door.

"You are mine, Celia," Simon went on inexorably. "The moment I first saw you, I knew you were for me, whatever you may think. I'll never let you go. I'll never give you up."

She looked at him, her eyes enormous. "Simon, what are you saying?"

"I won't let you do this to me, Celia. I won't let you do this to us. Not again. You shall *not* marry him. I'll kill him where he stands before I let him have you."

"Oh no-no-no-no-no-no!" cried Fitzclarence, waving his hands. "My lord! There's been a mistake! I am not—"

Simon glanced at him, his gaze cool and green and contemptuous. "Oh, I know that, boy," he said softly.

Fitzclarence swallowed hard. "What I mean is, I am not—I am not going to marry Celia—Miss St. Lys, I mean."

Simon snorted. "Of course you're not, boy. I just said so, didn't I? See how easily he gives you up? *That*'s the paltry, puking excuse for a man you choose for your husband?"

Celia folded her arms and glared at him. "You idiot!"

"Is that where you were on Sunday?" Simon demanded. "I know you were not in London. Where did you go? Were you with *him*, hatching your plans?"

"What business is it of yours where I go or who I am with?" she retorted. "What do you care? You have your virgin to keep you warm. You only show up here when you want a bit of rough. I'm just your rumpy-pumpy girl, that's all I am."

"Please," Fitzclarence whispered. "Please, just let me out of here."

"For God's sake," Simon said angrily. "You know damn well Belinda means nothing to me! You know damn well it's you I cannot live without."

"You'll live to get over it," she snapped. "Just as you got over it three years ago. You sent her *my* wildflowers! You should not have done that."

"Don't be ridiculous," he snapped. "I only wanted you to feel jealousy. I see I only injured your pride, however. Still, it is no reason to marry this—this jackanapes."

"You don't actually think I would, do you?" she said. "Lord, he's only a child. Marry Clare? Do I look like a cradle robber to you?"

"I beg your pardon," Fitzclarence said indignantly.

Simon caught his breath. Crossing the room, he seized Celia's hands. "You mean . . . you're not going to marry him?"

"Of course not, you ass," she answered. "It's *his* wedding day, not mine."

"Yes," said Fitzclarence, moving to the unblocked door, "and I if I do not leave now, I shall miss it."

"Wait!" Celia caught the young man at the door and smoothed his lapels. "There!" she said, satisfied. "I wish you joy, Clare."

"Thank you," he murmured, watching Simon warily out of the corner of his eye as she fussed over him.

"Oh yes! You look gorgeous, Clare," she said, her eyes suddenly full of tears. "Your mother would be so proud, if she were here. Are you quite sure this is what you want? You can still change your mind, you know."

"Of course it's what I want, you silly girl," he said, laughing. "Lord! I never knew you were so sentimental! It's my wedding, not my funeral."

"I know," she said, trying to smile.

"I'll see you again very soon," he promised.

He kissed her cheek and was gone.

Celia stood for a moment in the doorway, waving to the young man as he departed. Then she quietly closed the door and locked it. "What am I going to do with you?" she said, walking toward him. "You keep turning up like a bad penny."

He went to her swiftly, but softly, and taking her face in his hands, took her lips in a long, luxurious kiss. "Where did you go?" he whispered against her forehead. "I wanted you so much. I searched for you everywhere. I waited at my club for hours, but you did not send to me. Why did you not send to me?"

But she could not answer, for his mouth had closed over hers again. The kiss grew wild, and whirling her around in his arms, he lifted her off her feet and carried her up the stairs to her bedroom. They undressed each other eagerly, expertly, and fell to the hearthrug, panting with desire. They knew each other so well, there was little to communicate. He knelt between her thighs and she waited, unresisting, her lips parted, understanding perfectly what he wanted. Though as practiced a lover as any he had ever known, she knew when to let a man be a man. He drove into her, rigid as iron, and took his pleasure, knowing she would find her own. Her body pulsed with his, her womb opening and closing, and they arrived together at the very summit of pleasure. He fell, spent, into her arms, glazed in sweat. She caught her breath first and said, "If we go on like this, my lord, there will be a child. There will be no help for it."

He was still inside her, and his member stirred again at her words.

"Is it what you want?" she asked, in wonder.

He raised himself on his elbows to look into her huge, glimmering eyes. "Would it be so terrible?"

She drew her finger along his jaw and smiled. "Oh, I think I could bear it, my lord," she said softly. "I think I might bear you a dozen children very gladly."

"Perhaps," he murmured, cupping one perfect breast with his palm, "not all at once. And perhaps, not right away. I do not want to share you—not yet, not even with my own babe."

"Then we must be more careful."

"It is difficult to love you cautiously," he grunted, moving against her again.

"We need not be cautious now, after all," she panted, catching his rhythm. "The damage is done."

Sometime later, they moved to the bed, and she nestled in his arms.

"How I missed you when you were gone!" he murmured. "I missed your strength. I missed the sound of your voice. I missed your laughter. I missed your bad temper."

"You missed my golden hair and perfect breasts," she retorted.

"I missed them, too," he admitted. "Where did you go?"

"I went down to the country with—with friends," she answered. "I could not bear to see you with Belinda. Though I understand I missed quite a comedy!" she added, laughing.

"Miss Archer is a foolish child," he said.

"And you are a bully."

"I did not bully her," he protested. "She is a helpless little fool, frightened of her own shadow. You know I have no patience with such creatures. She expected me to coddle her, I suppose, but as she was only there to make you jealous, and as you were not there to see it, I had no reason to fawn over her."

"Brute!"

"No indeed. I was polite but distant. You were the one I wanted to hurt. I cannot bend you to my will, and it drives me mad," he confessed. "You need no one. You have a life of your own, apart from me completely."

"You are wrong," she cried out softly. "I am not so remote as all that. I need you. Oh, I do need you."

She kissed his mouth until they were both breathless. "Oh, Simon! I realized my mistake almost at once, with Armand. I thought he loved me—perhaps he did—but it was chiefly my money he wanted. I wanted so badly to go to you then."

"Why didn't you?"

"Would you have taken me back?"

"Of course. I would have punished you a little, perhaps, but yes, I would have taken you back."

"But it was too late. You had someone else at Brighton. And by summer's end, you had been posted to Vienna for the Congress."

"You should have come to me at Vienna—or Brussels, when the war started up again."

She sighed. "I had no money. Armand took everything I had. I could not—I would not go to you a pauper! I have my pride, too, you know."

"When I came home, after Waterloo, I wanted—Dear God, how I wanted you! But I would not allow myself to go to you. I refused to compete with Fitzclarence."

"Clare was never my lover," she said quickly. "I swear it. You have no rival. No one has ever compared to you. No one even comes close."

"Not even Tom, your garden bench?"

"You were never jealous of him, surely?"

"Wasn't I?"

"But he is just a boy."

"An eager boy who worships the ground you tread upon."

"I thought I was the jealous fool," she laughed. "I thought you were fascinated by Belinda. I have made myself miserable. You chose your weapon well. I know she can give you the one thing I can't."

"What is that?"

"Her virginity," Celia said simply.

He caught his breath. "I should have liked to have been the first man who ever loved you," he said. "I would have gloried in taking your innocence. But I couldn't care less about hers. She can die a virgin for all I care."

Celia laughed. "Then I have no rival?" she said happily.

"No indeed. *She* was never of interest to me. I was more interested in her mother, as a matter of fact. But when I saw how jealous you were, I could not resist."

"You were interested in Sybil Archer?" she exclaimed, laughing. "Good God, why?"

"She claims to have a letter from . . . a *certain gentleman*."

Celia understood perfectly to whom he was referring.

"She claims he made her certain promises. I was hoping to get a look at this letter, if it exists."

"And does it?" Celia asked, always eager for any gossip that touched on the royal family.

"I cannot say. She tells me it is the sort of thing she would show only to a potential son-in-law. When Belinda becomes engaged, I may have something to do. Until then . . . we must let sleeping dogs lie."

She sat up and looked at him. "You are amazing," she declared. "Does Prinny even know all the things you do for him?"

"I hope not," Simon replied with a faint smile. "The shock might very well stop his heart, and I would not want that. I am rather fond of him, you know."

"He is lucky to have you," she said. "But not," she added, grinning as she burrowed under the covers, "as lucky as I am!"

In the morning, Celia was hungrier than she had ever been. Leaving Simon still asleep, she dressed quietly and went down to eat breakfast. When she returned, bearing his breakfast on a tray, he was just stirring. She set the tray beside the bed and leaned over to kiss him.

"Taking a flyer?" he said, observing that she was dressed to leave the house.

"I have an early rehearsal," she apologized.

"Nonsense," he growled. "You never get up before noon."

He reached for her, but she eluded him easily. "I wish I could stay," she said. "But the new actress only arrived yesterday, and our first night is the day after tomorrow."

He sat up. "What time is it?"

"Eight o'clock," she told him.

"I have an appointment."

"I have a hackney waiting for me. May I set you down?"

He shook his head. "I am to meet my brother at Berkshire House. I can walk."

Getting out of bed, he looked around for his clothes. They had been scattered over the floor, but Celia had picked them up for him and placed them on the chair near the fire. His saber leaned against the chimney piece. "I may have some news that will please you," he said as he began dressing. "A certain gentleman may be attending the play on Thursday. He has a mind to see St. Lys in breeches."

Her face lit up. "Really? That would be wonderful!"

"You mustn't tell anyone," he said quickly. "The movements of princes are best kept a secret. And besides, he has been known to change his mind at the last minute."

"I shan't breathe a word," she promised. "Will I see you tonight?"

He shook his head. "I shall be on duty, I'm afraid. To-morrow?"

"I shall be in rehearsals all day, and I play that night."

"Send to me at my club and I will come to you."

"I'll do better than that," she said, opening the little reti-cule that hung from her wrist. "I shall give you my key. Then you can come and go as you please." She placed it on the breakfast tray, kissed him again, and left.

That same morning, the Dowager Duchess of Berkshire dressed carefully, ate a light breakfast from a tray in her boudoir, and went down to the library to await the arrival of her two sons.

The night before, Dorian had dragged her out of bed and forced her to sign a sheaf of papers. Naturally, she had protested, but he had shown her a piece of paper. With a shock she had recognized the hand of her dead husband. It was the will she had believed destroyed forever. She thought she had burned the only copy, in the library at Ashlands a decade before, but she had been deceived. And now, it seemed, she had been betrayed. The man Crutch-ley had kept the original, a document she had not even known existed. And at Ashlands the servants obviously had talked. It was only a matter of time before Dorian found out about Sarah Hartley—if, indeed, he didn't know already.

Naturally, she had denied everything. Of *course* Hotchkiss had not seen her burning anything in the library at Ash-lands on the day that her husband had died. The very idea was absurd. She knew nothing about this new will. She had never seen or heard of it before.

But Dorian, to her shock, had not believed his mother.

Dorian always believed his mother. She had signed the papers to appease him, but he was not appeased. He wanted her out of Berkshire House. She had been ordered to pack her things and go. If she left quietly and gave him no more trouble, he would not expose her, he said.

"But my dear Dorian!" she had cried. "You do not seriously believe that I hid this from you? You take the word of a servant over mine? I am your mother."

He had looked at her with such hatred that she had recoiled in real fear. "I wish to God it were not so," he had said, and there could be no doubt that he meant it.

What had happened to turn him against his own mother so completely? She vowed never to rest until she found out. After he had departed, taking the will and all the papers with him, she had called up all the servants and questioned them thoroughly. By dawn, she knew everything.

When the door opened and Simon entered the room, she was at first taken aback. She had been planning what she would say to Dorian. But on second thought, it would not be such a bad thing to bring Simon to her side first. Then, together, they might be able to save Dorian.

"Good God! Who died?" Simon asked, catching sight of her.

She had dressed for effect, in black from head to toe. Jet ornaments glittered at her ears and throat, and a large brooch containing a white lock of her late husband's hair had been pinned at her throat. She looked pale and frail. In short, she had reclaimed all the pathetic dignity of her widowhood.

"It is the anniversary of your father's death."

"Is it? I thought my father died in the summer."

"You may have heard of his death in the summer," she replied sternly. "You were in India at the time. I always wear black on this day."

"I see," he said briefly. "Where is Dorian? He wanted to see me about something, but I'm afraid his message was somewhat cryptic. Is he not here?"

"He still keeps at his club," she said. "But I expect he will return when he has put me out!"

Simon raised a brow. "Put you out? What do you mean?"

"First he stripped me of my jewels. Now I am to be thrown out of my home!"

"But why? What did you do?" he asked, suppressing a laugh. "It must have been dreadful indeed to make Dorian angry enough to toss you out on your . . . er . . . ear."

"It's lies," she said angrily. "All lies! He thinks I have done terrible things, but it's not true. I've done nothing wrong. Everything I did was for the best. Everything I did was to protect my family. But *she* has turned him against me. I fear we may have lost him forever."

"What are you talking about?" he said impatiently. "Less drama, madam, and more detail. Who has turned Dorian against you? What does she say you have done?"

Her green eyes lit with fury. "Her name is Sarah Hartley!"

"And who is she?"

"She is no one," said the duchess. "She is nothing. She was a penniless foundling when I took her under my wing."

"When you what?" he said in surprise. "I didn't know you had a charitable bone in your body."

"It was the fashion at the time," his mother explained.

"And why have I never heard of this person before?" Simon asked.

"I daresay I mentioned her in my letters; perhaps you should have read them," his mother replied tartly. "Of course you never met her. You were safe in the army when the wretched creature came into our lives. And you were in India still when I finally got rid of the nasty little gutter-snipe. Oh, your father tried to warn me! He didn't want her in his house at first. But she was such a pretty, sprightly, happy little thing, she soon had him eating out of her hand."

"I'm quite sure my father never ate from anyone's hand," said Simon dryly.

"You never saw her in action! She had him wrapped around her little finger in just a matter of days. He bought her a pony and taught her to ride. No one could resist her. Dorian taught her Shakespeare. She helped Joanna sort her silks. She brought soup to the servants when they were sick. She was quite the little mistress of the house! Everyone loved her!"

He frowned. "So what happened?"

"When your father died, I daresay she expected him to leave her a mountain of money. But she was disappointed. So she found another old man she could cozen. This one she seduced and married. Sir Terence Plunkett of Fishamble, he was called. He was old enough to be her grandfather, but he had money, which was all Miss Hartley wanted. He took her away to Ireland, and I thought that was the end of my ordeal."

"But it wasn't?"

"Oh no. Now she is back, greedier than ever. I suppose she has run through the great Plunkett fortune. She has her sights on something much greater. She has come back—with a piece of paper she claims to be your father's last will and testament."

"That is impossible. Such a thing could not have been hidden all these years."

"Of course it is impossible. It is nothing more than a clever forgery, but Dorian has allowed himself to be persuaded that his father wrote it. It is not witnessed, of course—she is too clever for that. She depends entirely on Dorian's good nature for her vile plan to succeed. He has already decided to give her thirty-five thousand pounds from his own pocket."

"What!" Simon said sharply. "Thirty-five thousand pounds? Let me see this will."

"Dorian keeps it with him."

"My father would not be so foolish," Simon said flatly. "Obviously, Dorian has been taken in by a clever adventuress. Thirty-five thousand pounds! It's incredible. Five thousand, perhaps, he might have left to a trusted and valuable servant. Ten thousand, possibly. But why should my father leave thirty-five thousand pounds to anyone not of his blood? Was he in love with her?"

"When he was dying, he called for her," said the duchess, her face cold and hard as she remembered. "He did not call for me. It was her face he wanted to see, not mine. She stayed with him all night. She read to him, and sang to him. He wanted no one else with him. He died holding her hand."

"That does not mean anything," said Simon, though he looked rather grim. "Anyway, you say the will was not witnessed. Therefore it is not valid. It need not be honored."

"Dorian is determined to do so. Indeed, he is determined to do *more* for her."

"What do you mean?" Simon asked sharply.

"According to this supposed new will, Miss Hartley was to have had twenty-five thousand pounds. But Dorian insists on giving her the interest as well. Ten years' worth of compounded interest."

"He told you all this?"

"No. I had to find out from the servants. When he returned from Ashlands yesterday, he brought one of the footmen back with him. It wasn't hard to get him to talk. I—" She hesitated, drawing his attention.

"There's more? Come, let's have it! What aren't you telling me?"

"There is one part of my conduct that troubles me," she said. "I did conceal from your brother the fact that Miss Hartley had eloped with Sir Terence. Perhaps that was wrong of me. But Dorian was still reeling from the shock of his father's death. His wife, too, had suffered another of her miscarriages. Under the circumstances, I felt it would be kinder to let him think Miss Hartley had died."

"Died?"

"He might have felt compelled to go after her, you see, and bring her back. Joanna was already jealous of the girl. It would have been quite disastrous."

"I see. Dorian also was in love with her. She sounds rather fatal."

"I did what I thought was best for everyone. But now she is back, and Dorian knows that I told a little fib. He won't hear my reasons, and perhaps it is just as well. Poor boy! He never even realized that he was in love with her. But of course, the moment he saw her again, she had him captivated. Now he won't hear a word against her. Simon, you will talk to him, won't you?"

"I certainly shall!" said Simon. "The damn fool. I shall talk to Miss Hartley, too, or Lady Plunkett or whatever it is she calls herself these days."

The duchess snorted. "These days!" she said. "Oh, these days she calls herself Celia St. Lys!"

Simon jerked about, the color draining from his face. "*What* did you say?"

"I did not recognize her when I met her at the theatre," said his mother, "but I suppose Dorian did. When I think that I actually encouraged him to make her his mistress, I could scream! Oh, she is clever! She waited until he was her lover, and then she sprang her trap."

"Celia St. Lys is this Sarah Hartley person? Are you quite certain?"

"Oh yes! He took her to Ashlands on Sunday. They dug up her grave, which, of course, was empty. After that, I am sure he was willing to believe anything she said, and to do anything she wanted."

"Dorian took St. Lys to Ashlands?" Simon repeated bitterly. "So that's where she was on Sunday! She told me she had gone to the country with friends."

"But at least we do not have to worry about him marrying her," said the duchess. "I have read in the papers only this morning that she is to marry Sir Lucas Tinsley! Her greed really does know no bounds. Thirty-five thousand pounds is nothing compared to the Tinsley fortune."

This was a new shock and a new blow to Simon's dignity. "St. Lys is to marry Sir Lucas? No! I cannot believe she would stoop so low as that."

"Why not? Because he is old and vulgar and physically repulsive? You never saw Sir Terence! He was hardly as rich as Sir Lucas, and twice as repulsive to behold, and she married him happily enough. He left her a tidy little sum when he died, and she was glad of it. Ah, well! At least Dorian is safe from her. Perhaps when he hears of her plans, he will come to his senses and see that she is no good."

"May I see that?" said Simon, and took the newspaper she handed to him. Yes, there it was, boldly printed, the announcement of the engagement of Sir Lucas Tinsley to Miss Celia St. Lys.

"Perhaps we should inform Sir Lucas that his bride is nothing more than a confidence trickster. He is not her first victim, after all."

"We shall do nothing of the kind," said Simon. "If Sir Lucas breaks with her, she will run straight to Dorian. God knows what she would then persuade him to do. Leave this to me. I will deal with Miss Hartley."

"Thank you, Simon! I knew that I could depend on you," she said. "And you should know, too, that I have decided to make over to you your inheritance. Indeed, I have signed the papers already."

To her surprise, he did not seem pleased. "You are too late, madam," he said coldly.

"Too late?" she asked, bewildered, but he had already gone.

Chapter 19

It was a somber party of actors that gathered on the stage of the Theatre Royal that morning. "She told me she had come into some money," Rourke said bitterly. "But she said she'd stay until the end of the season. What the devil are we supposed to do now?"

"She's come into some money, all right," Mrs. Archer said, her handsome face contorted with rage and envy. "Sir Lucas Tinsley must be worth millions! All that lovely coal."

"Ha!" said Miss Vane. "She'll never see a penny of his money. Just because a man is rich doesn't mean he's generous."

"You're right about that, Miss Vane," agreed Mrs. Archer. "I'd sooner see my Belinda the mistress of a generous man than the wife of a skinflint."

"Mama!" Belinda protested.

Rourke shook his head sadly. "I *thought* she had accepted an offer from the Duke of Berkshire, to become his mistress. His Grace is a most generous gentleman, a true lover of the arts, and the theatre."

"She'll be Lady Lucas," said Miss Vane. "That's something, I suppose."

"No, she won't," said Mrs. Archer. "She'll be Lady Tinsley."

"Is he a knight or a baronet?"

"What would he be knighted for?" Mrs. Archer said scornfully.

"Look here," Joe Grimaldi broke in. "This is all very interesting, but what are we going to do? She was to play tonight. Obviously this Sir Lucas isn't going to allow his betrothed to take the stage. Very likely, we'll never see her again."

"Fortunately," said Rourke, "we have Miss Vane. She has played Kate Hardcastle to great acclaim in Bath."

"Have you, my dear?" said Mr. Grimaldi to the actress. "I don't recall your mentioning that when you were rattling off your résumé yesterday."

"Well, no," said Miss Vane, lowering her lashes modestly. "I didn't think it tactful to mention it when Miss St. Lys asked me. She might have thought I was after the part."

"I saw her in the role myself," said Rourke. "It's why I brought her to London. She's every bit as good as St. Lys. In fact, she is better!"

"Oh la, sir!" Miss Vane said, blushing. "It's very kind of you to say so, I'm sure."

"Can you go on tonight in her place?" asked Joe Grimaldi, coming to the point. "Or shall we have to take the play off altogether, and put up something else? That is the question."

"I watched the performance last night from the wings, Mr. Grimaldi," Miss Vane assured him. "I daresay I can manage. I might even improve upon a few things."

"It's settled then," said Rourke. "Miss Vane shall play Miss Hardcastle tonight."

"What about Thursday?" cried the other actors. "What about *Twelfth Night*?"

"That won't be possible, I'm afraid," said Rourke. "Not now. We shall have to put up something else, or keep on with *She Stoops*."

There were groans all around.

"*Romeo and Juliet* is always a crowd-pleaser," said Mr. Charley Palmer. "If Miss Vane could take the role of Juliet . . ."

"Oh!" said Miss Vane, her beautiful eyes lighting up. "I was never more praised in Bath than when I played as Juliet!"

"I shall play your nurse," said Joe Grimaldi.

"And I, Mercutio," said Rourke, becoming excited.

"And I, Tybalt," said Richard Dabney.

There was a flurry among the curtains, the sound of footsteps, and Celia hurried onto the stage. "I see you are all here," she said briskly. "Let's get started, shall we?"

Her fellow actors all turned to stare at her, the footlights flinging queer shadows up to their faces. "What are *you* doing here?" Joe Grimaldi inquired coldly. "Traitress!"

"What?" Celia cried, her brows raised.

"You've got a bloody cheek coming here!" said Mrs. Archer.

"Is this some sort of joke?" said Celia, frowning. "If so, it's really not at all funny."

"When were you going to tell us?" demanded Palmer, the others forming an indignant chorus behind him.

Celia looked daggers at Rourke. "You told them? Yes; all right, everyone. I shall be leaving you at the end of the season—which is all the more reason that we get this right. I want to go out a success, not a failure. Shall we get started?"

They stared at her as if she had sprouted two heads.

"Won't your betrothed have something to say about that?" said Mrs. Archer.

"My *what*?" said Celia, startled.

"Your fiancé," said Rourke. "Surely he means to take you off the stage immediately?"

"No," said Celia. "No indeed. I don't know what you're about."

"My dear," said Mrs. Archer coldly, "there is no need to pretend with us. The news of your engagement is in all the morning papers!"

"The news of my engagement? But I am not engaged!" she said angrily, becoming red in the face. "He hasn't even asked me yet! Is it in the papers, truly? Oh! Of all the high-handed, arrogant, conceited, selfish, self-important—The man is a tyrant! How he could he do this to me? I would not marry Lord Simon Ascot if he were the last man on earth! I would rather be sold into slavery! It would amount to the same thing!"

"It's fortunate, then," said Mrs. Archer, "that you are engaged to Sir Lucas Tinsley."

"What?" said Celia, now quite cross. "Oh, you are joking. I am no more engaged to Sir Lucas Tinsley than I am engaged to Lord Simon. I'd sooner marry a Barbary ape."

"See for yourself," said Rourke, thrusting the newspaper under her nose.

"Yes! Miss St. Lys! What do you say to that?" cried Mrs. Archer.

Celia took the newspaper and studied it, frowning. Her mouth worked helplessly. After a moment, she was able to form words. "It's not true," she cried, looking at them. "I am not engaged to Sir Lucas Tinsley. I am not engaged to anyone. Lord! You don't think I'd do that to you? What you must have been thinking! What agonies you must have suffered! No, my friends, I would never leave you in the lurch. I know very well you could not do without me."

"Of course not, Celia darling," said Rourke. "We'd be entirely lost without you."

"Actually," Mrs. Archer said, "we'd be just fine. Miss Vane had already agreed to go on in your place tonight as Miss Hardcastle."

"Is that so?" Celia said, her eyes narrowed almost to slits.

"Of course, now that you are *here*, Miss St. Lys," Miss Vane murmured.

"And what about *Twelfth Night*?" Celia demanded. "I suppose you can do without me there, as well?"

"Indeed we could not," said Rourke. "We'd have to cancel it altogether."

"And do what? Another eight weeks of *She Stoops to Conquer*?"

"Miss Vane, it seems, was highly acclaimed in the role of Juliet," said Joe Grimaldi.

Celia glanced over Miss Vane coolly. "Highly acclaimed? In Bath?"

"Yes, Miss St. Lys."

"I see. Well, I'm sorry to disappoint you, Miss Vane, but I am still here."

"I'm very glad, I'm sure," said Miss Vane.

Celia returned the newspaper to Rourke, saying, "You'll have to send someone to Fleet Street. This report must be contradicted as soon as possible. I'll sue if it's not. It's obviously someone's idea of a joke." She clapped her hands together. "Now then! Let's just get to work, shall we? Clear the stage, please. Miss Vane, why are you not in costume?"

"I—I—" stammered Miss Vane. "Well, no one was quite sure what was going to happen, Miss St. Lys."

"Well, now you know," said Celia.

"Don't be angry with her, Miss St. Lys," said Mrs. Archer. "It's not her fault."

Celia laughed suddenly. "Did you *really* think you could just put her on in my place, and London would not notice the difference? They come here to see me, you know."

"I think I would have done a very good job, Miss St. Lys," said Miss Vane with dignity. "The audience might have been a little doubtful at first, but I would have won them over."

"Is that so?" said Celia. "Why don't we try it and see?"

"Now, now, ladies!" cried Rourke, stepping between them. "Let us not quarrel. We are all friends here, I trust. Go and get dressed, if you please, Miss Vane."

"Yes, Miss Vane. We have a lot of work to do on *Twelfth Night* if we are to be ready."

"Certainly, Miss St. Lys," Miss Vane said sweetly. "I'm sure you need the practice."

"No, my dear; but *you* do," Celia told her just as sweetly. "In our first scene together, when you lift your veil and I am unmoved by your beauty, your expression of feminine pique needs a little work. You look a little constipated; I'm not sure that's what the playwright had in mind."

"Is that so, Miss St. Lys?"

"And in act three, when you say, 'Love sought is good, but given unsought better'—"

"Yes, Miss St. Lys?" Miss Vane said, very coldly.

"I've been thinking about it, and I think you should *kiss* me, Miss Vane," said Celia. "Shall we try it, and see if it works?"

Celia was changing out of her costume when Simon arrived at the theatre. He went straight to her dressing room and without knocking, went in.

"Dismiss your servant," he commanded from the sitting room.

"You may go, Flood," Celia said immediately.

Simon did not speak again until Flood was out of the room, then he pushed aside the muslin curtain. "Oh dear," Celia murmured, belting on her comfortable old dressing gown. "You've seen that ridiculous announcement, I suppose?"

"I have," he said, looking at her with cold eyes. Not for the first time, he wished she was not so beautiful.

"You should not believe everything you read in the papers," she said.

"You mean it isn't true? You are not to be his—his wife?"

"No, of course not!" she said, smiling. "How could you ever believe such a thing? I ought to be furious with you," she added, wagging her finger at him. "Don't you know me better than that?"

"I don't," he said faintly, "think I know you at all."

"What?"

"Why shouldn't you marry Sir Lucas? He is rich. He wouldn't be the first rich old man you've tricked into marriage with your charm and your beauty. Isn't that so, Lady Plunkett?"

She took a step back as if she had been pushed. "What did you call me?" she whispered.

"You do remember your first victim, don't you? Sir Terence Plunkett? Or was he your second victim? Was your first my father? Was it Dorian? How many men have you deceived in your splendid career?"

She could not speak, her throat was so constricted.

"Have you nothing to say, actress? Have you no lines for this scene?" he taunted her. "You have been found out."

"I don't understand," she said, shaking her head. "What are you saying to me?"

"I know who you are," he said flatly. "You are Sarah

Hartley. You were dropped in the streets by your parents, whoever they may have been. You were fortunate indeed that my mother took a fancy to you. She brought you into her home and made a lady of you, didn't she? And how did you repay her? By stealing the affections of her husband, her son, and God only knows who else! As for this—this *will* of my father's you claim to have discovered—you won't get away with it. You'll never see a penny of that money, I promise you, my girl."

"I never—I never wanted the money," she uttered, forcing out the words. "I never knew anything about it. Dorian—"

"Ah yes! Dorian! I was coming to that. Did you think I would not find out you were at Ashlands together? How cozy that must have been! Did you enjoy pretending you were mistress of that great house?"

Celia gave a guilty start. Her knees buckled, and she groped for the stool at her dressing table and sat down. "Who has told you this? Not Dorian!"

He gave a short laugh. "No! No, not Dorian. He brought a servant back with him from Ashlands. That is how my mother found out who you are."

Celia passed her hand across her brow, where beads of sweat had appeared. "She knows, then," she whispered. "It is done."

"Were you thinking of my brother when you were in my arms?" he asked, his face contorted with pain and rage. "Did you think of *me* when you were in his? I have heard of a woman having two strings to her bow—one for use and one for pleasure—but you, madam! You are in a class of your own! You must have strings enough for an entire orchestra!"

Celia bowed her head as if she had been beaten by physical blows. "You won't believe me, of course," she managed to say, "but there is nothing between Dorian and me but the most innocent friendship. He is my friend."

"You're right," he said flatly. "I don't believe you."

"Then there is nothing more to say."

"I have something more to say. When you left me this morning, I had decided to marry you. Yes!" he went on bitterly, as she lifted amazed eyes. "Yes! I, Lord Simon Ascot, had made up my mind. I would stoop to marry a girl out of the playhouse. I loved you, Celia. Oh God! When I think how I have loved you!" he went on bitterly. "With all my soul I have loved you. Against my will, I have loved you. But it was a dream I loved. I fell in love with the part you played, that is all. Now I see you for what you really are. There is not enough beauty in the world to cover such ugliness."

"You are wrong about me," she said.

"I wish to God I was," he retorted. "You are a cold-hearted, merciless mercenary, madam. Your parents knew what they were about when they dropped you in the gutter. Clearly it is where you belong. I could almost pity Sir Lucas!"

Her eyes flashed. "Yes, my lord, I came from the gutter," she said. "But I won't be going back there, whatever you may have to say about it."

"Oh, I shan't give you away," he said. "You can marry Sir Lucas; I shan't interfere. But you will give up your hold on my brother. You will give up this ridiculous scheme of extorting money from him. In exchange, I won't say a word to Sir Lucas about your past, or indeed about your present. He can repent at leisure for having married you, and you can enjoy his money. Do we have an understanding?"

"No, my lord," she said coldly. "We do not. I shall do exactly as I please. Your threats do not frighten me in the least."

"Then I shall ruin you!"

"You must do what you think is best," she said.

"I shall!" he said sharply, and left her.

Flood returned to find her mistress at her dressing table, filing her nails. "What did he want, madam?" she anxiously inquired. "Sure his face was as black as thunder."

"Was it?" said Celia, with a faint smile. "I can't say I noticed."

The next person to come to her door was Eliza London. When admitted into the sitting room, she asked timidly if Celia could give her any news of Fitzclarence.

"No," Celia replied. "Not since he came to my house very early this morning. He must be married by now," she added carelessly.

To her dismay, Eliza turned the color of ashes and slumped down into a chair. "Married? Wot? My Clare? 'E never said a word to me about it! Not a ruddy word. I've not seen 'im in two days!"

Celia bit her lip. "I'm sorry, my dear," she murmured. "I thought you knew."

Eliza shrugged. "I suppose I knew 'ow it would be. 'E could've told me! I 'ad a right to know."

"Did he leave you with any money?" Celia asked gently.

Eliza shook her head wearily. "No, and the man's locked me out of the room."

"Never mind," said Celia quickly. "You can come home with me after the play tonight. We might go to Crockford's first, and have a little supper."

"Lord love you, Miss St. Lys," said Eliza, with a faint laugh. "I can't play tonight; I 'ave to work!"

"Playing *is* work," said Celia firmly.

"I mean, I 'ave to earn a living, don't I? Playing is great fun, and I do love it, but it don't pay, if you see what I mean—not enough to keep body and soul together. There's not even a part for me in the new play."

"No," Celia admitted. "But there are other theatres, you know. The Haymarket will be doing *The Beggar's Opera* this summer—that would be perfect for you. You can't just give up, you know. You're too talented. And I won't let you be swallowed up by the streets again. You can come and stay with me until you get on your feet. I'll look after you better than any man ever could. I'll arrange for you to have lessons."

"Lessons?" Eliza said, wide-eyed. "Lessons in what?"

"In everything," said Celia. "Singing, dancing, speaking. You've got that natural spark, you know; you just need a little polish. You're young; you'll pick it up very quickly, I promise. You *do* want to be rich and famous, don't you?"

"Sure," said Eliza, "but—"

"But nothing," Celia said fiercely. "Just because some man has let you down is no reason to give up on life. It's up to you to make the life you want. Believe me, it's better if you earn it. If a man gives it to you, what's to stop him from taking it away again? I am sorry about Clare," she added. "I do know what it's like to be . . . disappointed. But you can't let a man ruin your life. Don't give him the satisfaction, my dear. A year from now, when Clare is married to that cross-eyed cow, and you are the toast of London, he will weep bitter tears for you."

"I don't much feel like playing tonight," said Eliza.

"What does feeling have to do with it? You will go out there. You will make them laugh. I don't care if you're crying on the inside. You're an actress now. That's the job. You don't see me crying, do you?"

"No, Miss St. Lys."

"No! And you never will."

They were interrupted by a knock on the door. "I'm very popular today," Celia murmured as Eliza opened the door to admit the Duke of Berkshire.

"My dear girl," he murmured, crossing the room swiftly to take Celia's hands. "Do tell me it isn't true! It can't be!"

She smiled at him. "Well, if it can't be true, then I'm sure it isn't, Your Grace. I believe you have met my friend Miss London?"

"Oh yes, how do you do?" he murmured.

"Your Excellency," Eliza said, giving him a sort of curtsy before banging the door shut.

Dorian hardly seemed to notice her departure. "This thing in the paper," he began haltingly. "I don't like to call it an announcement. It can't be true. You are not—Tell me at once that you are not engaged to Sir Lucas Tinsley!"

"I am not engaged to Sir Lucas Tinsley," she said. "I am not engaged to anyone. That beastly joke will be corrected in tomorrow's edition."

"Joke!" he exclaimed.

"Yes. What else could it be? Sir Lucas hasn't even proposed to me. Indeed, I hardly know him. We met a few times at the studio of Sir Thomas Lawrence. We have spoken perhaps five times, but that is all."

"I am relieved! When I saw it in the paper, I went to your house, but you were already gone."

"Yes, I had an early rehearsal."

"From your house, I went to Sir Lucas's. He was not at home, either. I'm sorry to say, I entertained some very foolish ideas. I allowed myself to become quite frantic."

"I can tell you exactly where Sir Lucas is," said Celia. "Today is his daughter's wedding day. She married Captain Fitzclarence at Bushy House this morning. I daresay Sir Lucas has not yet returned to London."

"So that's it! But . . . who would do such a thing? Who would make such a joke?"

Celia shrugged. "The world is full of jokesters," she said. "I wouldn't be surprised if it wasn't Captain Fitzclarence. Frankly, it's the sort of juvenile prank I might expect from him."

Dorian shook his head.

"I just hope this doesn't affect attendance tonight," said Celia. "If London thinks I am engaged to be married, they won't expect me to play. We'll have to put up an enormous sign over the front door: Yes! The Saintly One plays tonight."

"Soon you will be free of all this," said Dorian. "You are about to become a very rich young woman. But I never asked you: How would you like the matter to be arranged? Shall you have the money all at once? Or shall I put it in four-percents? Would you like some of it now, and the rest held in trust? However you'd like it, so it shall be arranged."

Celia moved away from him and sat down on the sofa. "As to that . . ." she said. "Your brother is of the opinion that the will is a forgery."

Dorian frowned. "What do you mean? Simon hasn't even seen it. By the time I made it to Berkshire House, he had been and gone. How do you know what he thinks?"

She laughed shortly. "He was good enough to tell me what he thinks. I am a coldhearted mercenary, if you please. The will is a forgery. I am a confidence trickster. I should marry Sir Lucas for his money, just as I married Sir Terence"—she had to force the name out—"for his. My parents were right to drop me in the gutter. Oh, he had an opinion on everything! He knows that I am Sarah Hartley, and he despises me."

"But how? I never said a word about it to anyone."

"Apparently your mother questioned the servants. You brought one of the footmen with you from Ashlands. I was foolish," she added, "to think it could be kept a secret. My God, Dorian, he practically accused me of—of seducing your father—and you!"

"What!"

"He said I had repaid your mother's kindness to me by stealing her husband's affections. I can hardly deny that I craved his approbation. I wanted everyone to love me."

"But he has only heard my mother's version. I hope you told him the truth."

She shook her head. "I could say nothing. I was struck dumb by his accusations. What could I say to him, anyway, that he would believe? He knows I went with you to Ashlands, and he—he thinks the worst of me now. I shall never change his mind."

"But why should you care what Simon thinks?" he asked. "I hope you will come to Ashlands with me again very soon, and stay longer. We need not care what Simon thinks about it. His opinion means nothing."

"Oh, I wish to God that were true," she said faintly, her eyes fixed and staring. "But it seems his is the opinion that does matter. I do care what he thinks. I care very much. I am sorry, Dorian, but if your brother truly believes that the will is a forgery and that I am a trickster, I cannot confirm that view by accepting any money from you. I cannot."

"But, my dear, the money won't be coming from Simon; he has no share in my father's estate. You must allow me to do what I know to be right, whatever he may think."

She shook her head. "He may have no share in your father's estate, but he has an equal share of your father's heart. If he is against it, then I'm afraid I cannot accept the bequest. I shall stay where I am and remain an actress. It's not such a bad life, you know. As a matter of fact, it's rather fabulous being me."

That night, the theatre was packed to the rafters. Despite reports of St. Lys's engagement, her name was still on the marquee. The crowd was breathless with anticipation as the curtain went up, but when Miss Hardcastle made her entrance, it wasn't St. Lys.

She was a lovely blonde with an excellent figure. Her voice was pure and sweet. She had grace and talent and charm, but she was not St. Lys. The audience, at first puzzled, became unruly. "Who the 'ell are you?" someone shouted from the gallery.

Where was St. Lys? They had been promised St. Lys!

Then out came Miss Neville, a tall, shapely brunette with a saucy walk and a rich, husky voice that filled the theatre. She paused, crossing one ankle over the other and planting the toe of one shoe so that those seated in the pit could clearly see that the sole of her slipper was bright pink. "It's St. Lys!" someone called out in disbelief. And Celia gave that very clever fellow the wink he deserved.

Chapter 20

Morning was a horrible business, as it usually is when one has drunk too much champagne the night before. It is even worse when one has never drunk champagne before, as was the case with Miss Eliza London. Flood grumbled no end at having to do for two such sorry creatures, but she managed to have them both up and dressed by the appointed time. They had even eaten a little. The hackney carriage appeared at the door promptly at eight o'clock, and Flood herded them downstairs. They looked demure and ladylike in their coats and bonnets and gloves.

Tonecho opened the front door for them, and as he did so, a large, angry man was coming toward them. It was Sir Lucas Tinsley, shifting his bulk up the steps. Celia had just entered the hall, with Eliza in tow. He saw her at once and she saw him. His face was red as a cock's crown, and his left eye was dashing back and forth. As there could be no escaping the meeting, Celia fixed a smile on her face and said warmly, "Sir Lucas! How very nice of you to visit me. But, as you can see, I am on my way out."

He stopped short of the threshold, staring at her in confusion. The warmth of her greeting, her beauty, and the charm of her smile had dampened most of his anger.

"Miss St. Lys! What, pray, is the meaning of *this*?" he implored as he held out the newspaper in his hand.

"I see you have read that silly announcement," Celia said briskly. "How tiresome! My dear sir, it seems that you and I have been the victims of a practical joke. I know it is hard, but we must bear it as best we can."

"P-practical joke?" Sir Lucas stammered, after a moment. "Are you saying—"

"What else could it be but the work of some prankster?" she said reasonably. "*I* certainly did not do it, if that is what you think. And if *you* did not do it . . ."

"No! Oh no! I hope you do not blame *me*?"

"Not at all," Celia assured him. "I blame no one. Let us simply agree that it was a harmless prank. One looks so silly getting all lathered up about such foolishness. Don't you agree, Sir Lucas?"

Sir Lucas stood, embarrassed, uncertain how to proceed. "I . . . er . . . yes!"

Celia smiled. "Now you must excuse me, Sir Lucas. I am wanted at the theatre."

"The theatre!" Sir Lucas exclaimed. "No, my dear! You can never go back there again."

"I beg your pardon," said Celia, signaling to her manservant with a glance, a slight widening of the eyes, that her visitor might require pacification.

"That life is all behind you now, my dear," said Sir Lucas, his thick, fleshy lips curved in a grotesque smile. "I am come to take you home with me to my mansion in South Audley Street."

"How very kind of you to invite me," said Celia, "but I'm afraid I really must be getting to the theatre now."

"But, my dear, if you are to be my wife—" cried Sir Lucas.

At that moment, Tonecho sprang, imprisoning Sir Lucas in his strong arms.

Celia held up her hand as a signal to Tonecho. As a result, the manservant did not throw Sir Lucas into the street but merely continued to hold him. "You are confused, Sir Lucas," she told her visitor. "I am not to be your wife. The announcement of our engagement has been most firmly contradicted in this morning's paper. I'm afraid I won't be going with you to your mansion in South Audley Street or anywhere else. Do you understand?"

Sir Lucas ceased to struggle against his captor and stared at her, astounded. "What? But, my love! You said that was a practical joke!"

"Yes, certainly," she said, becoming impatient. "The announcement of your engagement to me *must* have been a practical joke. Anything else would be unthinkable!"

"No!" he cried. "It was the announcement this morning that there was no engagement—*that* was the practical joke."

"No," she insisted. "That was all right. I put that in myself. It was the original announcement that was the joke."

"No," he said, beginning to frown. "I made the announcement."

"I beg your pardon?" said Celia, blinking at him. "Why should you do such a thing? Are you mad?"

"Mad?" he cried, becoming red in the face. "Do you deny that you agreed to marry me?"

"What are you talking about?" Celia gasped. "I never agreed to any such thing. As a matter of fact, you never even made me an offer of marriage. Your offer, I seem to recall, was something rather different!"

"That was a mistake," he said. "Lord Simon is to blame for that. He told me—"

"Never mind! I can guess what he told you! The fact remains, Sir Lucas, that you thought you could buy me."

"No," he protested weakly.

"Yes, you did," she said. "I liked you so much when we first met."

"Y-you did?" he said incredulously.

"Yes. I enjoyed our conversations," she said. "I thought you were different from the others. You really seemed to listen to me when I talked. You made me feel clever. I thought we were friends! Then you sent me that horrid, horrid necklace, and I realized you were just like all the other rich men I have met in my life. You thought you could buy me."

"No!" he gasped, horrified.

"Yes, you did! You thought you could buy me—with some tawdry trinket. Well, I am not for sale, Sir Lucas."

"But I don't want to buy you," he protested. "I want to marry you! Indeed, I have announced to the world my intention to marry you. You shall be Lady Tinsley."

"I shall be no such thing!" she said angrily. "You did not have my permission to make any such announcement. It was an insufferable presumption! Did you not think I would contradict you? No, of course not! You thought I would be glad to have you, I suppose."

"But you wore the necklace," he protested. "You wore the collar of pink diamonds I gave you."

Celia frowned. "What does that signify?" she asked impatiently.

"That was our signal," he told her.

"Signal?"

"I wrote in my letter," he hurried on rather desperately, "that if you were willing, you were to wear the necklace. And you did. You wore it."

"You proposed to me in a *letter*?" she said, incredulous. "Of all the nonsensical—"

Sir Lucas hung his head. "I was afraid I might lose my nerve if I saw you in person, so I dropped it in the post."

"You dropped it in the post," she repeated, fighting the urge to laugh. "Have you any idea, Sir Lucas, how many letters I get in a day? I could not possibly read them all."

"Then . . . you did not get my letter?"

"I'm sure it's here somewhere," she said. "But I have not read it, no."

"I see. Then you—?"

For a moment, he looked so forlorn that she almost felt sorry for him. "I just happened to wear the necklace that night. That is all. It wasn't a signal. It was very kind of you to want to marry me," she went on gently. "I'm flattered, of course, that you think me worthy of such an honor, but I cannot possibly accept."

Sir Lucas suddenly seemed to realize the ridiculousness of his position. His face slowly turned the color of mahogany. "Take your hands off of me, you bloody dago," he snarled at Tonecho.

"The door, Tonecho," Celia said quietly. "Sir Lucas is just leaving."

"Not quite," said Sir Lucas, thrusting out his jaw. "I am not finished with you, my dear. I will have my necklace back, if you please. I will not be made a fool by an actress."

"I'm sorry I cannot oblige you, Sir Lucas," she replied. "You see, I live by the Golden Rule. Do unto others as you would have them do unto you. If I were ever as stupid, cowardly, and mean as you, I would want to be taught a lesson. Show the gentleman out, Tonecho, *por favor*! *Sacarlo de aquí*."

The huge Spaniard picked up Sir Lucas as if he were nothing, tossed his bulk over one shoulder, and flung him down the steps.

"Good morning, Sir Lucas," said Celia, marching past

him to step into the waiting hackney. "Come along, Miss Eliza!"

Eliza gave Sir Lucas a wide berth and jumped into the hackney.

For Celia, there was no champagne after the play that night. The following night was to be the first night of the new play, and she never indulged on the eve of such an important event. She went straight home. Eliza, who still had not heard anything from Captain Fitzclarence, came home with her. In silence, they ate a cold supper in the kitchen, then went to bed.

Celia's hand shook as she gave Eliza her bedroom candle.

"You're not nervous, are you, Miss St. Lys?" Eliza cried.

"I'm always nervous before a first night," Celia confessed. "I doubt I shall sleep a wink."

"No, nor I," said Eliza. "I suppose 'e's off on 'is 'oneymoon with '*er*."

"Mind your H's," Celia told her.

"Yes, Miss St. Lys."

Dorian, after setting down Celia and her protégée in Curzon Street, continued on to Berkshire House, where the butler informed him that Lord Simon was waiting to see him. Dorian went up to the library and found his brother brooding in a chair, a glass of brandy in his hand. "Good evening, Simon," he said civilly, as he poured himself a drink.

Simon was in no mood to observe the social niceties.

"Am I to understand," he said, setting down his glass, "that you have put my mother out on the street?"

"Hardly," said Dorian. "She checked in to the Pulteney Hotel this morning. I believe her stay there will be of some duration. Beyond that, I do not concern myself."

"My mother cannot live at the Pulteney Hotel," said Simon. "She is the Dowager Duchess of Berkshire. It is ridiculous."

"She has money of her own. She is free to set up her own establishment."

"You know damned well that this late in the season it will be difficult to find her suitable accommodation."

"She can live with you, presumably."

"With me?" Simon echoed, very much taken aback.

"The lady has two sons, I believe."

"I have nothing but bachelor rooms at Carlton House."

"You have your house in Green Park."

"I couldn't possibly evict my tenants."

Dorian shrugged. "There are some very nice trees in Hyde Park, I believe. She can build a nest in one of those. But she will never set foot in my house again. After what she did to Sally—"

"What she did to Sally!" Simon said roughly. "What did she do to the little guttersnipe? From what I hear, Sally owes her benefactress a debt of gratitude. You seem to think it is the other way around! Not only is she an ungrateful, wretched girl; she is a fraud and a liar."

Dorian's eyes flashed with anger. "You will not speak of her like that."

"I shall speak of her anyway I choose," Simon replied. "I know her, Dorian, better than you ever could. I know all her tricks. You seriously cannot be thinking of giving thirty-five thousand pounds to her! Why, for God's sake? Because she is beautiful? Because she smiles at you? Because she promises you heaven? Because she gives you her body?"

"Certainly not," Dorian said coldly. "You are despicable even to suggest such a thing. If you knew her at all, you could never say such things about her. The money is hers because my father willed it so. That is all."

"Oh yes," Simon said softly. "My father's famous last will and testament! Hidden away all these years. Don't be such a gull, Dorian. Obviously it's a forgery."

"I think I know my father's handwriting," Dorian said sharply. "But you may judge for yourself." Setting down his glass, he went to his desk and unlocked the center drawer. From this he brought forth a piece of paper, brown with age, which he gave to his brother. "In any case," he went on, as Simon looked at the document, "it doesn't concern you. Sally's inheritance will come out of my pocket, not yours."

Simon stared at the paper in his hands.

"It is the last thing he ever wrote," said Dorian. "You see there that he wasn't only concerned with Sally's portion. In the first lines, he appoints me as your guardian, instead of our mother."

"Yes, I see that," Simon said faintly.

"If it were a forgery, why would anyone care about you and your inheritance?"

"It is not a forgery," said Simon. "I had letters enough from my father when I was a young man. He filled them with advice and instruction. I don't think I benefitted much from the advice and instruction, but I do know his hand. I know my father's hand as well as you, Dorian."

Dorian breathed a sigh of relief. "I am glad that's settled," he said, sitting down. "I was afraid I was in for a battle royal. You know what this means, of course. If I had known of the existence of this will, you would have gotten your inheritance when you came of age. The very *day* you came of age. I know it is not a proper will, as the law would have it. It was not witnessed. But that would not have mattered to me. His intentions were clear as crystal. I would have plagued the woman's eyes out until she gave you control of your inheritance. I can be quite firm when I know I am right."

"She has made it over to me, finally," Simon murmured. "I have my inheritance now. She told me yesterday that she had done it, and today I have seen the papers."

"Yes, but only because I forced her to do it!" said Dorian. "When I confronted her, she knew she had no choice but to sign the papers I put in front of her. She would have been quite ruined otherwise. She didn't tell you that, did she?"

"No," Simon said. "She did not. I still do not understand," he continued after a slight pause. "How did this come to be in—in *Sally's* possession? And why did she keep it a secret all these years?"

"I'm afraid you've got the wrong end of the stick," Dorian told him. "I didn't get this from Sally. I got it from Crutchley. He's an attorney in Ashland Heath. Our father sent to him when he was on his deathbed. His clerk made a copy of the will. It was to be signed and witnessed the day our father died, but he was not in time. It was the *copy* our mother burned, not the original, thank God!"

"What do you mean? She burned my father's will?"

"Oh yes. Hotchkiss saw her do it. Fortunately for us, she never knew of the existence of the original. She did not tell you that, either, I suppose?"

"No."

"I thought not. Now at least you understand why I must give Sally her money. It is what our father wanted."

"Yes," said Simon, returning the paper to him. "In your place, I expect I would do the same."

"Good," said Dorian. "I am glad we agree. Sally refused to accept any of it unless we were agreed. And the interest, too. Are we agreed there, also?"

"Under the circumstances, I believe that our mother must pay the interest," said Simon. "Celia might even be entitled to damages."

"That is what I said, too. But Sally would not hear of it. She would not take a penny from our mother."

Simon shrugged. "We cannot force her. By all means, let her have her twenty-five thousand pounds, as set down in the will. I suppose she earned it, by making an old man happy."

"I beg your pardon?" said Dorian, frowning.

"I don't judge her," said Simon. "She came from the gutter, with nothing. She must have been delighted when my mother took such an interest in her—more so when my father did. I suppose the temptation was too great to resist—on both sides. Was he the first to have her? Or did you get there before him?"

"What?" Dorian was on his feet, his face quite pale. "What the devil are you saying?"

"I can't say I blame you," Simon went on. "She's beautiful. She must have been quite something when she was innocent. Why, if I had been there, I might have been tempted myself."

"Stand up!" said Dorian, moving swiftly across the room. "Stand up! For I cannot hit you when you are sitting down. How dare you imply that I—that our father—There was nothing untoward in that relationship. My father adored her. He delighted in her company."

Simon remained where he was. "Obviously," he drawled. "Why else would he leave her so much money?"

"You are despicable!" said Dorian, clenching his fists. "For God's sake, she was only a child! She was but fourteen

years of age when our father died. What you are suggesting is too vile even for words!"

Simon had the grace to look ashamed. "Fourteen? I was
led to believe that she was older—much older."

"Led to believe!" Dorian repeated bitterly. "Yes, by our
mother! What exactly did the old hag tell you?"

Simon passed his hand over his eyes. "That the girl seduced everyone in the house. That both you and my father
were in love with her. That your wife was wild with jealousy. Is any of this true?"

"No indeed," Dorian said furiously. "Of course we all
loved Sally. She was such a sweet, clever child. My wife?
Jealous of her? She was the child Joanna wanted so desperately but could never have, poor woman. It seems to me that
the only one who was jealous of Sally was our mother!"

"But she also told me that, when our father died, the
child seduced another rich old man. This one married her.
She was married before, was she not? You told me that
yourself."

"Oh God!" Dorian groped for a chair. "How could she be
so wicked? Here is what happened. When our father died,
Sally was but fourteen. Our mother found out about the will
and burned it. She must have decided then and there to get
rid of the girl. She arranged for her to be married. She sent
Sally to Ireland. This man—this Sir—Sir—"

"Sir Terence Plunkett," Simon said calmly.

"Sally had never met him before. She was left with him
at his house, a rather bleak and remote place from what I
understand. She had no friends, no money, no one to help
her. She had no choice but to marry the man."

"At the age of fourteen?" cried Simon.

"He married her on her fifteenth birthday," Dorian said
quietly. "I need hardly tell you the marriage was not a
happy one. In the meantime, my mother told us Sally had

died. I never even looked for her. I thought she was buried in the churchyard. How she must have suffered!"

Simon's head was in his hands. "What have I done?" he murmured.

"It's not your fault," Dorian said. "You couldn't have known. The worst of it is, she told Sally it was what I wanted. All these years, she blamed me. And I had no idea she was even alive. And I cannot even punish the person responsible! She sits in comfort in her rooms at the Pulteney Hotel—and thinks herself quite ill-used, I daresay."

"Yes, she does," said Simon, his face set and grim. "Not half as ill-used as she will think herself in the very near future, however."

"What do you mean? I know what you are thinking, Simon, but no! We cannot expose her without exposing Sally. It would be a humiliation to her if anyone knew she had been married to that—that Irish oaf! She doesn't want anyone to know she was my mother's pet charity case."

"I have something very different in mind," said Simon. "There really is only one way to make amends for all the pain and misery my mother has inflicted upon her. The money's not enough. There's not enough money in the world to make up for what she has suffered."

"What are you going to do?"

"I am going to marry her, of course," said Simon, "if she will have me."

Dorian coughed gently. "That's a very good thought, Simon, but you see, I have already offered her the protection of my name, and she has declined the honor. Somehow, I don't really think she'll have you."

"But I am not going to offer her the protection of my name," said Simon. "I offer her my heart."

"Your what?" said Dorian incredulously.

"I do have one, you know."

"I'll take your word for it," said Dorian. "But, Simon, you don't even like her!"

"I love her," Simon said simply.

"Well, I don't think she loves you! In fact, I'm sure she doesn't."

"I hope to God you are wrong," said Simon. "I shall look a bloody fool if you are right."

The next day, the Theatre Royal was a hive of noisy activity as players and stagehands, painters and carpenters, all gathered to put the last touches on the play.

"Me, I cannot work like this!" cried Monsieur Alexandre, in the alcove of Celia's dressing room, after a particularly large crash, followed by shouts. "*Je dois avoir tranquillité pour mon travail! J'ai besoin de silence . . . sauf si vous voulez finir par ressembler à . . . un hérisson,*" he added ominously.

Celia was seated at her dressing table and caught his eye in the mirror. "*Un hérisson!*" she cried. "No, monsieur, I most certainly do not want to look like a hedgehog! Flood! Go and tell them to be still for twenty minutes."

Presently, a deep and profound silence reigned over the theatre.

Monsieur took a deep breath and picked up his golden scissors.

St. Lys was having her hair cut.

Flood stood in the shadows of her mistress's dressing room, helplessly weeping as monsieur made the first cut. The Irishwoman let out a wail of grief as the long golden curl fluttered to the floor. Even monsieur seemed to lose his nerve.

"*Est-ce que vous voulez vraiment, mademoiselle?*" he asked, almost pleading.

But Celia did not hesitate. "Yes, of course it is what I want. *Coupez*," she commanded. "*Faites de moi un beau garçon.*"

Monsieur sighed, and seemed almost in tears himself as he began to crop her hair. Twenty minutes later he was done. Celia opened her eyes and looked in the mirror. Her eyes widened in shock. "Monsieur!" she breathed, running her fingers rapidly through the woefully short curls. "*Qu'avez vous fait? Mon Dieu! Vous m'avez scalpé!* I would rather you made me look like a hedgehog than a shorn sheep!"

"*Jamais! Pas du tout!* The effect, it is most charming," monsieur assured her, hastily putting away his scissors. "*Vous ressemblez à la Pucelle d'Orléans.*"

"Butcher!" cried Flood, chasing him out of the room. When he was dispatched, she hurried back to her mistress. Falling to her knees, she began gathering up the golden curls that had fallen to the floor. "Oh, madam!" she cried. "Whatever were you thinking?"

"Actually," said Celia, smoothing her hair down into a smooth, golden cap, "it's not so bad. I suppose I do look a bit like Joan of Arc. I just never knew my head was *shaped* like that. Anyway, it's the right look for the part, and what's done is done."

"Aye! 'Tis done, all right!" said Flood. Having gathered Celia's hair in her apron, she climbed to her feet. "And what are you going to do in the last scene, when you're supposed to reveal to everyone that you're a girl?"

"I shall take the duke's hand and place it on my breast," said Celia.

"Sure won't Davey Rourke like that," Flood said darkly.

There was a knock on the door. "Hurry! Help me get the wig on," cried Celia, snatching her blond wig from the stand. "No one can see me like this. It's a surprise."

There was another knock, louder, and suddenly the door opened. "Celia darling? Are you decent?"

"What is it, Mr. Rourke?" Celia called from behind the curtain.

"Lord Simon is here—"

"Is he? Tell him to go away!" said Celia. "I won't see him. How dare he come here, today of all days! He knows I am busy."

"Yes, Miss St. Lys," said Simon, coming into the room. "I know you are busy. I won't take up much of your time. As you may have heard, His Royal Highness means to attend the play tonight . . ."

Celia jumped from behind the curtain, her shorn head concealed under a blond wig and her body wrapped in her old dressing gown. "Don't tease me!" she said. "My nerves cannot take it. Is he really coming?"

"Yes. I know it is an inconvenience, but—"

"Inconvenience!" she cried, astonished. "How can you say that? It is a very great honor. Why, it practically guarantees the house a successful run. We are all delighted, are we not, Mr. Rourke?"

"Oh yes! We're all beside ourselves with glee," said Rourke.

"I did not mean that the prince's coming here would be an inconvenience," said Simon. "But I'm afraid the theatre will have to be searched quite thoroughly from top to bottom. *That* may indeed inconvenience you all."

"You're searching the theatre?" cried Celia. "Whatever for?"

"The last time His Royal Highness went to a play, someone took a shot at him," Simon reminded her. "Needless to say, I was not in charge of the prince's security on that occasion. I am determined that there be no unpleasantness like that this evening."

"But that was just some wretched lunatic!" Celia protested. "Anyway, what do you expect at Covent Garden? *This* is the Theatre Royal. You don't really think we're harboring assassins here, do you?"

"We've already confiscated half a dozen powder kegs and made four arrests."

"What!" she cried, startled.

"They'll be after hanging all the Irish," said Flood, shivering. "So they will!"

"I beg your pardon," said Simon. "That was my little joke."

"Very funny," Celia said coldly. "Mr. Grimaldi should put you in his act."

"Shall I perform the search now? Would that be convenient?" he asked.

Celia looked at him, wide-eyed. "But surely you don't mean to search the dressing rooms, Lord Simon!"

"Yes; all of them, Miss St. Lys," he replied.

"What? The ladies' rooms, as well as the men's?"

"Yes. All."

"Not *my* room, surely?"

"I'm sorry . . . I can make no exceptions."

"Who asked you to?" she snapped. "Go on, then. *Search.*"

"You may have one of my junior officers, if you prefer," he offered.

Celia tossed her head. "I'm sure I don't care which of you paws my petticoats and which of you reads my love letters. Just get on with it, if you please. I have a lot to do."

"What's in this cupboard?" he asked, starting for the wardrobe, only to find that Flood had thrown herself in front of it.

"Costumes," Celia said smartly. "Stand aside, Flood. In fact, you'd better wait outside."

"I'll not leave you, madam," cried Flood.

Celia pushed her out into the corridor, saying, "We'll leave the door open."

"Is this what you are wearing tonight?" Simon asked, observing Viola's masculine disguise, which had been placed on a tailor's dummy to preserve its shape.

"Yes."

"What's this for?" he asked, pulling the rapier free of its sheath. The blade was of painted metal, probably tin, certainly not steel. Simon tested the dull edge with his finger.

"It's only for show," she told him coldly. "It's *Twelfth Night*, for heaven's sake. It's not *Hamlet*. There will be no bloodshed."

"No. It is a comedy, I believe."

She frowned at him, detecting criticism where perhaps there was none. But then, her nerves were very raw today, as they always were before a first night. "What of it?" she snapped. "People like me in a comedy."

"Yes, of course they do," he replied, sheathing the blade. "Who would want to see you suffer, after all?"

"No one, I trust," she said, snatching the rapier from him. Compared to his saber, certainly, it was a silly article and she was suddenly ashamed of it. "What do you suppose I might do with it? Suddenly take a flying leap off the stage and pierce the prince's heart?"

"You would not have to leave the stage to do that, Miss St. Lys," he said. "Your beauty is enough to pierce any man's heart."

She looked at him sharply. "Now you are mocking me! Perfect. That's just what I need."

"I do not mock you, Celia," he said gently. "No one who

ever saw you could deny your beauty. I have been a fool, Celia—"

"Yes, I know *that*, my lord."

He frowned. "Do not interrupt me. I am attempting to apologize."

"I don't want to hear it. Why should you apologize for saying what you felt? Now at least I know what you really think of me."

"No. When I saw you—when I said those things to you, I had not yet spoken to my brother. I had not seen the will. I have seen it now. Obviously it is genuine. But I should not have accused you."

"You spoke to Dorian?"

Simon was pleased; at least she was listening to him. "Yes. I saw him last night. He explained everything."

"You did not want to hear *my* explanation."

"No," he admitted. "I gave you no chance to defend yourself. Can you forgive me?"

"I don't know."

"You shall have your inheritance," he explained quickly.

"Is that what you think this is about?" she cried. "I don't care about that! Of course I am pleased that your father was thinking of me, but I never wanted his money."

"I know that, child." He reached for her.

"No!" she said violently, blinking back tears. "I can't think about this now. I have a play to think about, and it is a comedy, not a bloody funeral. Please! Just finish your searching and leave me in peace. It would be a fine thing if I forgot my lines, wouldn't it?"

"Of course," he said, bowing. "We can talk later."

"Yes, perhaps," she said. "If I am not too busy."

Taking a seat at her dressing table, she put her back to him and began trimming her nails. Behind her, he was rummaging in the drawers of her wardrobe.

"My lord?"

Celia turned at the sound of a male voice and discovered, to her annoyance, that one of Simon's officers had come into the room. The muslin curtain between the sitting room and the alcove stood open, and he had a clear view of St. Lys in her dressing gown.

Going out to meet the other guardsman, Simon jerked the curtains closed. "Yes, what is it, Osborne?"

"I beg your pardon, Miss St. Lys," the young man called to the actress. Celia, naturally, ignored him. "I'm so sorry to disturb you."

"Lieutenant!" Simon barked, focusing the officer's attention on himself.

"My lord, we've apprehended a suspicious character. He was trying to sneak out of the theatre. He won't tell us his name or his business. But Lieutenant West says he's definitely French. He could well be a Bonapartist agent. He's got a locked case with him."

"I'll vouch for him," Celia said quickly, poking her head through the opening in the curtains.

Simon frowned at her. "Who is he?"

"He's certainly not a spy or an assassin. He's an old friend."

"What is his name, madam?" Simon demanded, as Lieutenant Osborne hid a smile.

"I shan't tell you, you great bully. Just let him go!"

"Perhaps you would be good enough to identify him," Simon said coldly. "Lieutenant! Have the prisoner brought here—and his locked case."

"Prisoner! This is ridiculous," Celia complained.

Lieutenant West of the Life Guards appeared with the prisoner and the locked case, having refused to relinquish his prize to Lieutenant Osborne of the Royal Horse Guards.

"Tom! What are you doing?"

"Oh, hullo, Miss St. Lys. I caught this Frog sneaking out of the theatre!" West told her proudly. "I'm sure he has a bomb in his case."

"That is ridiculous, Tom. If he came here to plant a bomb, he wouldn't be leaving the theatre with it, now, would he?" Celia said impatiently.

"Zees eez an outrage!" Monsieur Alexandre raged as he was pushed into the room. "Take your 'ands off of me, you big stupid rosbif!"

"Yes, Tom," said Celia. "This is my friend. I vouch for him."

"But who is he?" Simon asked curtly. "What's he doing here?"

"He's not doing anything here. He'd like to leave."

Simon picked up the case. It was something like a physician's black bag, and it was indeed locked. "What's in here?"

"Zat eez none of your business, monsieur!"

"Mind how you talk to his lordship!" said Lieutenant Osborne, giving him a push.

"Look here!" Tom West said sharply. "He's my prisoner, not yours. I'll shove him if he wants shoving."

Simon held up his hand. "Give me the key, monsieur," he warned the Frenchman, "or I shall be obliged to break it open."

"No! Please!" Celia cried, as the Frenchman let loose a stream of curses in his native tongue. "There's nothing in there that need concern you, my lord. I vouch for him! I give you my word. Is that not enough?"

Simon smiled thinly. "I'm afraid not, Miss St. Lys. You do understand."

"I understand perfectly," monsieur said bitterly. "Never should I 'ave come to zees bloody country. Zee English! Zey are rude and stupid."

"I'll tell you who he is, my lord," Celia said hastily, her cheeks pink with embarrassment. "But I must tell you in private."

"Very well!" Simon snapped, motioning to his lieutenant. "I will speak to Miss St. Lys and the prisoner in private!" When he had cleared the room of everyone but Celia and her Frenchman, he said, with tolerable calm, "Well, madam? Who is this man?"

"Monsieur Alexandre," she confessed, whispering, "is my hairdresser."

"Your hairdresser?" he repeated incredulously. "If that is so, madam, then why all this secrecy?"

Celia groaned. "I promised him no one would ever find out that he is the man who did *this* to me." Squeezing her eyes shut, she pulled off her wig, revealing her smart new haircut.

Dead silence greeted the revelation, and she cautiously opened her eyes.

Simon was staring at her in horrified fascination. He looked as though all the blood had been drained from his body. Monsieur, it seemed, could not even bear to look at his handiwork. His face was turned away as if from a most pitiful sight.

"For God's sake," Celia said angrily. "It's only hair. It will grow back."

Simon shook his head. "You were butchered," he said flatly.

"Oh yes?" she snapped. "I happen to think I look like Joan of Arc. It's supposed to be a surprise," she went on impatiently, "for the play. Now will you please let him go?"

"I ought to lock him up for what he's done," Simon muttered. "Very well, monsieur, you may go." Going to the door, he informed his officers of his decision.

Meanwhile, Celia hastened to her dressing table to

replace her wig. Was it really so bad? she wondered. *He* certainly thought so. *Oh well*, she thought. *It's too late now*.

His shadow fell across the mirror and she looked up at him belligerently. "You must admit it did look suspicious," he said.

"Even after I vouched for him? I suppose your officer thinks monsieur is my lover."

"Very likely," he said.

Celia sighed. "Please, just finish your search and go. My nerves are completely shattered. I shall be a candidate for Bedlam by the end of the night."

"I'm almost finished. What's in here?" he asked, opening another cupboard. "More costumes?"

"Aren't you the clever one."

"And this?" he asked. Taking up a small, narrow box perhaps nine inches long, he opened it before she could stop him. Inside, nestled in velvet, was a fairly realistic version of the male member, executed in white leather. Shocked, Simon closed the box quickly and put it back in the wardrobe.

"It's not what you think," Celia said quickly. She could not be certain, but she rather thought that his lordship was blushing. "It's just my little . . . codpiece, if you like."

"Yes, of course it is," he said quickly. "There's really no need to explain."

"But it's for the play, my lord," she said firmly. "You see, I'm playing the part of Sebastian—"

"I thought you were Viola," he said.

"I am to play both parts," she explained. "They are twins, you know, but when I am onstage as Sebastian, I need a little something extra, if you see what I mean. There's a special sort of pocket it fits into. Meyer informs me that his less endowed clients often request such . . . enhancements."

"I would not know anything about that."

"No, my lord."

He frowned. "You mean you have discussed this with the tailor?"

"Of course, my lord. Who do you think made it for me?"

"I have to go," Simon said abruptly. "I shall return with the prince at—at the appointed time. While I am gone, there will be guards posted at all the entrances and exits. During the performance, there will be guards posted on either side of the stage: one officer of the Life Guards, and one of my own, Mr. Osborne, but they will not be in the actors' way."

"And where will you be?" she said.

"I shall be with the prince, of course."

"Of course," she said, seeing him to the door. "I hope you enjoy the play."

"I'm sure I will," he answered, "unless, of course, someone tries to assassinate His Royal Highness, and then I shall have to take a bullet."

"Right," she said.

Chapter 21

"I shall never see him again," Celia murmured, as Flood hurried back into the room.

"God willing," Flood murmured.

"Celia darling," called a familiar voice from the doorway.

Celia's nerves, quite badly frayed, abruptly gave way. "What now?" she practically snarled at David Rourke.

"Is this a bad time?" he asked innocently.

"No! Not at all! Bring a friend!"

"I don't think I have any left at this point," he murmured. "Everyone's snapping at me! One of the officers broke Mrs. Archer's mirror, and you would think that I—"

Celia gasped. "Not her *lucky* mirror? The one she always looks into right before she goes onstage?"

"The very one."

"Oh no," Celia groaned, dropping her head in her hands.

"Never mind all that, darling. I was wondering what you mean to wear for 'God Save the King.'"

With the prince regent in attendance, it was customary for the anthem to be played by the orchestra and sung by the entire company before the curtain went up on the first act.

Celia caught her breath. "Oh dear! I hadn't thought . . . Flood—"

"The audience ought not to see you in costume before the play starts," said Rourke.

"No, to be sure," Celia murmured.

"I was thinking . . . His Highness is very fond of the military style. He'll probably be wearing his field marshal's uniform. You've a Life Guards habit, don't you?"

"Yes, of course," said Celia. "I shall have to send Flood home for it."

"That leaves Miss Vane."

"What about her?"

"Poor child! She was only wondering if she might borrow something from you, Celia darling. She has really nothing suitable for mingling with royalty. Olivia's in mourning in the first act—she can't go out all in black to sing 'God Save the King'!"

"No," Celia agreed. "She can borrow my Life Guards habit. I shall wear my Royal Horse Guards habit."

"Madam," Flood protested. "His Lordship won't like that one bit!"

"I know," said Celia, "but what can I do? I can't go out there naked—that would completely spoil the surprise of my first scene."

The plan hit a snag, however, when Lieutenant Osborne of the Royal Horse Guards refused to allow Flood to leave the theatre. Lieutenant West of the Life Guards gamely offered to escort the dresser there and back again. A loud argument ensued between the two young officers, which might have come to blows had Captain Fitzclarence not intervened.

"Clare!" Celia exclaimed in astonishment. And after Tom West and Flood were on their way, she peppered him with questions. "What are you doing here? Where is your bride? Why are you not on your honeymoon?"

"That's all over, I'm afraid," he said, pulling a long face. "My father and her father could not come to terms, and the whole thing is to be annulled. That's two days of my life I'll never get back."

"You wanted too much money," Celia guessed.

"Sir Lucas said he would give her ten thousand pounds and not a penny more!"

"So little?" cried Celia. "That is shocking."

"Anyway, she only agreed to run off with *me* because she thought her father was going to marry *you*. Now that that's off—"

"My dear boy," she protested. "'Twas never on. But I do know one young lady who will be very glad to know you are not married."

"Oh yes?" He grinned. "Who?"

"Miss London, of course! She has been crying her eyes out for two days."

"Oh yes, the amusing little Cockney. Is she here?"

"She is at my house," said Celia. "But I left a *billet d'entrée* for her with the porter."

"Then I shall see her after the play tonight," he said.

Leaving him, Celia hurried along to Mrs. Archer's dressing room. "I heard of your tragedy," she said, when Mrs. Archer's dresser reluctantly had admitted her. "I know nothing can ever replace your lucky mirror—"

"It belonged to Mrs. Barry herself, the first actress ever to grace the English stage."

"I've got a lucky handkerchief, if you want to borrow it," Celia offered. "It was woven by a two-hundred-year-old sibyl. The pattern of strawberries was printed with the blood of virgins."

Mrs. Archer stared at her. "Yes, I can see that, Miss St.

Lys. I cannot accept. That is your handkerchief. You carried it in *Othello*, when you were Desdemona."

"And so did you, Mrs. Archer," Celia said, pressing the silken square into the other actress's hands, "when *you* were Desdemona. It's really *your* handkerchief; I've just been looking after it. And how is Belinda?" she went on, peeking toward the back of the room. The curtains of the little daybed had been drawn, but she assumed that Belinda was inside, as she was not in sight.

"Oh, Miss St. Lys," cried Belinda, starting up out of the bed. "Have you heard the terrible news? The Prince of Wales is coming—to the play—tonight! Can nothing be done to prevent him?"

"Why should we want to do that?" cried Celia. "It is an honor! It will guarantee that the play is a success. You want the play to succeed, don't you, Belinda?"

"Yes, of course she does," said her mother, shepherding Celia from the room. "It's just nerves, Miss St. Lys. You'd know that if you were an actress. Thank you for returning my handkerchief to me. I *did* wonder who had stolen it."

Pushing Celia out into the corridor, she closed the door firmly.

At half-past six, half an hour before the curtain was slated to rise, disaster struck. The Prince of Wales was not late, as everyone expected—as everyone had the right to expect. No, His Royal Highness arrived early. The theatre was embarrassingly empty. Nothing had been prepared for his entertainment before the play. Little could be offered in the way of refreshments. Left to his own devices, the regent expressed a desire to meet the cast.

"Of course!" cried Celia when she heard. She knew who was to blame: Lord Simon. He had done it on purpose, too, she was sure, to catch them all off guard, and make her look ridiculous. Fortunately, she was mostly dressed.

Hardly anyone else was ready, but it would have been unthinkable to delay the prince. They all hurried into their clothes and rushed to the stage just as the prince arrived, flanked on one side by Captain Fitzclarence and on the other by Lord Simon.

Simon's eyes widened in surprise as he saw what St. Lys was wearing. The dark blue habit, richly laced in gold, was the feminine version of his own uniform.

He probably thinks I wore it for him, Celia thought sourly, stiffening as he gave her a smile. *What nonsense! It just so happens I look better in blue than scarlet.*

Miss Vane, now a brunette, stood beside her in the Life Guards habit. Her figure was not as tall and athletic as Celia's, and it fit her perhaps a little tight across the bust, but that is no great defect in a man's eyes. His Royal Highness clearly liked what he saw, and though he politely went down the line, greeting each member of the cast, his glance strayed more than once toward the two lovely girls in the middle.

Rourke was quite right; His Royal Highness was inordinately fond of the military style. He had indeed chosen to wear his field marshal's uniform, the splendor of which hid somewhat the increasing corpulence of his figure. He was wearing his best brown wig, too, and his blue eyes looked especially sharp. Celia somehow resisted the strong urge to make certain that her own wig was perfectly in place, and as the sovereign stopped before her, she sank into a graceful curtsy.

"Your Royal Highness."

"Miss St. Lys," he said. Taking her hand, he raised her up, and kept her hand. "Are you thinking of joining my Royal Horse Guard?"

"Have you a commission for me, sir?" she answered.

He laughed pleasantly. "Oh, now that *would* be a scandal, would it not? Beautiful workmanship," he went on, running his hand down the length of her sleeve from shoulder to wrist. "Weston made it for you, I suppose."

"No, sir. Mr. Schweitzer."

"Oh yes," he said, fondling her other sleeve. "I see it now. The lace is extraordinarily fine—really quite beautifully done."

"Thank you, sir. Monsieur Nugee was responsible for the lace."

His Royal Highness expressed surprise. "Monsieur Nugee? But surely he has gone back to France."

"Yes, sir. I had the habit made three years ago, but I never had the occasion to wear it—until tonight."

"Oh?" he said. "And what is so special about tonight?"

"Why, Your Royal Highness is with us tonight," she replied.

"And I suppose three years ago you had fallen in love with a handsome young officer of the Royal Horse Guard," the prince went on, giving her a wink, "and you had it made to please him? And where is he now?"

"Sir! It was all so long ago," Celia murmured, blushing.

Simon leaned forward and murmured in the prince's ear.

"I see," His Royal Highness said gravely. "Forgive me, my dear. I did not know."

"Didn't know what, Your Royal Highness?" Celia asked, very much alarmed.

"I was just telling His Royal Highness that the young man fell at Waterloo."

"What a terrible pity," said the prince, pressing Celia's hand.

"I happen to know," Simon said, surprising both Celia and the prince, "that as he fell, he thought of no one but you, Miss St. Lys. And later, when he was lying in his bed, feverish from his wounds, it was your name he called out. At least," he added, "that is what his valet told me."

Celia stared at him in disbelief. "Now?" she breathed. "You tell me this now?"

"You've overset her," the prince complained. "There, there, my dear. Time heals all wounds. And the lace really is quite splendid!"

"Thank you, sir," she said, recovering her composure. "May I present my dear friend Miss Julia Vane? Miss Vane comes to us from Bath and we were very lucky to get her. Tonight marks her official London debut . . ."

The prince and his entourage passed on.

Promptly at seven o'clock, Dorian stepped out of his carriage and walked up to the doors of the Theatre Royal. "Please, sir!" cried a young woman, catching hold of his sleeve. "Won't you 'elp me? They won't let me in!"

"I am not a bit surprised," Dorian said coldly, but as he was removing her hand from his sleeve, he recognized Celia's friend. "Oh, it's you, Miss Eliza."

"Begging Your Hexcellency's pardon, sir! Miss St. Lys left a ticket for me at the door, but the soldiers say they won't honor it—not tonight, because the prince is coming, you see."

"Never mind," he said, tucking her hand in the crook of his arm. "I'll look after you."

"Oh!" she said. "Thank you ever so!" and stuck out her tongue at the guards as she sailed past them on the Duke of Berkshire's arm.

Finally, after what seemed like two eternities of torment, the actors took their places, the curtain rose, and the play began. Celia waited in the wings, listening for her cue, then ran lightly up the steps to the stage. Right before she went on, the stage boy flung a bucket of ice-cold water over her, drenching her from head to toe. Instantly, her gown of white muslin was rendered almost completely transparent, and she had just a few seconds to artfully arrange some blue tatters over her breasts before going out.

There was an audible gasp from the audience, as good as a standing ovation to Celia. All at once her nervousness left her, and she was supremely confident. She was Viola, an innocent, noble maiden, washed onto the shores of Illyria after a cruel shipwreck. She was frightened and alone; her dear brother presumably was dead, lost at sea, as she herself might have been. Glancing up, she saw Eliza London and the Duke of Berkshire in the latter's stage box. How had that come about? she wondered, but there was no time for conjecture. Her teeth chattered as she spoke her lines, but that was not acting; the water in that bucket had been bloody ice-cold.

Fortunately, the scene was a short one.

When next she appeared, she was better dressed, in male attire. In her scarlet coat and scandalously tight white breeches, she looked a very pretty toy soldier. But it was her cropped head, when she removed her shako, that made the audience gasp.

It's only hair, she wanted to shout at them. *It grows back.*

The rest of the play passed in a dream, punctuated by a few frenzied, nightmarish bits.

In the third act, she had a long break, during which she had planned to enjoy a lie-down and a cup of tea. Instead, she was greeted with the horrifying news that Belinda, who only had to go on in the last scene, had split her breeches.

"Would you happen to have another pair, Miss St. Lys?" asked the desperate dresser. "A spare pair?"

"No!" said Celia. "No, I don't have a spare pair. I gave her my spare pair! They cost me sixty guineas. Can't you just sew them up?"

"I tried. I've torn the bloody leather! I'm not a tailor, you know," the dresser protested.

"Oh God."

"Oh, you just had to have those fancy white leather breeches, didn't you?" the dresser said bitterly. "Just like the Household Cavalry, you said."

Celia caught her breath, and so did the dresser, for they had both had the same idea at once. Lieutenant Osborne was posted at the stage-right stairs, but eschewing him, Celia ran around to fetch Tom, who was posted stage left. "Tom!" she called to him sotto voce, and beckoned.

"Sorry, Miss St. Lys; I can't leave my post. I'm to make sure no one goes onstage except the actors."

"I just need your breeches," Celia explained, running to him. "Or rather, Miss Archer needs them for the last scene."

"But then I should be out of uniform," he protested, going red in the face.

"Strip," she commanded him. "I'll find you something to wear."

Someone found a kilt for the young officer, and Celia ran to Belinda's dressing room with the precious breeches. Belinda was in the daybed, crying. "What if I split these, too?" she asked.

"But you're not going to split them, are you? Now stop crying and put them on."

"Ugh!" said Belinda. "They're warm!"

"Of course they're warm," Celia snapped. "I just took them off Mr. West!"

Belinda gasped. "What? These are Tom's breeches? Oh no! Miss St. Lys, I could not possibly wear Tom's breeches.

It wouldn't be decent—and still warm from his body, too. Oh, I couldn't!"

Celia's eyes narrowed. "Oh yes, you could. You will put them on, or I will kill you. Do you understand me, Miss Archer?"

Belinda blinked at her. "Yes, Miss St. Lys," she said meekly.

She was perhaps too harsh with the girl, for by the time she left the stage in act four, with the interval to follow, Belinda Archer had disappeared from the theatre, taking Tom's breeches with her. "This is all your fault, Miss St. Lys," Mrs. Archer said accusingly.

"But I don't understand," said Celia. "No one was to be allowed in or out of the theatre! Lord Simon's orders!"

"She was dressed as a soldier—a Life Guard," Rourke explained. "What the devil are we going to do?"

"Don't panic!" said Celia, breathing hard. "Tom will just have to do it. He'll have to play Sebastian in the last scene. It's only a few lines he'll have to learn, but there's enough of a resemblance. He could be my brother."

"I should be very glad to help, Miss St. Lys," said Tom, when asked, "but you forget, I have no breeches! I cannot go out there—in a skirt!"

"It's a kilt, Tom, I swear," Celia said quickly. "It's a kilt, from *Macbeth*."

The fatal word slipped from her lips before she knew what she was saying.

The other actors all gasped in horror. "You did *not* just say that!" Mrs. Archer said severely. "I did not hear you."

"No, of course not," said Celia, in a voice tinged with hysteria. "I said the Scottish play. It is a kilt from the Scottish play."

"Whatever it is," said Tom West rather sullenly, "it ain't breeches!"

* * *

"No!" said Lieutenant Osborne, when asked. "Absolutely not! No, you most certainly may not have my breeches, Miss St. Lys! What a thing to ask!"

"But it's for the play, Mr. Osborne," she pleaded. "I'll give them back to you, I promise. And look, here's a lovely kilt for you to wear in the meantime."

"Madam, I beg of you—Please!"

"If Lord Simon were here," she said desperately, "he would order you to do as I say!"

"Would I?" asked the man himself, coming out of the shadows.

Celia jumped in fright. "Oh! My lord! I did not see you there," she murmured in dismay. "Shouldn't you be with the prince?"

"Fitzclarence can look after him for a few minutes, I am almost certain," Simon replied. "Is there a problem?"

"No! Of course not. Not really. Nothing for you to worry about. Yes."

"May I help?"

Celia took a deep breath. "I need Mr. Osborne's breeches," she confessed, not daring to look at him. "That is to say, Mr. West needs them."

"Why?" Simon asked, not unreasonably. "What happened to Tom's breeches?"

"I took them already," said Celia, almost in tears. "You see, Belinda split her breeches, and that was my only spare pair, so I borrowed Tom's. But now Belinda has run away with them—the breeches, I mean. Anyway, what I need now more than anything are Mr. Osborne's breeches on Tom West's arse! Does no one understand? *It's for the play!*"

"You heard the lady, Mr. Osborne," said Simon, with scarcely a pause. "And that is an order, Lieutenant."

"Yes, my lord."

Celia looked up at Simon incredulously.

"Anything else?" he asked.

"Well, yes," she said. "As a matter of fact, Tom will need permission to leave his post in the last scene. I shall need him onstage."

"I'll see that he is relieved."

"Thank you, my lord."

"Anything else?"

"No, my lord. Wait!" she added, as he turned to go. "Why did you come backstage? Did His Royal Highness send you? Have we—have we offended him in some way? It was the kiss, wasn't it?" she fretted. "I should never have urged Miss Vane to kiss me. Indeed, it is all my fault. I alone am to blame."

"It wasn't the kiss," he assured her. "We all quite enjoyed that, as a matter of fact."

"Then what—"

"I just wanted to ask you something," he said, "but I can see that you are busy—"

"I am not busy at all," she protested, taking a step toward him.

He chuckled. "It will keep," he said, walking away.

Celia stood looking after him for a moment, then, recalling herself to her surroundings and the problem at hand, snapped at Lieutenant Osborne. "Haven't you got them off yet?"

The play hurtled along to its happy conclusion with no further calamity. Tom West took the stage as Sebastian, and with liberal aid from the prompter, was able to stammer out his lines, of which there were mercifully few. Then Orsino turned to the leading lady and, holding out his hand, said, "'Cesario, come—For so you shall be when you are a man; but when in other habits seen, Orsino's mistress and fancy's queen.'"

Or so he would have spoken, had he been allowed to.

"Stop!"

Rising from his seat beside the Prince of Wales, Lord Simon moved to the end of the stage and, with scarcely any effort at all, jumped onto the stage, making rather a loud noise. The principal actors, all of whom were gathered on the stage for the finale, stood paralyzed as his lordship strode across the stage.

"You cannot marry her, Orsino!" said Simon, drawing his saber. "Unhand her, ye yeasty varlet. Draw your weapon, coward, and fight me if you dare!"

Mr. Rourke, strangely enough, did not seem very eager to accept the challenge. "Take her," he said, releasing Celia.

"Simon, what are you doing?" Celia whispered fiercely.

"You cannot marry Duke Orsino," said Simon, loud enough for the whole theatre to hear. "He doesn't even love you. Yesterday he was in love with—with—"

"Olivia," Miss Vane said helpfully.

"With Olivia, yes," said Simon. "Tomorrow he'll be in love with some other person, no doubt. But I . . . I have never loved anyone but thee. I love you, Celia St. Lys! I have loved you from the first moment I saw you. You were Desdemona, strangled in your bed by Mr. Kean. Like every other man in the place, I longed to storm the stage and rescue you from your fate. But I was too cowardly to follow my heart. I let you go."

"Simon, I don't know what to say," Celia murmured. "Everyone is looking," she added foolishly.

"Of course they are," he said. "I want them to look. I want everyone to know how much I love you. Celia St.

Lys," he went on, going down before her on one knee, "will you marry me?"

Celia stared in shock. "Don't be a fool, Simon," she whispered. "You don't have to marry me; I am yours."

"I shall indeed look like a fool if you don't say yes," he said, talking through a forced smile. "I am asking you," he went on loudly, "before all these witnesses, before His Royal Highness, the Prince of Wales, and all the rest of them, will you do me the honor of becoming my wife?"

"Yes!" she said quickly, stretching out both hands to him.

Climbing to his feet, he took both her hands in his. Together they faced the audience.

The Prince of Wales looked very grave. The theatre fell silent as the sovereign stood. All the ladies on the stage curtsied, and all the men bowed.

"Your Royal Highness," said Simon, bowing. "I— Would it be impertinent of me to ask for your blessing?"

"Do you need my blessing?" asked the prince.

"I should very much like to have it, sir," Simon replied.

"But, dear boy!" said the prince. "What about this other fellow that she was in love with? The one who died at Waterloo?"

"He did not die, sir," Simon replied. "He only fell. He is . . . on his feet again at last," he added.

"I see," said the prince, looking at them. "In that case, not only do I give you my blessing, but I offer myself as your best man, Lord Simon. Tomorrow I create you Earl of Sutton, and you shall take the oath to me in the House of Lords. But on Saturday," he went on, "on Saturday you shall take the oath to this young lady. And I trust," he added, with a slight bow to Celia, "that you will bring Lady Sutton with you to court very often."

"Thank you, sir. I shall."

"Kiss!" cried a voice from the stage boxes. It was Eliza London alone, but the rest of the audience soon took up the chant. "Kiss! Kiss! Kiss!"

"Well, my dear?" Simon murmured. "Shall we give them what they want?"

Celia laughed. "I think we'd better, don't you?"

On Sunday, the following notice appeared in the London papers:

> Married, at Berkshire House, London, the Right Honorable, the Earl of Sutton to Miss Celia St. Lys of the Theatre Royal, Drury Lane, and ward of His Grace, the Duke of Berkshire, who gave the bride away; His Royal Highness, the Prince of Wales, standing as best man to the bridegroom.